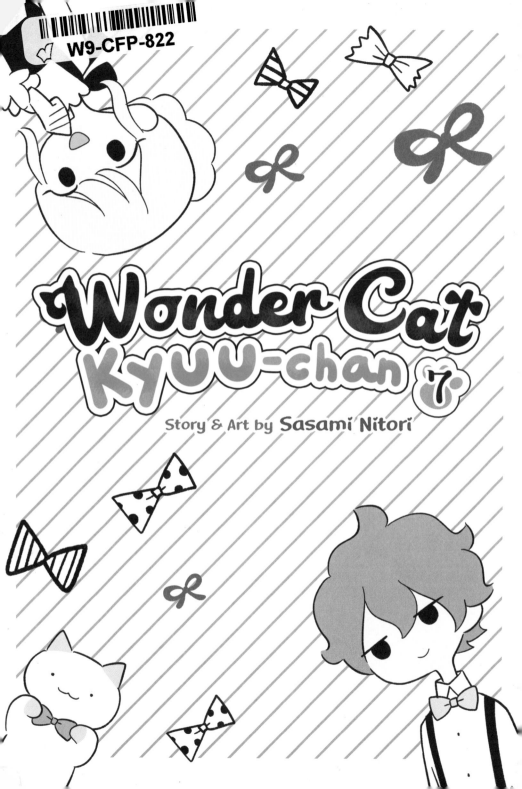

# Wonder Cat Kyuu-chan 7

Story & Art by **Sasami Nitori**

Wonder Cat Kyuu-chan

# SLEEP HABIT FORECAST

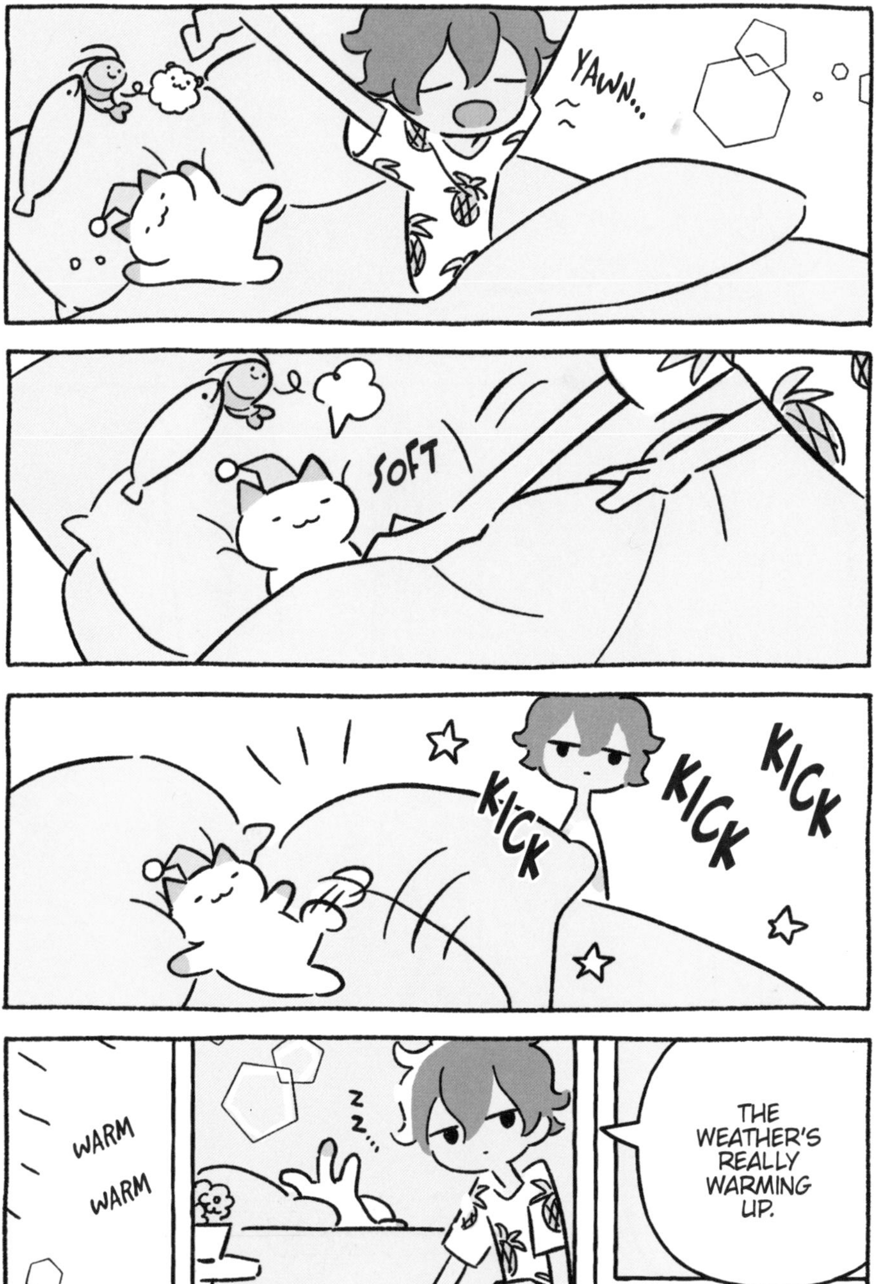
YAWN...
SOFT
KICK
KICK
KICK
THE WEATHER'S REALLY WARMING UP.
ZZ...
WARM
WARM

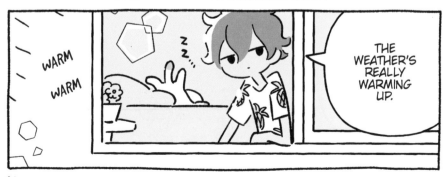

# LAZY MORNING

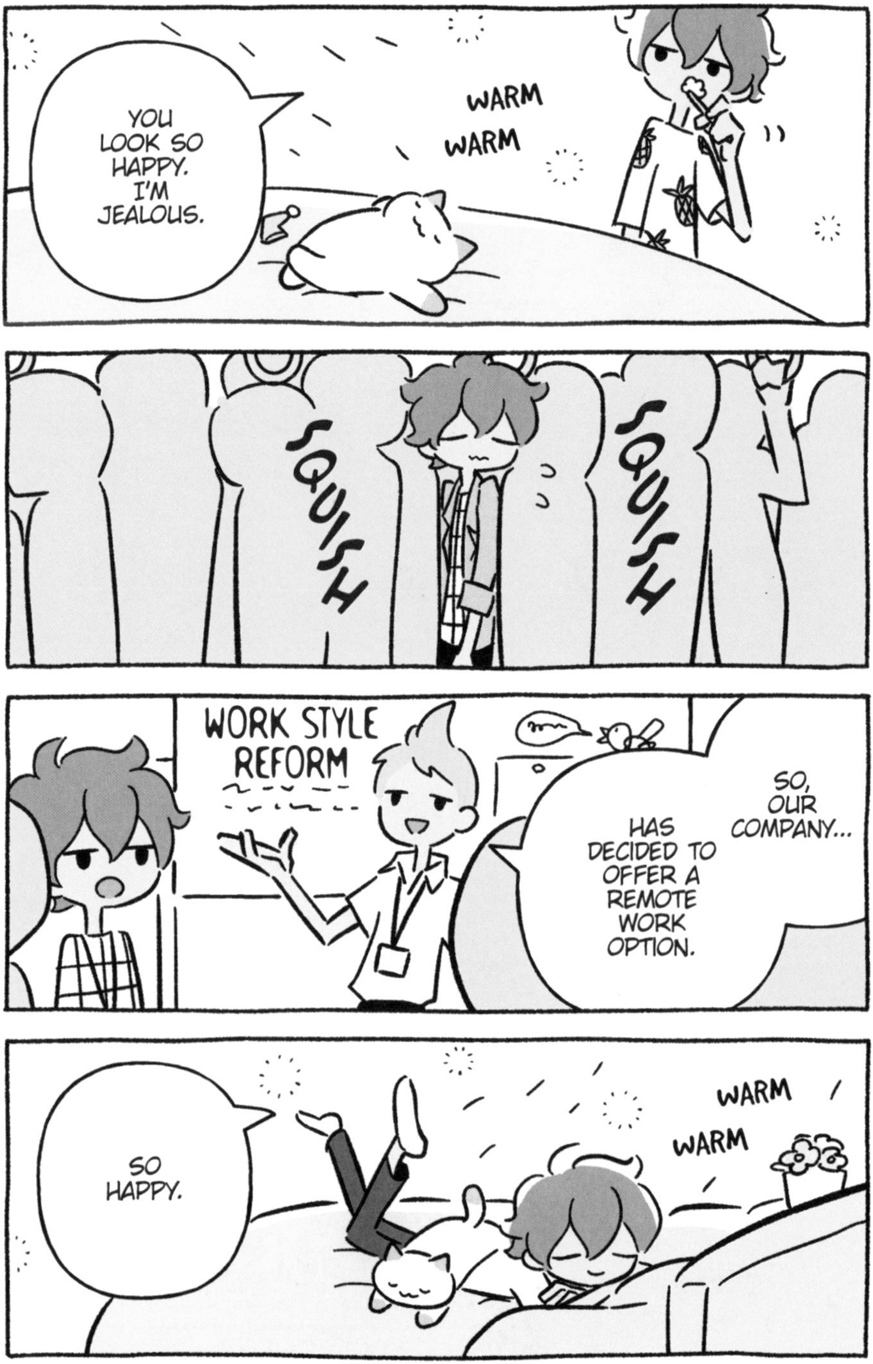
WARM
WARM
YOU LOOK SO HAPPY. I'M JEALOUS.
SQUISH
SQUISH
SO, OUR COMPANY...
HAS DECIDED TO OFFER A REMOTE WORK OPTION.
WORK STYLE REFORM
WARM
WARM
SO HAPPY.

# REMOTE WORK

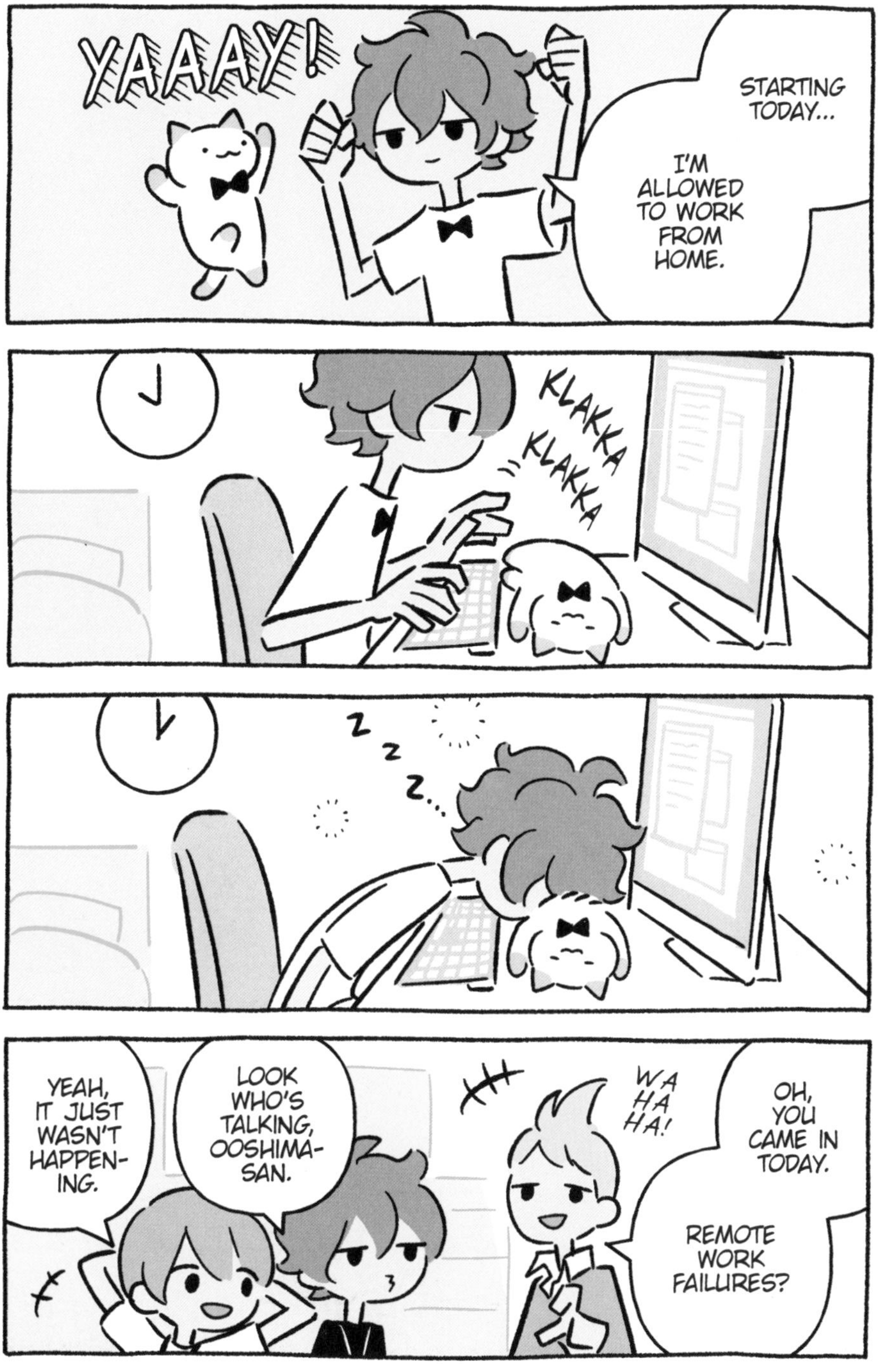

STARTING TODAY...
I'M ALLOWED TO WORK FROM HOME.
YAAAY!
KLAKKA KLAKKA
Z Z Z...
OH, YOU CAME IN TODAY.
REMOTE WORK FAILURES?
WA HA HA!
LOOK WHO'S TALKING, OOSHIMA-SAN.
YEAH, IT JUST WASN'T HAPPEN-ING.

# GUIDING

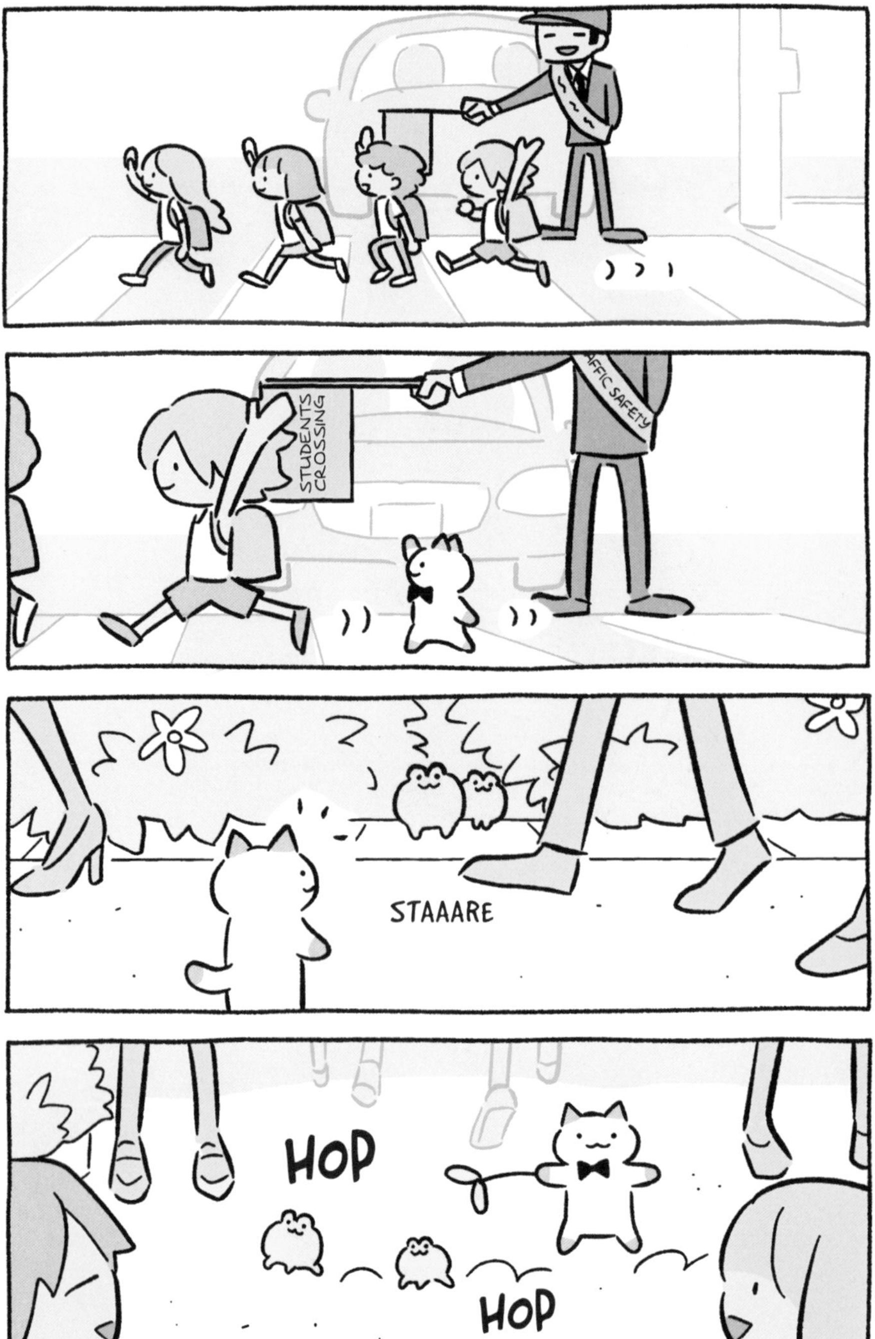

STUDENTS CROSSING
AFFIC SAFETY
STAAARE
HOP
HOP

# THE PIZZA FAIRY

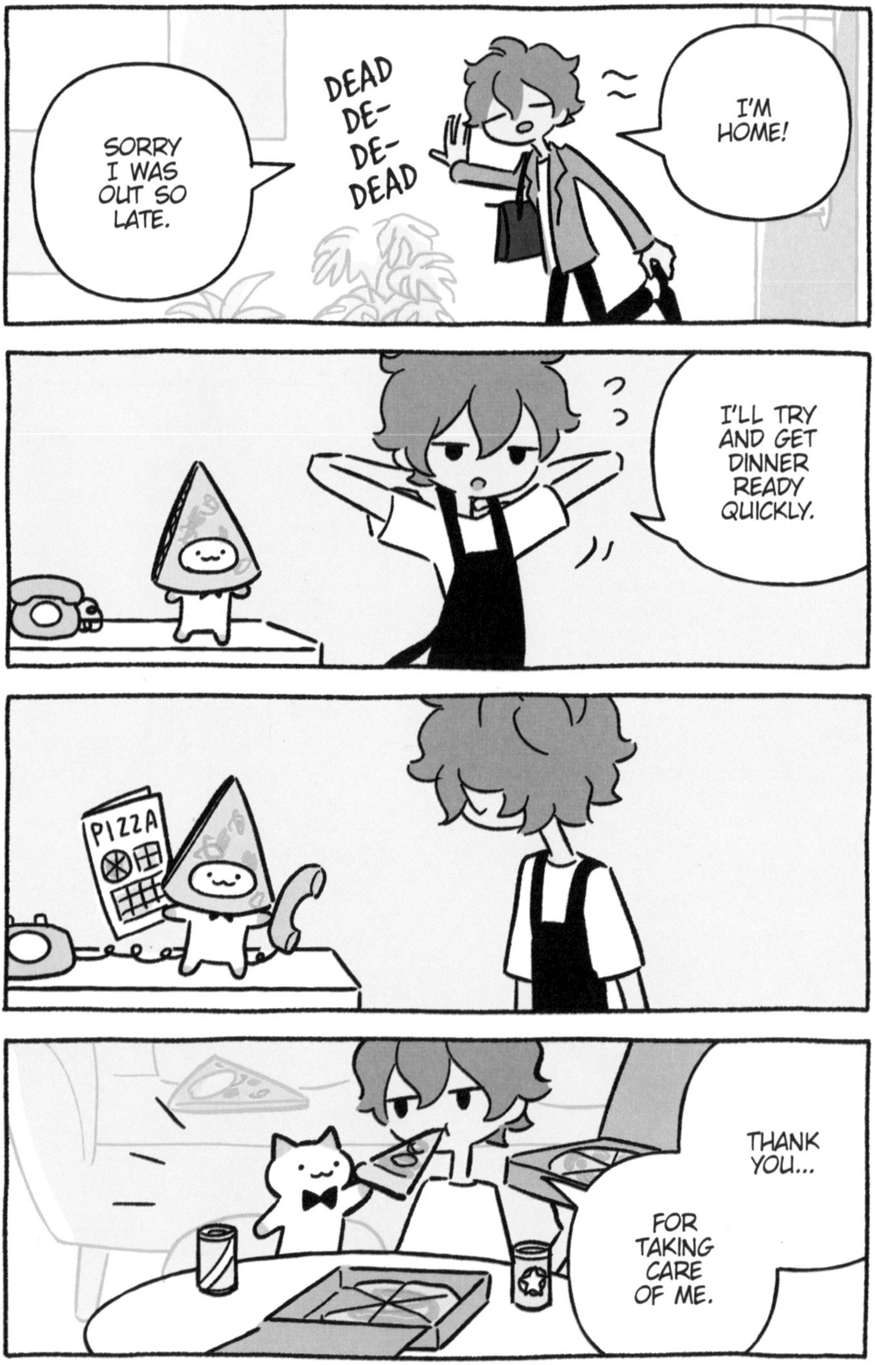
I'M HOME!
DEAD DE-DE-DEAD
SORRY I WAS OUT SO LATE.
I'LL TRY AND GET DINNER READY QUICKLY.
PIZZA
THANK YOU...
FOR TAKING CARE OF ME.

# SCRATCH

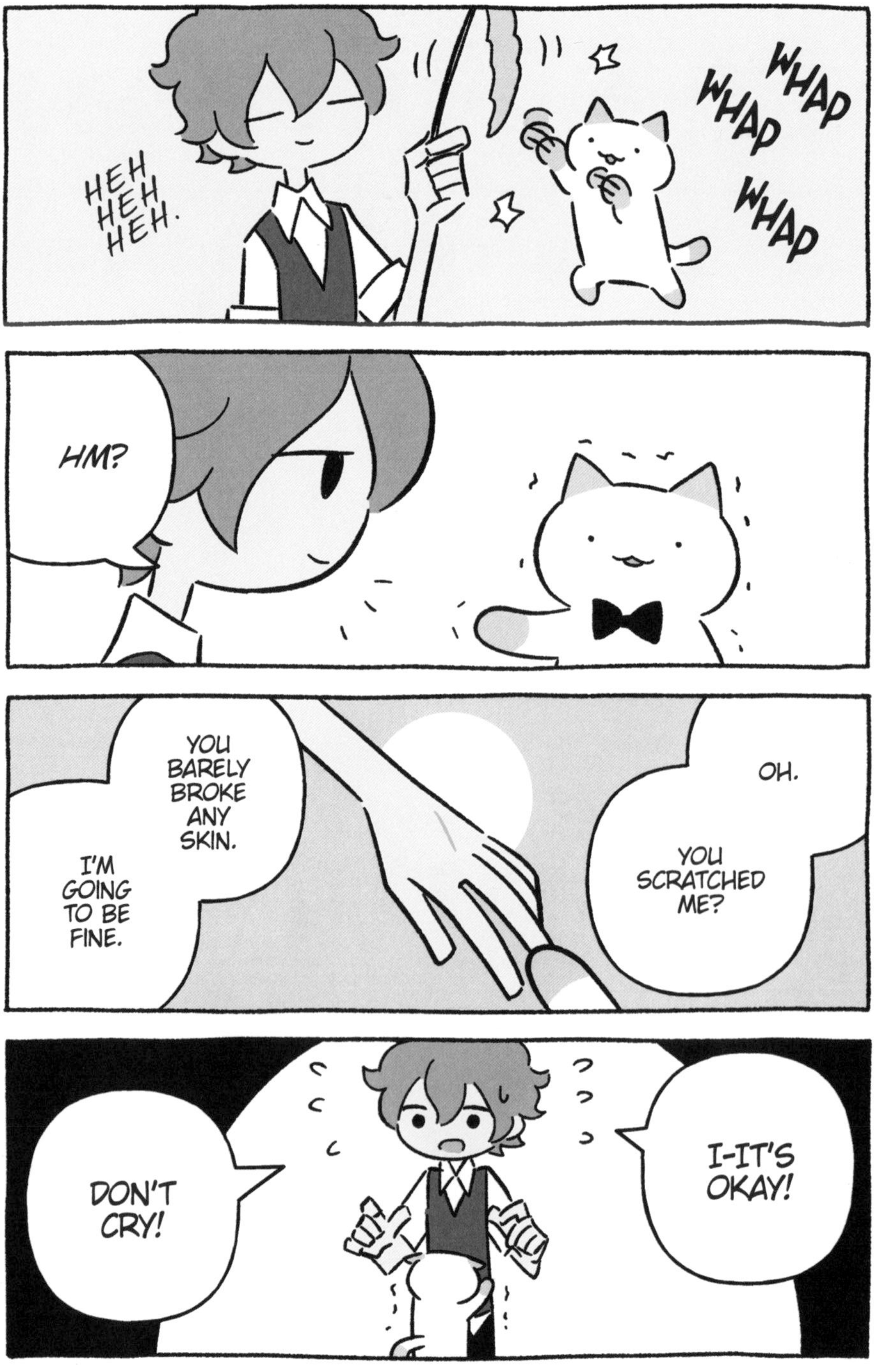
WHAP WHAP
WHAP
HEH HEH HEH.
HM?
OH.
YOU SCRATCHED ME?
YOU BARELY BROKE ANY SKIN.
I'M GOING TO BE FINE.
I-IT'S OKAY!
DON'T CRY!

# LET ME BANDAGE IT UP

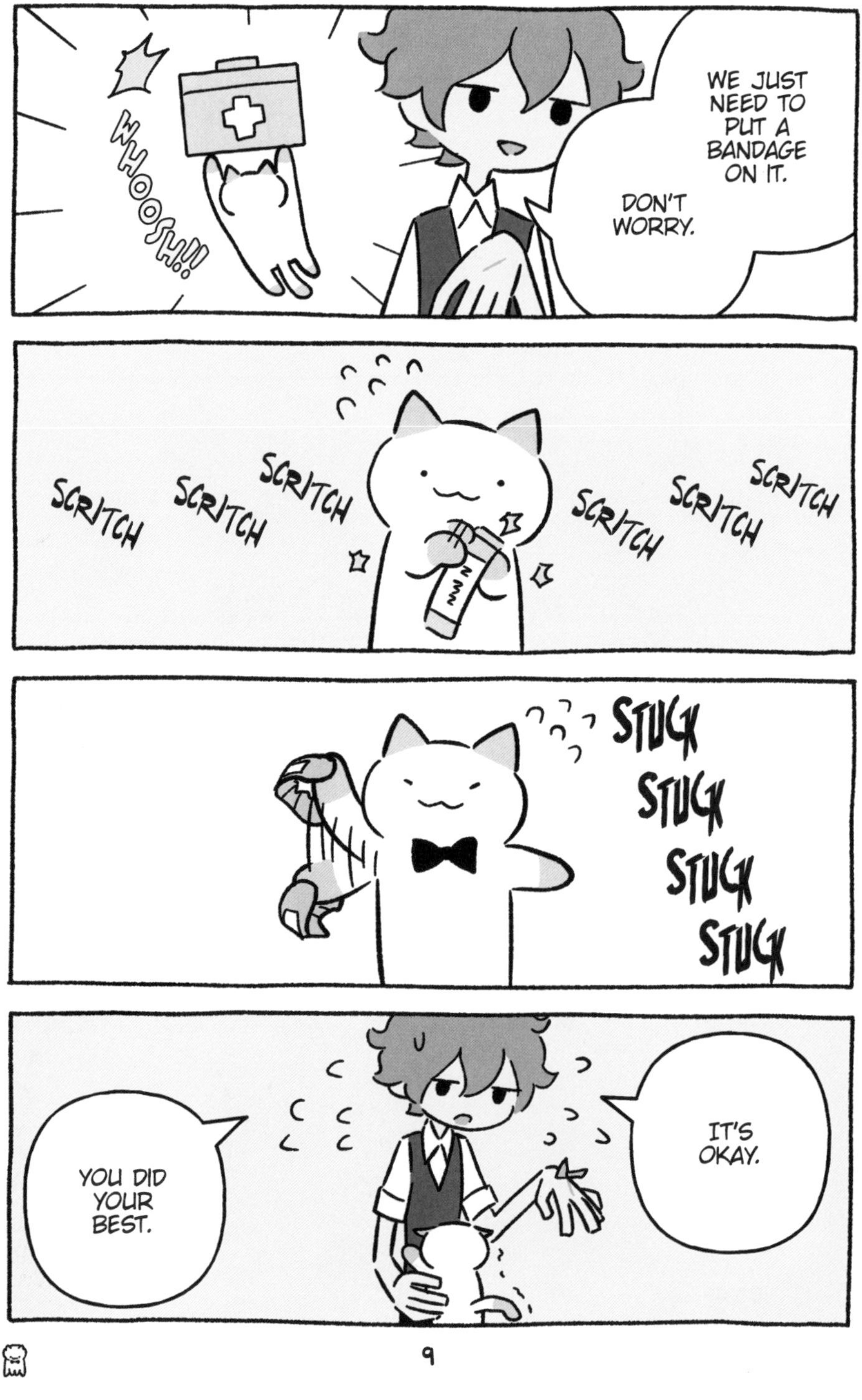
WE JUST NEED TO PUT A BANDAGE ON IT.
DON'T WORRY.
WHOOSH!!
SCRITCH
SCRITCH
SCRITCH
SCRITCH
SCRITCH
SCRITCH
STUCK
STUCK
STUCK
STUCK
IT'S OKAY.
YOU DID YOUR BEST.

# DOING WITHOUT

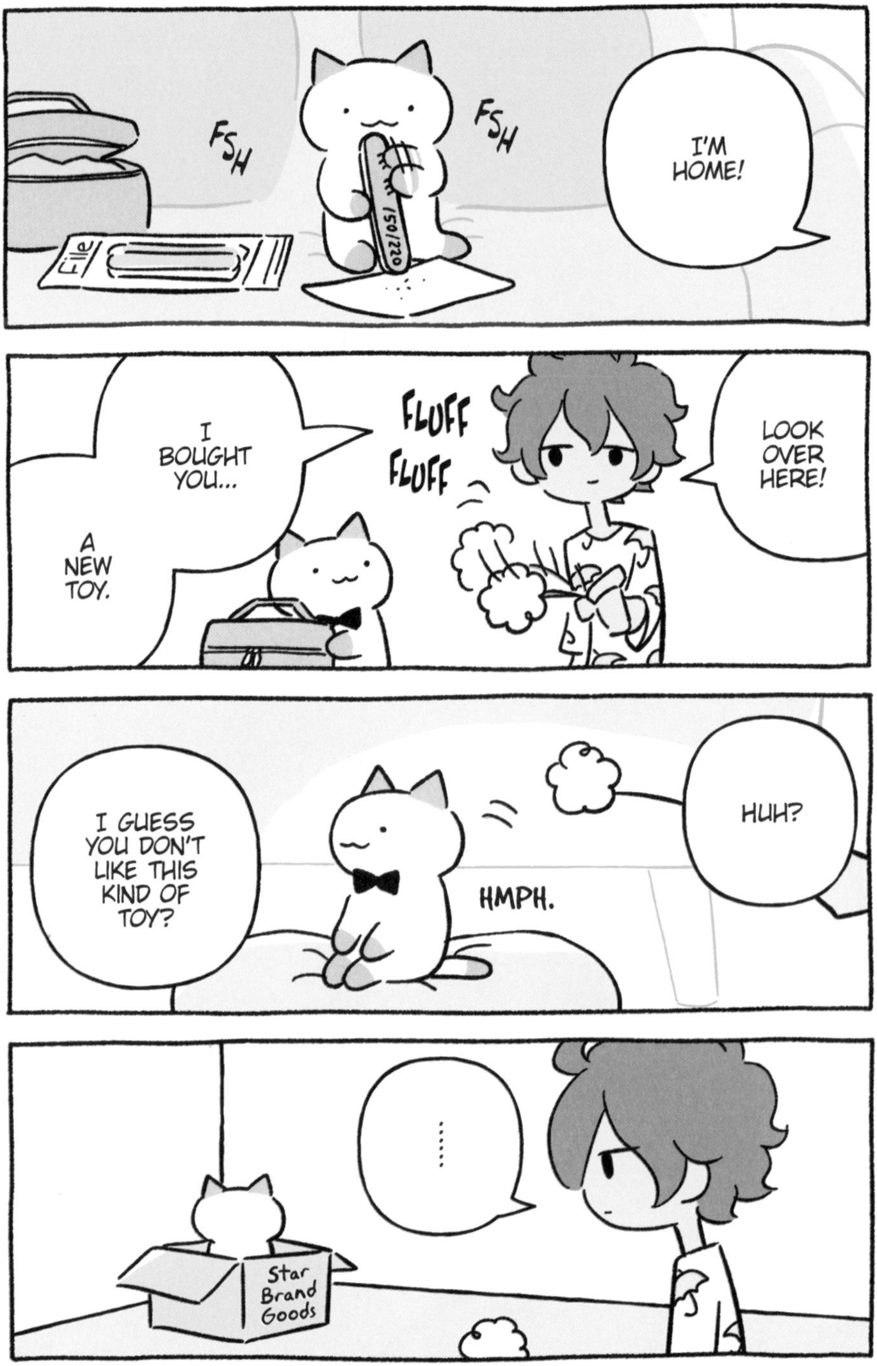
I'M HOME!
FSH
FSH
150/220
File
LOOK OVER HERE!
FLUFF
FLUFF
I BOUGHT YOU...
A NEW TOY.
HUH?
HMPH.
I GUESS YOU DON'T LIKE THIS KIND OF TOY?
......
Star Brand Goods

# IT DOESN'T HURT

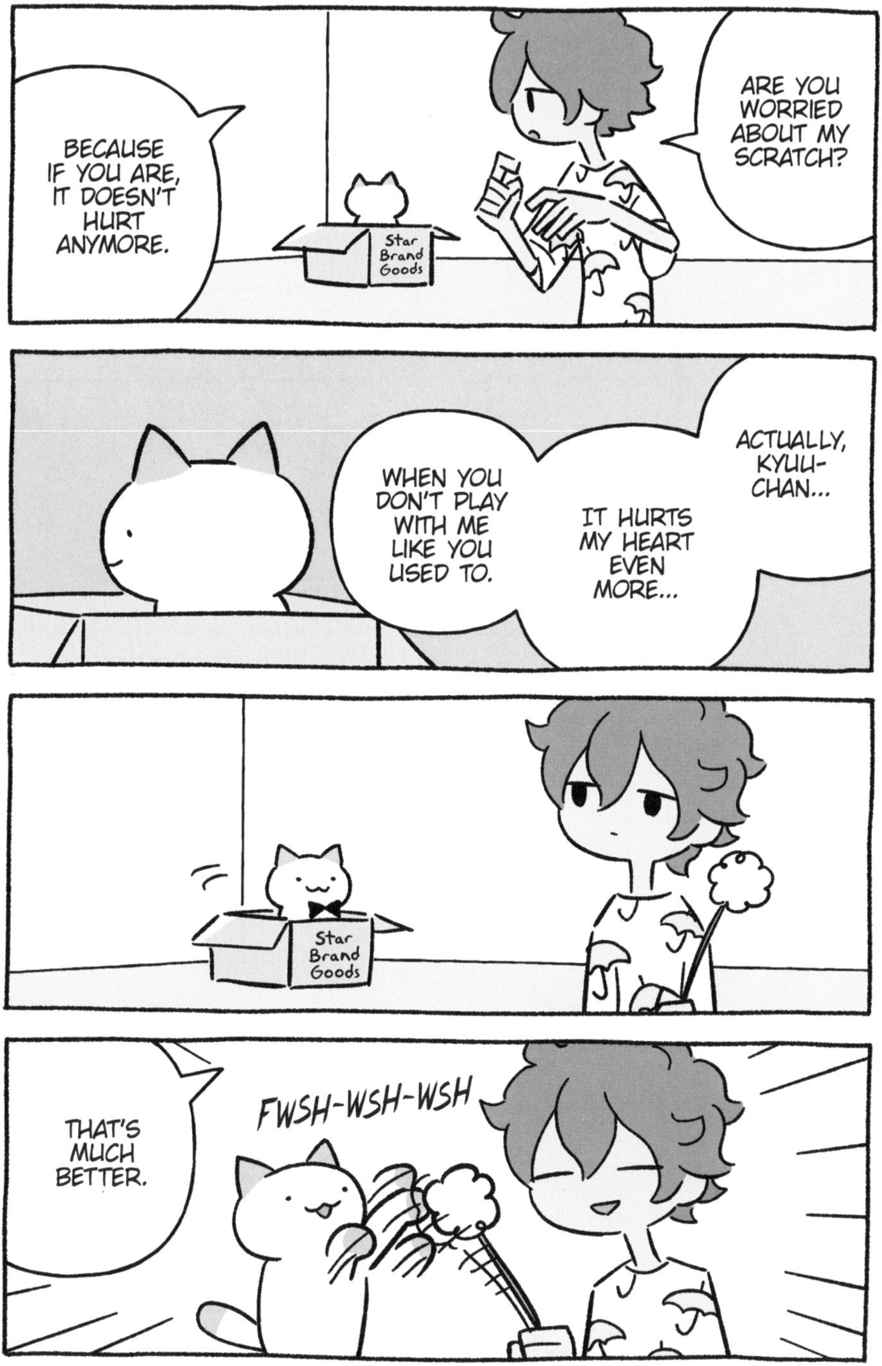
ARE YOU WORRIED ABOUT MY SCRATCH?
BECAUSE IF YOU ARE, IT DOESN'T HURT ANYMORE.
Star Brand Goods
ACTUALLY, KYUU-CHAN...
IT HURTS MY HEART EVEN MORE...
WHEN YOU DON'T PLAY WITH ME LIKE YOU USED TO.
Star Brand Goods
FWSH-WSH-WSH
THAT'S MUCH BETTER.

# COME ON OUT

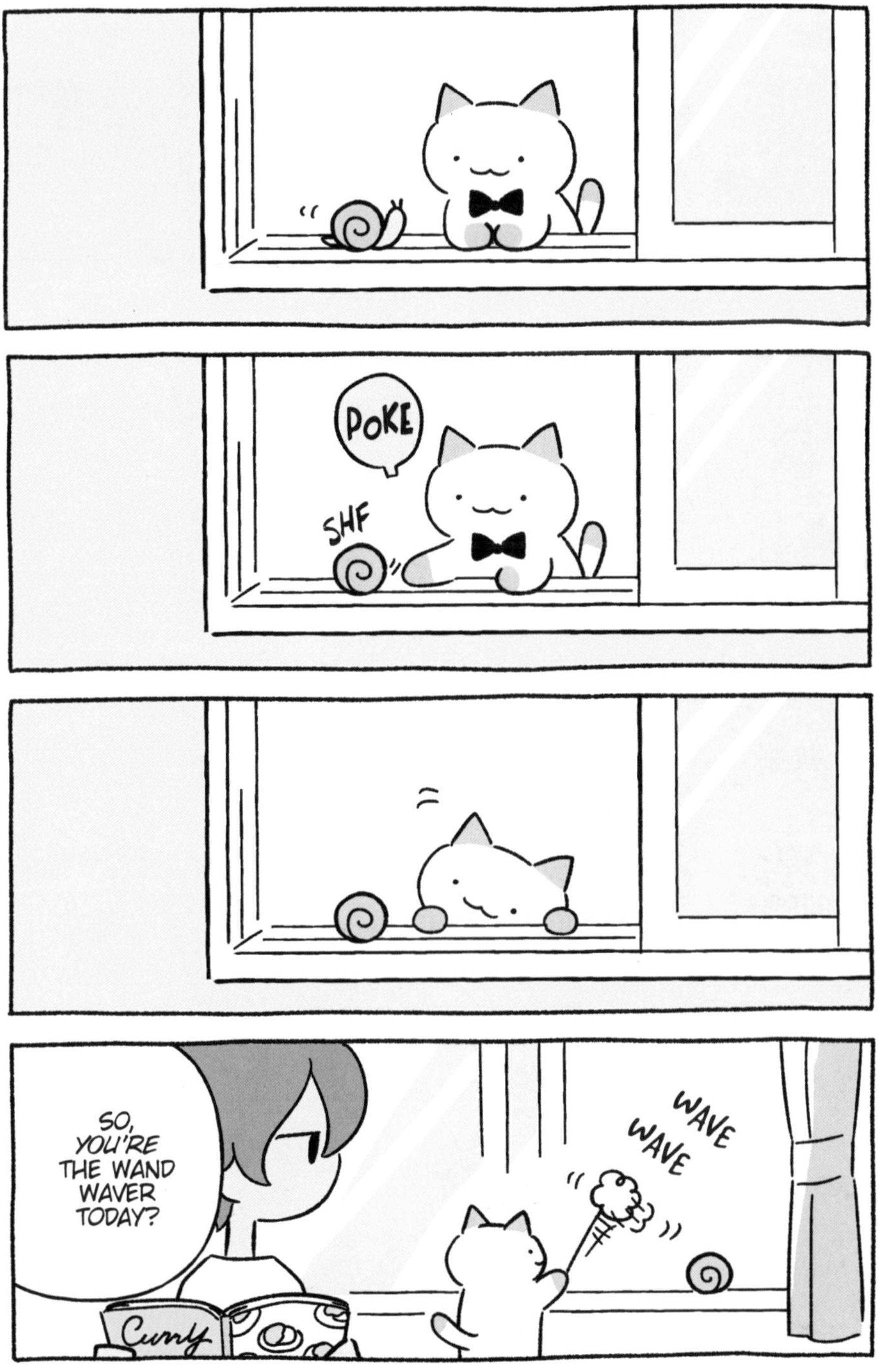
POKE
SHF
WAVE WAVE
SO, YOU'RE THE WAND WAVER TODAY?

# COOKING TOGETHER ①

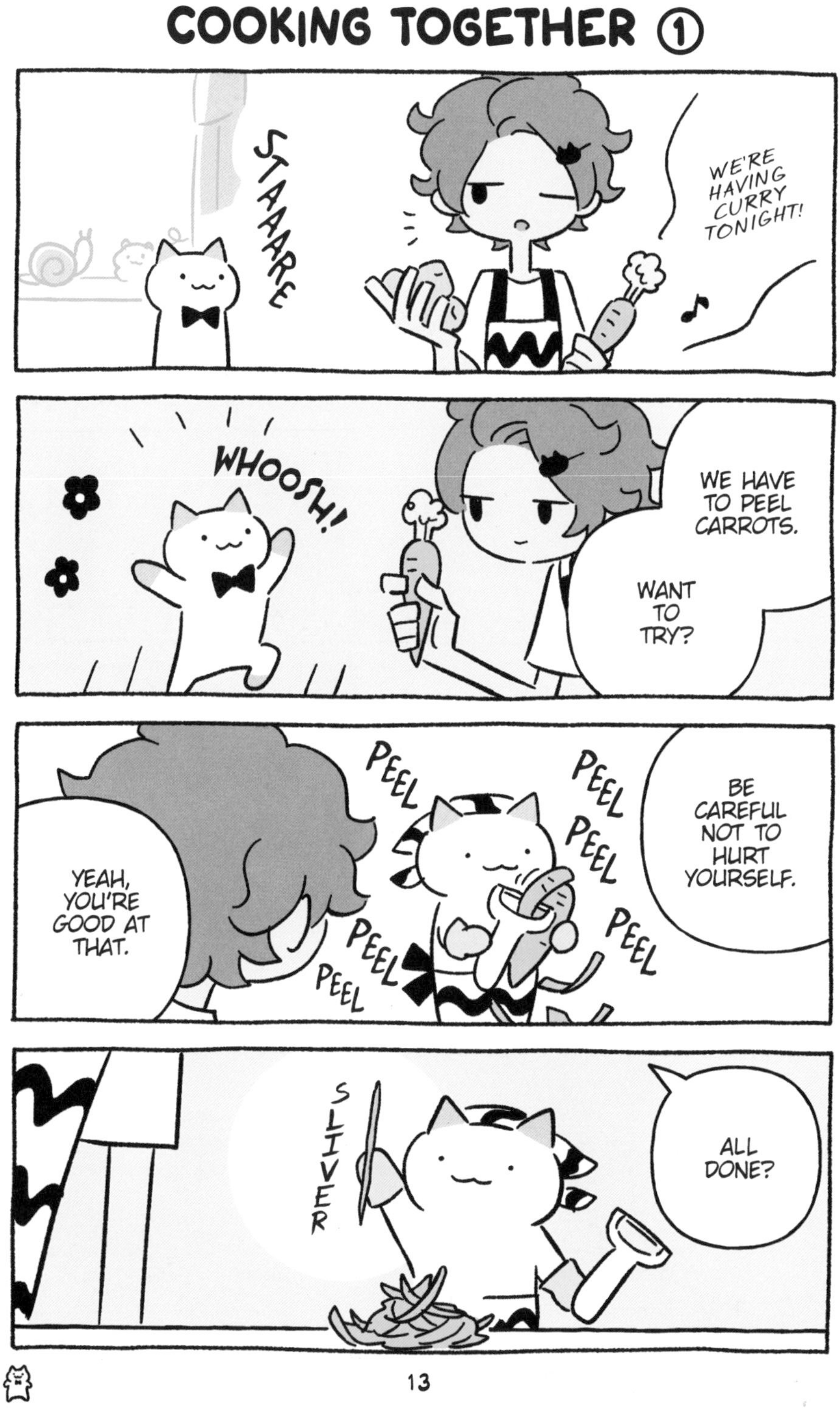
WE'RE HAVING CURRY TONIGHT!
STAAAARE
WE HAVE TO PEEL CARROTS.
WANT TO TRY?
WHOOSH!
BE CAREFUL NOT TO HURT YOURSELF.
PEEL
PEEL
PEEL
PEEL
PEEL
PEEL
YEAH, YOU'RE GOOD AT THAT.
ALL DONE?
SLIVER

# COOKING TOGETHER ②

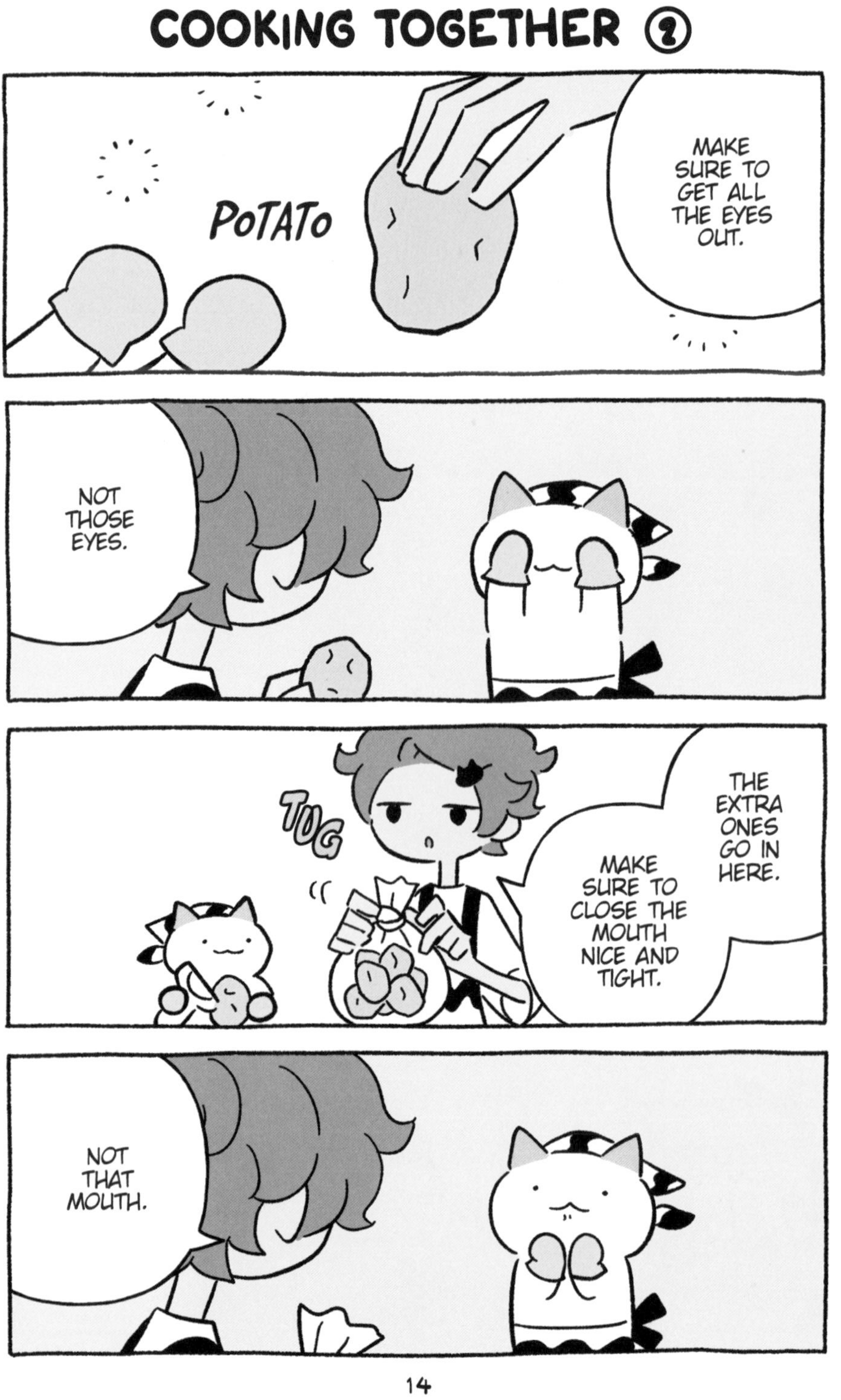

MAKE SURE TO GET ALL THE EYES OUT.
POTATO
NOT THOSE EYES.
THE EXTRA ONES GO IN HERE.
MAKE SURE TO CLOSE THE MOUTH NICE AND TIGHT.
TUG
NOT THAT MOUTH.

# HAVING YOU HERE

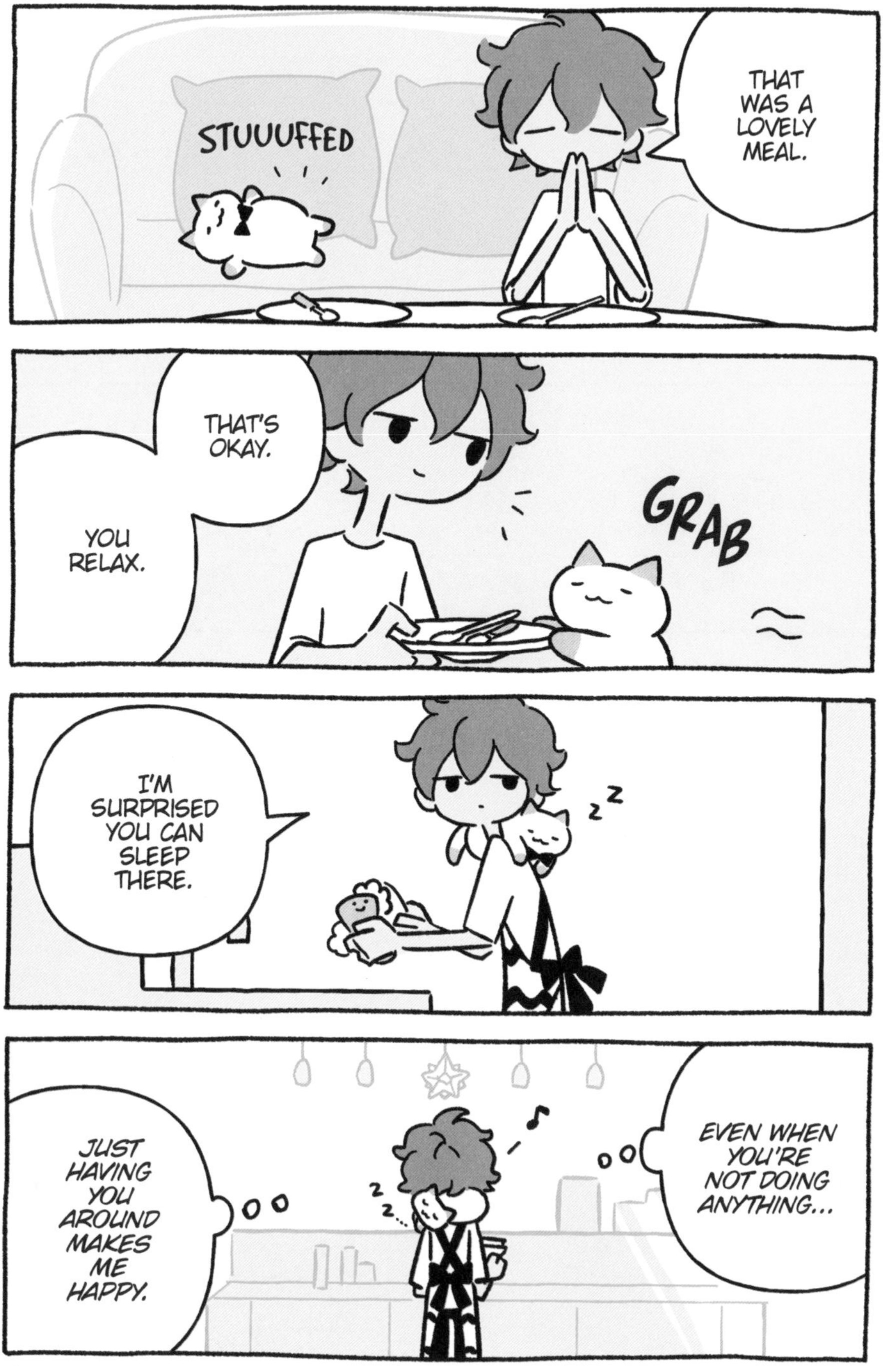
THAT WAS A LOVELY MEAL.
STUUUFFED
GRAB
THAT'S OKAY.
YOU RELAX.
I'M SURPRISED YOU CAN SLEEP THERE.
EVEN WHEN YOU'RE NOT DOING ANYTHING...
JUST HAVING YOU AROUND MAKES ME HAPPY.

# WHIPPED CREAM ARTIST

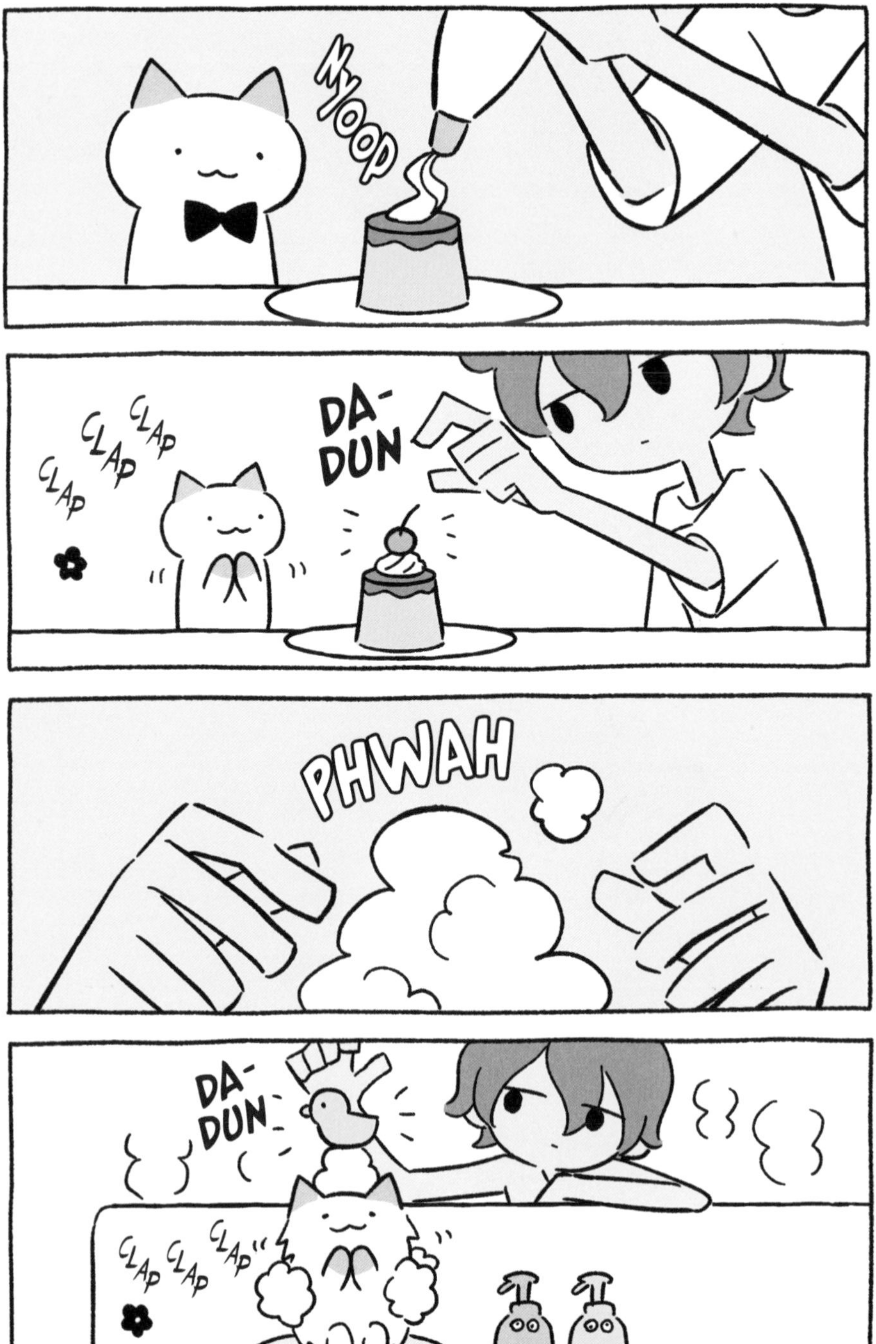
NYOOP
DA-DUN
CLAP CLAP CLAP
PHWAH
DA-DUN
CLAP CLAP CLAP

# SHORTCUT

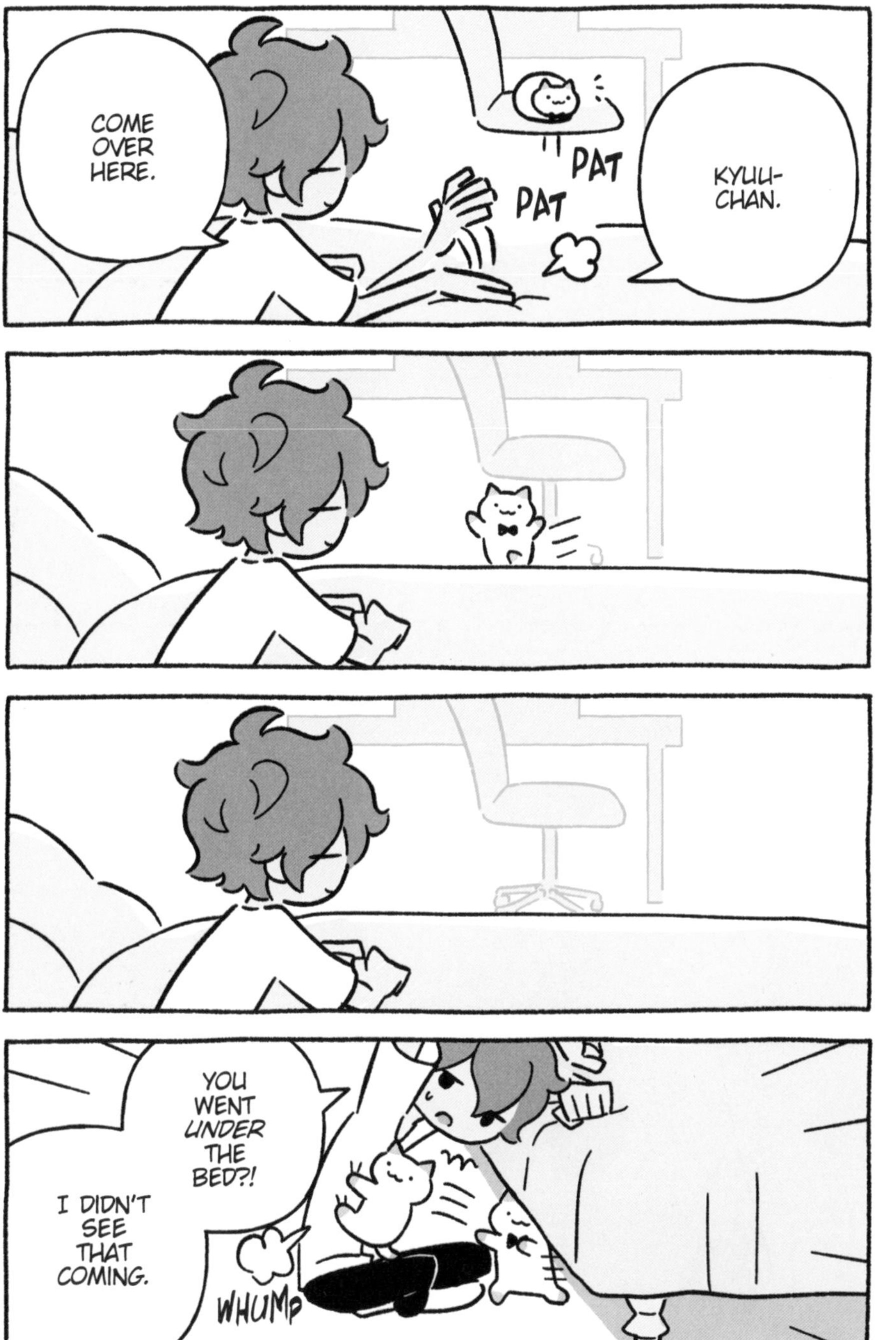

KYUU-CHAN.
PAT
PAT
COME OVER HERE.
YOU WENT *UNDER* THE BED?!
I DIDN'T SEE THAT COMING.
WHUMP

# HAND CLAPPING GAMES

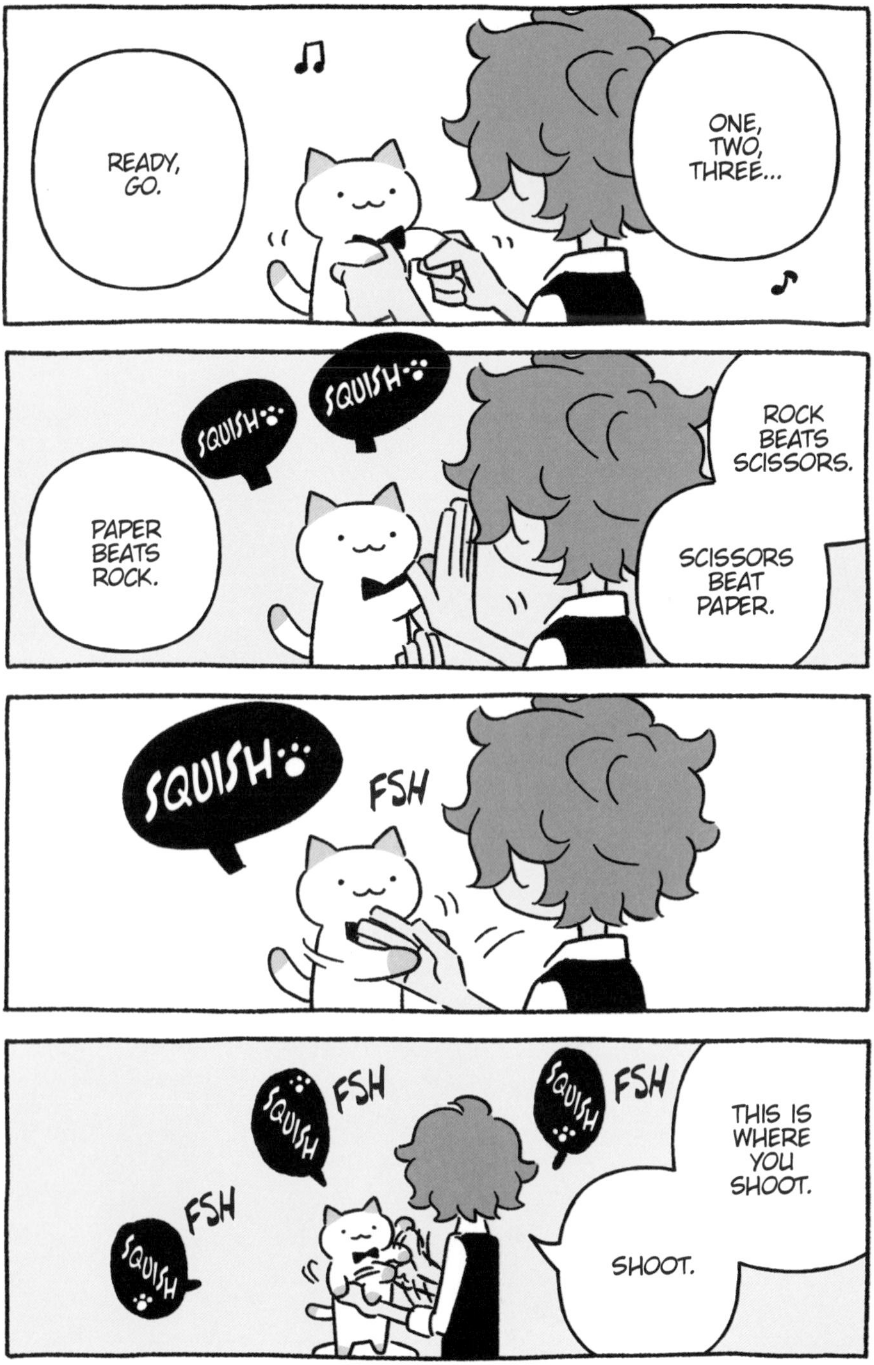

ONE, TWO, THREE...
READY, GO.
ROCK BEATS SCISSORS.
SQUISH
SQUISH
SCISSORS BEAT PAPER.
PAPER BEATS ROCK.
SQUISH
FSH
THIS IS WHERE YOU SHOOT.
FSH
SQUISH
FSH
SQUISH
SHOOT.
FSH
SQUISH

# ALL FISH ALL THE TIME

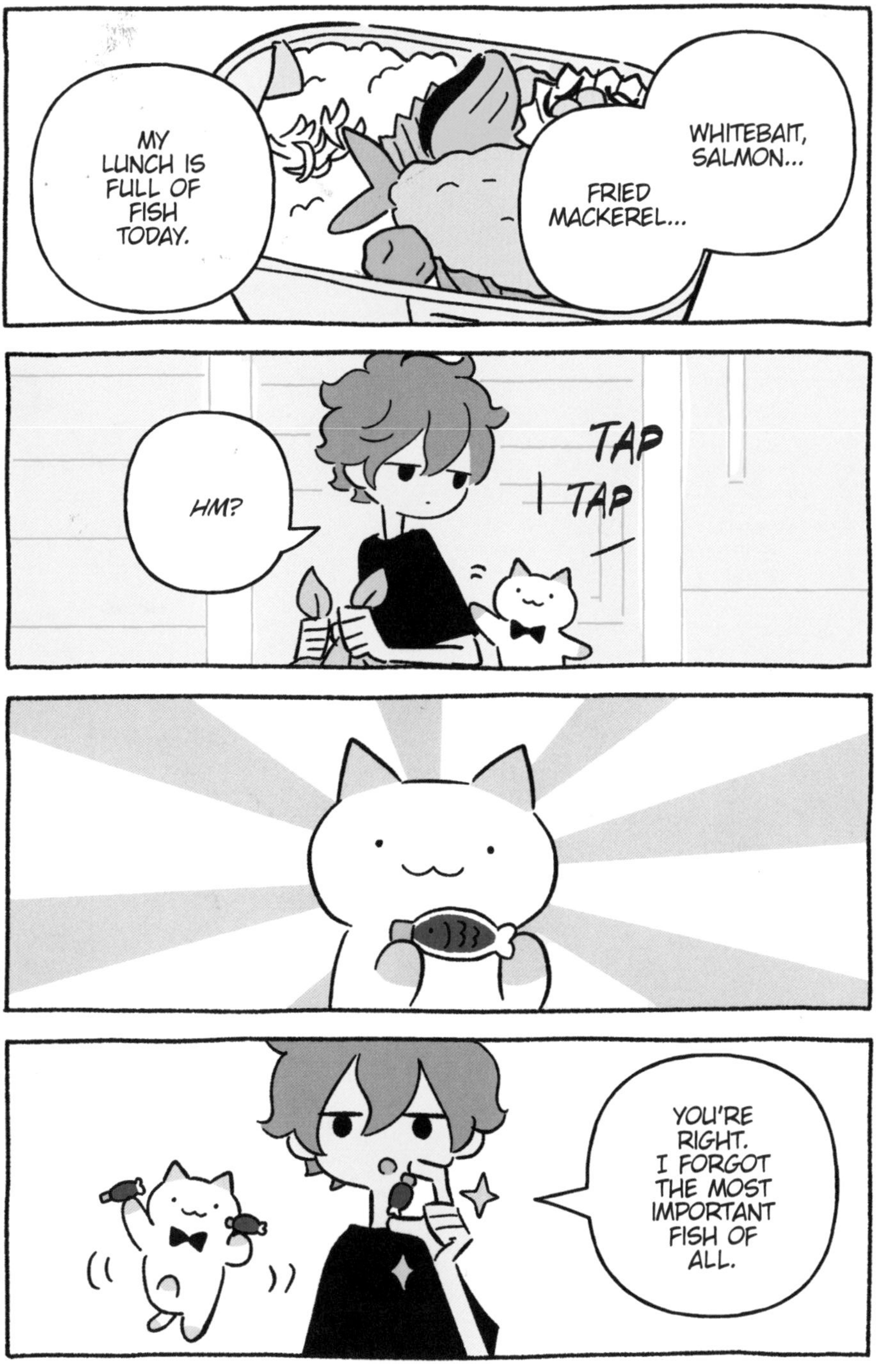
WHITEBAIT, SALMON...
FRIED MACKEREL...
MY LUNCH IS FULL OF FISH TODAY.
TAP TAP
HM?
YOU'RE RIGHT. I FORGOT THE MOST IMPORTANT FISH OF ALL.

# DOWNPOUR

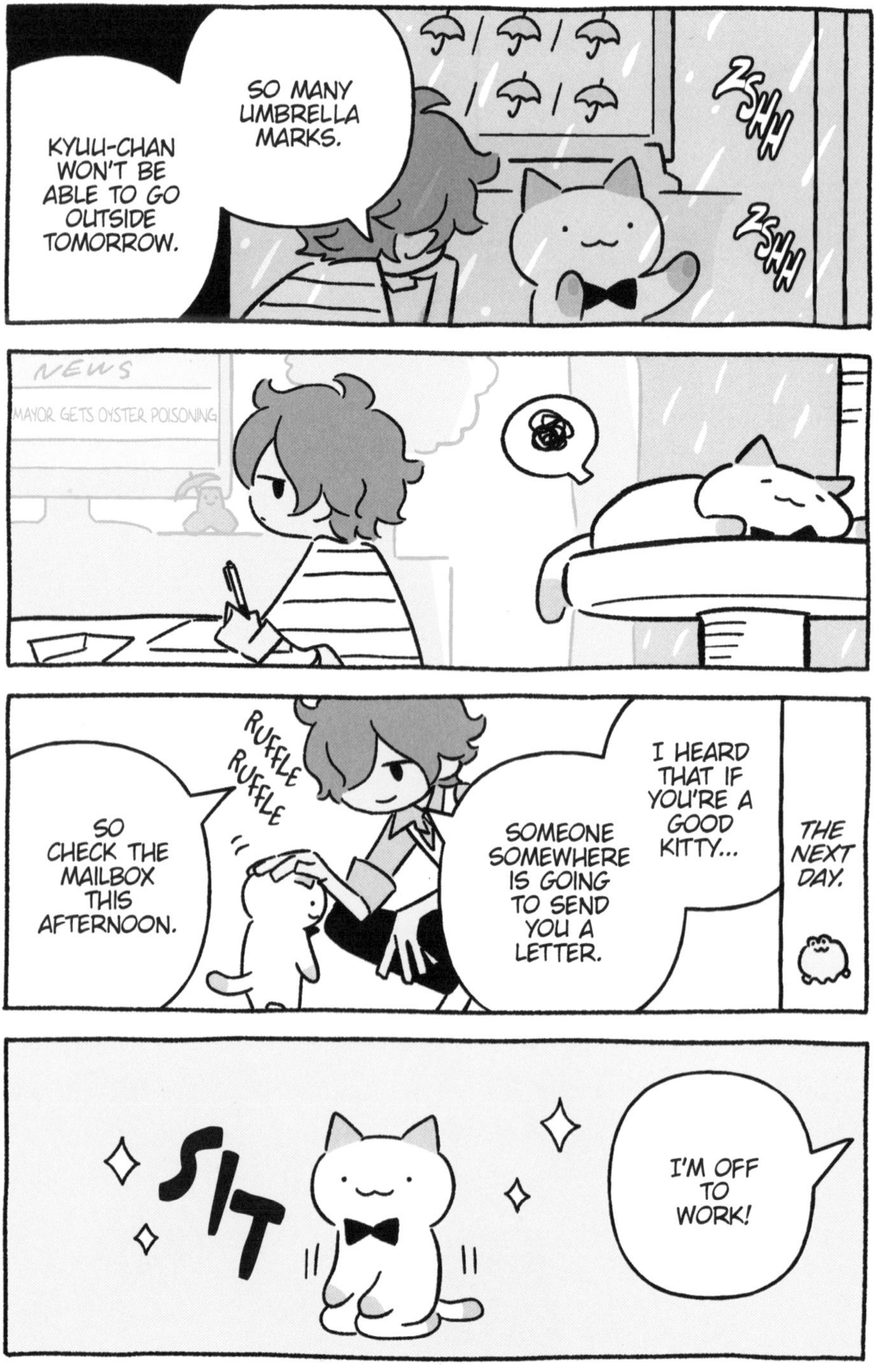

ZSHH
SO MANY UMBRELLA MARKS.
ZSHH
KYUU-CHAN WON'T BE ABLE TO GO OUTSIDE TOMORROW.
NEWS
MAYOR GETS OYSTER POISONING
THE NEXT DAY.
I HEARD THAT IF YOU'RE A GOOD KITTY...
SOMEONE SOMEWHERE IS GOING TO SEND YOU A LETTER.
RUFFLE RUFFLE
SO CHECK THE MAILBOX THIS AFTERNOON.
I'M OFF TO WORK!
SIT

# GOOD KITTY

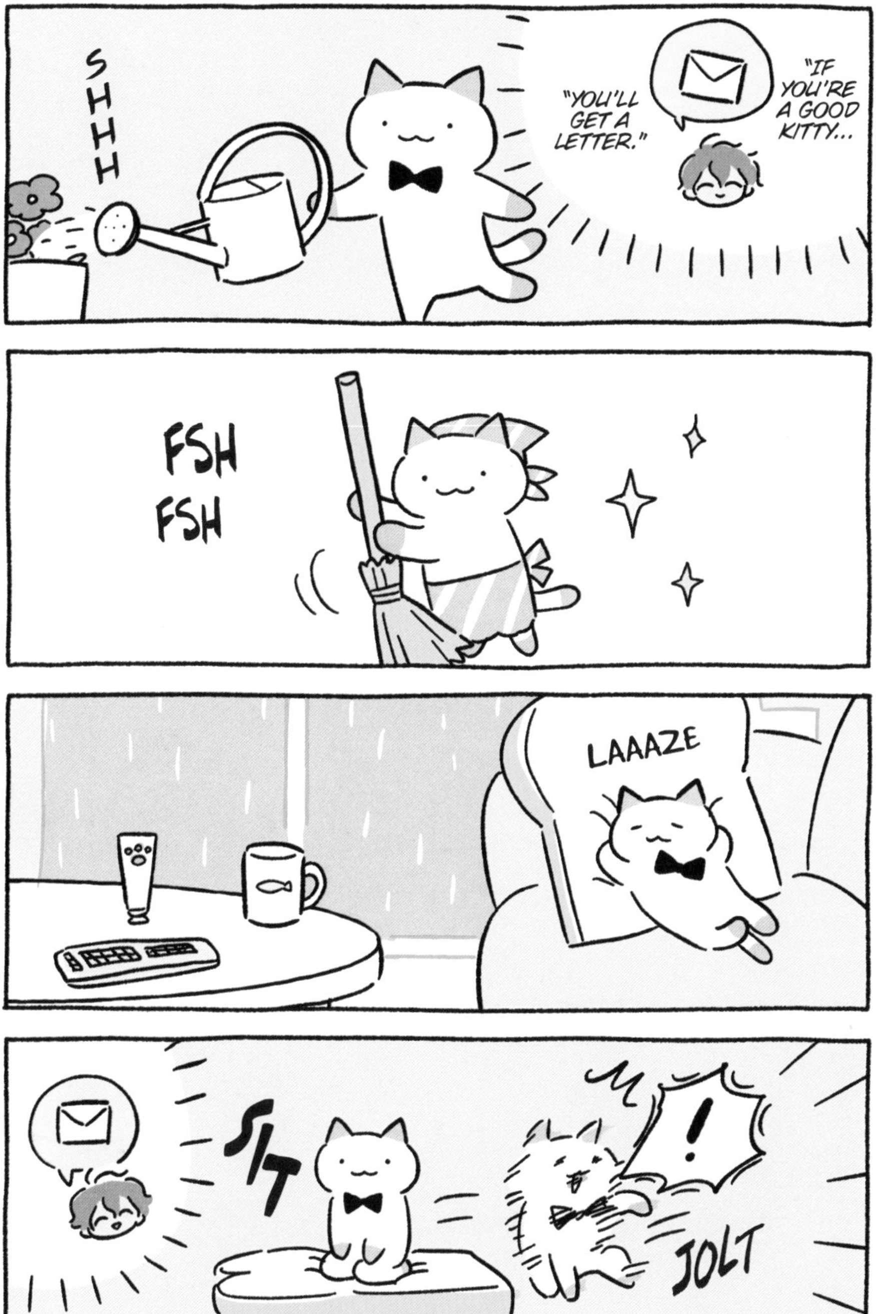

"IF YOU'RE A GOOD KITTY...
"YOU'LL GET A LETTER."
SHHH
FSH
FSH
LAAAZE
!
JOLT
SIT

# KYUU'S CLUES

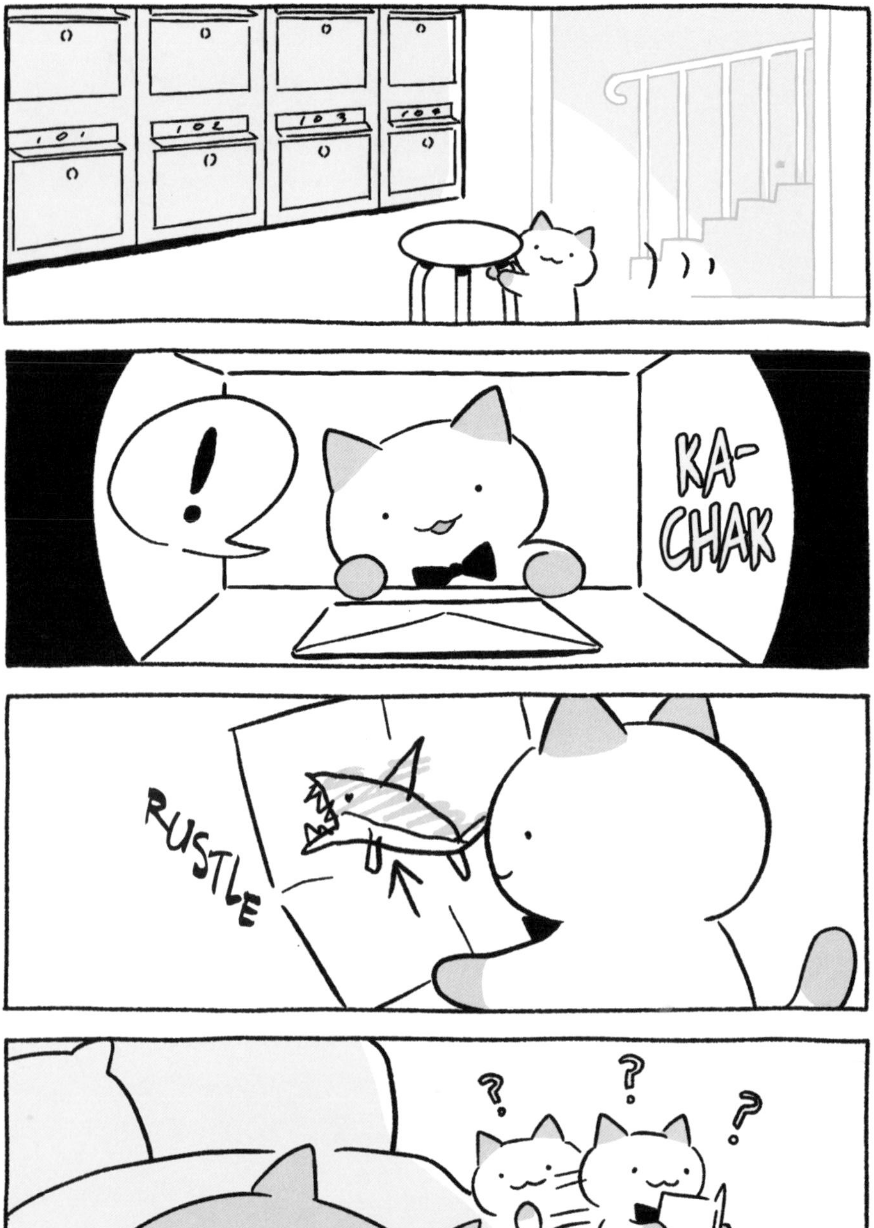
!
KA-
CHAK
RUSTLE
? ? ?

# COOKIE

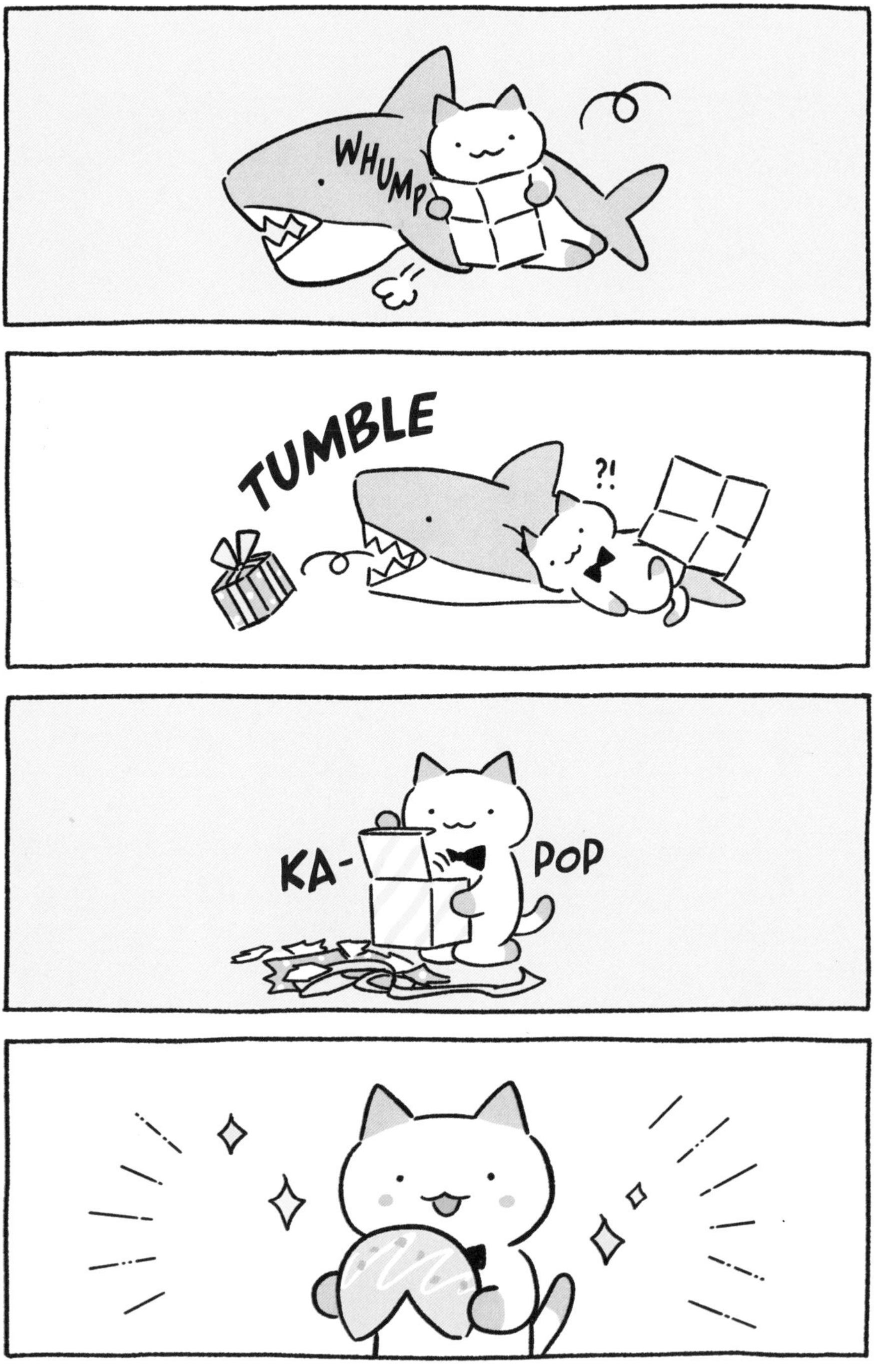
WHUMP
TUMBLE
?!
KA-
POP

# KYUU'S CLUES REVISITED

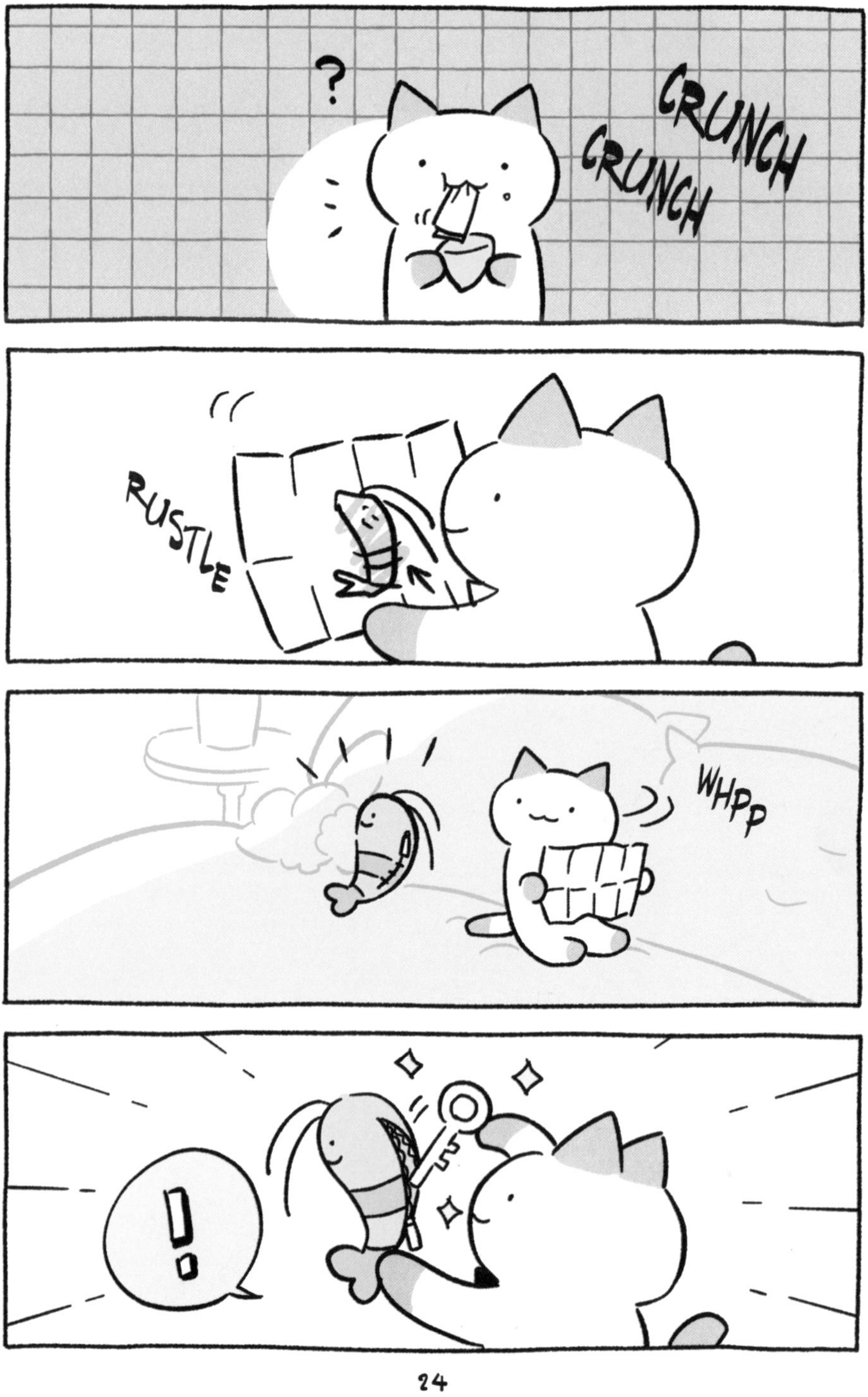
CRUNCH
CRUNCH
?
RUSTLE
WHPP
!

# COLLABORATOR

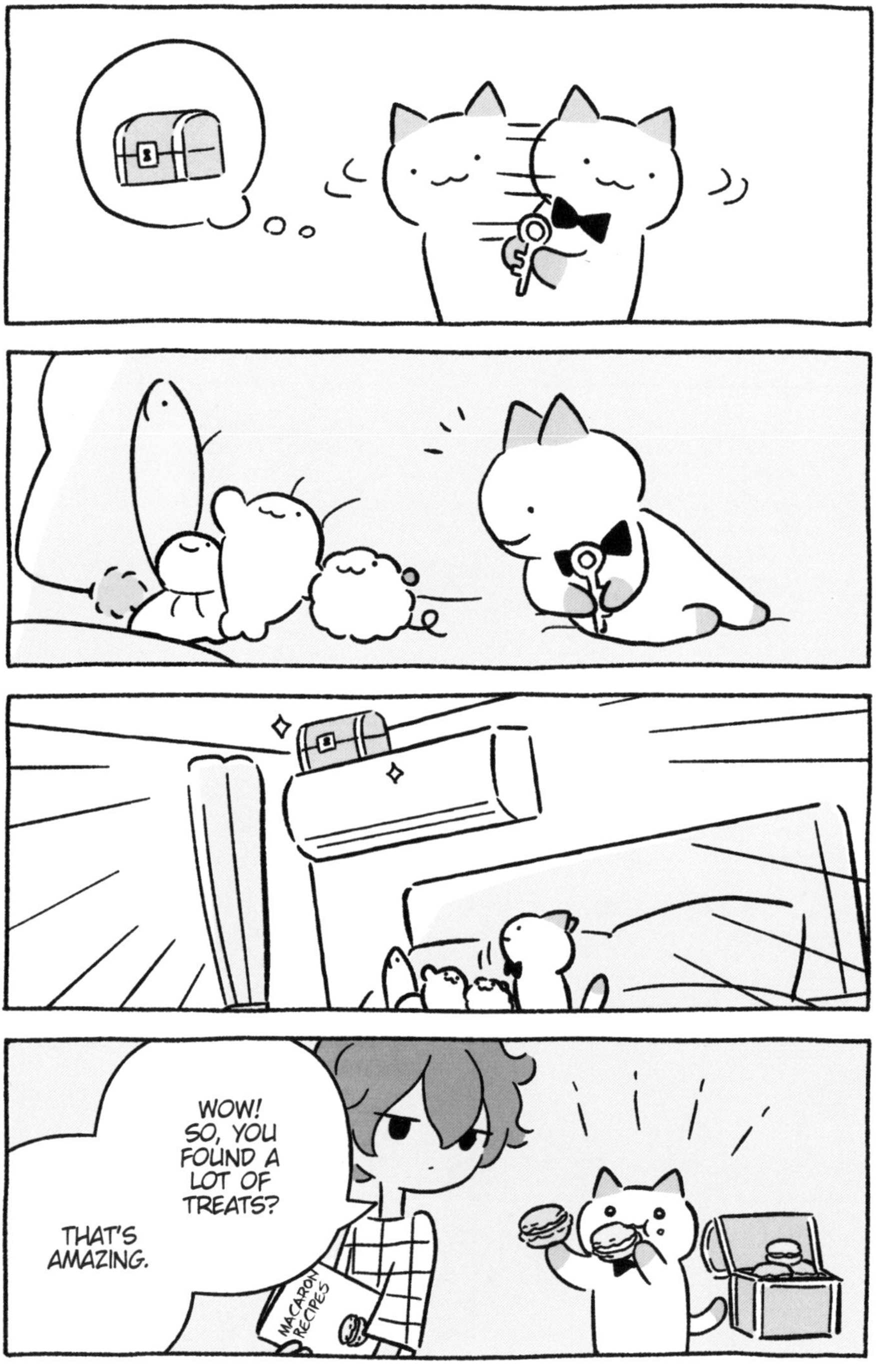
WOW! SO, YOU FOUND A LOT OF TREATS?
THAT'S AMAZING.
MACARON RECIPES

# RUSSIAN ROULETTE PUFFS

I MADE SOME RUSSIAN ROU-LETTE PUFFS.
RMB
RMB
ALL OF THEM HAVE CUSTARD CREAM EXCEPT ONE...
RMB
RMB
RMB
GULP
WHICH HAS FLAN!!
YUMMY!

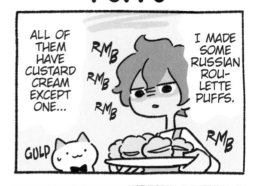

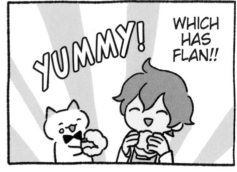

# AGING SOCIETY

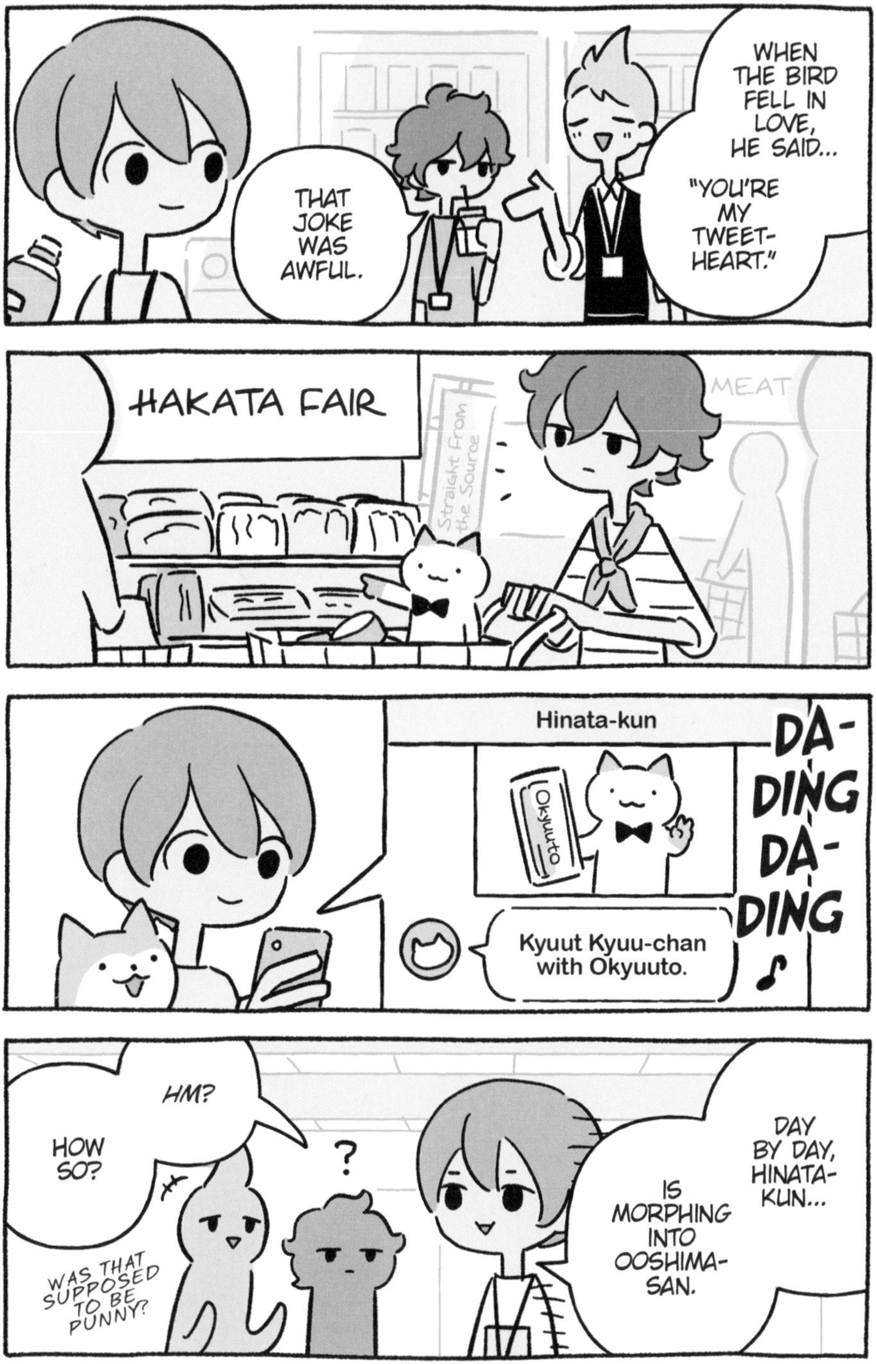
WHEN THE BIRD FELL IN LOVE, HE SAID... "YOU'RE MY TWEET-HEART."
THAT JOKE WAS AWFUL.
MEAT
Straight From the Source
HAKATA FAIR
DA-DING DA-DING ♪
Hinata-kun
Okyuuto
Kyuut Kyuu-chan with Okyuuto.
DAY BY DAY, HINATA-KUN... IS MORPHING INTO OOSHIMA-SAN.
?
HM? HOW SO?
WAS THAT SUPPOSED TO BE PUNNY?

# WORK FROM HOME

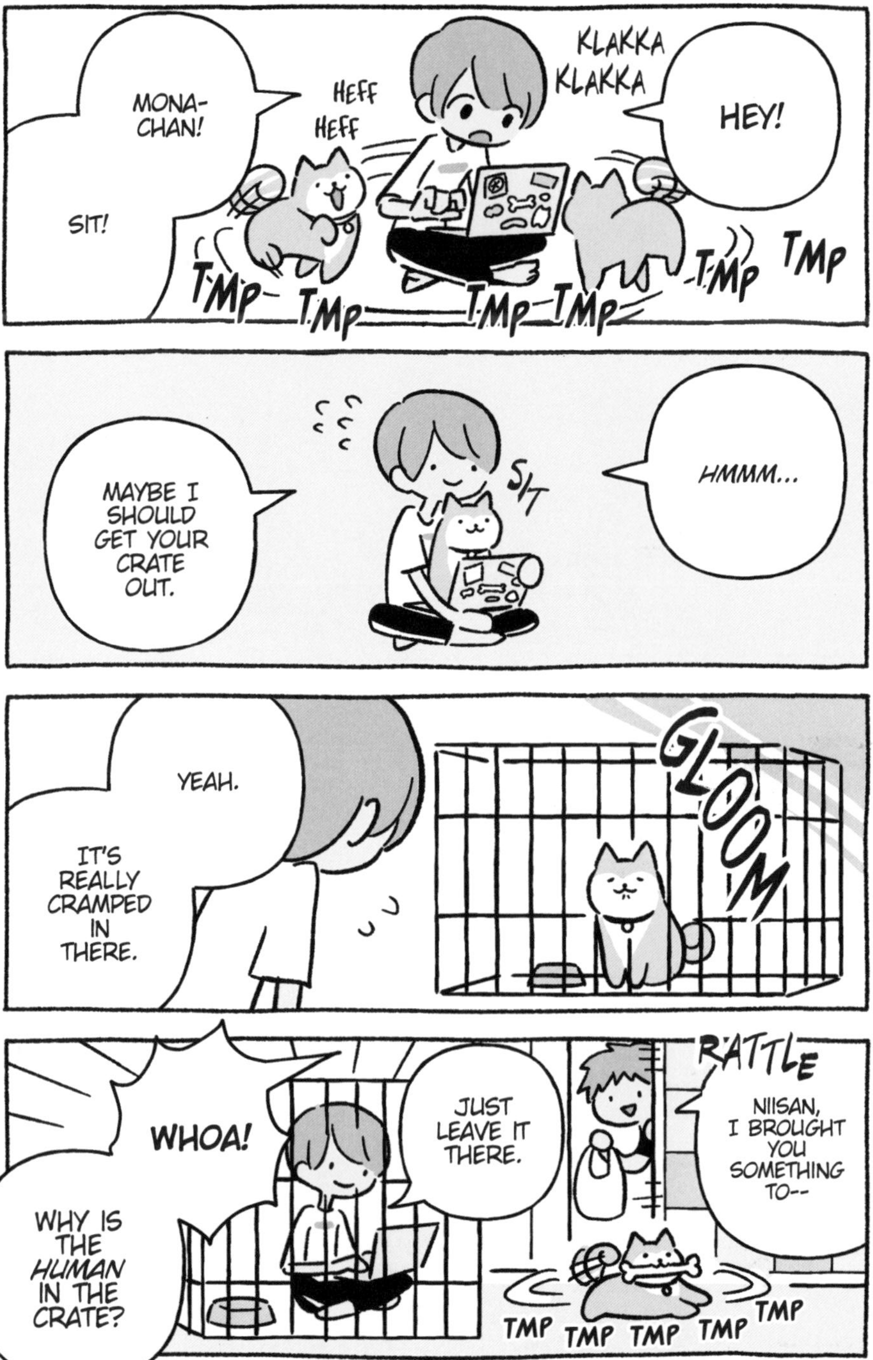
KLAKKA KLAKKA
HEY!
HEFF HEFF
MONA-CHAN!
SIT!
TMP TMP TMP TMP TMP TMP
HMMM...
SIT
MAYBE I SHOULD GET YOUR CRATE OUT.
GLOOM
YEAH.
IT'S REALLY CRAMPED IN THERE.
RATTLE
NIISAN, I BROUGHT YOU SOMETHING TO--
JUST LEAVE IT THERE.
WHOA!
WHY IS THE *HUMAN* IN THE CRATE?
TMP TMP TMP TMP TMP

# FEINT

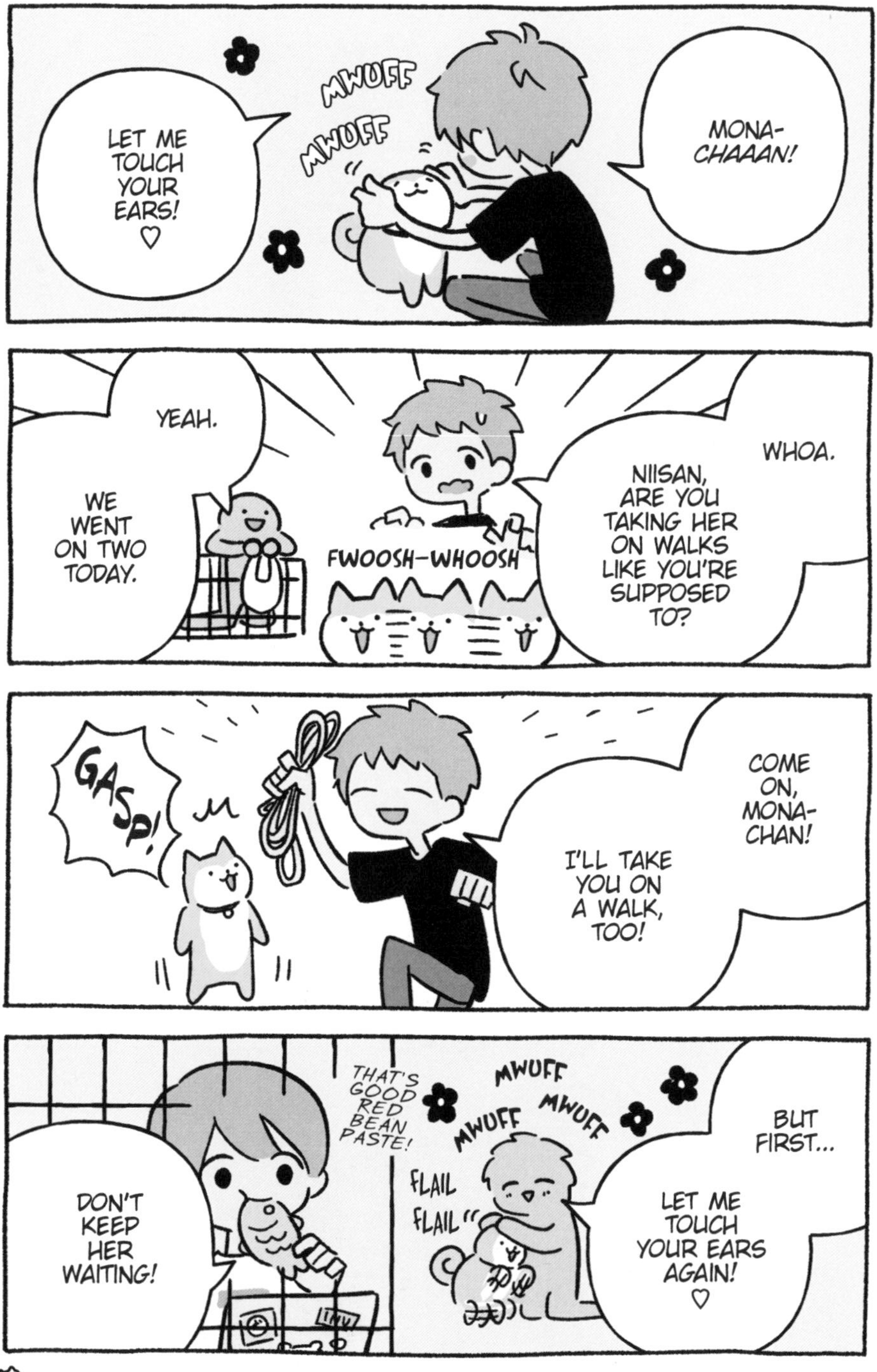

MONA-CHAAAN!
MWUFF
MWUFF
LET ME TOUCH YOUR EARS! ♡
WHOA.
NIISAN, ARE YOU TAKING HER ON WALKS LIKE YOU'RE SUPPOSED TO?
FWOOSH-WHOOSH
YEAH.
WE WENT ON TWO TODAY.
COME ON, MONA-CHAN!
I'LL TAKE YOU ON A WALK, TOO!
GASP!
BUT FIRST...
LET ME TOUCH YOUR EARS AGAIN! ♡
MWUFF
MWUFF
MWUFF
FLAIL
FLAIL
THAT'S GOOD RED BEAN PASTE!
DON'T KEEP HER WAITING!

# FULL-POWER MONA-CHAN

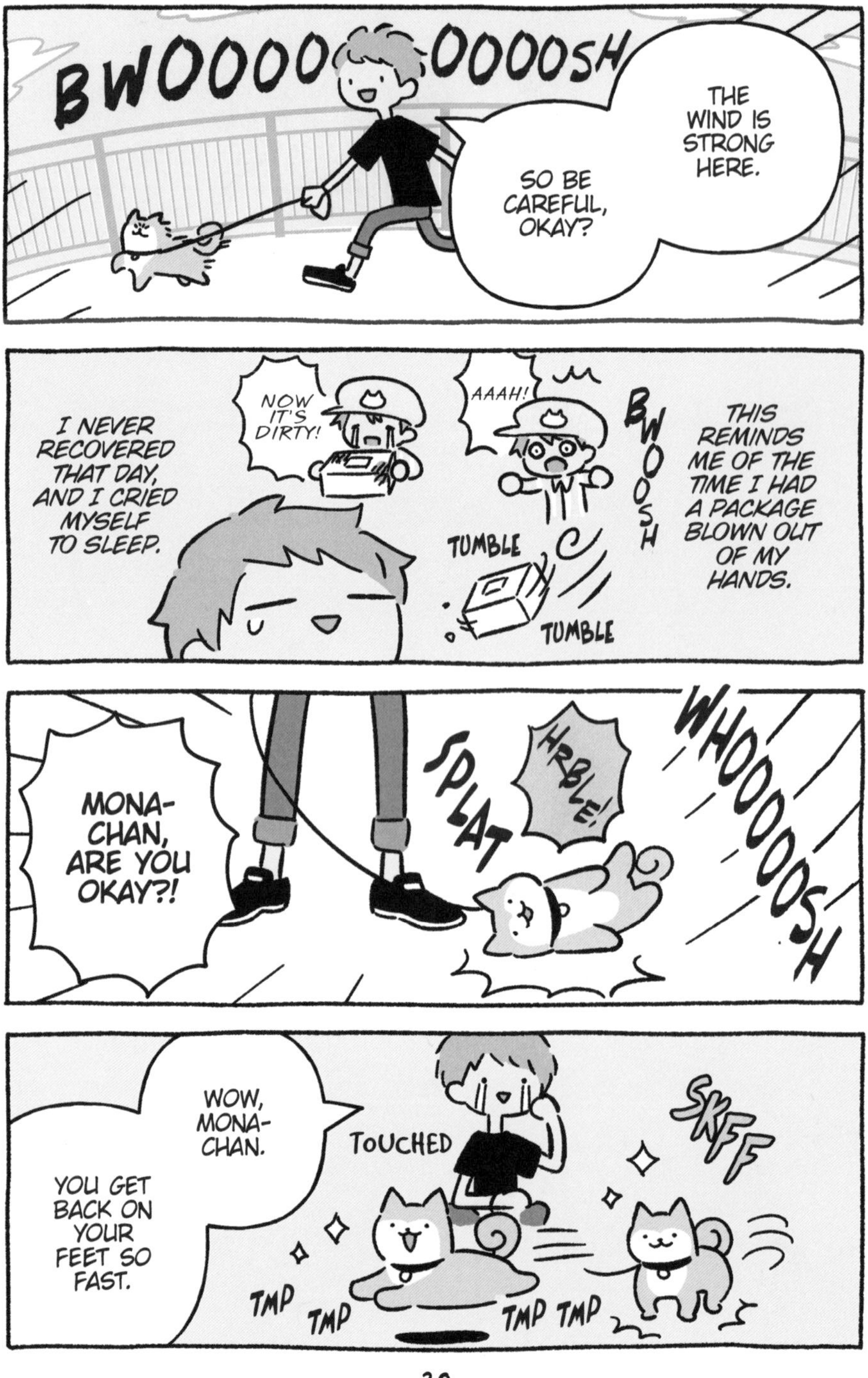
BWOOOOOOOOOSH
THE WIND IS STRONG HERE.
SO BE CAREFUL, OKAY?
THIS REMINDS ME OF THE TIME I HAD A PACKAGE BLOWN OUT OF MY HANDS.
BWOOOSH
AAAH!
NOW IT'S DIRTY!
TUMBLE
TUMBLE
I NEVER RECOVERED THAT DAY, AND I CRIED MYSELF TO SLEEP.
WHOOOOOOSH
HRBLE!
SPLAT
MONA-CHAN, ARE YOU OKAY?!
SKFF
WOW, MONA-CHAN.
TOUCHED
YOU GET BACK ON YOUR FEET SO FAST.
TMP TMP
TMP TMP
TMP
TMP

# BACK ON FEET CONTEST

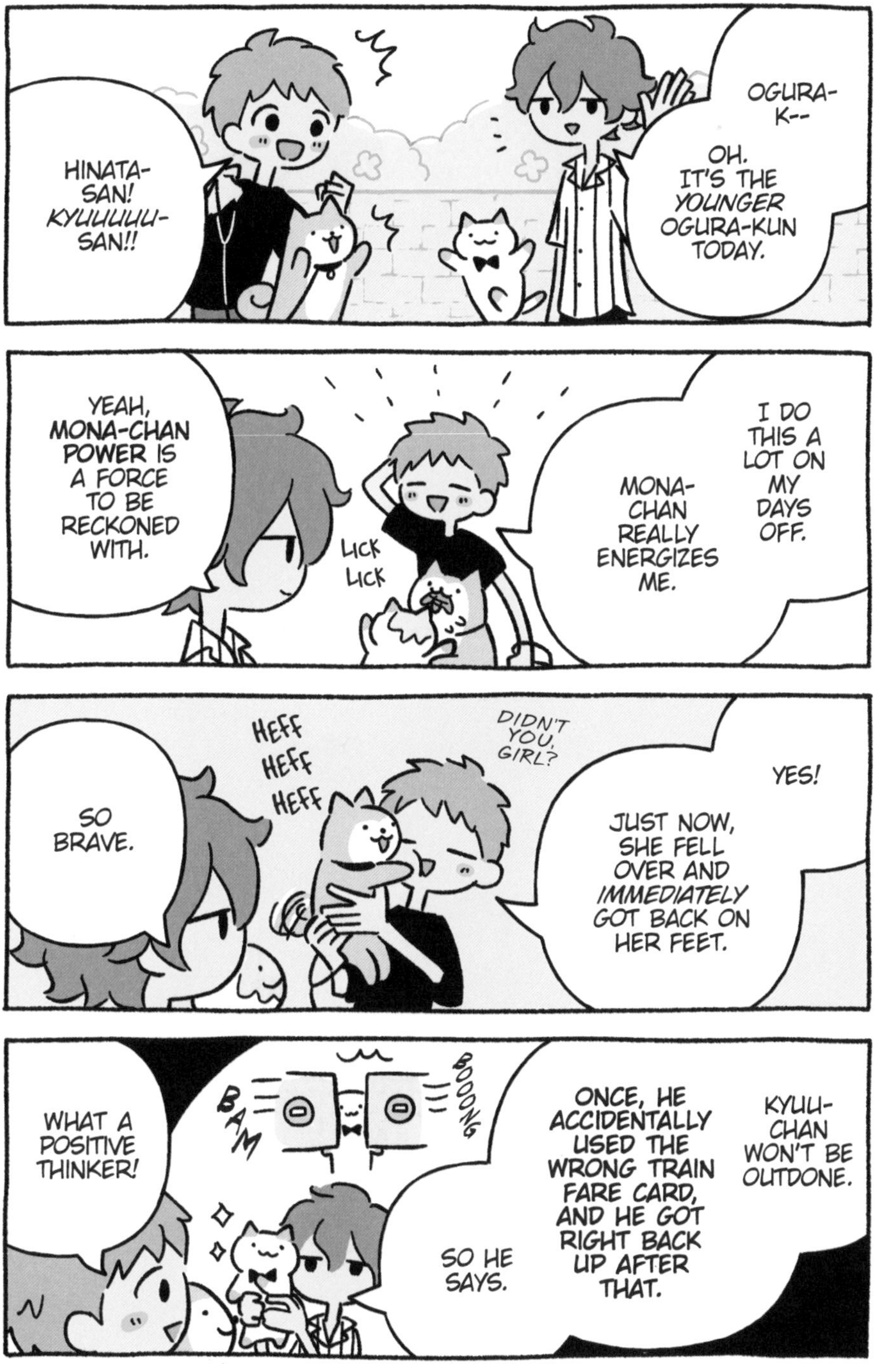
OGURA-K--
OH. IT'S THE *YOUNGER* OGURA-KUN TODAY.
HINATA-SAN! KYUUUUUU-SAN!!
I DO THIS A LOT ON MY DAYS OFF.
MONA-CHAN REALLY ENERGIZES ME.
LICK LICK
YEAH, **MONA-CHAN POWER** IS A FORCE TO BE RECKONED WITH.
YES!
DIDN'T YOU, GIRL?
JUST NOW, SHE FELL OVER AND *IMMEDIATELY* GOT BACK ON HER FEET.
HEFF HEFF HEFF
SO BRAVE.
KYUU-CHAN WON'T BE OUTDONE.
ONCE, HE ACCIDENTALLY USED THE WRONG TRAIN FARE CARD, AND HE GOT RIGHT BACK UP AFTER THAT.
BOOONG
SO HE SAYS.
BAM
WHAT A POSITIVE THINKER!

# SOOTHING ANIMALS

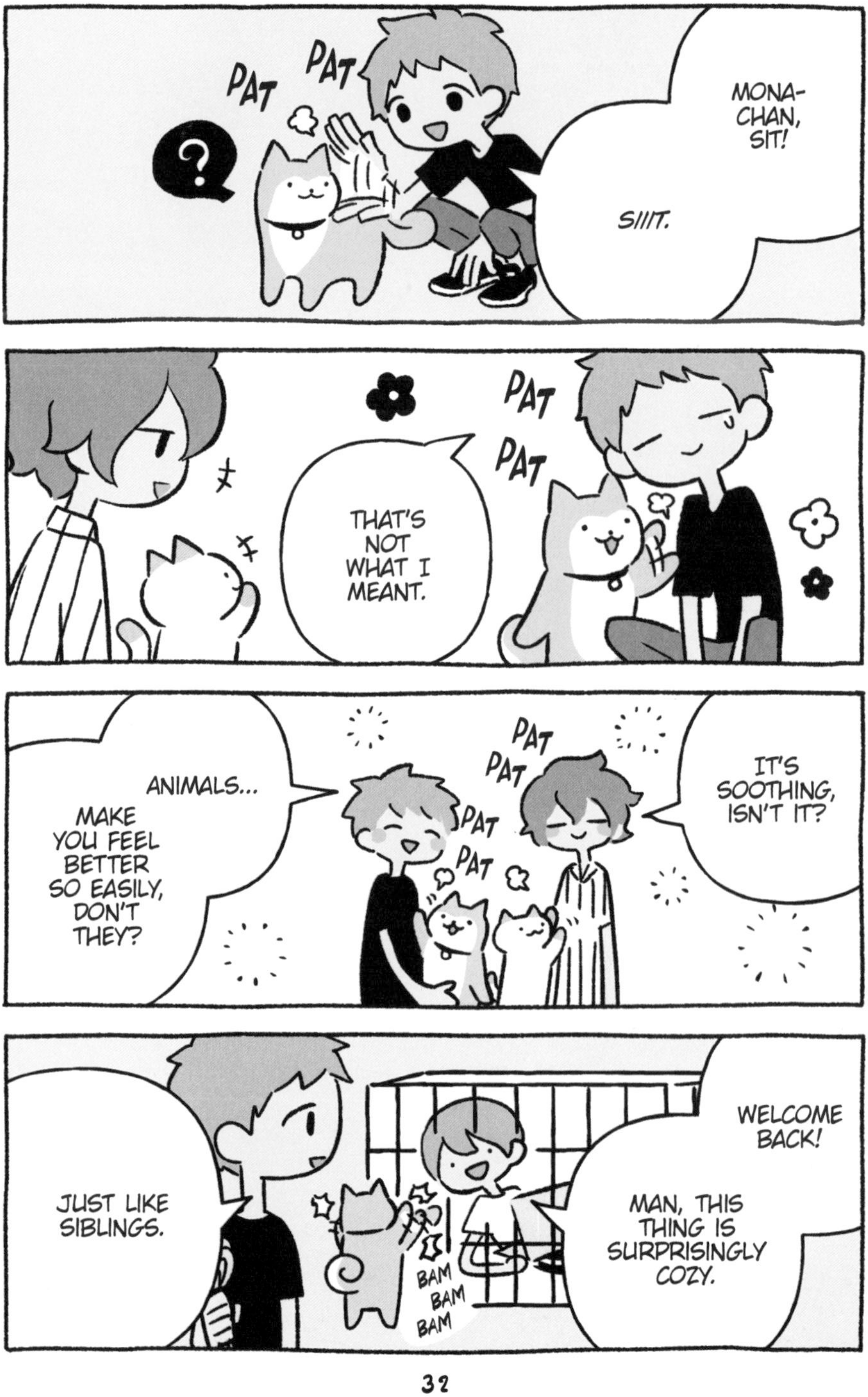
MONA-CHAN, SIT!
SIIIT.
PAT
PAT
?
PAT
PAT
THAT'S NOT WHAT I MEANT.
IT'S SOOTHING, ISN'T IT?
PAT
PAT
PAT
PAT
ANIMALS...
MAKE YOU FEEL BETTER SO EASILY, DON'T THEY?
WELCOME BACK!
MAN, THIS THING IS SURPRISINGLY COZY.
BAM
BAM
BAM
JUST LIKE SIBLINGS.

# PERCEPTIVE

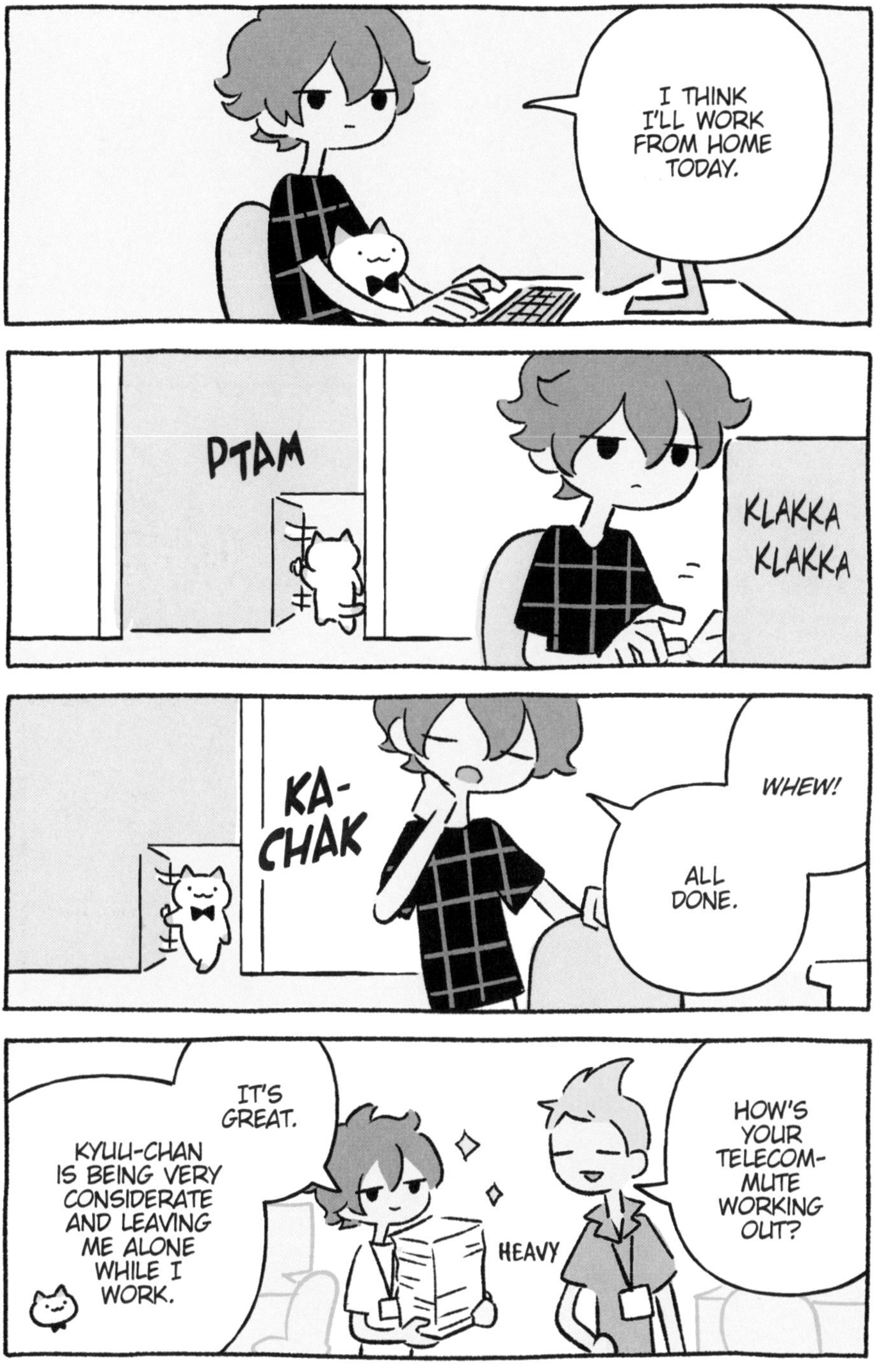
I THINK I'LL WORK FROM HOME TODAY.
KLAKKA KLAKKA
PTAM
WHEW!
ALL DONE.
KA-CHAK
HOW'S YOUR TELECOM-MUTE WORKING OUT?
IT'S GREAT.
KYUU-CHAN IS BEING VERY CONSIDERATE AND LEAVING ME ALONE WHILE I WORK.
HEAVY

# ENTRANCING HEAD TILT AND SMILE

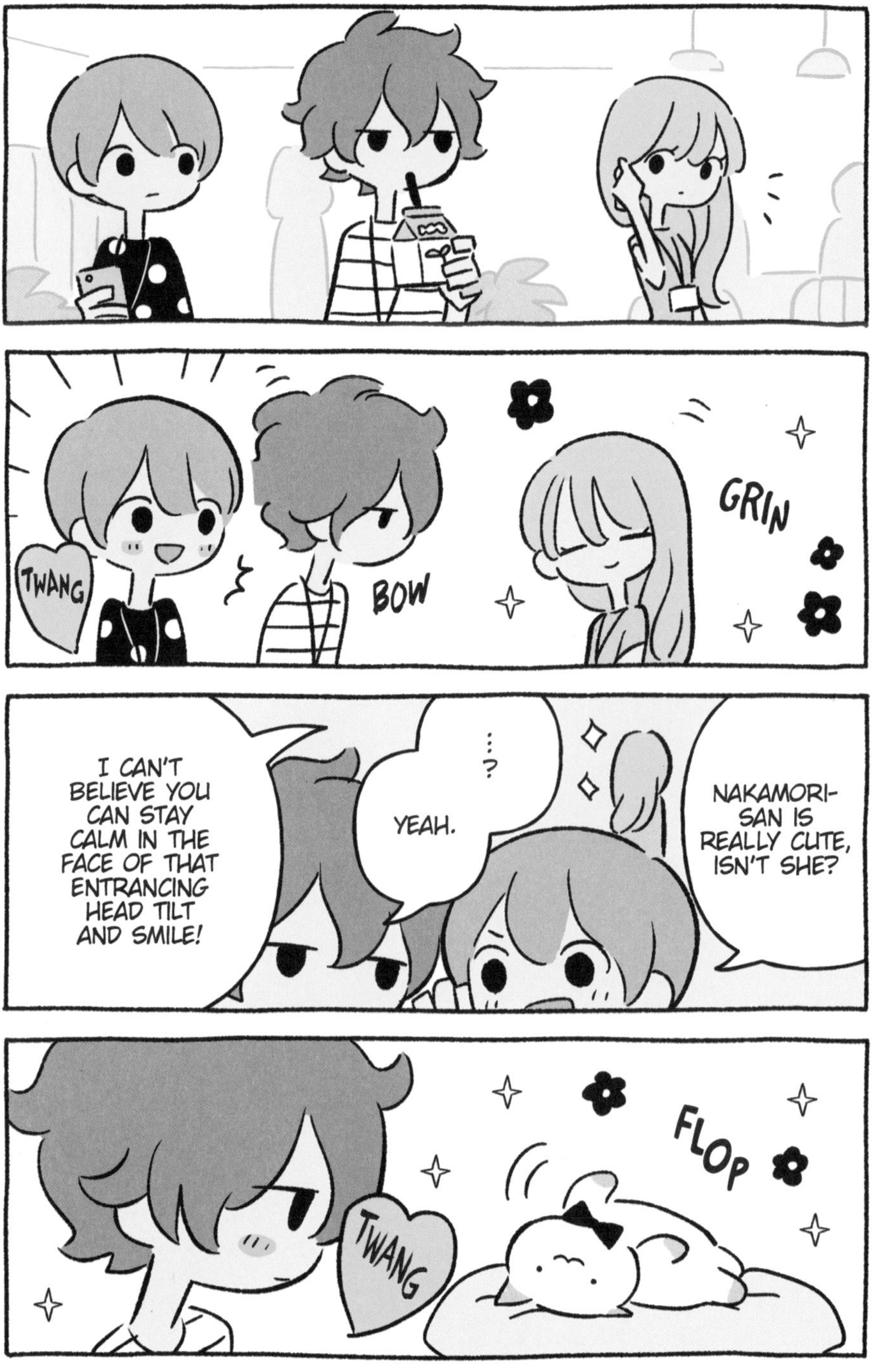
GRIN
BOW
TWANG
NAKAMORI-SAN IS REALLY CUTE, ISN'T SHE?
...?
YEAH.
I CAN'T BELIEVE YOU CAN STAY CALM IN THE FACE OF THAT ENTRANCING HEAD TILT AND SMILE!
FLOP
TWANG

# SUNNY SPOT

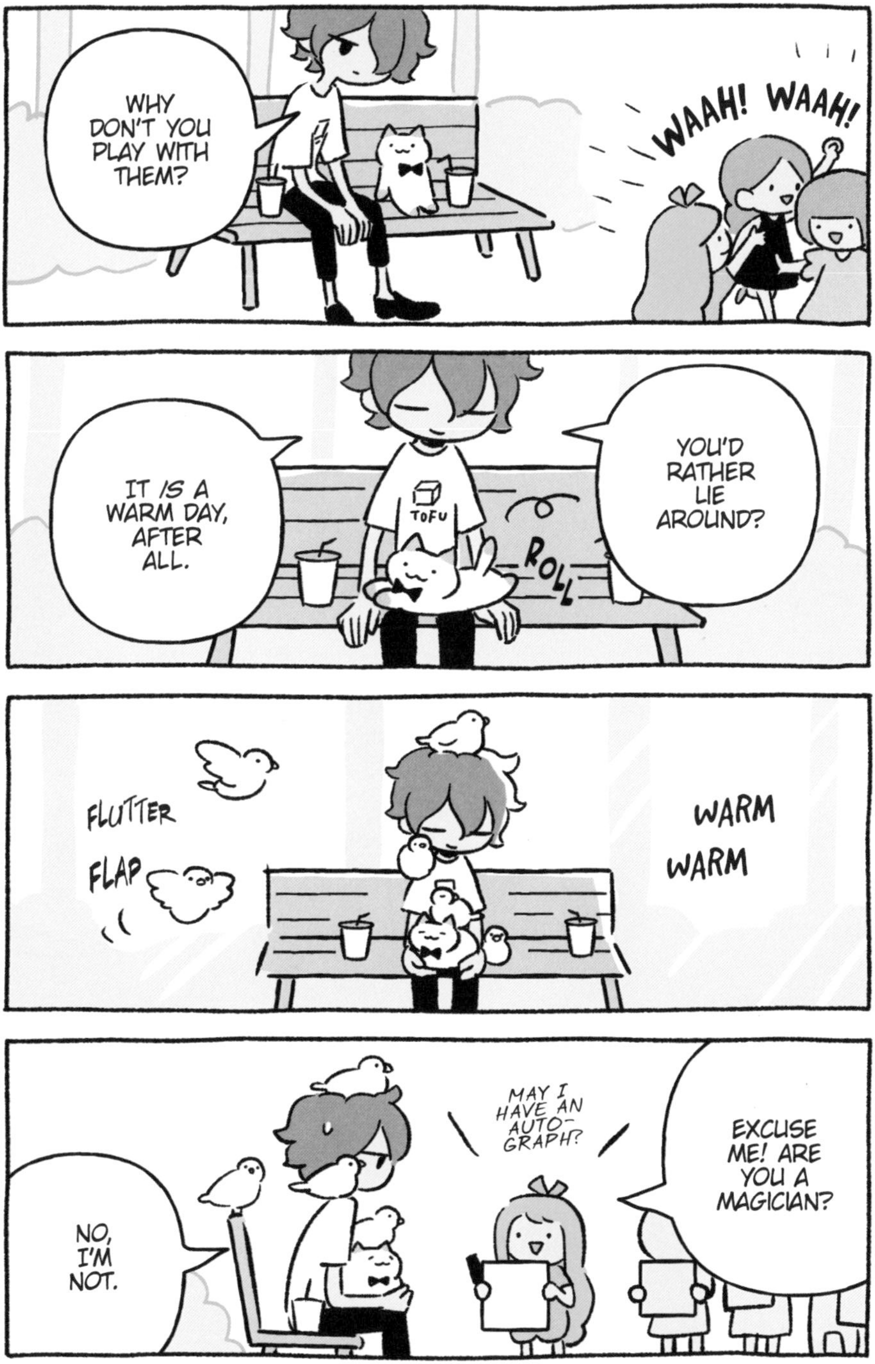
WAAH! WAAH!
WHY DON'T YOU PLAY WITH THEM?
YOU'D RATHER LIE AROUND?
ROLL
IT IS A WARM DAY, AFTER ALL.
WARM
WARM
FLUTTER
FLAP
EXCUSE ME! ARE YOU A MAGICIAN?
MAY I HAVE AN AUTO-GRAPH?
NO, I'M NOT.

# SOURNESS DETECTOR

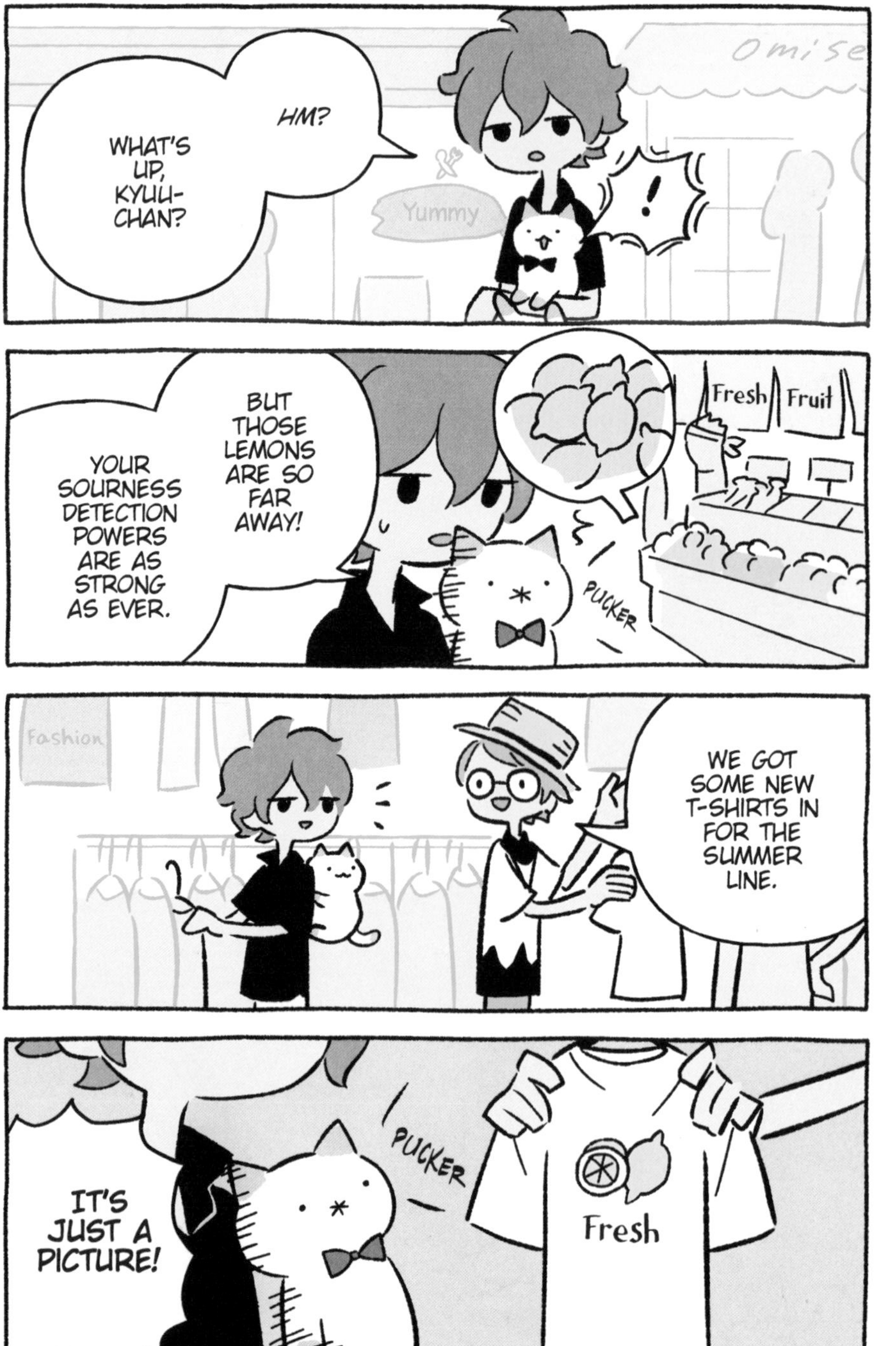

Omise
HM?
WHAT'S UP, KYUU-CHAN?
Yummy
!
Fresh Fruit
PUCKER
BUT THOSE LEMONS ARE SO FAR AWAY!
YOUR SOURNESS DETECTION POWERS ARE AS STRONG AS EVER.
WE GOT SOME NEW T-SHIRTS IN FOR THE SUMMER LINE.
Fashion
Fresh
PUCKER
IT'S JUST A PICTURE!

# PAPER MUNCHING

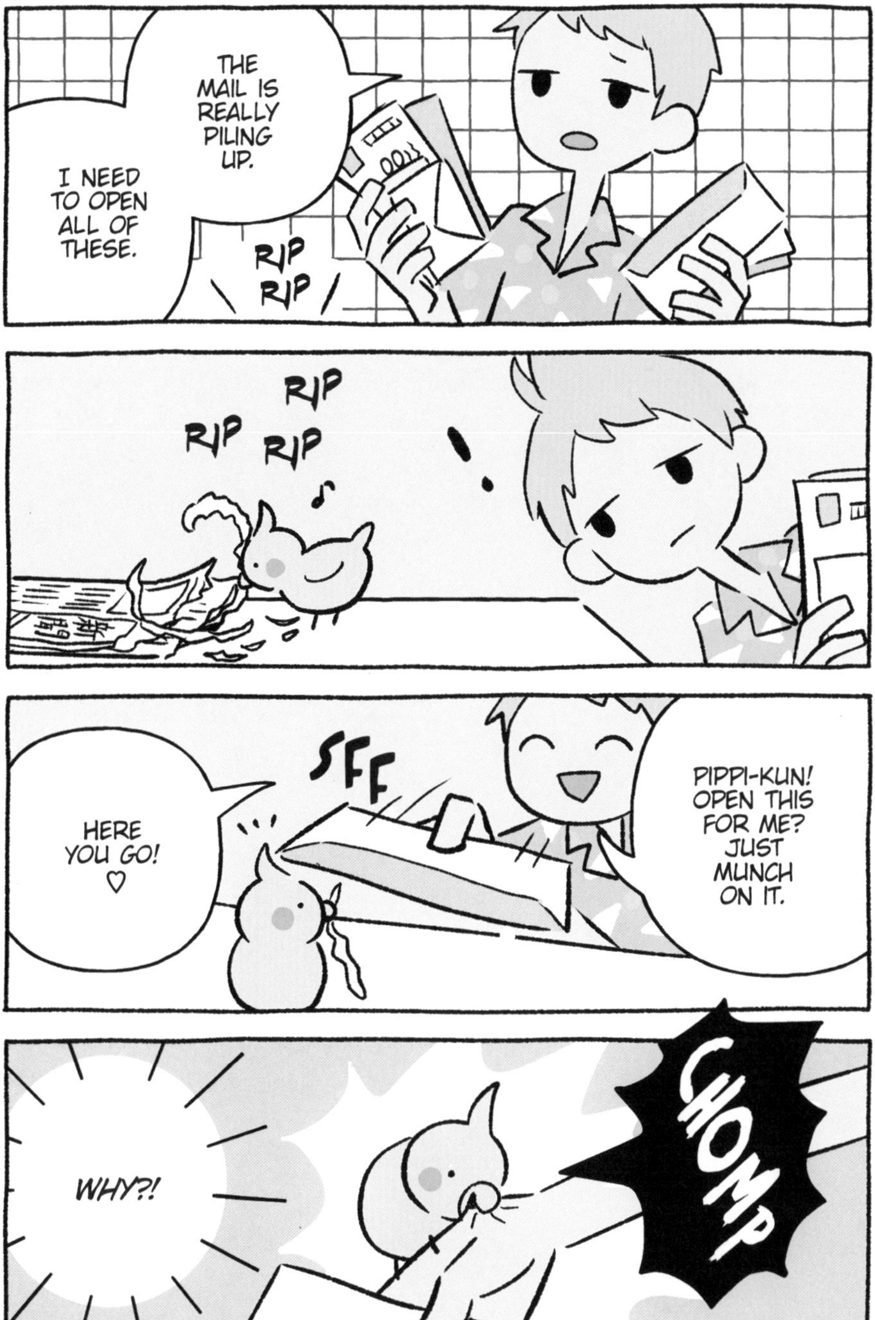
THE MAIL IS REALLY PILING UP.
I NEED TO OPEN ALL OF THESE.
RIP RIP
RIP
RIP RIP
!
PIPPI-KUN! OPEN THIS FOR ME? JUST MUNCH ON IT.
SFF
HERE YOU GO! ♡
CHOMP
WHY?!

# CHIN POWER

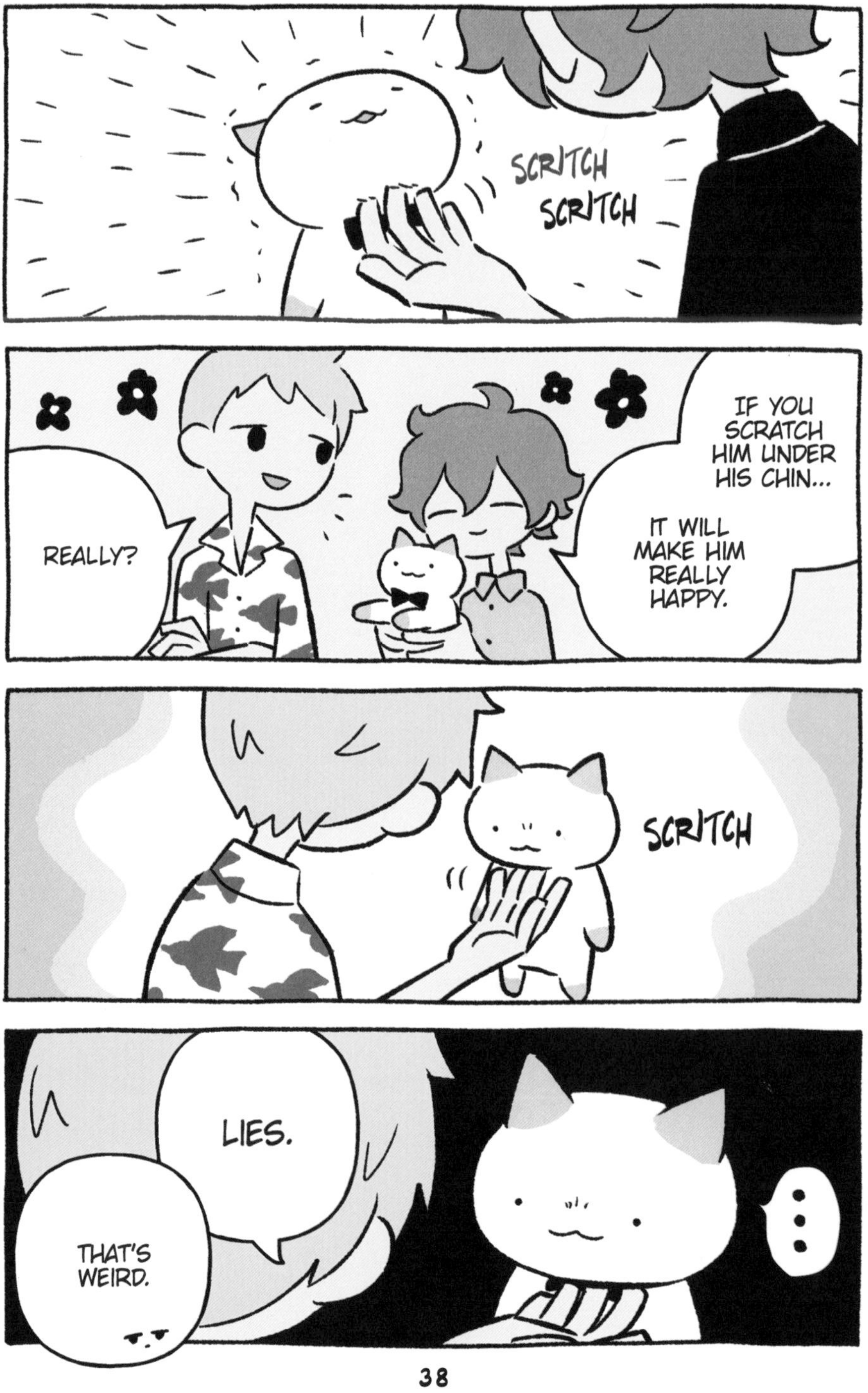
SCRITCH
SCRITCH
IF YOU SCRATCH HIM UNDER HIS CHIN...
IT WILL MAKE HIM REALLY HAPPY.
REALLY?
SCRITCH
...
LIES.
THAT'S WEIRD.

# KICKING BACK

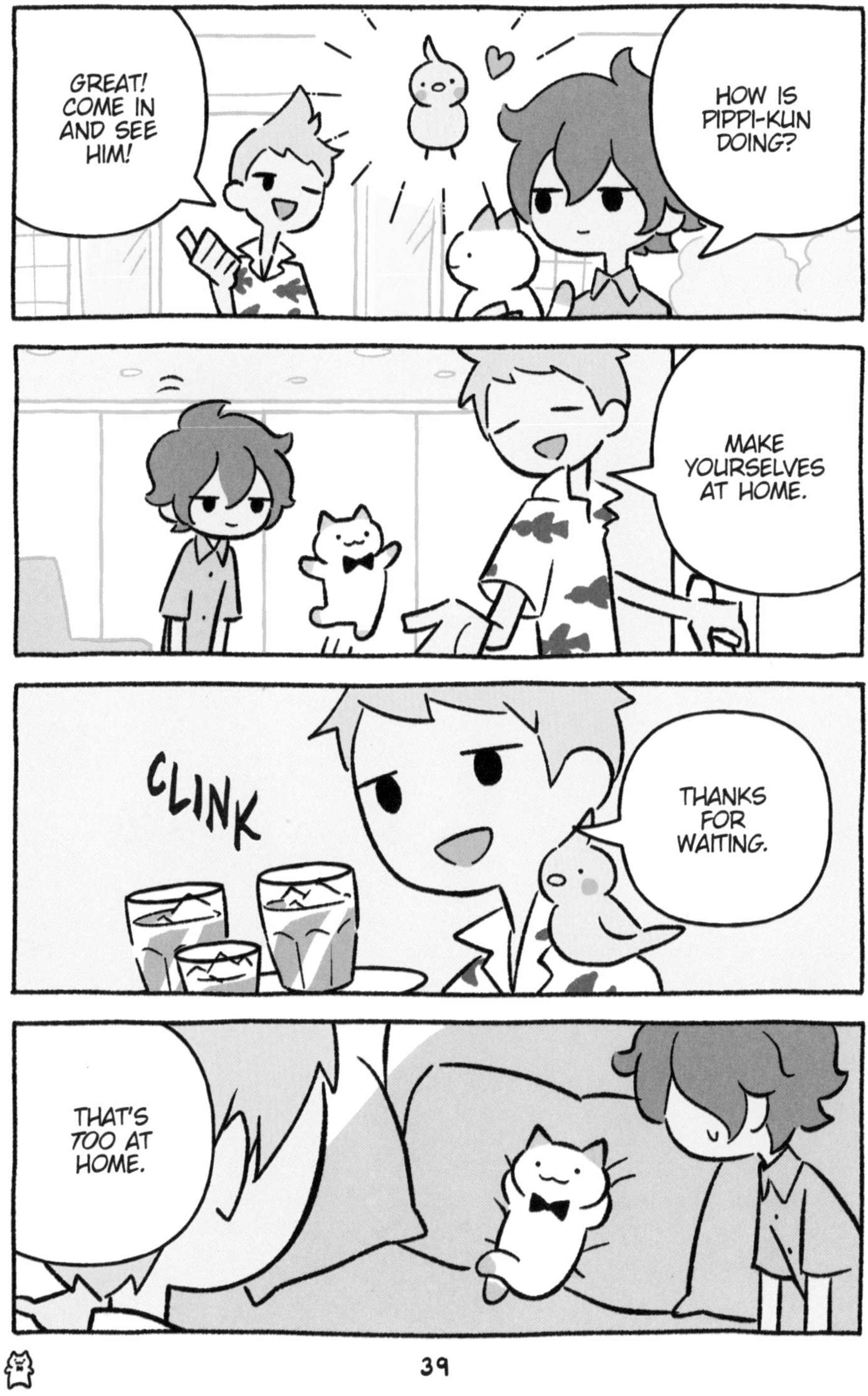

HOW IS PIPPI-KUN DOING?
GREAT! COME IN AND SEE HIM!
MAKE YOURSELVES AT HOME.
THANKS FOR WAITING.
CLINK
THAT'S *TOO* AT HOME.

# TRUST

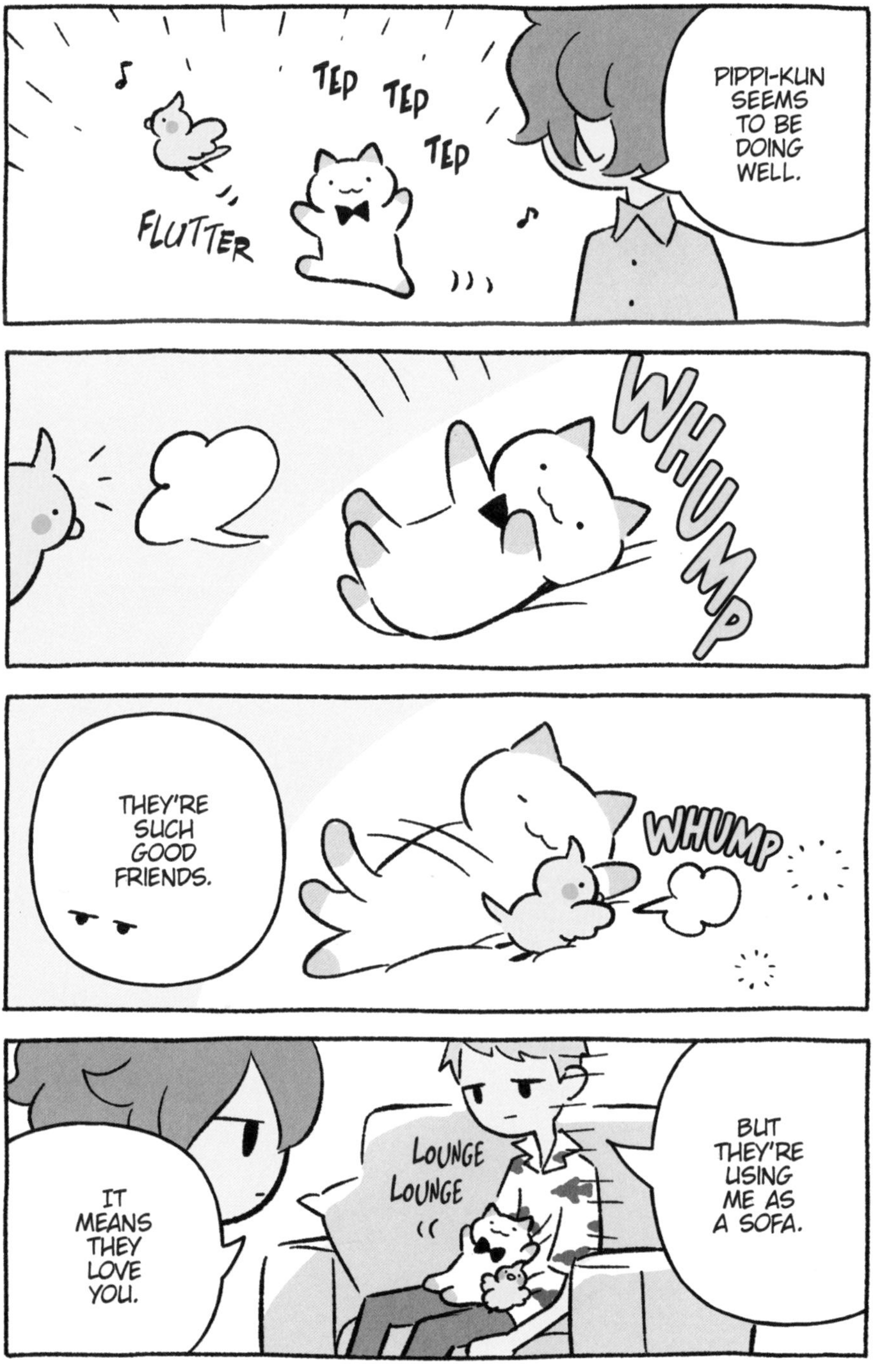
PIPPI-KUN SEEMS TO BE DOING WELL.
TEP TEP TEP
FLUTTER
WHUMP
WHUMP
THEY'RE SUCH GOOD FRIENDS.
BUT THEY'RE USING ME AS A SOFA.
LOUNGE LOUNGE
IT MEANS THEY LOVE YOU.

# PI-TAN

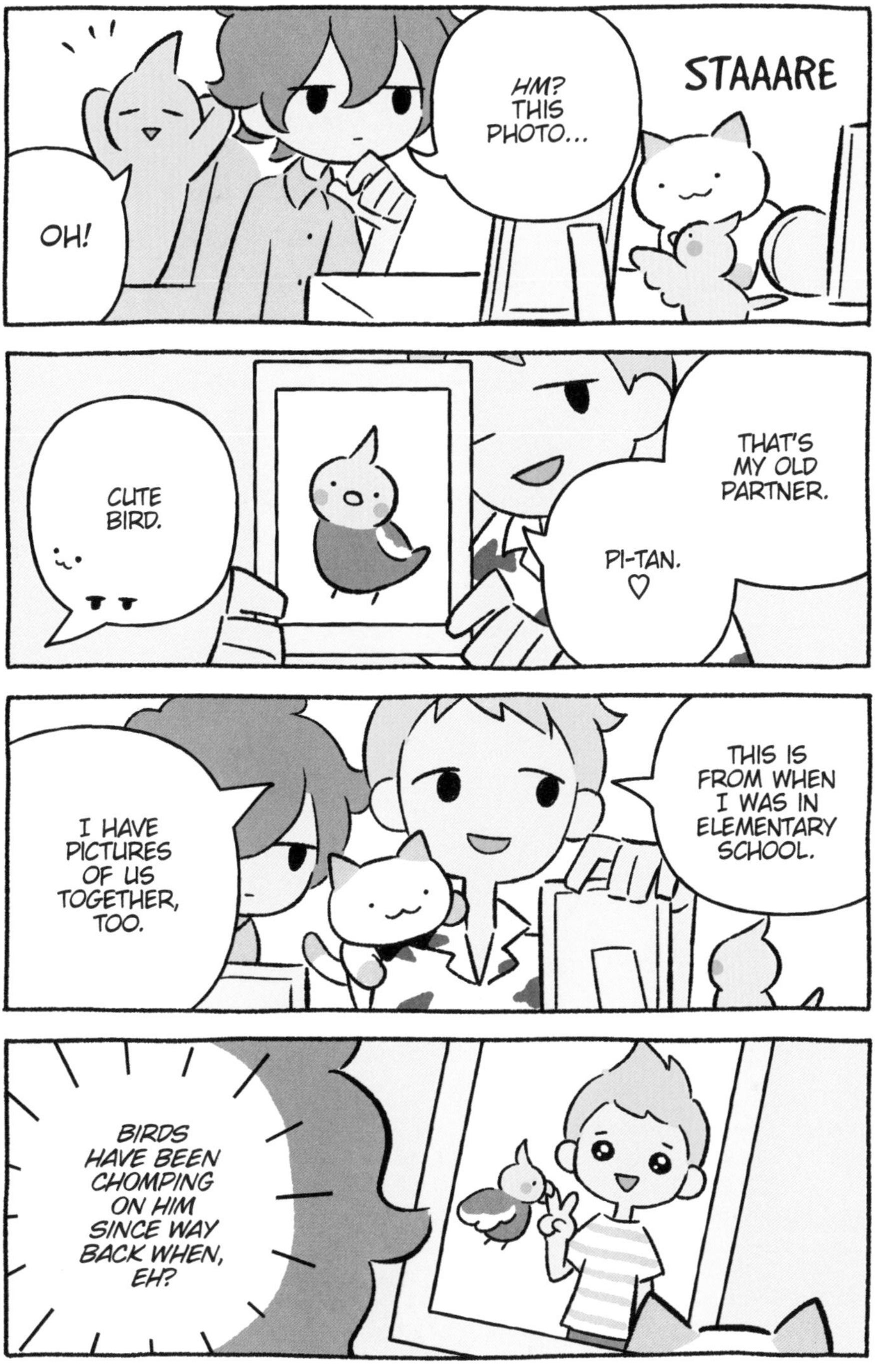
STAAARE
HM? THIS PHOTO...
OH!
THAT'S MY OLD PARTNER.
PI-TAN. ♡
CUTE BIRD.
THIS IS FROM WHEN I WAS IN ELEMENTARY SCHOOL.
I HAVE PICTURES OF US TOGETHER, TOO.
BIRDS HAVE BEEN CHOMPING ON HIM SINCE WAY BACK WHEN, EH?

# STUBBORN REFUSAL

42

# RAIN

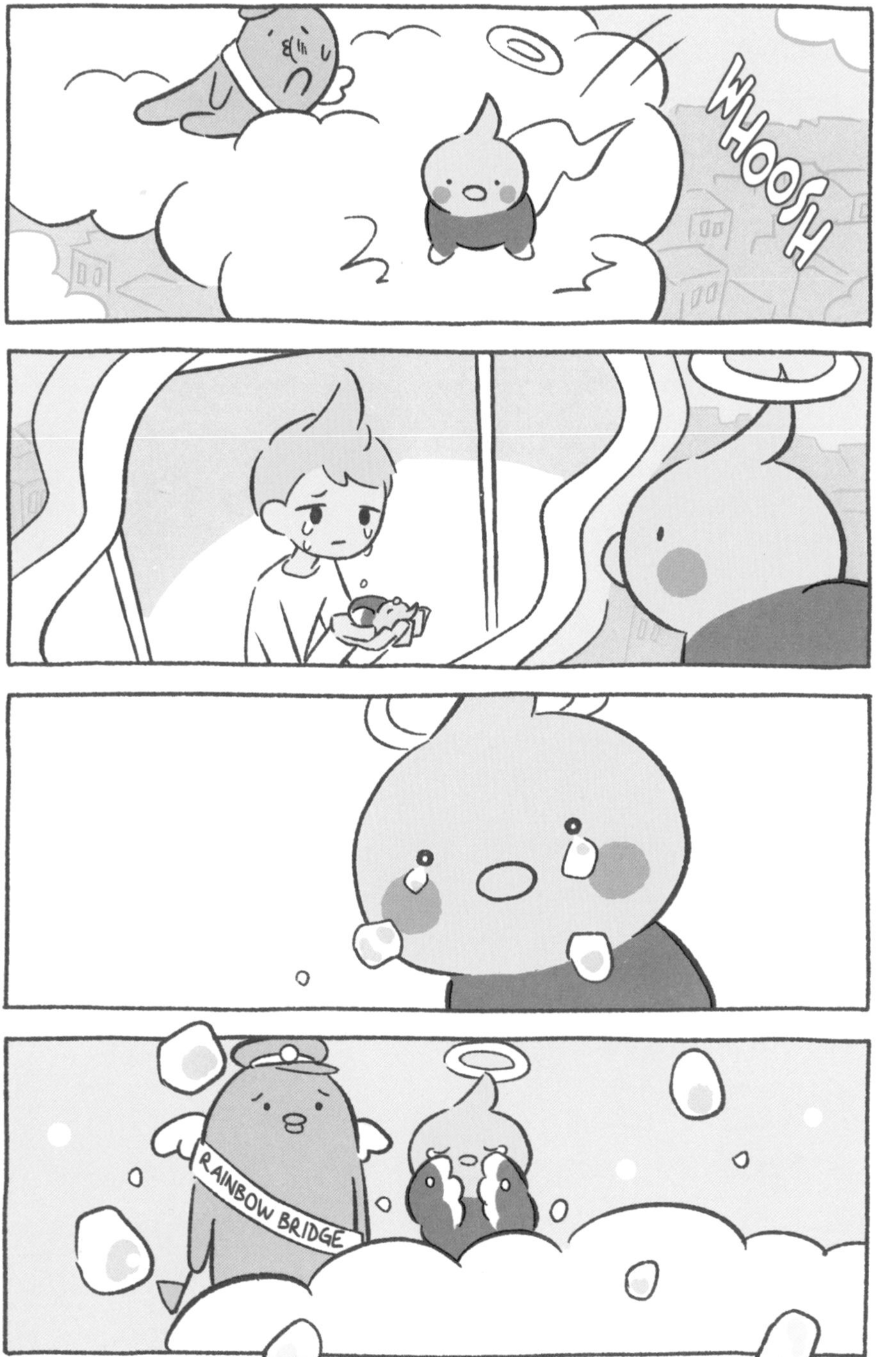
WHOOSH
RAINBOW BRIDGE

# DON'T TELL ANYONE

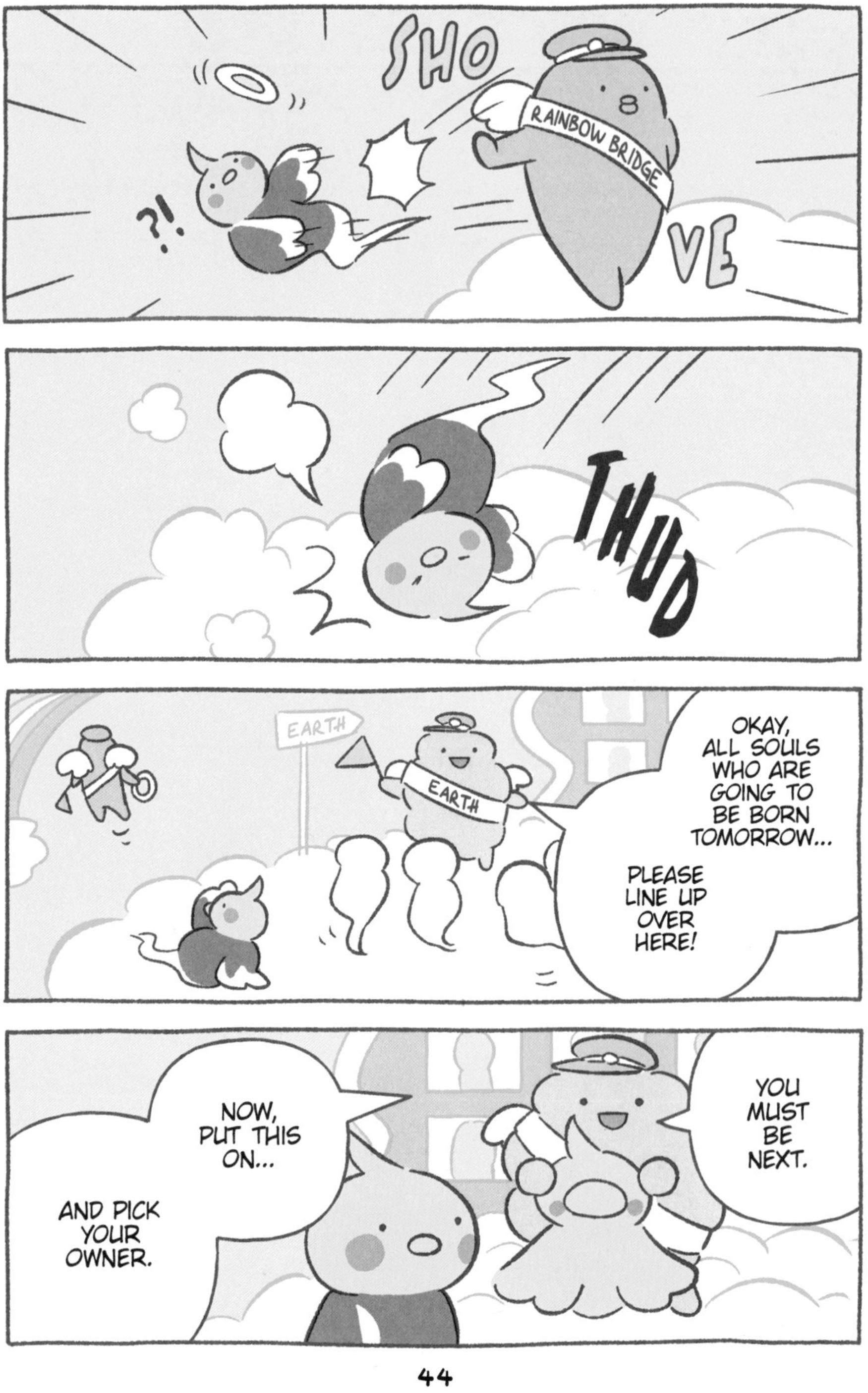
RAINBOW BRIDGE
SHO
VE
?!
THUD
OKAY, ALL SOULS WHO ARE GOING TO BE BORN TOMORROW...
PLEASE LINE UP OVER HERE!
EARTH
EARTH
YOU MUST BE NEXT.
NOW, PUT THIS ON...
AND PICK YOUR OWNER.

# TOGETHER FOREVER

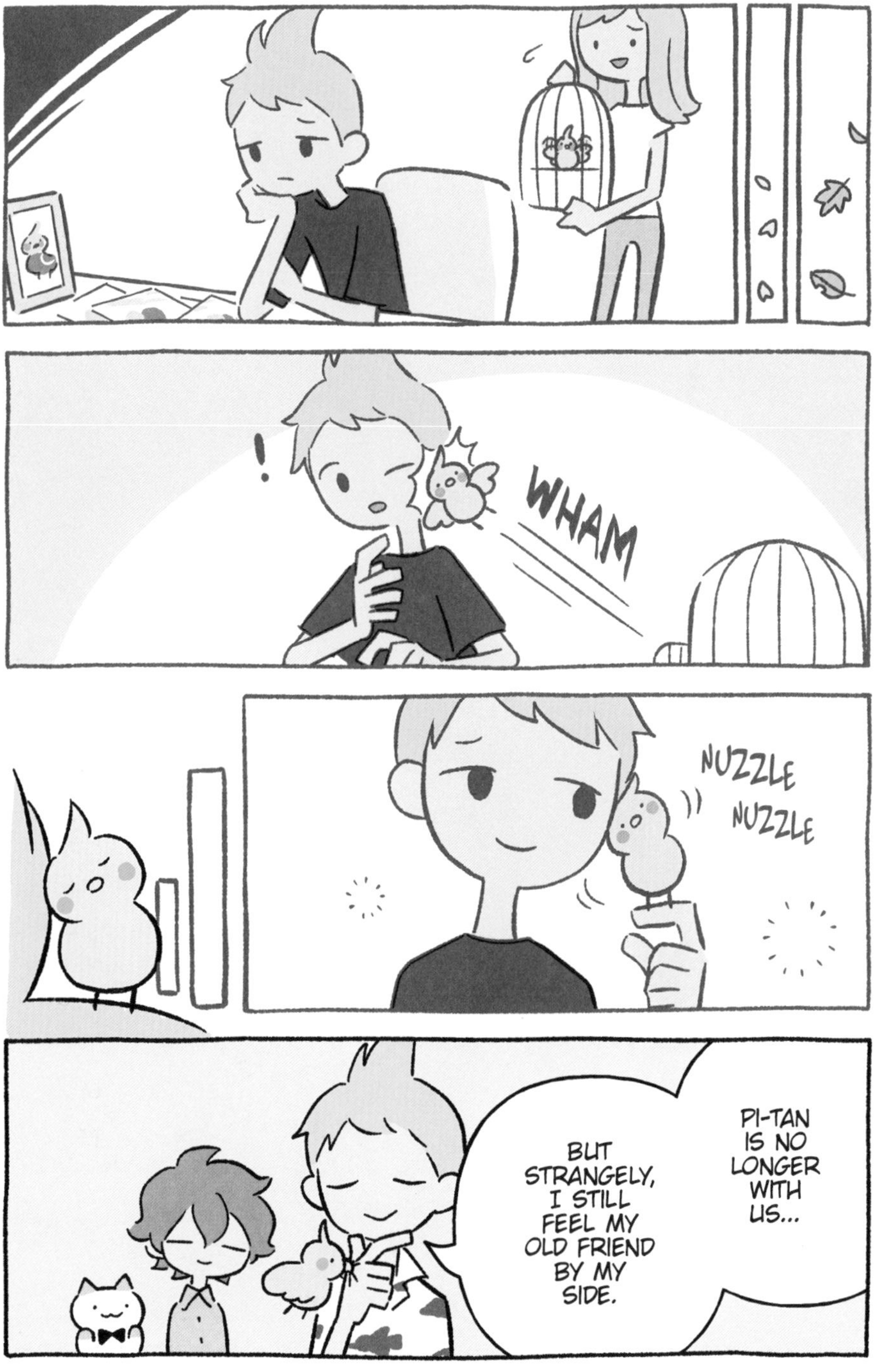
!
WHAM
NUZZLE
NUZZLE
PI-TAN IS NO LONGER WITH US...
BUT STRANGELY, I STILL FEEL MY OLD FRIEND BY MY SIDE.

# ARTISTE

I WANT TO SEE KYUU-CHAN GO ALL AT A LEMON PICTURE AGAIN.
ALL DONE!
...?
NOTHING
SHOCK

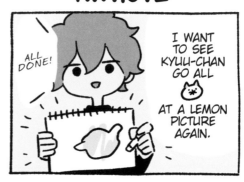

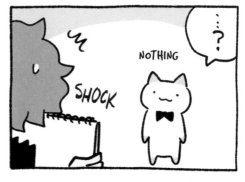

# I ALWAYS WANTED TO WEAR A NECKTIE

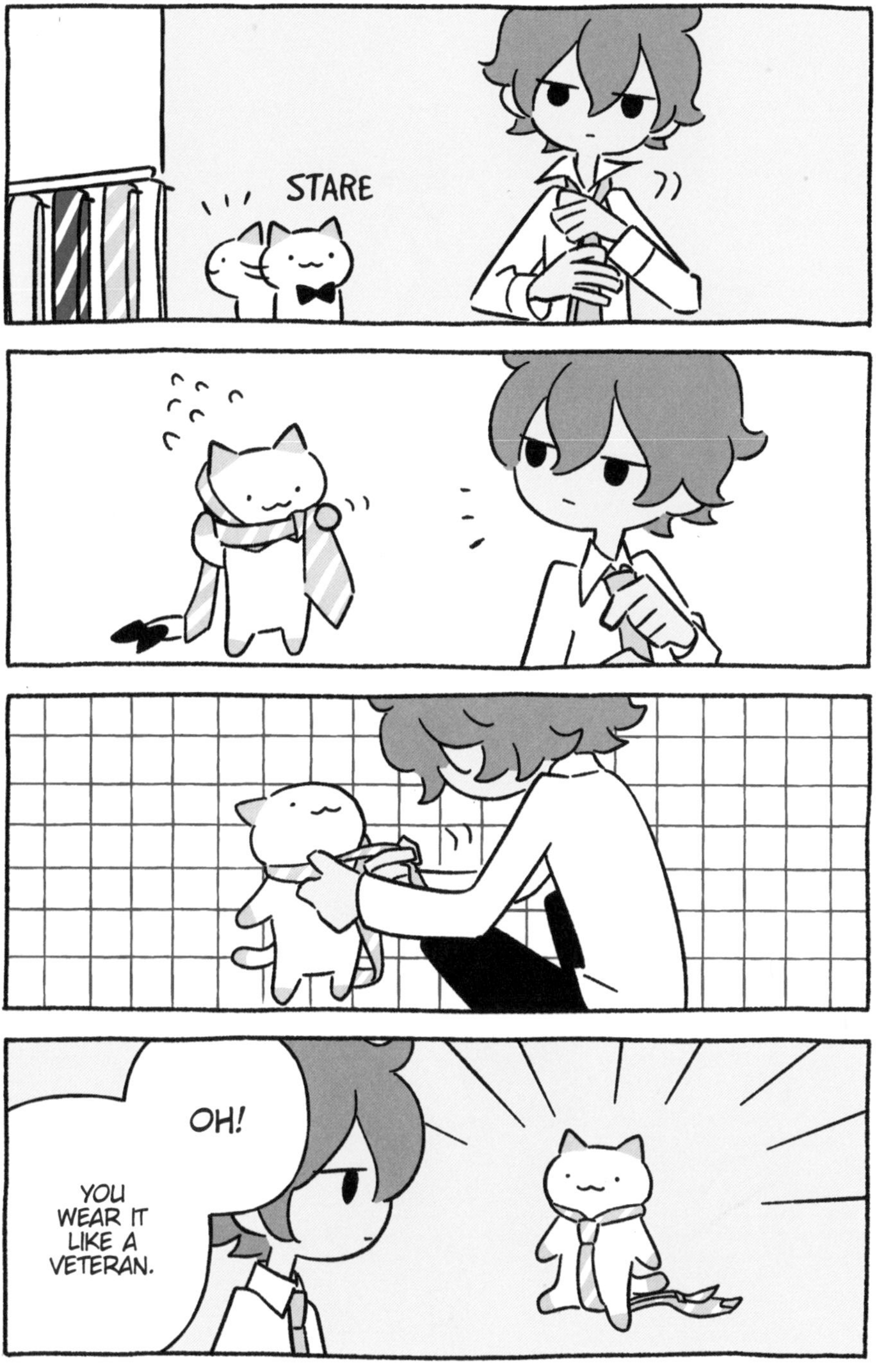
STARE
OH!
YOU WEAR IT LIKE A VETERAN.

# GENTLEMAN

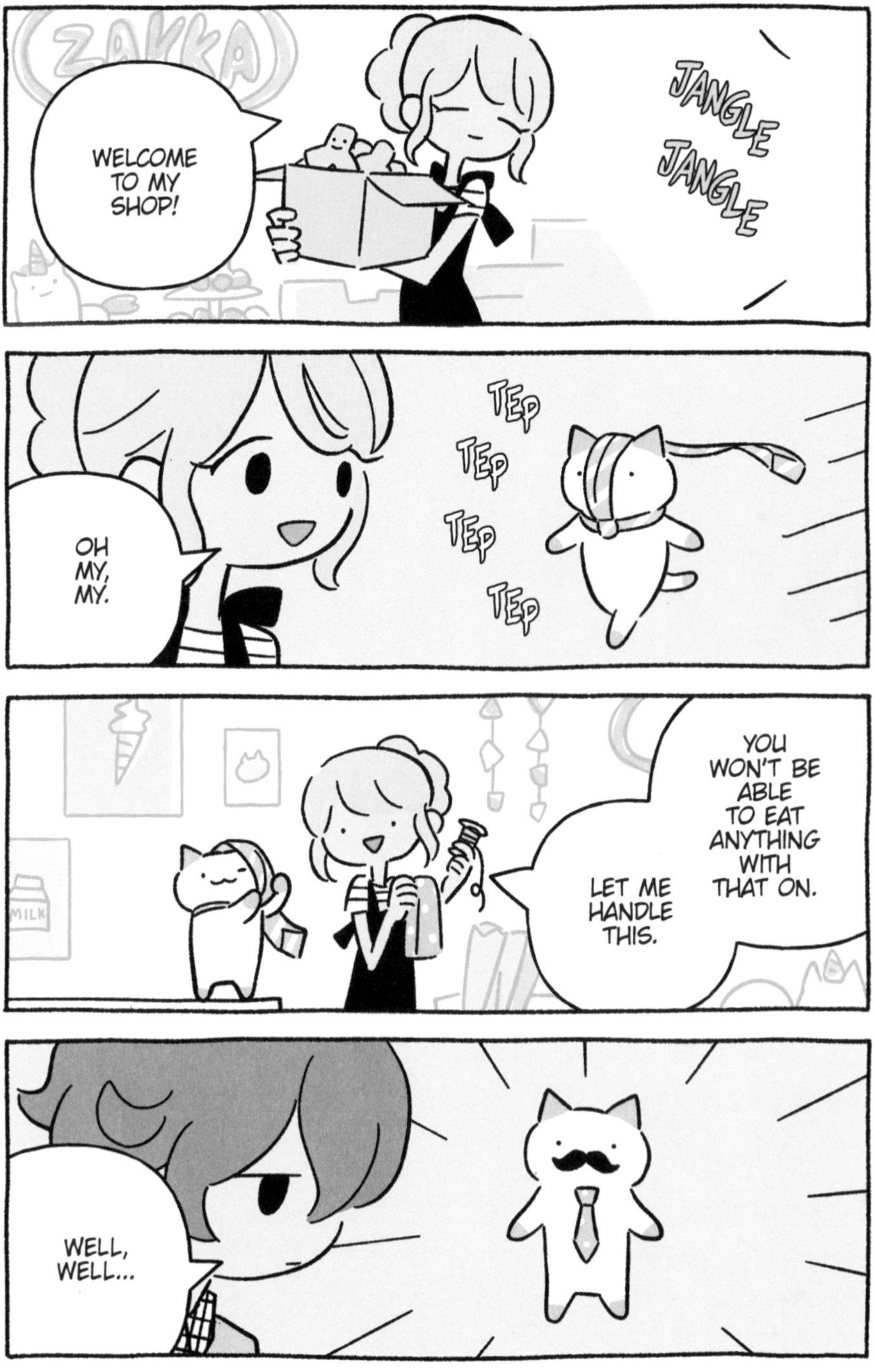
JANGLE JANGLE
WELCOME TO MY SHOP!
TEP TEP TEP TEP
OH MY, MY.
YOU WON'T BE ABLE TO EAT ANYTHING WITH THAT ON.
LET ME HANDLE THIS.
WELL, WELL...

# LETTER

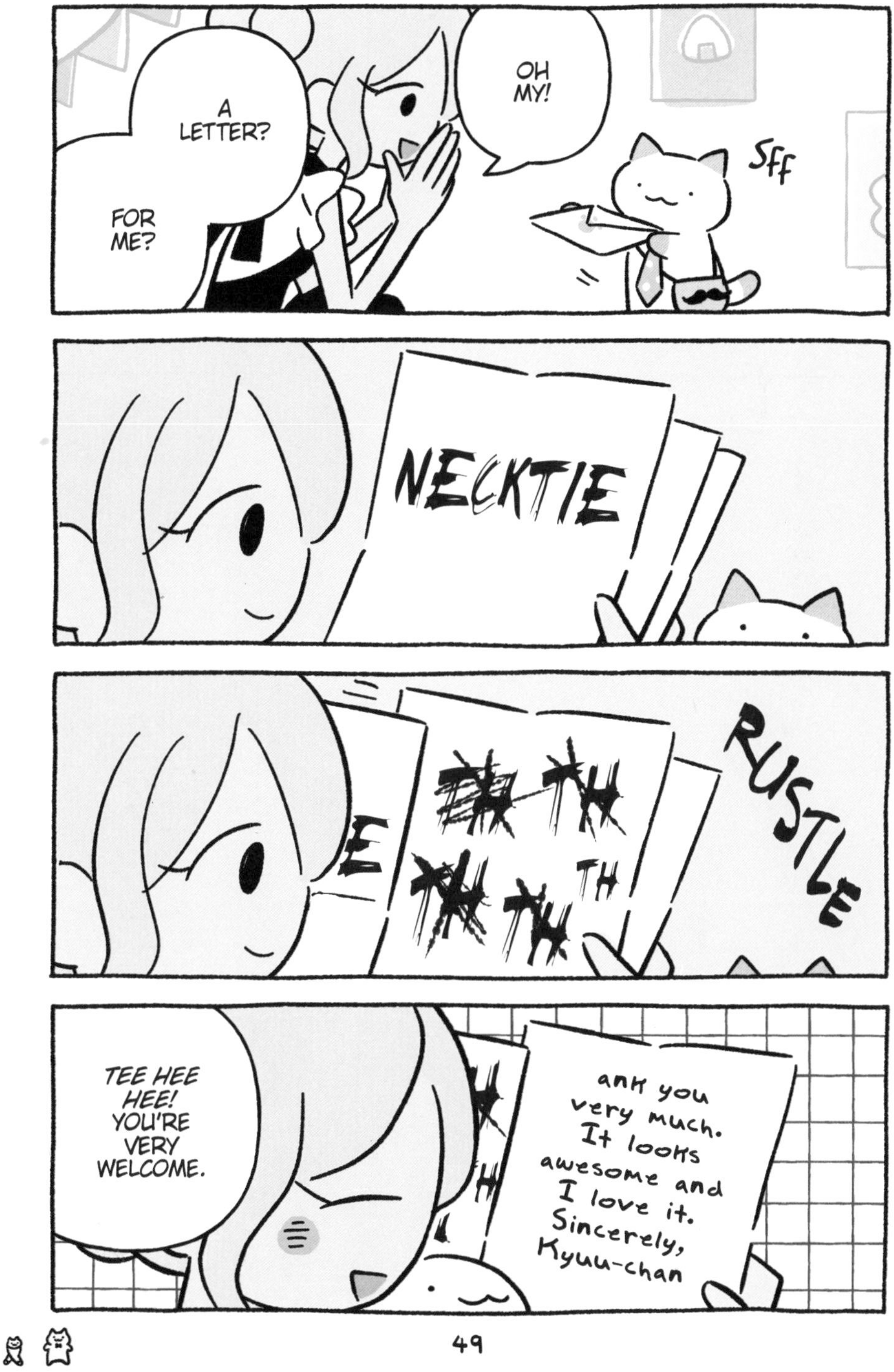
OH MY!
SFF
A LETTER?
FOR ME?
NECKTIE
RUSTLE
TH
ank you very much. It looks awesome and I love it. Sincerely, Kyuu-chan
TEE HEE HEE! YOU'RE VERY WELCOME.

# GATHERING OF FRIENDS

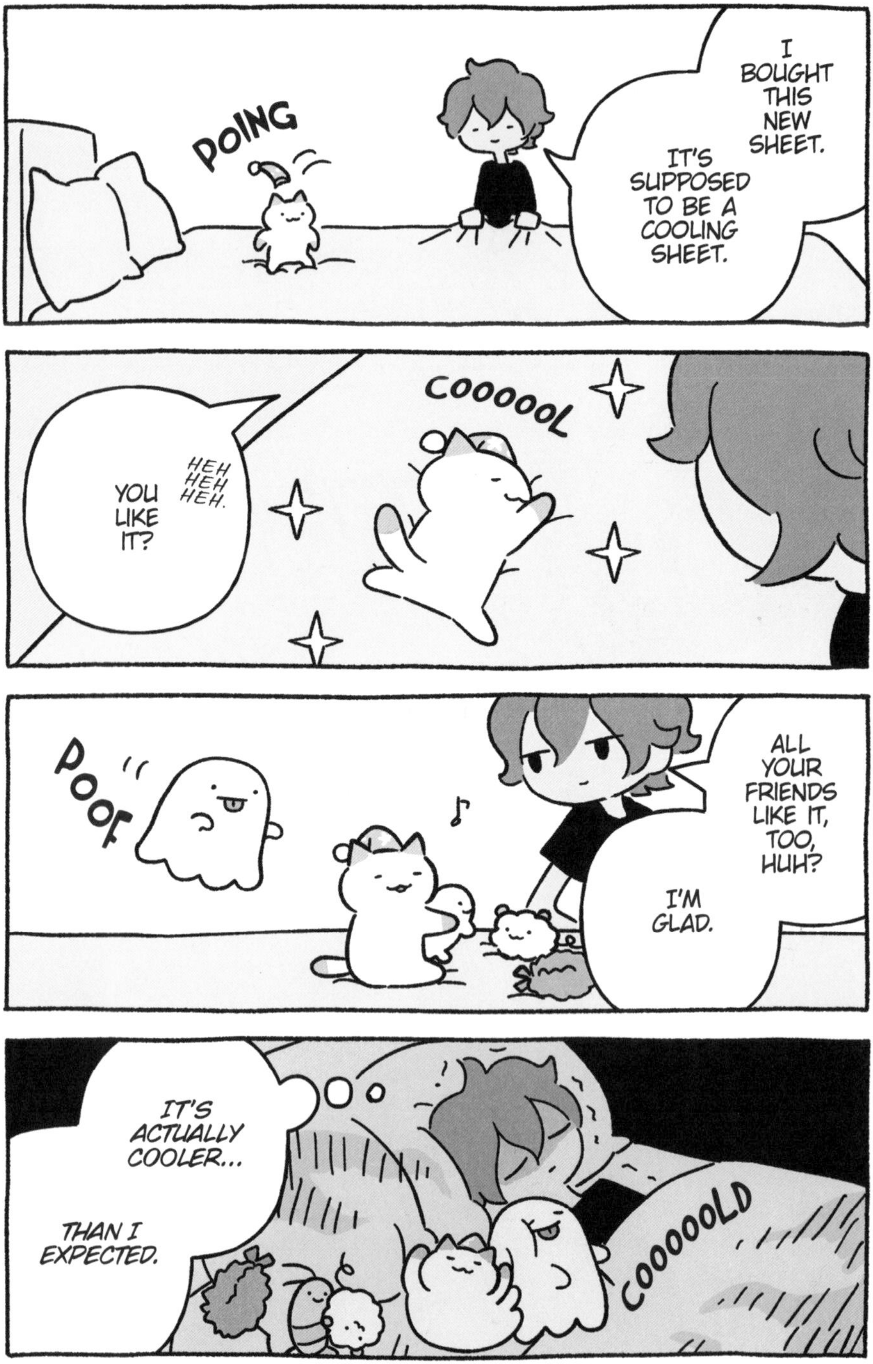
I BOUGHT THIS NEW SHEET.
IT'S SUPPOSED TO BE A COOLING SHEET.
POING
COOOOOL
HEH HEH HEH.
YOU LIKE IT?
ALL YOUR FRIENDS LIKE IT, TOO, HUH?
I'M GLAD.
POOF
COOOOOLD
IT'S ACTUALLY COOLER...
THAN I EXPECTED.

# LEFT HAND

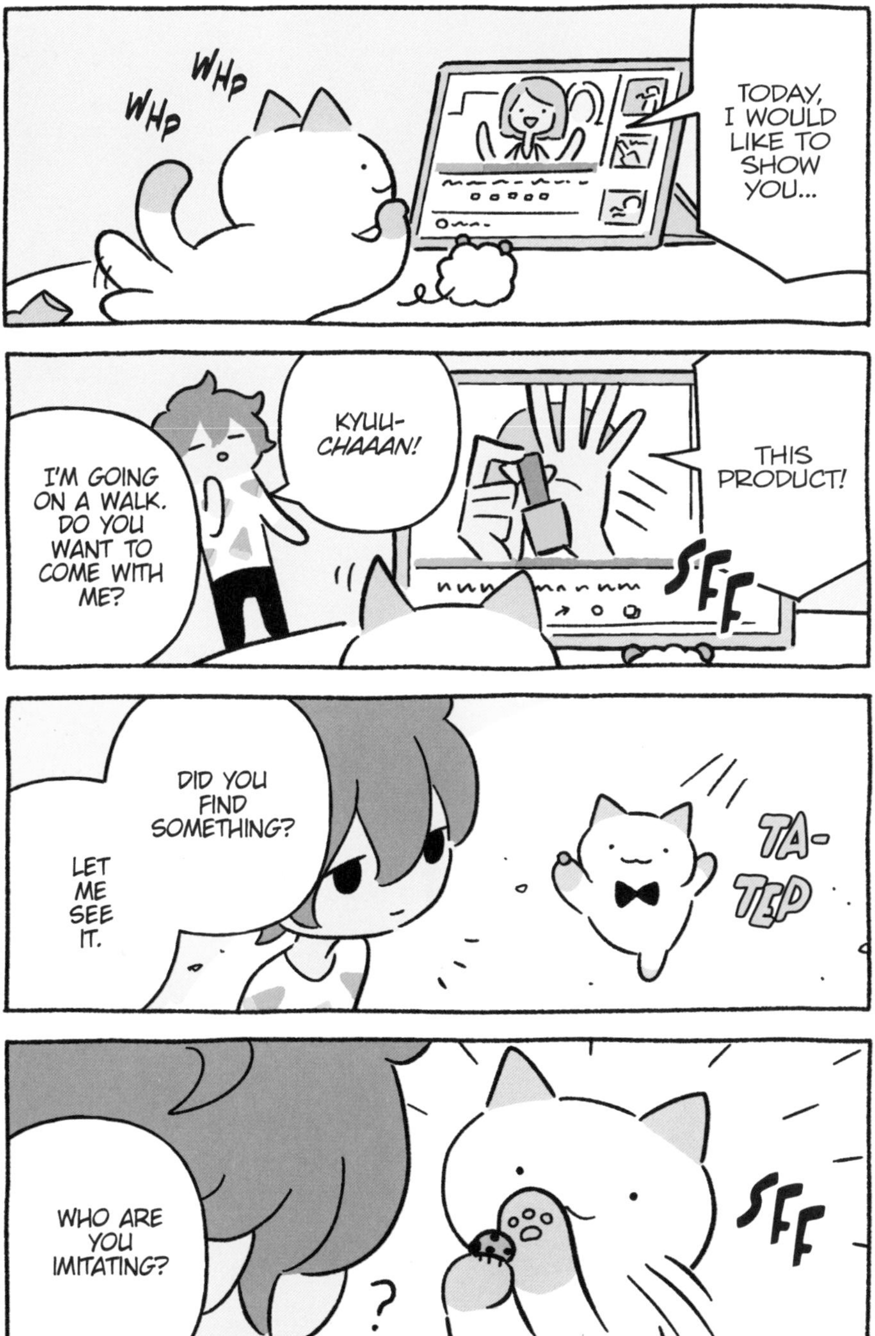
TODAY, I WOULD LIKE TO SHOW YOU...
WHP
WHP
THIS PRODUCT!
SFF
KYUU-CHAAAN!
I'M GOING ON A WALK. DO YOU WANT TO COME WITH ME?
TA-TEP
DID YOU FIND SOMETHING?
LET ME SEE IT.
SFF
?
WHO ARE YOU IMITATING?

# WATERMELON SMASH

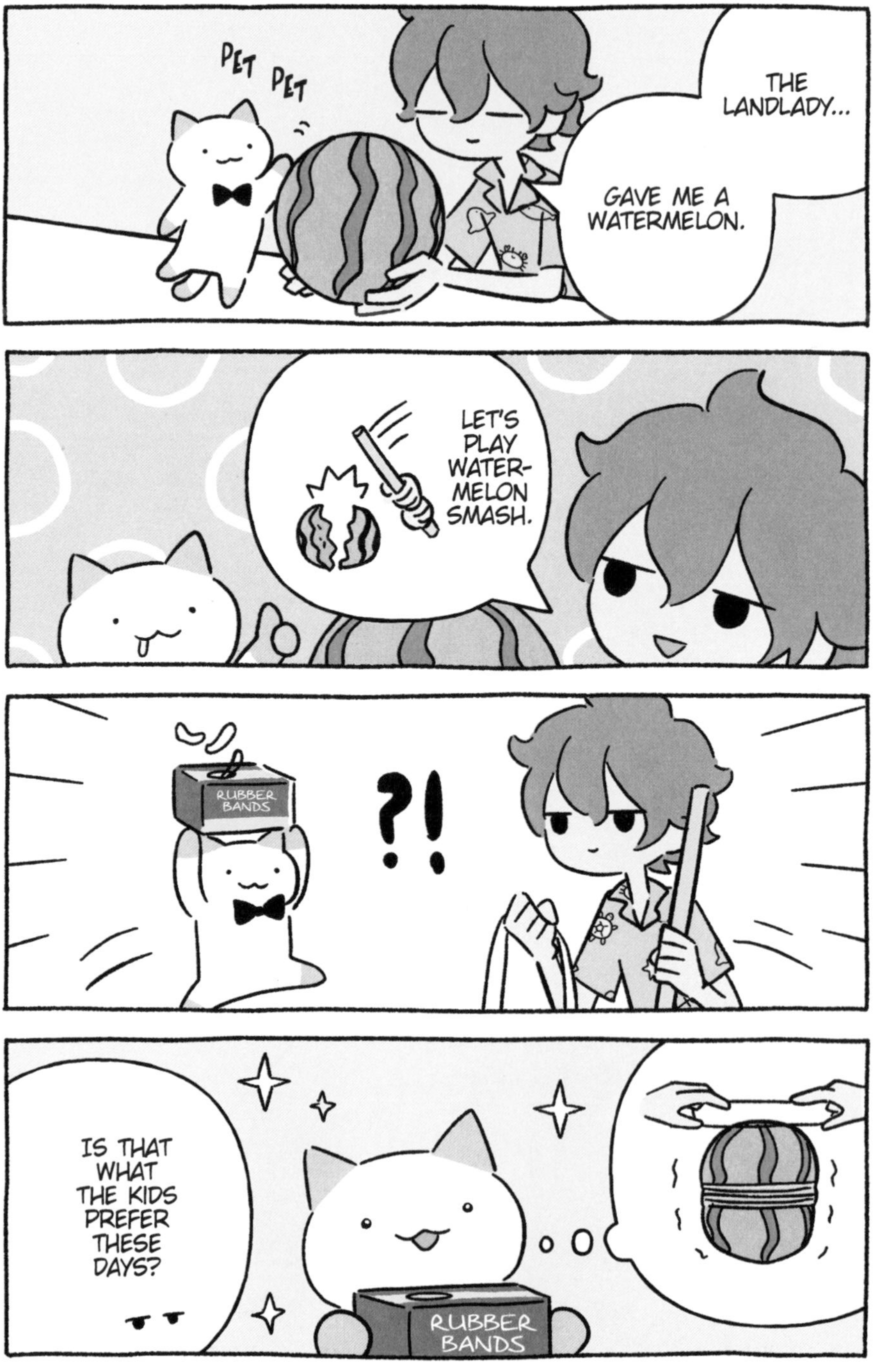
THE LANDLADY...
GAVE ME A WATERMELON.
PET PET
LET'S PLAY WATER-MELON SMASH.
RUBBER BANDS
?!
IS THAT WHAT THE KIDS PREFER THESE DAYS?
RUBBER BANDS

# GO BIG

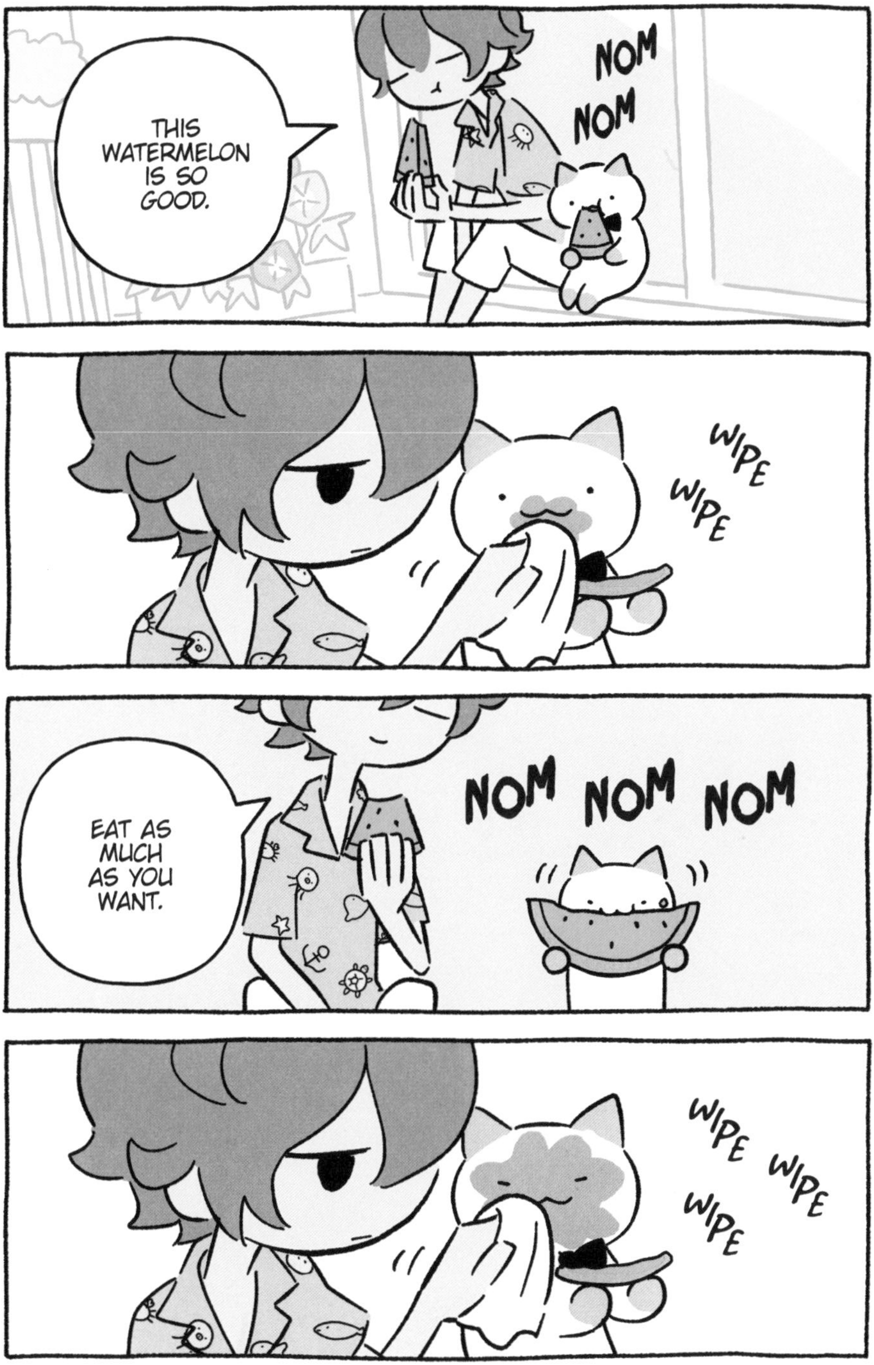
NOM
NOM
THIS WATERMELON IS SO GOOD.
WIPE
WIPE
NOM NOM NOM
EAT AS MUCH AS YOU WANT.
WIPE WIPE
WIPE
WIPE

# SNOOT CHALLENGE

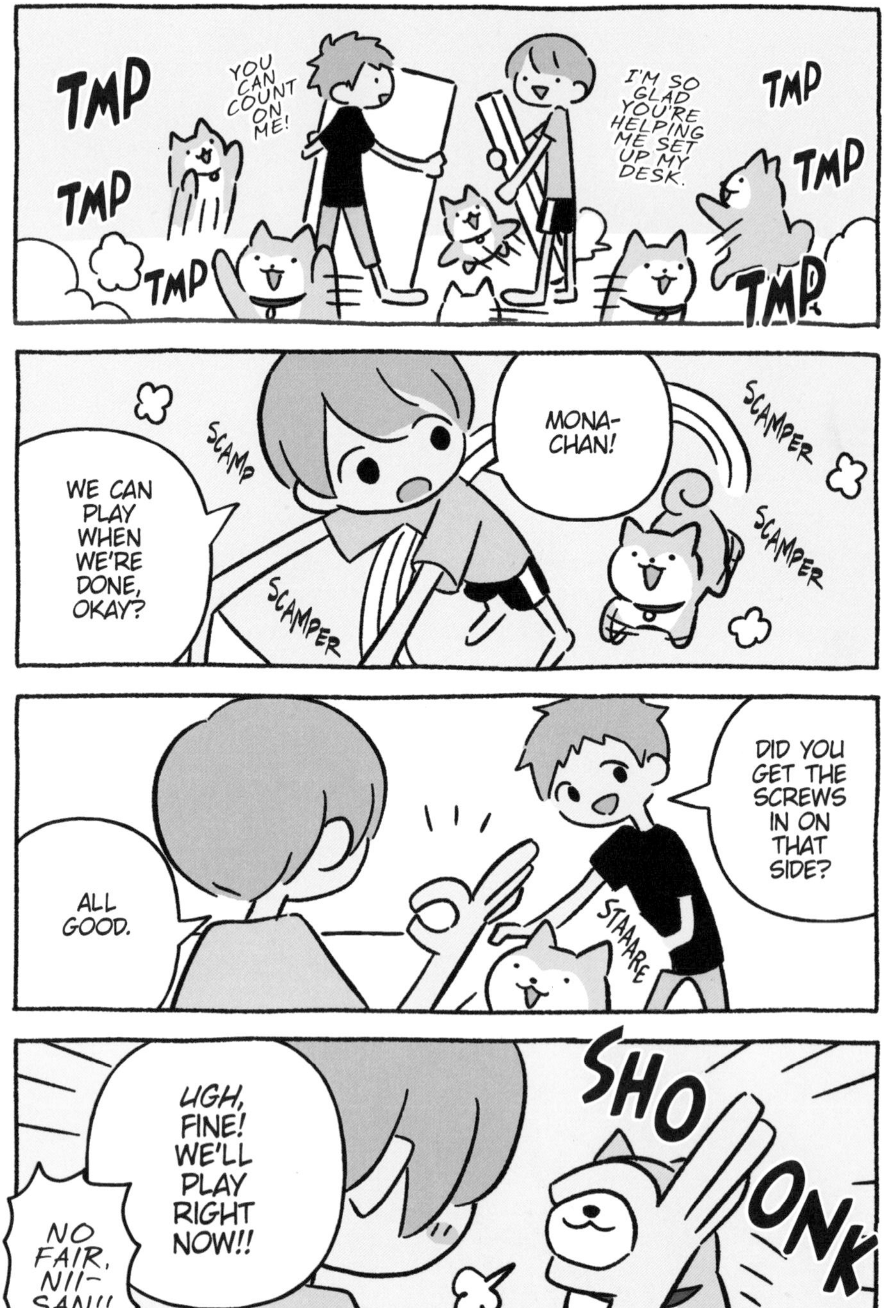
TMP
I'M SO GLAD YOU'RE HELPING ME SET UP MY DESK.
TMP
TMP
YOU CAN COUNT ON ME!
TMP
TMP
TMP
TMP
SCAMPER
MONA-CHAN!
SCAMPER
SCAMP
WE CAN PLAY WHEN WE'RE DONE, OKAY?
SCAMPER
DID YOU GET THE SCREWS IN ON THAT SIDE?
STAAARE
ALL GOOD.
SHO
ONK
UGH, FINE! WE'LL PLAY RIGHT NOW!!
NO FAIR, NII-SAN!!

# INFINITE COFFEE

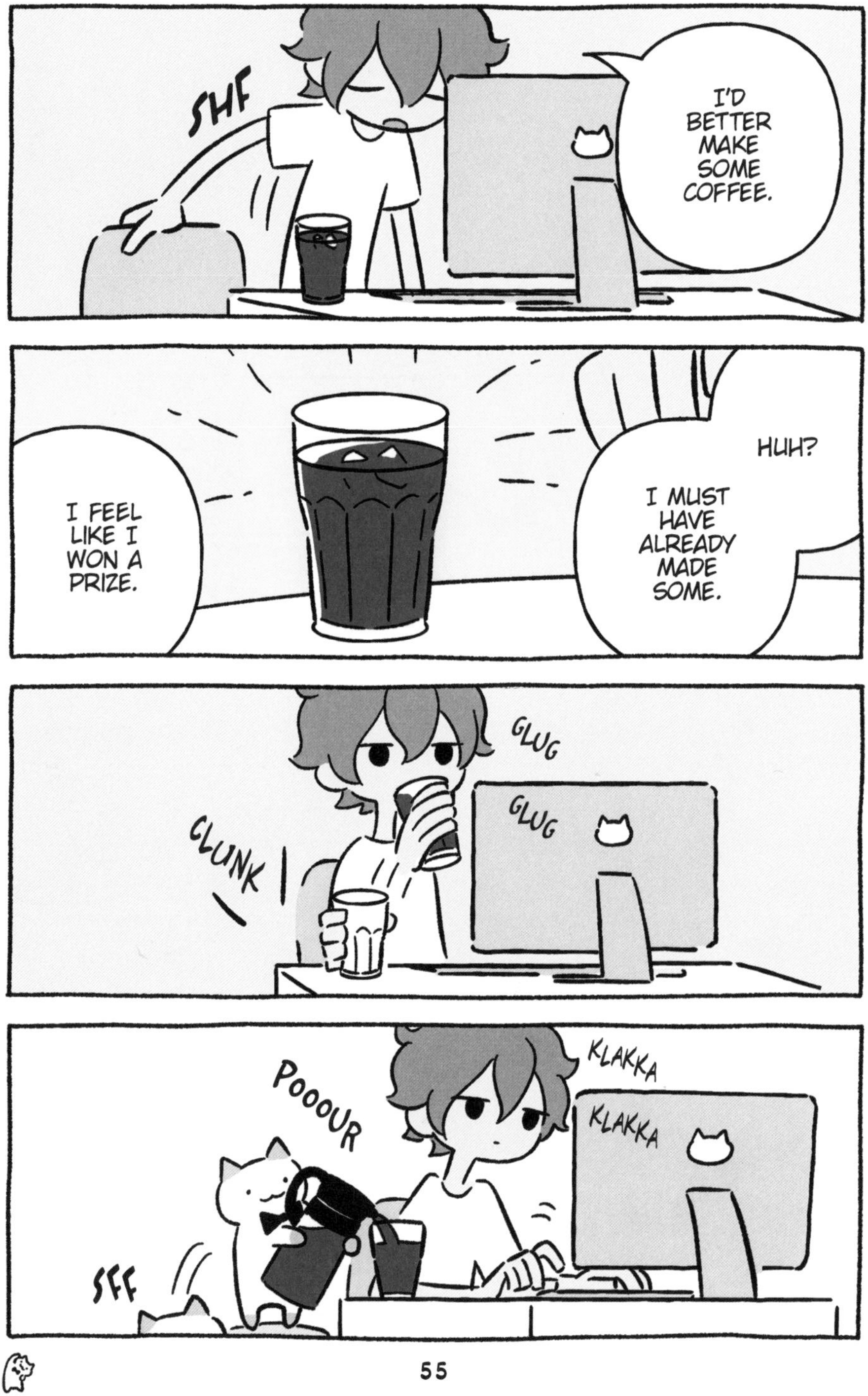
I'D BETTER MAKE SOME COFFEE.
SHF
HUH?
I MUST HAVE ALREADY MADE SOME.
I FEEL LIKE I WON A PRIZE.
GLUG
GLUG
CLUNK
KLAKKA
KLAKKA
POOOUR
SFF

# I'M HERE

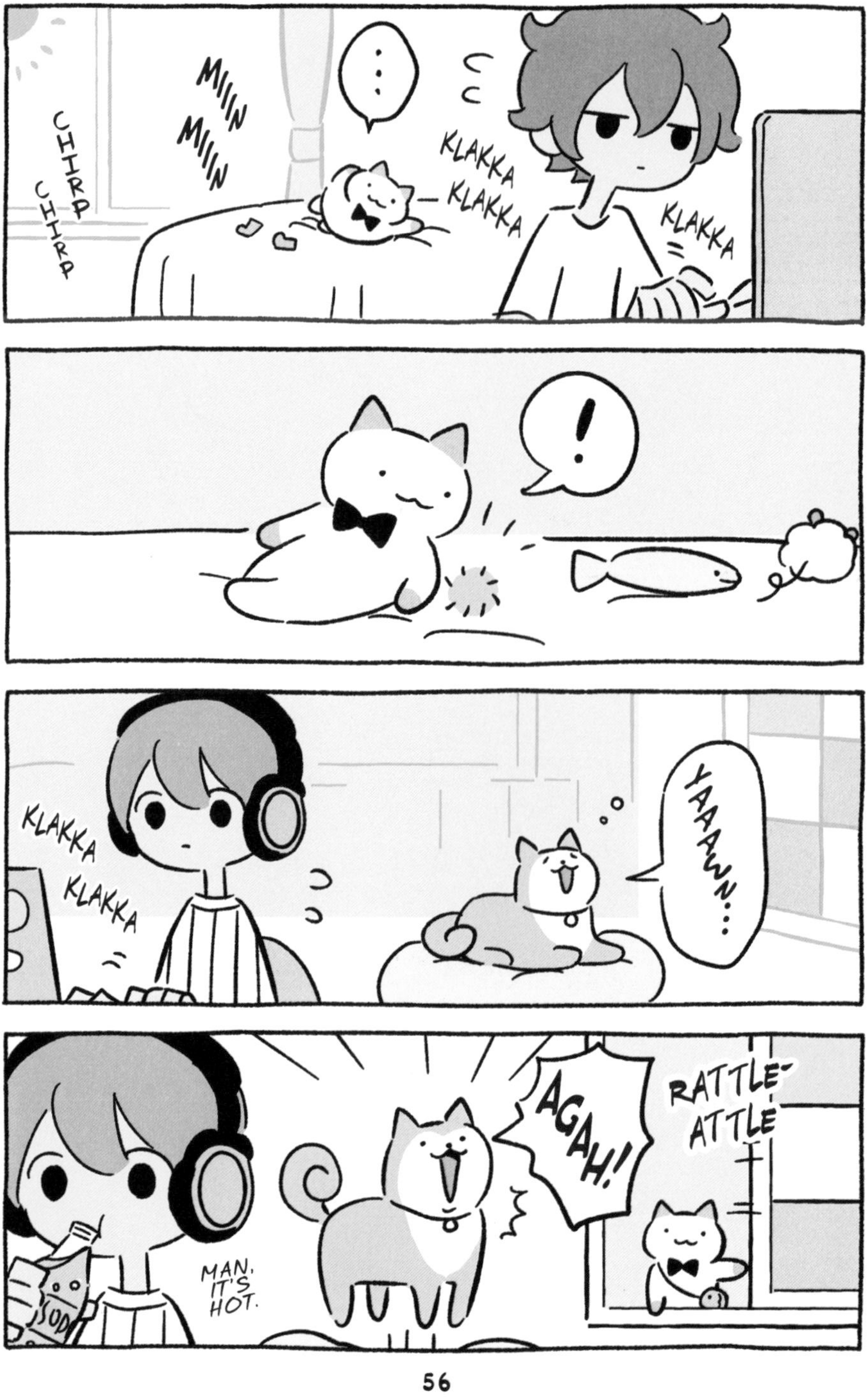
KLAKKA
KLAKKA KLAKKA
...
MIIIN MIIIN
CHIRP CHIRP
!
YAAAWN...
KLAKKA KLAKKA
RATTLE-ATTLE
AGAH!
MAN, IT'S HOT.

# LET'S OBEY TRAFFIC LAWS

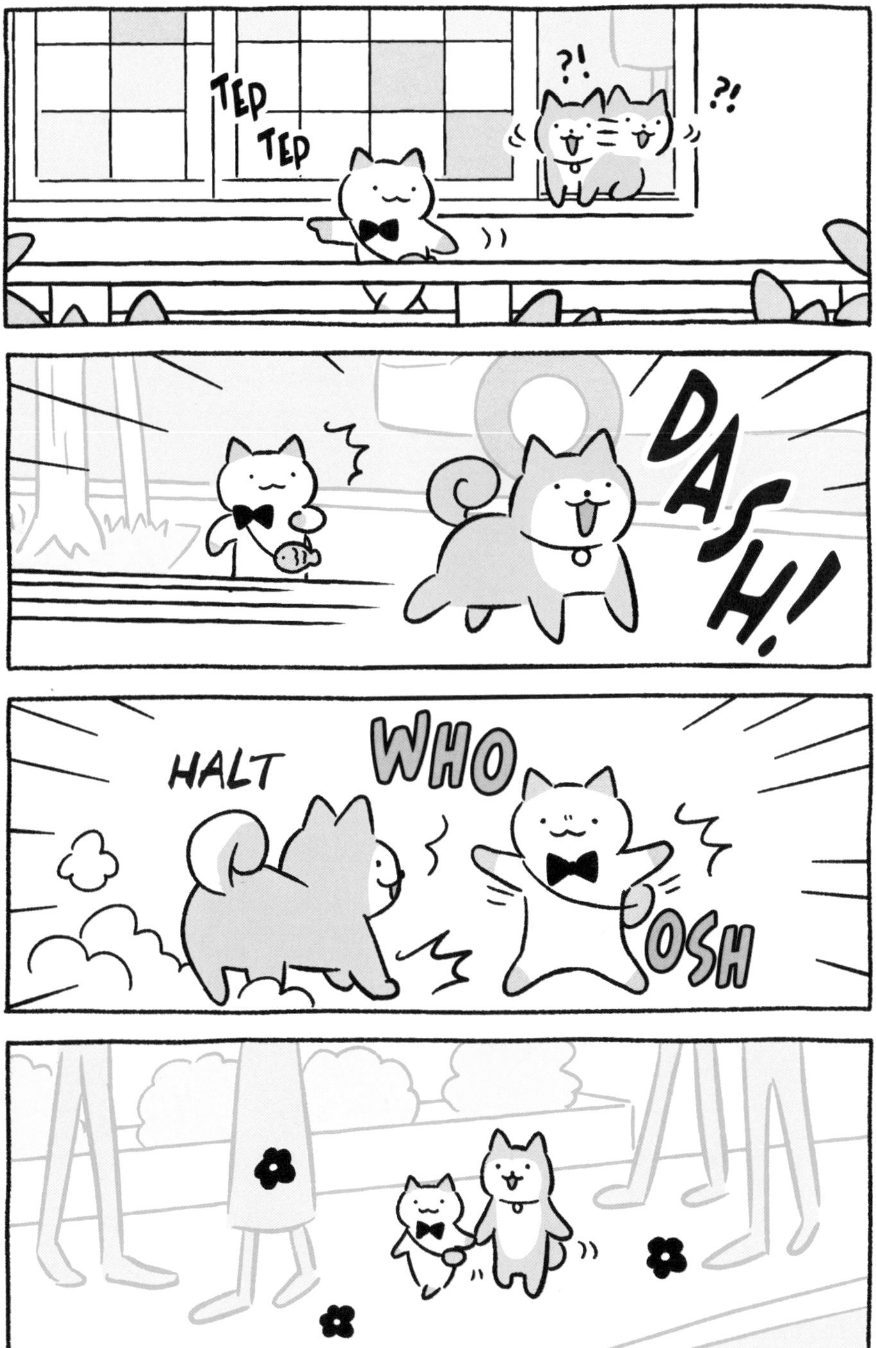
?!
?!
TEP
TEP
DASH!
WHO
OSH
HALT

# AT THE SUPERMARKET

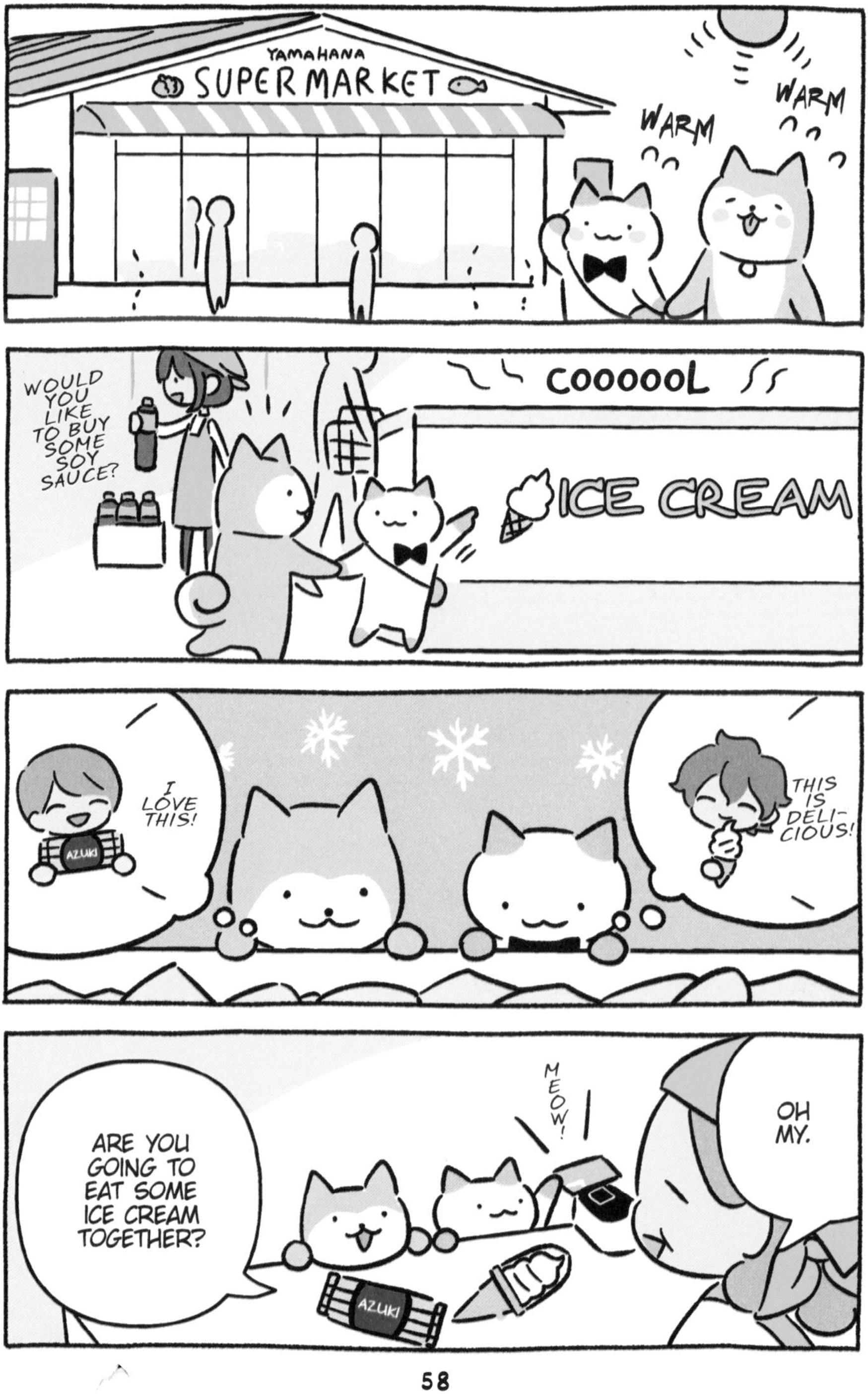
YAMAHANA
SUPERMARKET
WARM
WARM
COOOOOL
ICE CREAM
WOULD YOU LIKE TO BUY SOME SOY SAUCE?
THIS IS DELICIOUS!
I LOVE THIS!
AZUKI
OH MY.
MEOW!
ARE YOU GOING TO EAT SOME ICE CREAM TOGETHER?
AZUKI

# INFINITE ICE CREAM

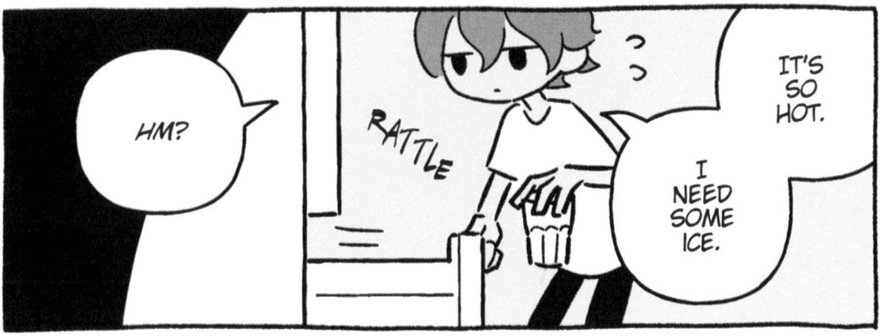
IT'S SO HOT.
I NEED SOME ICE.
RATTLE
HM?

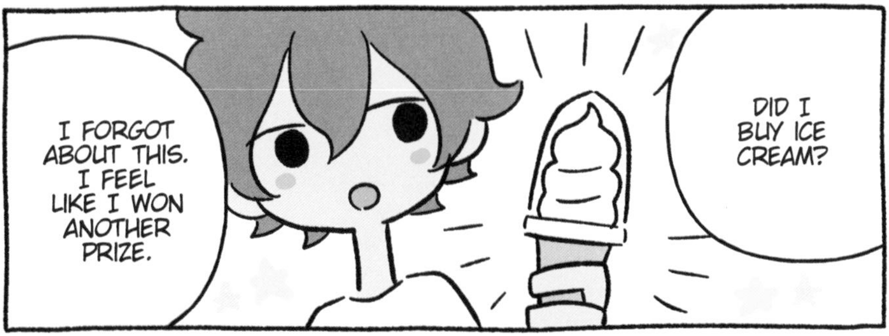
DID I BUY ICE CREAM?
I FORGOT ABOUT THIS. I FEEL LIKE I WON ANOTHER PRIZE.

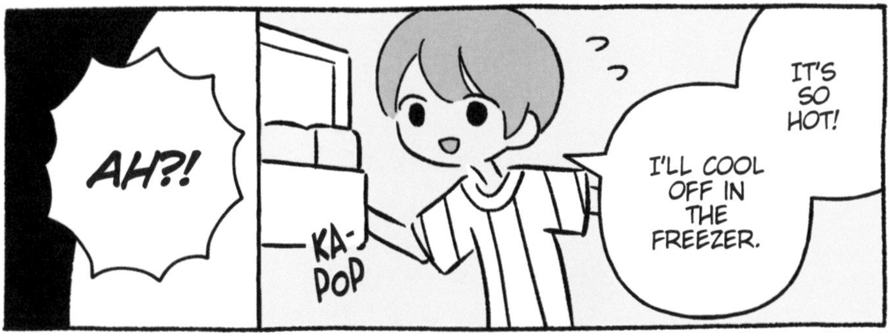
IT'S SO HOT!
I'LL COOL OFF IN THE FREEZER.
KA-POP
AH?!

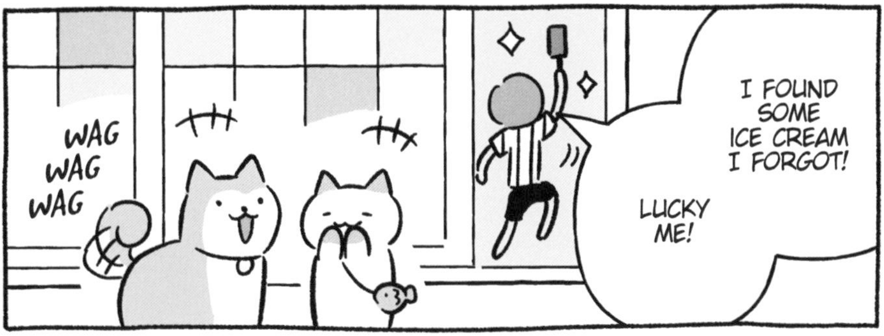
I FOUND SOME ICE CREAM I FORGOT!
LUCKY ME!
WAG WAG WAG

# PICTURE BOOKS OF ALL KINDS

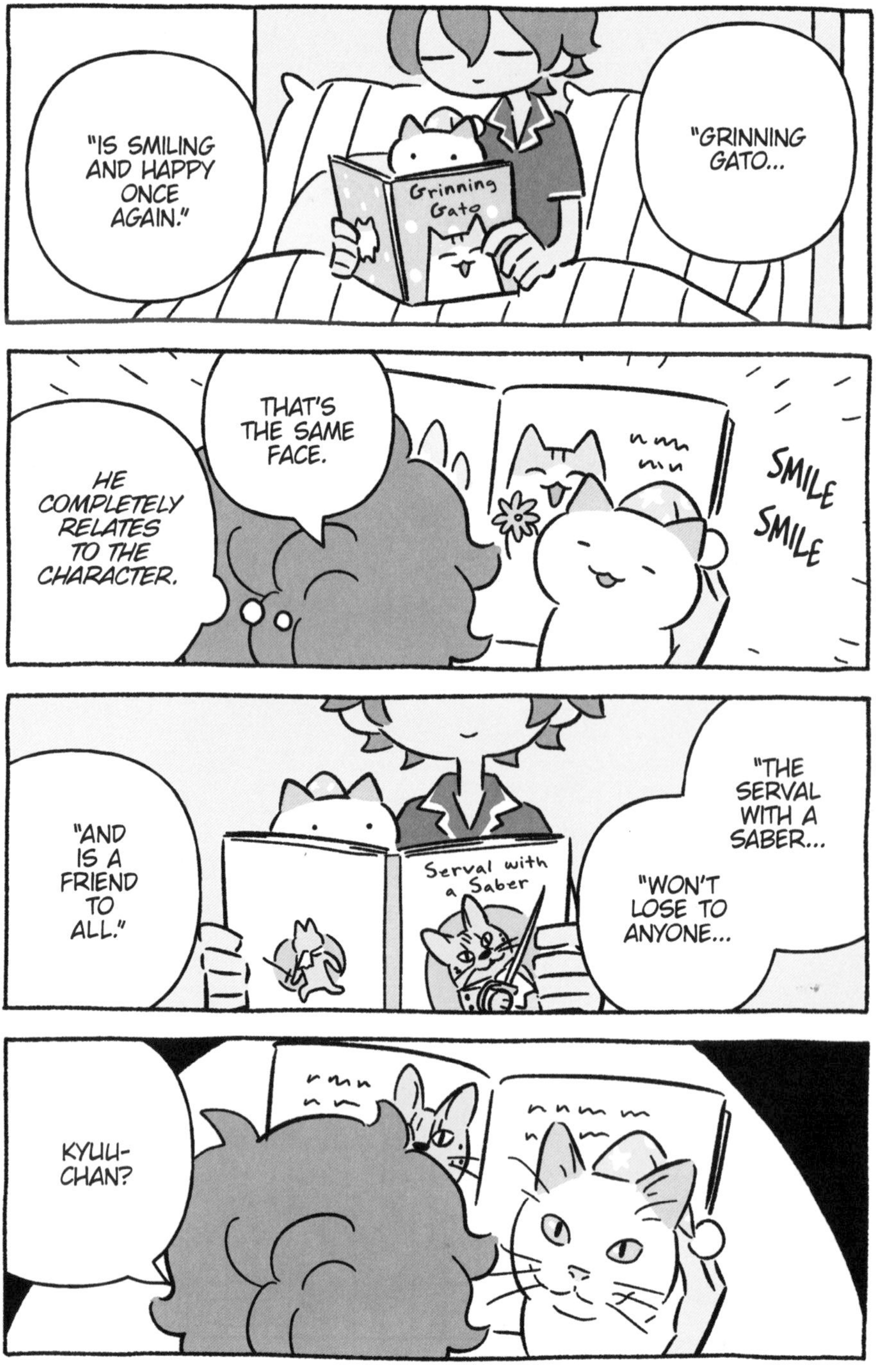
"GRINNING GATO...
Grinning Gato
"IS SMILING AND HAPPY ONCE AGAIN."
SMILE SMILE
THAT'S THE SAME FACE.
HE COMPLETELY RELATES TO THE CHARACTER.
"THE SERVAL WITH A SABER...
"WON'T LOSE TO ANYONE...
Serval with a Saber
"AND IS A FRIEND TO ALL."
KYUU-CHAN?

# MR. SHARK

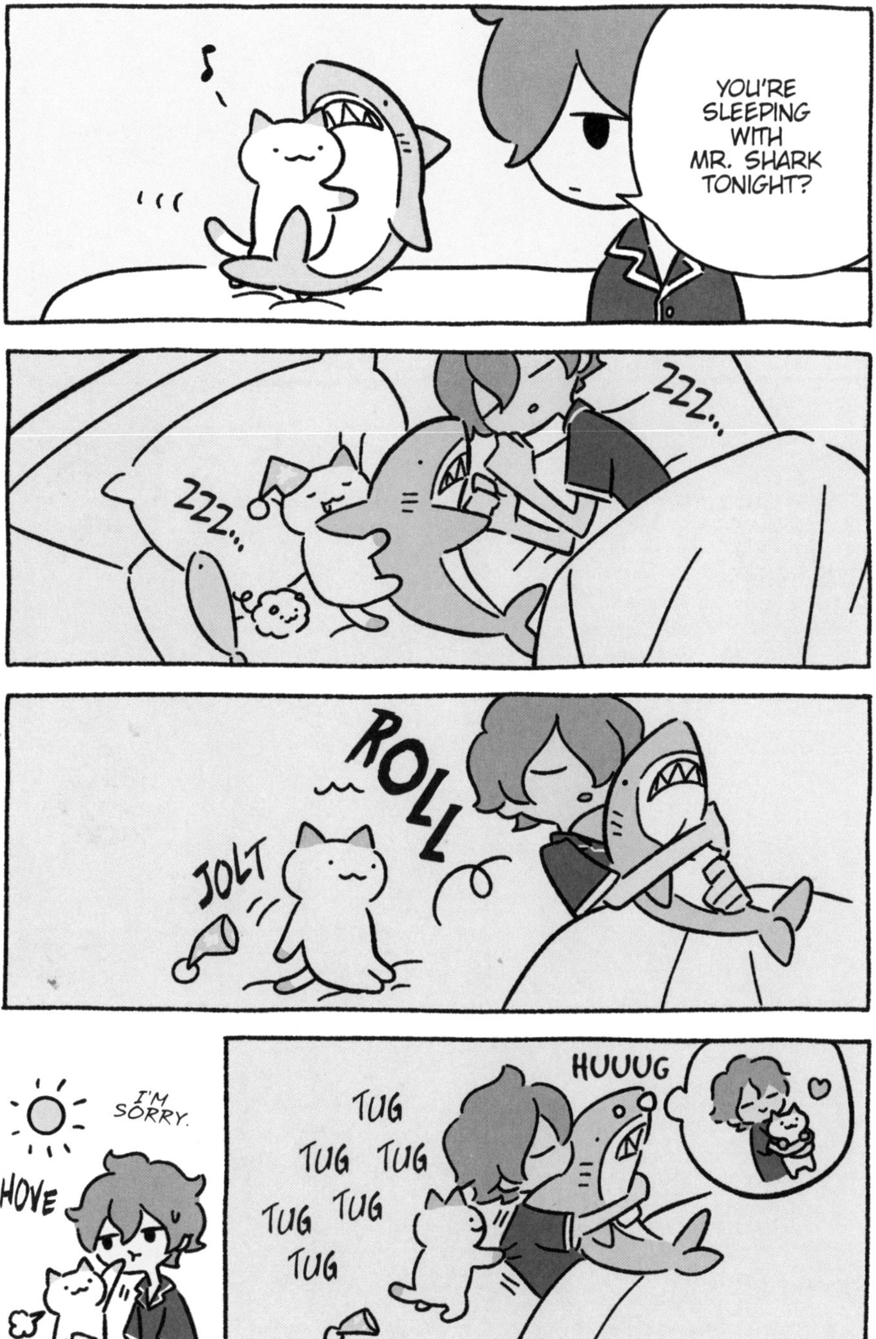
YOU'RE SLEEPING WITH MR. SHARK TONIGHT?
ZZZ...
ZZZ...
ROLL
JOLT
HUUUG
TUG
TUG TUG
TUG TUG
TUG
I'M SORRY.
SHOVE

# GOODBYE?

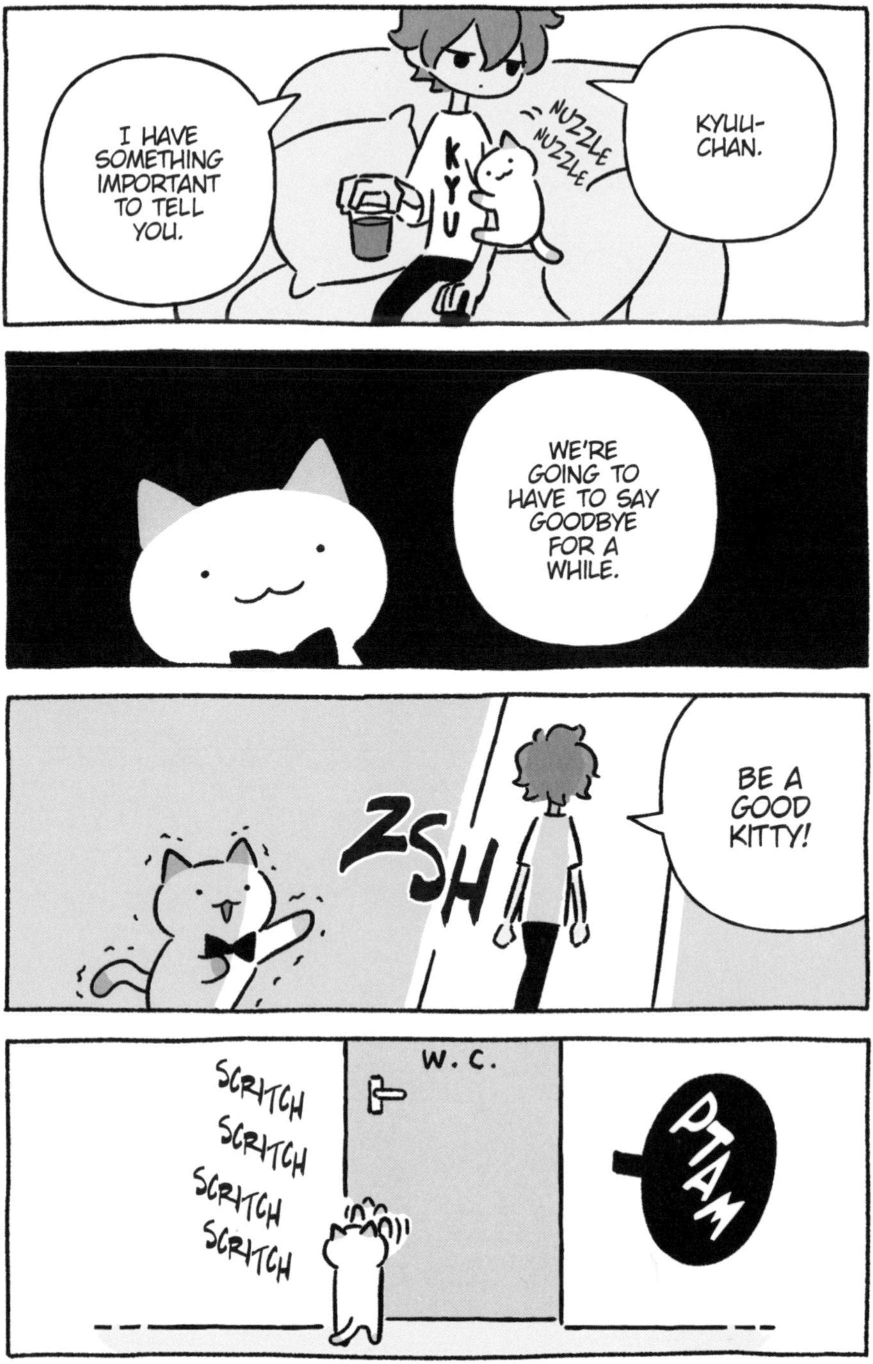
KYUU-CHAN.
NUZZLE NUZZLE
I HAVE SOMETHING IMPORTANT TO TELL YOU.
WE'RE GOING TO HAVE TO SAY GOODBYE FOR A WHILE.
BE A GOOD KITTY!
ZSH
PTAM
W.C.
SCRITCH SCRITCH SCRITCH SCRITCH

# TRICK FOR BUYING TIME

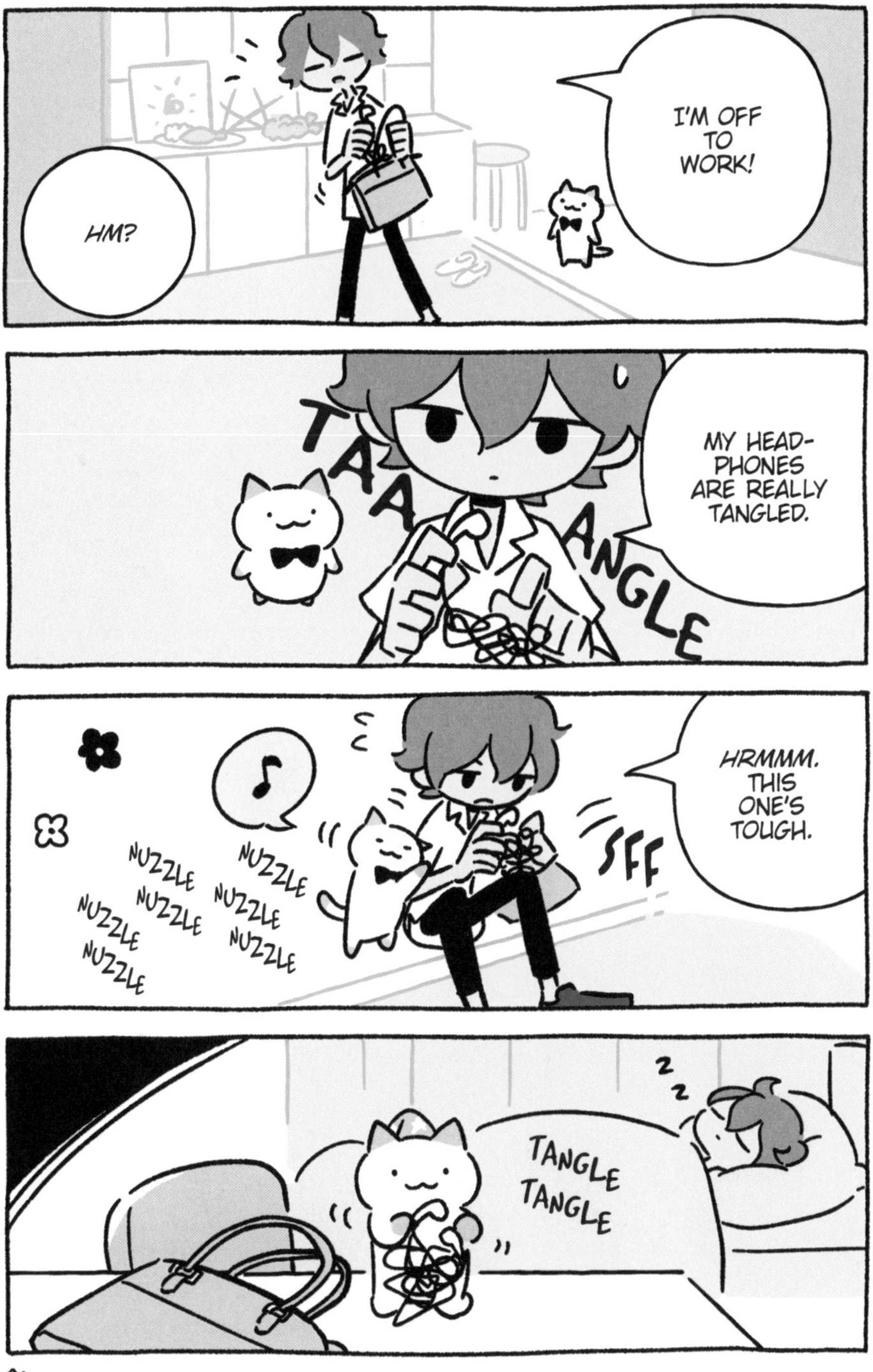
I'M OFF TO WORK!
HM?
MY HEAD-PHONES ARE REALLY TANGLED.
TAAANGLE
HRMMM. THIS ONE'S TOUGH.
SFF
NUZZLE NUZZLE NUZZLE
NUZZLE NUZZLE NUZZLE NUZZLE
Z Z
TANGLE TANGLE

# BUBBLES ①

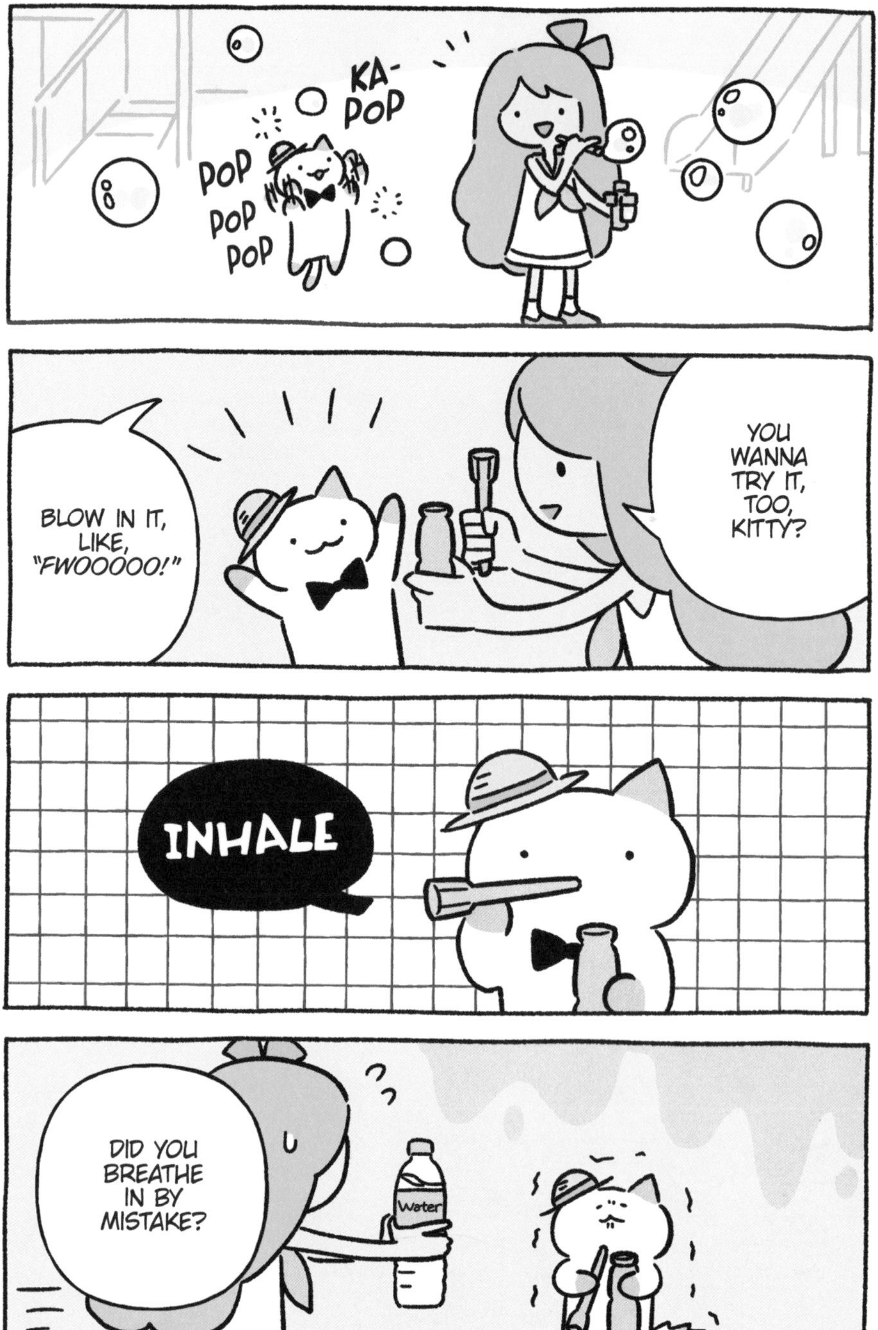
KA-POP
POP
POP
POP
YOU WANNA TRY IT, TOO, KITTY?
BLOW IN IT, LIKE, "FWOOOOO!"
INHALE
DID YOU BREATHE IN BY MISTAKE?
Water

# BUBBLES ②

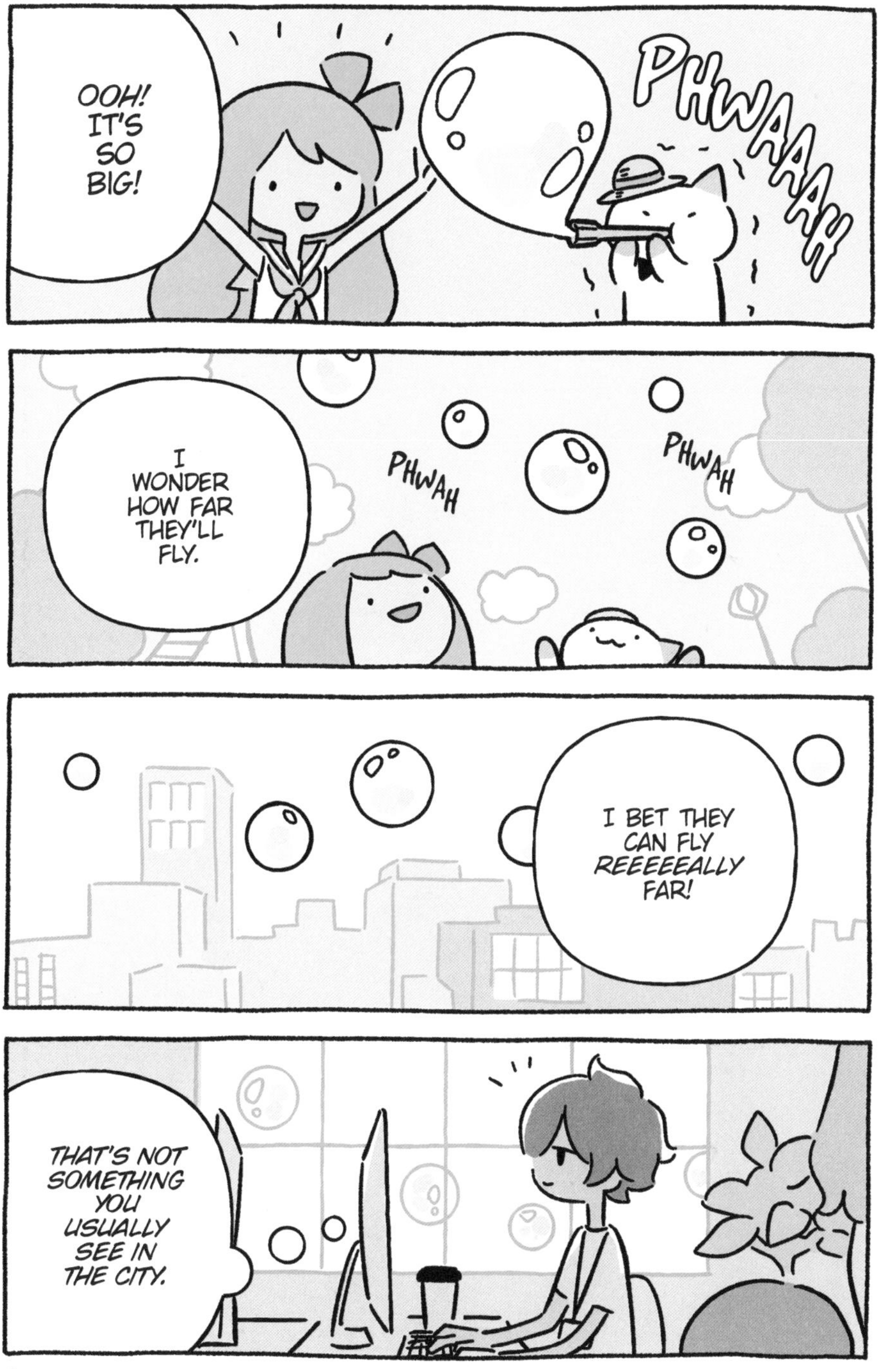
OOH! IT'S SO BIG!
PHWAAAAH
I WONDER HOW FAR THEY'LL FLY.
PHWAH
PHWAH
I BET THEY CAN FLY REEEEEALLY FAR!
THAT'S NOT SOMETHING YOU USUALLY SEE IN THE CITY.

# HEADPHONES

YOUR HEADPHONES GET TANGLED? WHY NOT BUY WIRELESS ONES?
OH, GOOD IDEA.
KA-CHOMP
?!
I DON'T KNOW WHY, BUT I THINK I'LL PASS...
?

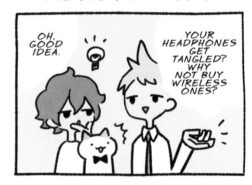

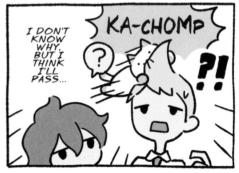

# SNEEZE

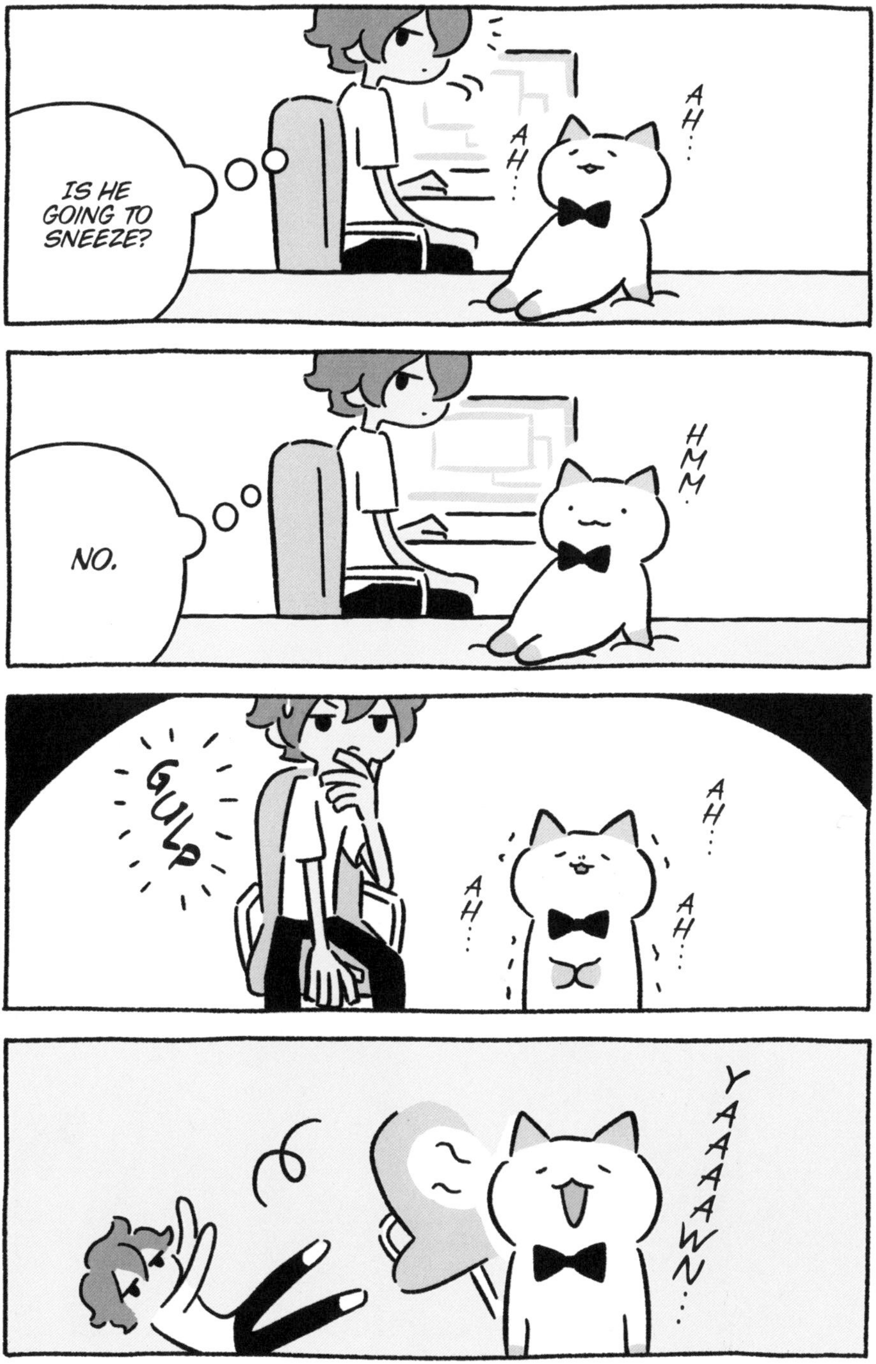

AH...
AH...
IS HE GOING TO SNEEZE?
HMM.
NO.
AH...
AH...
AH...
GULP
YAAAAAWN...

# I WANT TO GROW UP

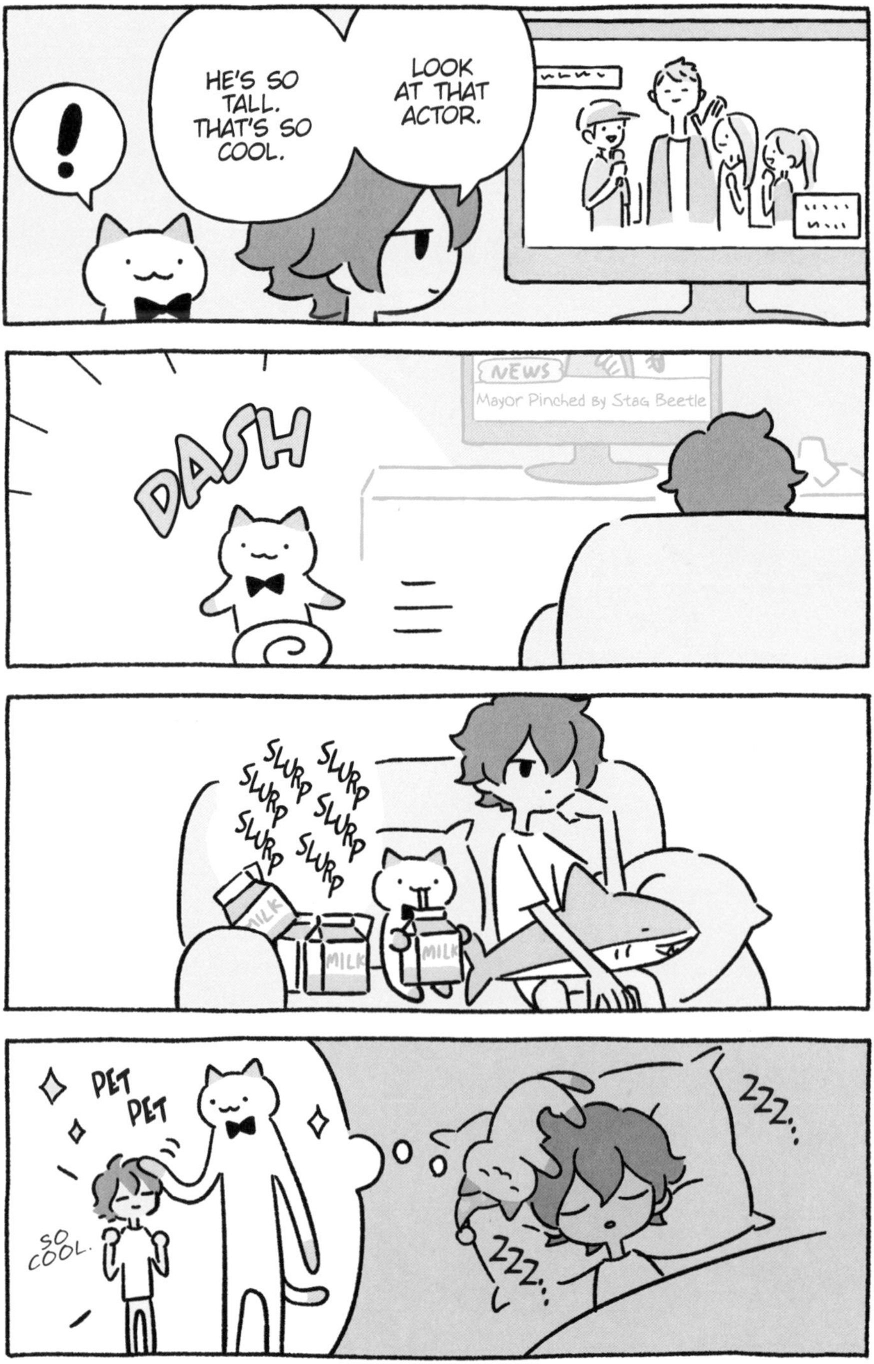

LOOK AT THAT ACTOR.
HE'S SO TALL. THAT'S SO COOL.
!
NEWS
Mayor Pinched by Stag Beetle
DASH
SLURP SLURP
SLURP SLURP
SLURP SLURP
MILK
MILK
MILK
ZZZ...
ZZZ...
PET PET
SO COOL.

# MOUTHWATERING CHICKEN

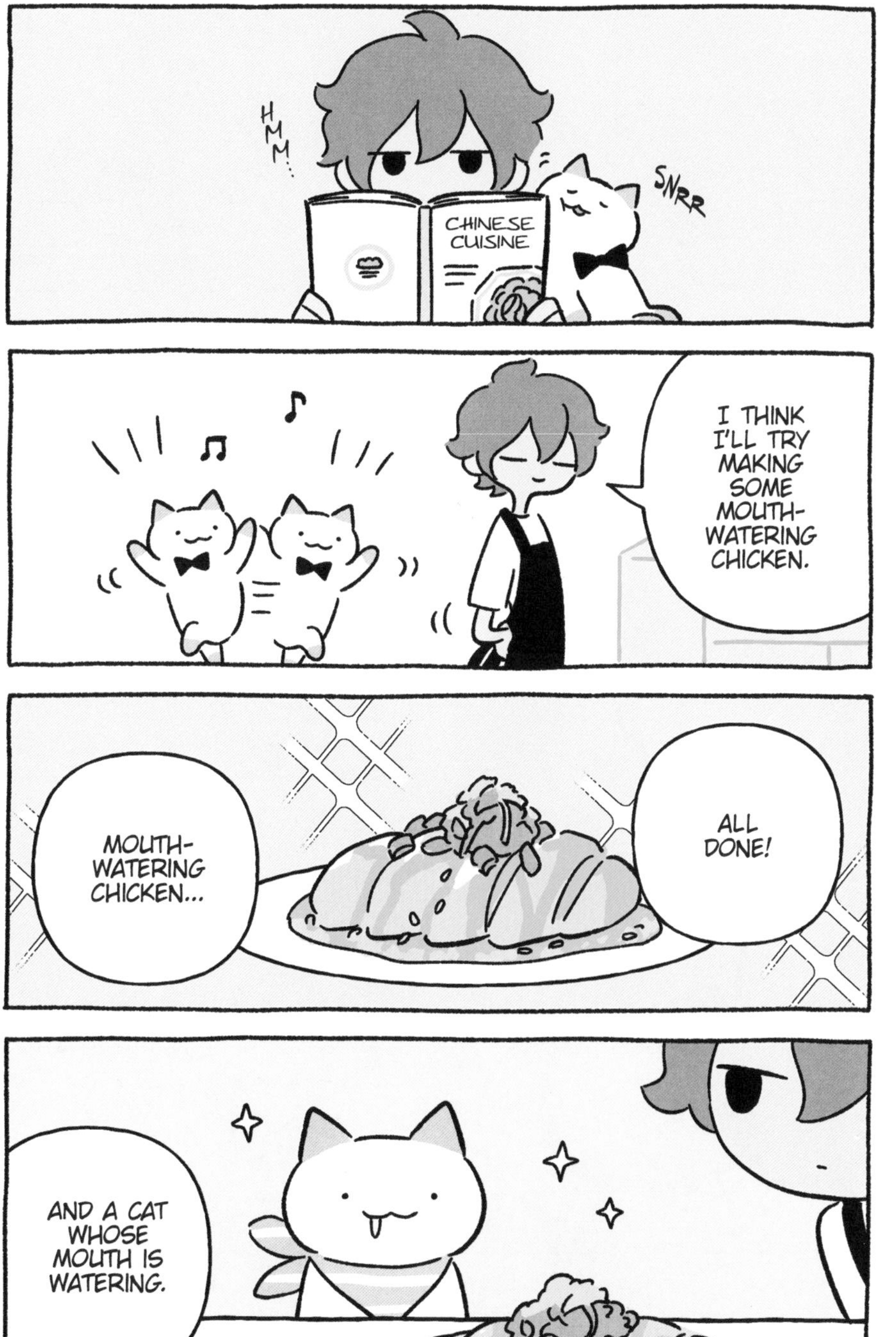
SNRR
CHINESE CUISINE
HMM...
I THINK I'LL TRY MAKING SOME MOUTH-WATERING CHICKEN.
ALL DONE!
MOUTH-WATERING CHICKEN...
AND A CAT WHOSE MOUTH IS WATERING.

# FIELD OF SUNFLOWERS

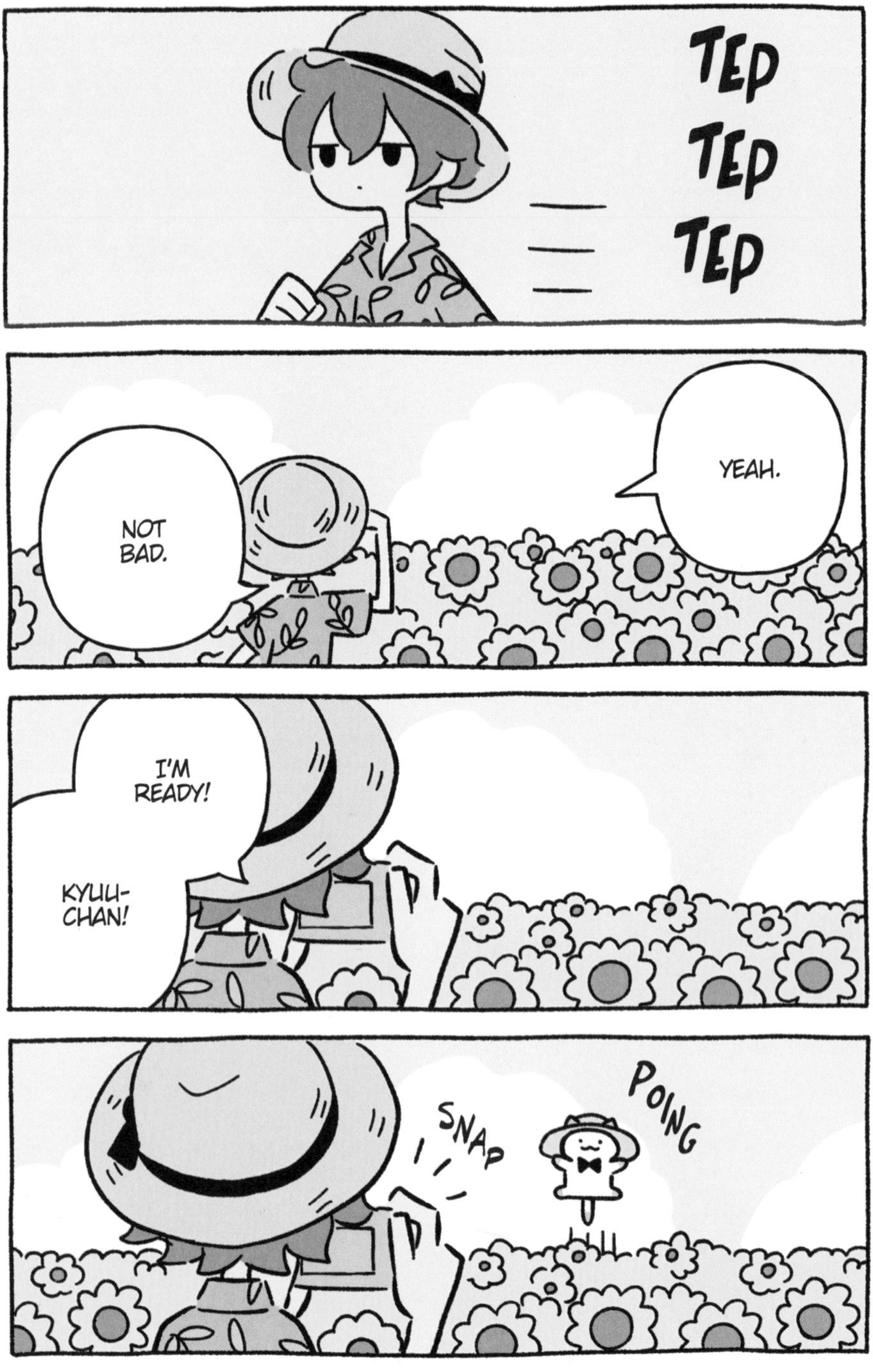
TEP
TEP
TEP
YEAH.
NOT BAD.
I'M READY!
KYUU-CHAN!
POING
SNAP

# RED HOT

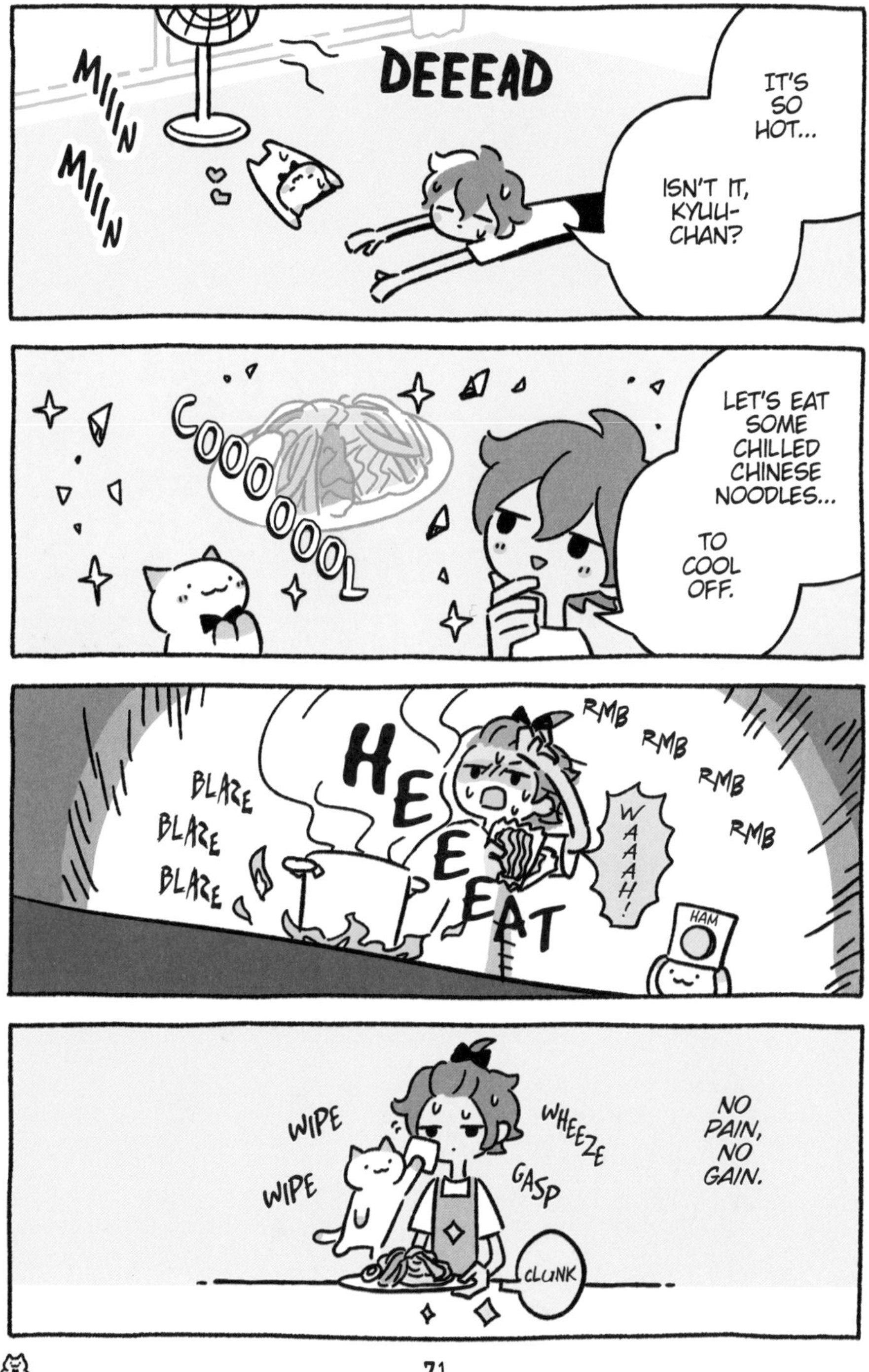
IT'S SO HOT...
ISN'T IT, KYUU-CHAN?
DEEEAD
MIIIN
MIIIN
LET'S EAT SOME CHILLED CHINESE NOODLES...
TO COOL OFF.
COOOOOOOL
RMB
RMB
RMB
RMB
WAAAAH!
HEEEAT
HAM
BLAZE
BLAZE
BLAZE
NO PAIN, NO GAIN.
WHEEZE
GASP
CLUNK
WIPE
WIPE

# SUMMER PLANS

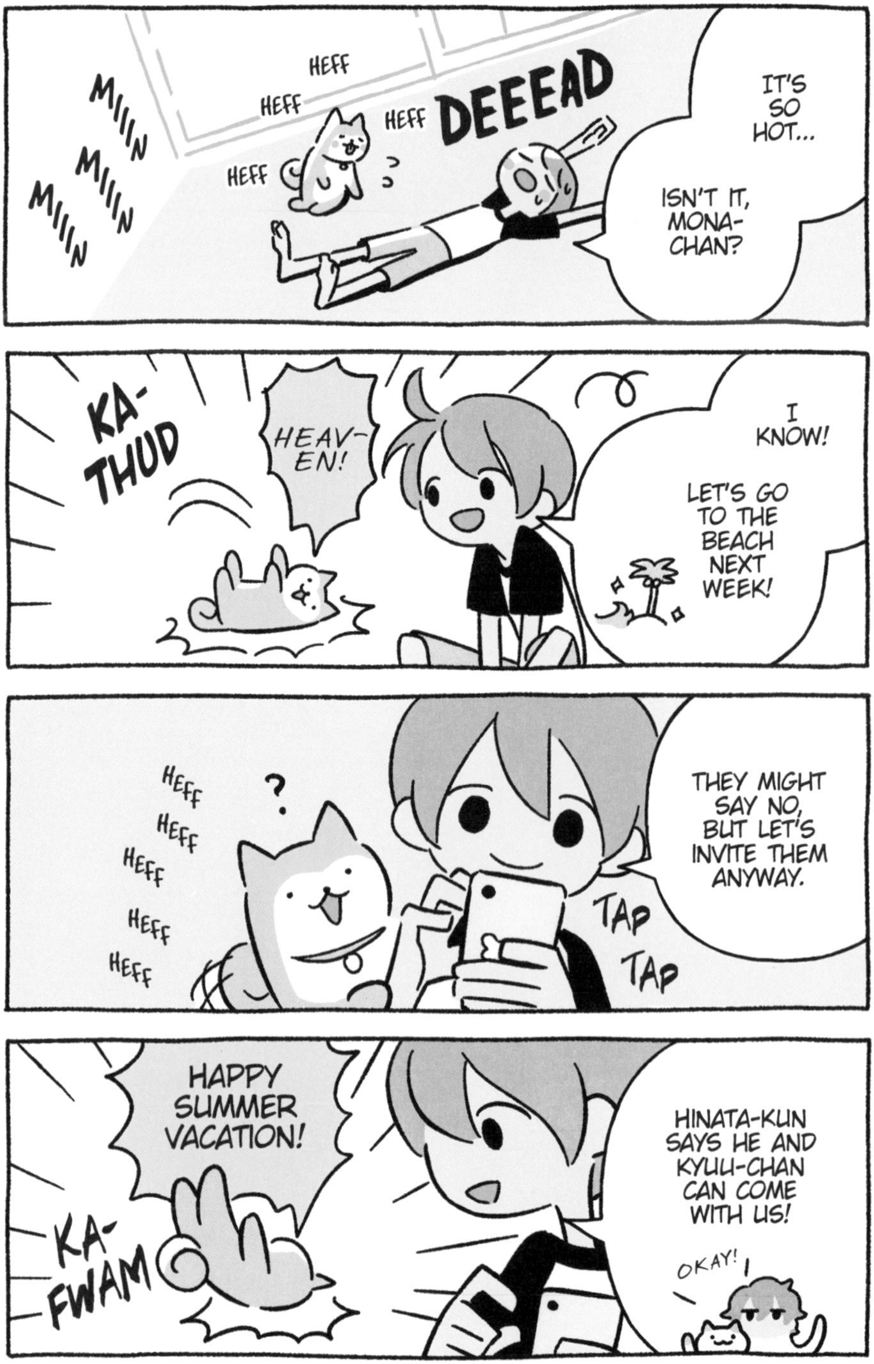
IT'S SO HOT...
ISN'T IT, MONA-CHAN?
DEEEAD
HEFF
HEFF
HEFF
HEFF
MIIIN
MIIIN
MIIIN
I KNOW!
LET'S GO TO THE BEACH NEXT WEEK!
HEAV-EN!
KA-THUD
THEY MIGHT SAY NO, BUT LET'S INVITE THEM ANYWAY.
TAP
TAP
HEFF
HEFF
HEFF
HEFF
HEFF
HINATA-KUN SAYS HE AND KYUU-CHAN CAN COME WITH US!
OKAY!
HAPPY SUMMER VACATION!
KA-FWAM

# THE BEACH

THE BEACH!
TODDLE
KA-SPLASH
WOO-HOO!
MEEP!
ZZSHHHH
SIT
WOW, YOU GUYS ARE LOW-ENERGY EVEN AT THE BEACH, HUH?

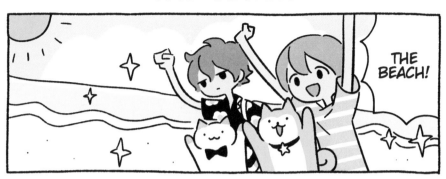

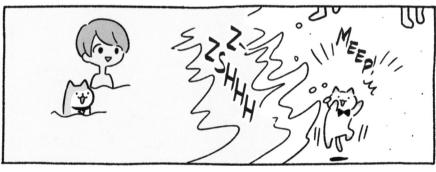

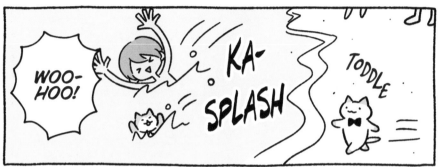

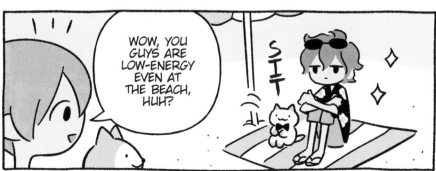

# BEACH VOLLEYBALL

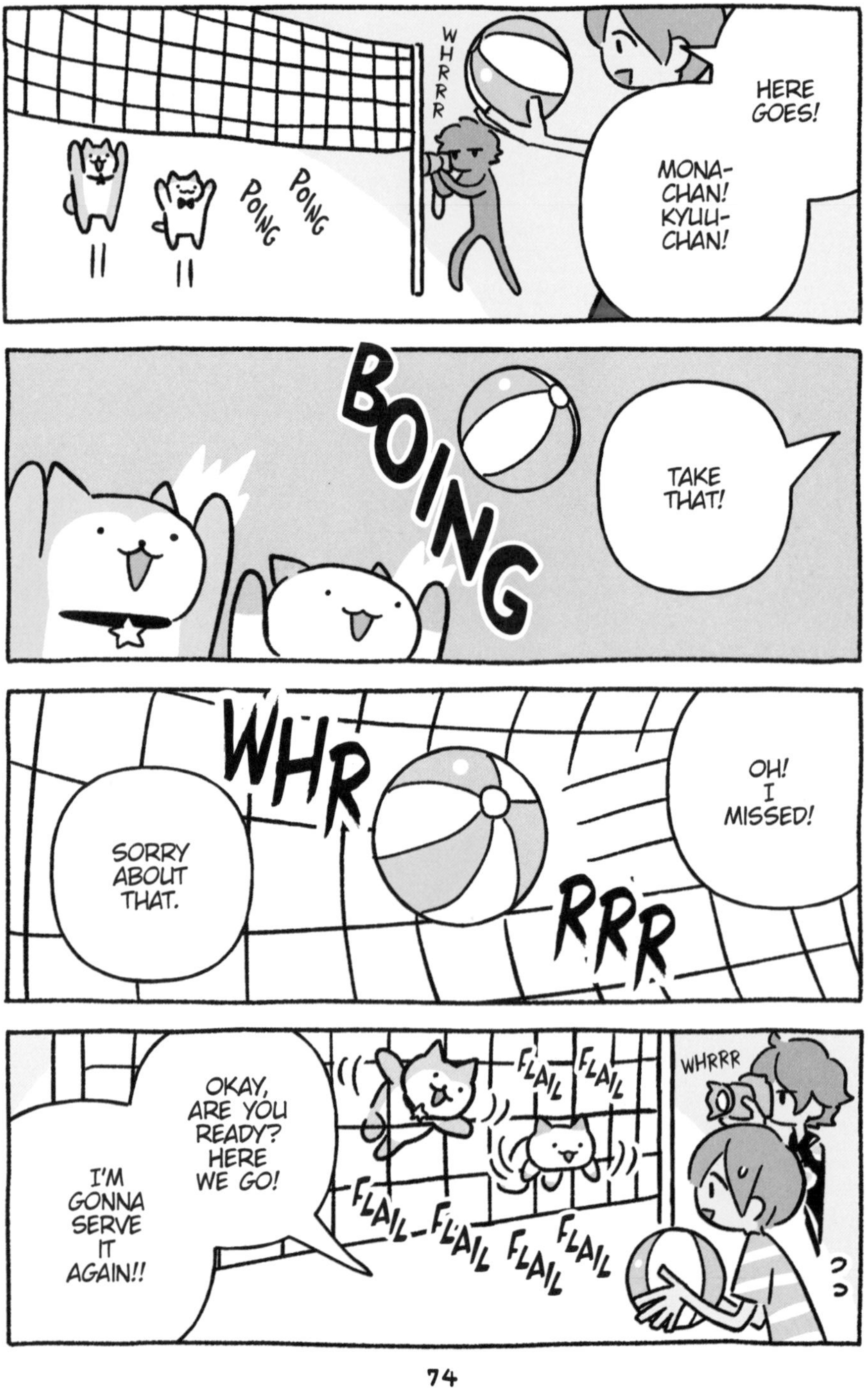
HERE GOES!
MONA-CHAN! KYUU-CHAN!
WHRRR
POING
POING
TAKE THAT!
BOING
OH! I MISSED!
WHRRRR
SORRY ABOUT THAT.
WHRRR
FLAIL FLAIL
OKAY, ARE YOU READY? HERE WE GO!
FLAIL FLAIL FLAIL FLAIL
I'M GONNA SERVE IT AGAIN!!

# UNDER THE RIGHT CIRCUMSTANCES

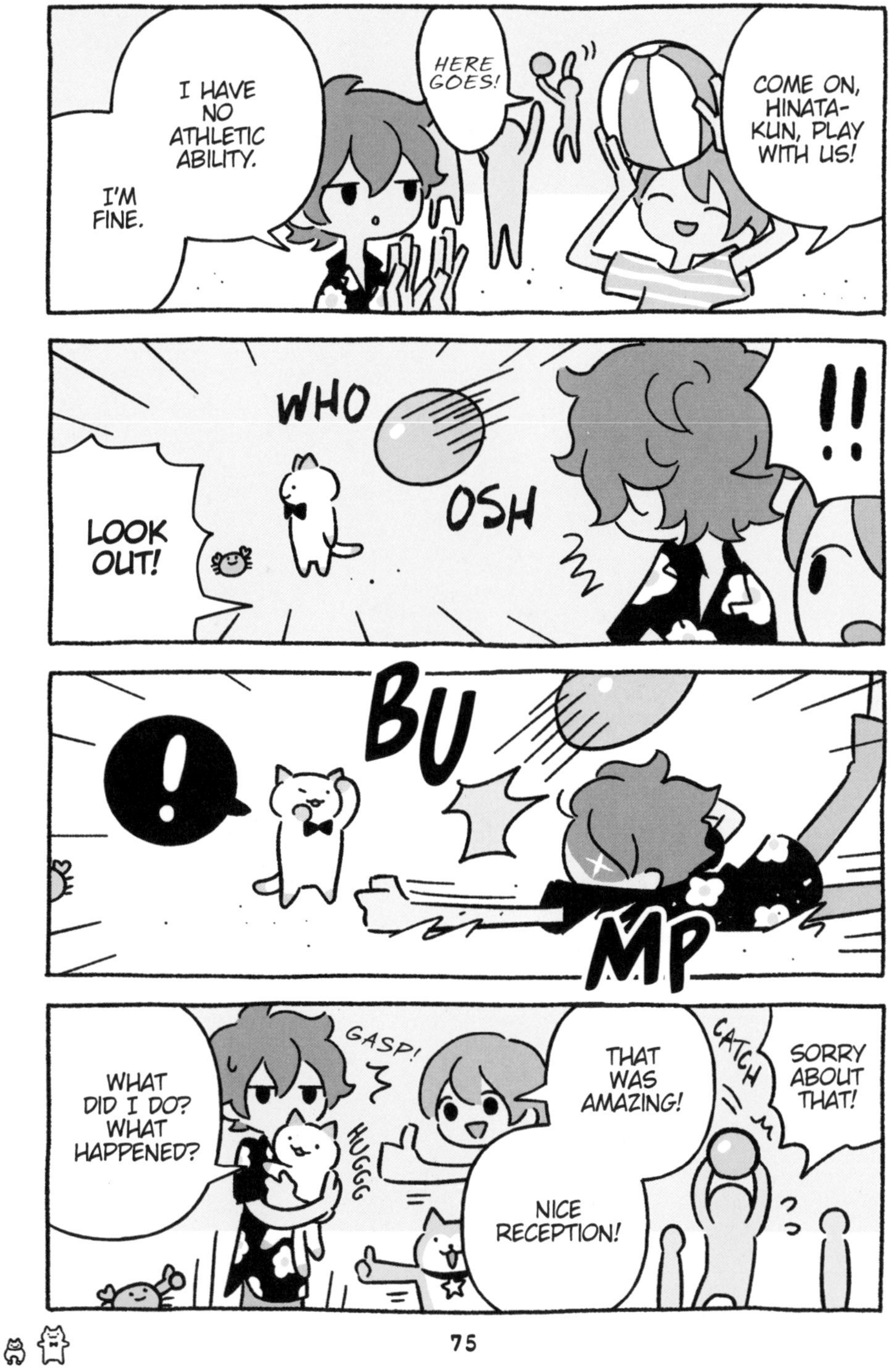
COME ON, HINATA-KUN, PLAY WITH US!
HERE GOES!
I HAVE NO ATHLETIC ABILITY.
I'M FINE.
!!
WHO
OSH
LOOK OUT!
BU
MP
!
SORRY ABOUT THAT!
CATCH
THAT WAS AMAZING!
GASP!
NICE RECEPTION!
HUGGG
WHAT DID I DO? WHAT HAPPENED?

# SEASHELLS

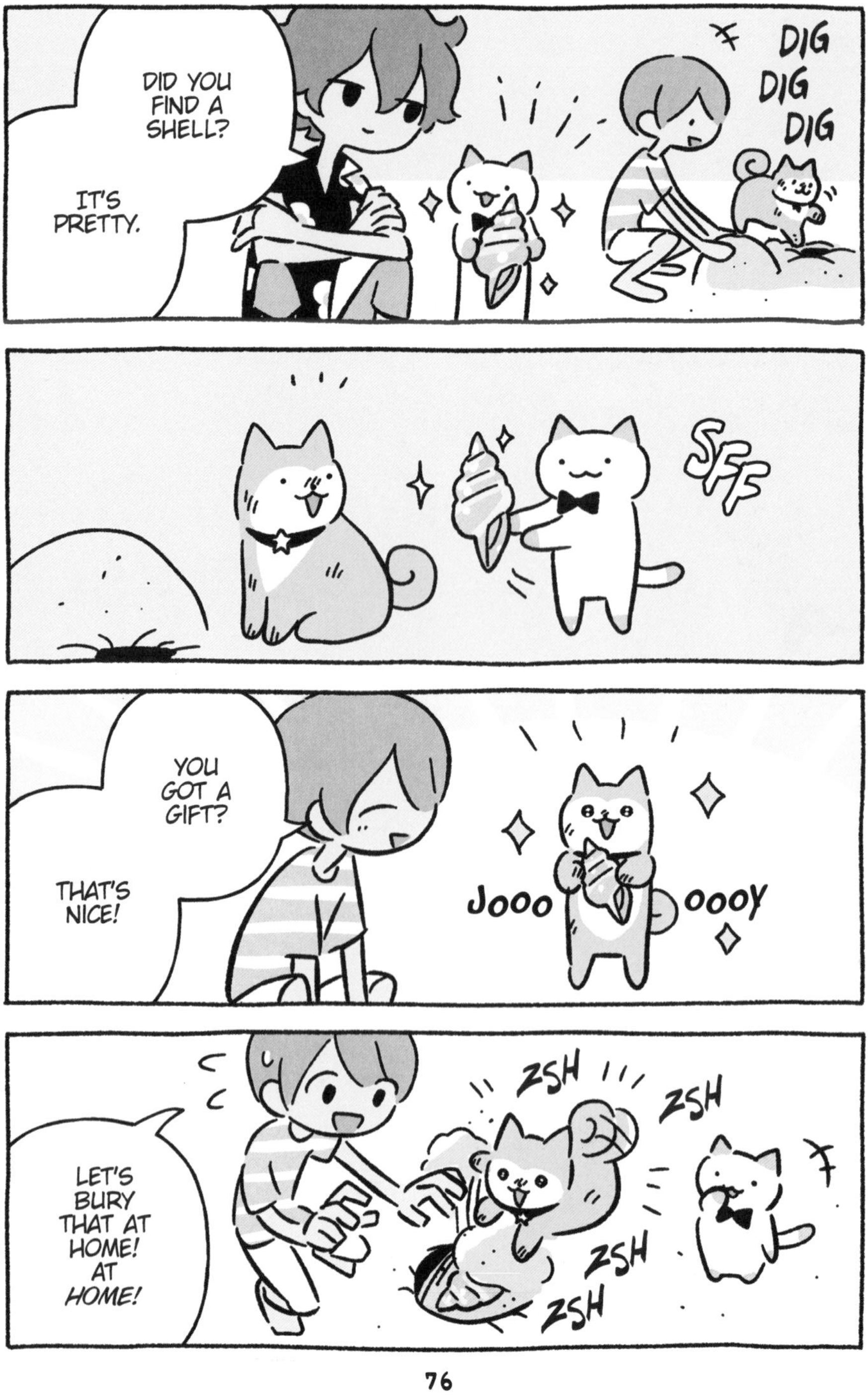

DIG DIG DIG
DID YOU FIND A SHELL? IT'S PRETTY.
SFF
JOOO OOOY
YOU GOT A GIFT? THAT'S NICE!
ZSH ZSH
ZSH ZSH
LET'S BURY THAT AT HOME! AT *HOME!*

# SUNTAN

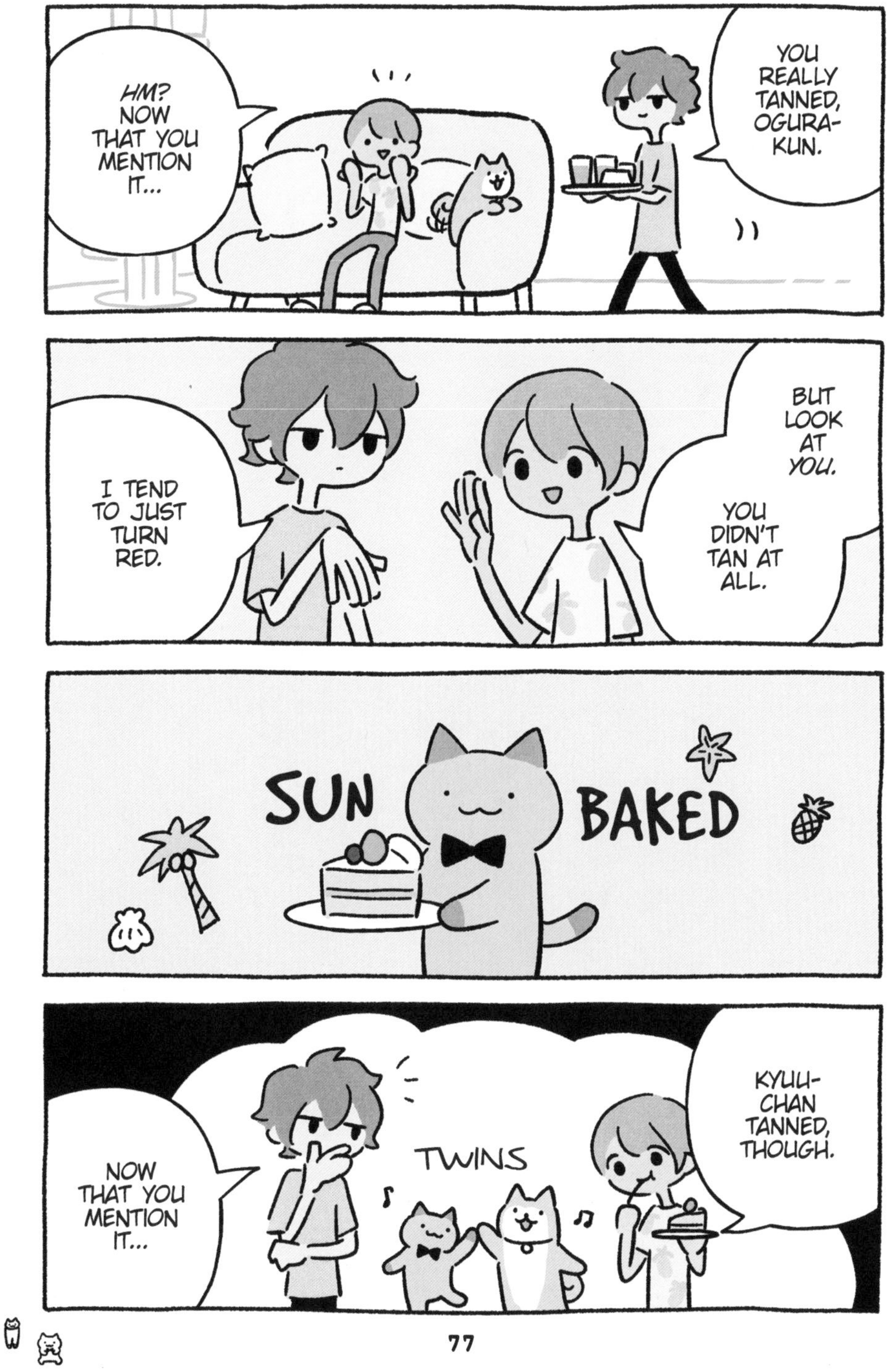

YOU REALLY TANNED, OGURA-KUN.
HM? NOW THAT YOU MENTION IT...
BUT LOOK AT YOU.
YOU DIDN'T TAN AT ALL.
I TEND TO JUST TURN RED.
SUN BAKED
KYUU-CHAN TANNED, THOUGH.
TWINS
NOW THAT YOU MENTION IT...

# LAMP

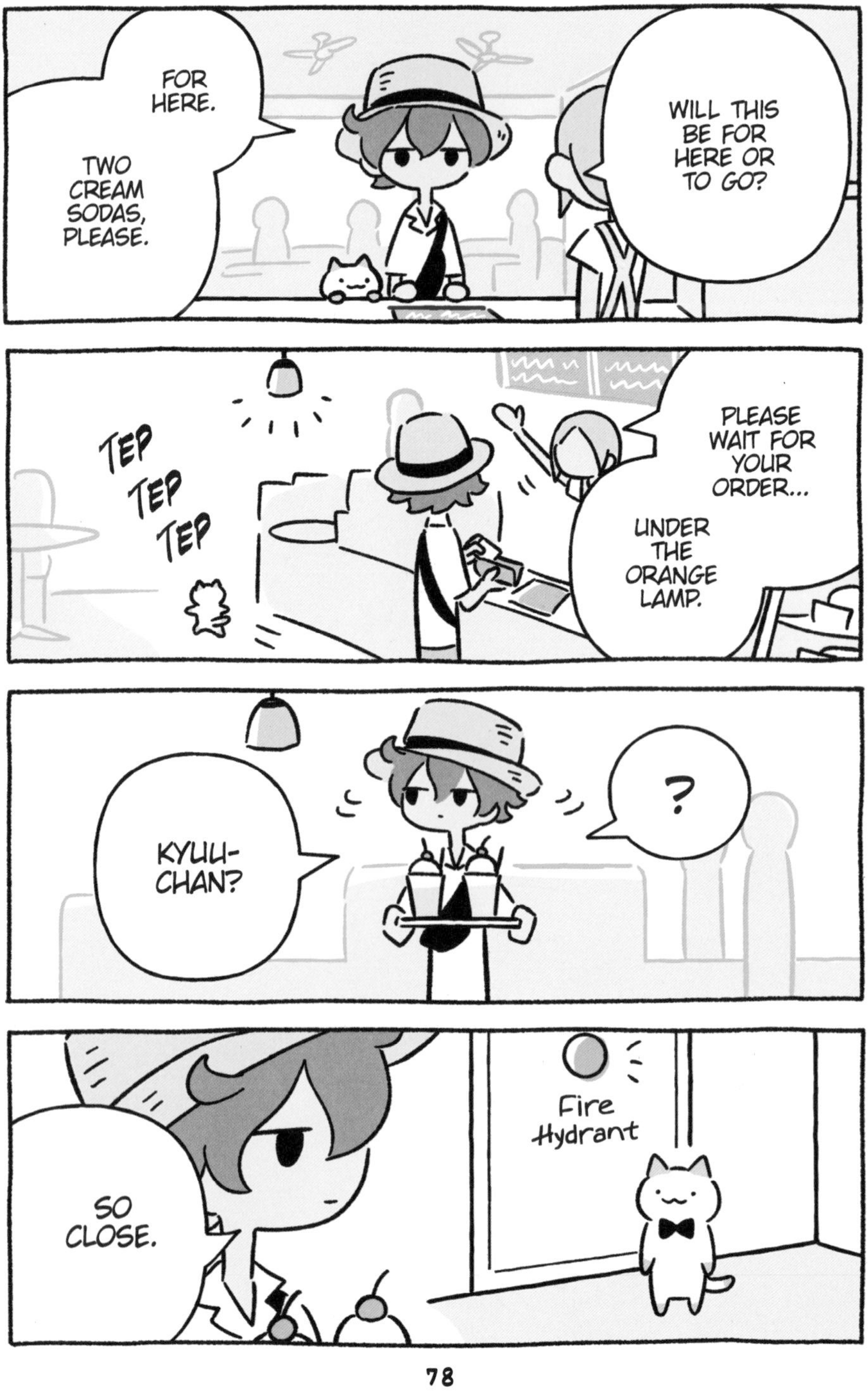
WILL THIS BE FOR HERE OR TO GO?
FOR HERE.
TWO CREAM SODAS, PLEASE.
PLEASE WAIT FOR YOUR ORDER...
UNDER THE ORANGE LAMP.
TEP TEP TEP
?
KYUU-CHAN?
Fire Hydrant
SO CLOSE.

# PLONK

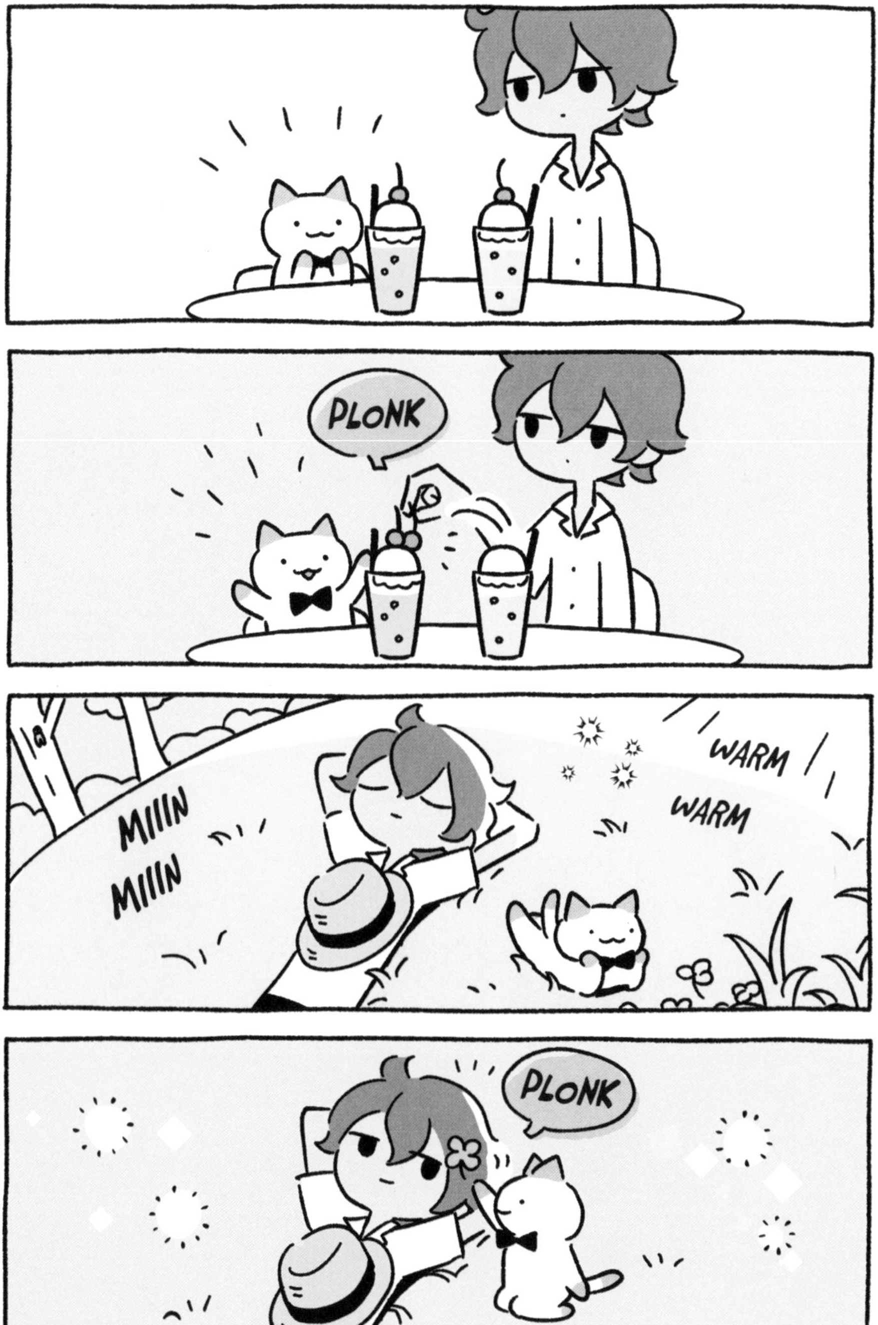
PLONK
WARM
WARM
MIIIN
MIIIN
PLONK

# CARELESS MISTAKES

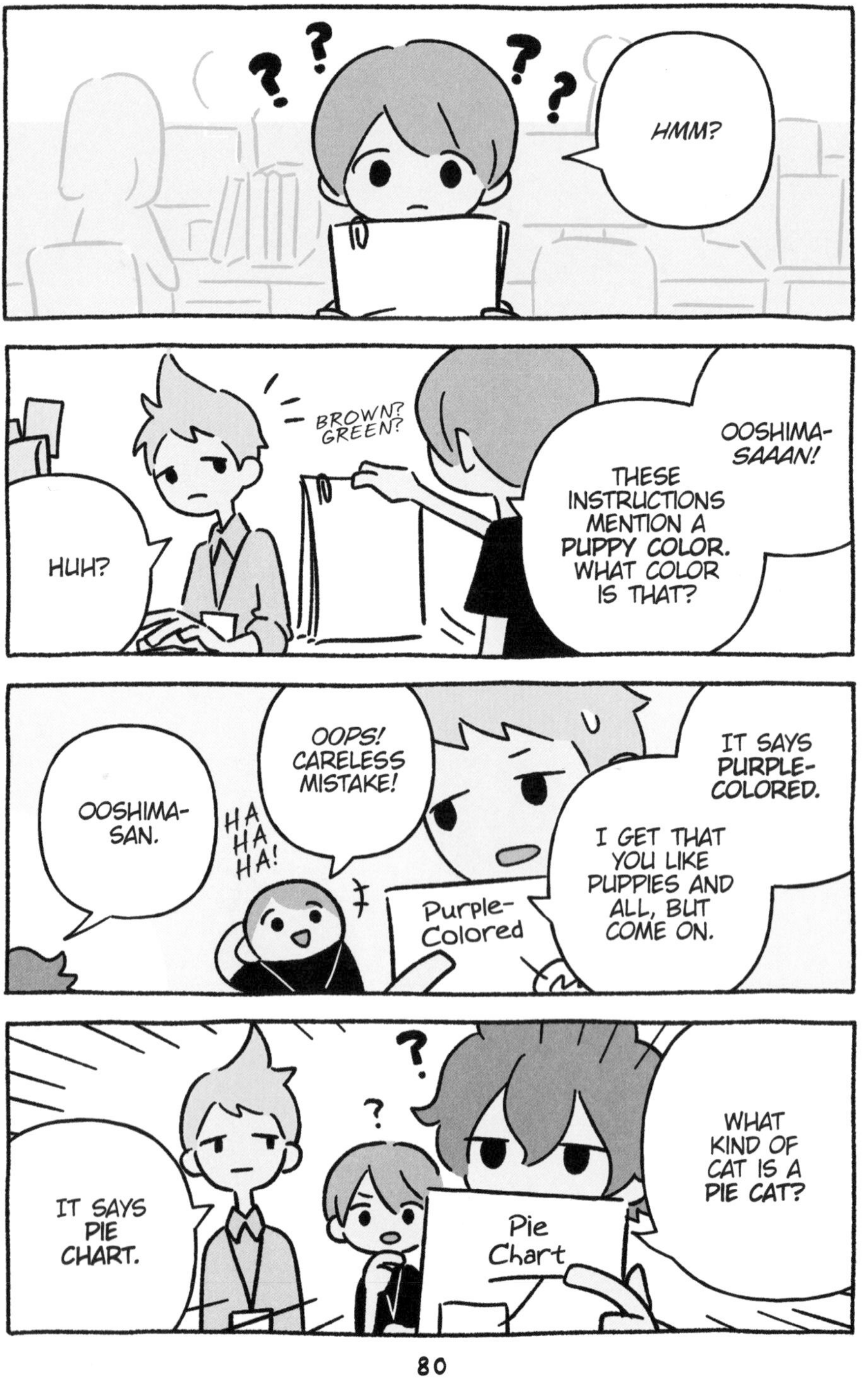
HMM?
OOSHIMA-SAAAN!
THESE INSTRUCTIONS MENTION A PUPPY COLOR. WHAT COLOR IS THAT?
BROWN? GREEN?
HUH?
IT SAYS PURPLE-COLORED.
I GET THAT YOU LIKE PUPPIES AND ALL, BUT COME ON.
Purple-Colored
OOPS! CARELESS MISTAKE!
HA HA HA!
OOSHIMA-SAN.
WHAT KIND OF CAT IS A PIE CAT?
Pie Chart
IT SAYS PIE CHART.

# UNMOVING

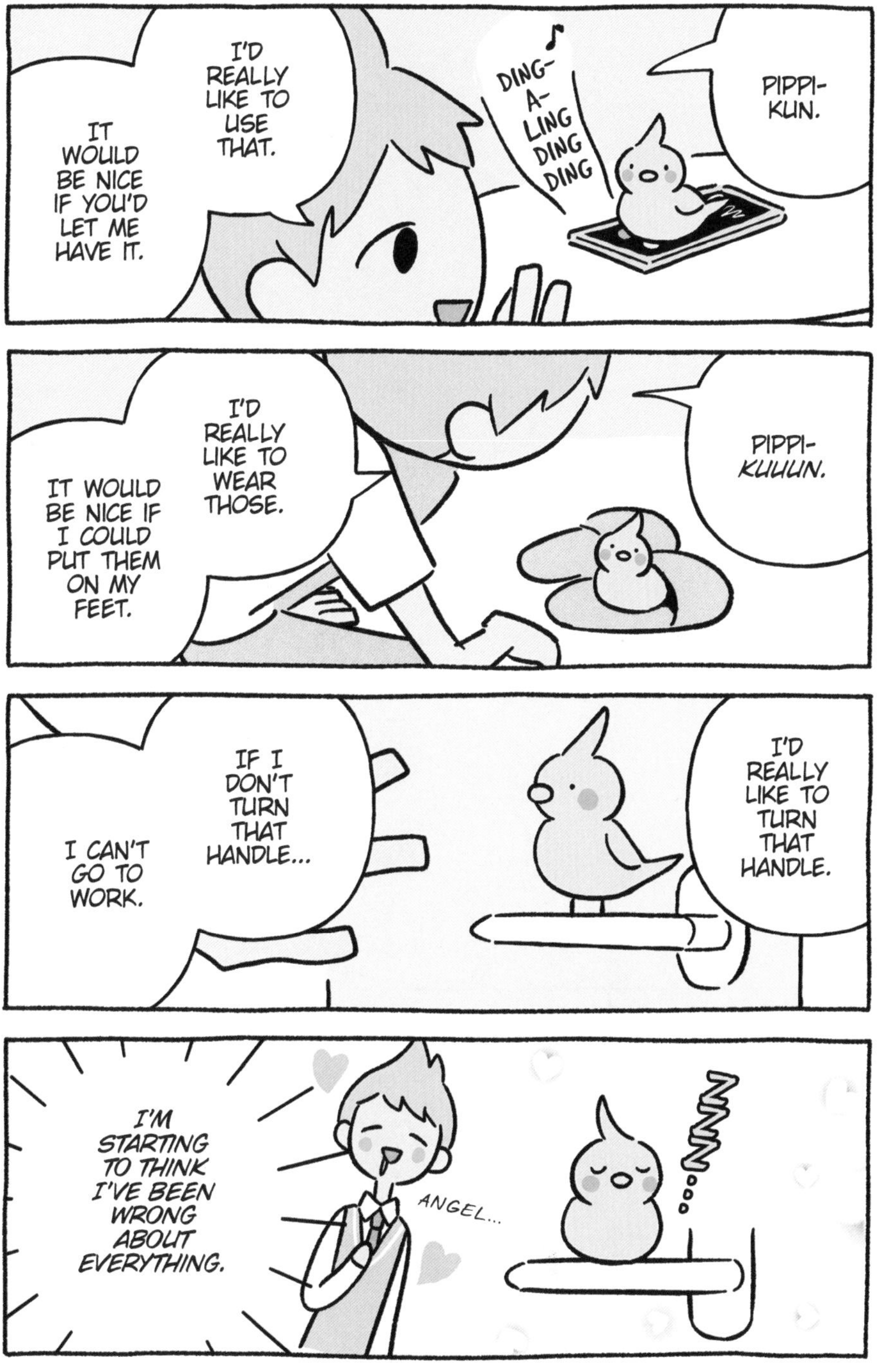
PIPPI-KUN.
DING-A-LING DING DING
I'D REALLY LIKE TO USE THAT.
IT WOULD BE NICE IF YOU'D LET ME HAVE IT.
PIPPI-KUUUN.
I'D REALLY LIKE TO WEAR THOSE.
IT WOULD BE NICE IF I COULD PUT THEM ON MY FEET.
I'D REALLY LIKE TO TURN THAT HANDLE.
IF I DON'T TURN THAT HANDLE...
I CAN'T GO TO WORK.
ANGEL...
I'M STARTING TO THINK I'VE BEEN WRONG ABOUT EVERYTHING.

# TIRELESS EFFORT

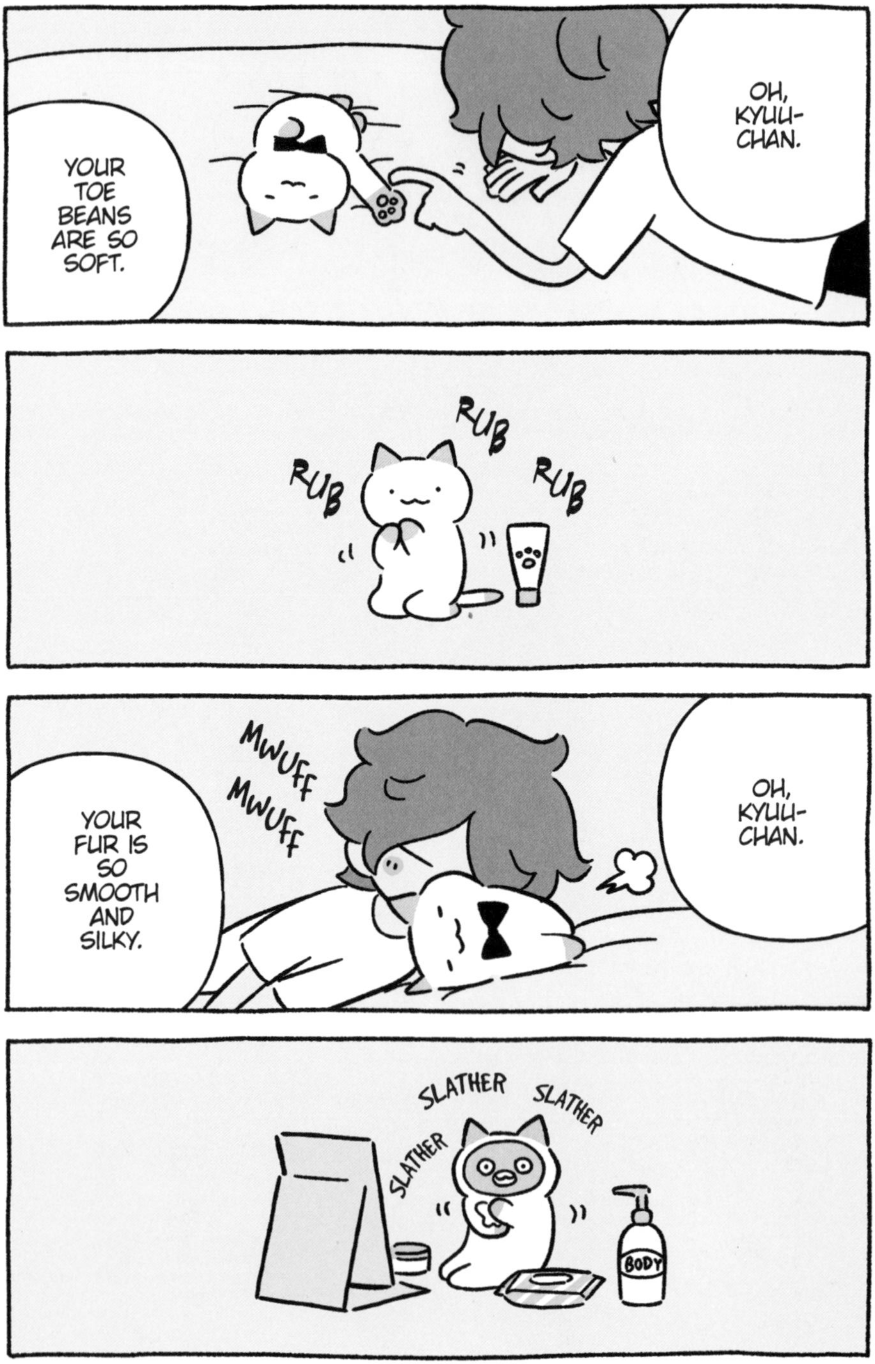
OH, KYUU-CHAN.
YOUR TOE BEANS ARE SO SOFT.
RUB
RUB
RUB
OH, KYUU-CHAN.
MWUFF
MWUFF
YOUR FUR IS SO SMOOTH AND SILKY.
SLATHER
SLATHER
SLATHER
BODY

# A HANDKERCHIEF AND...

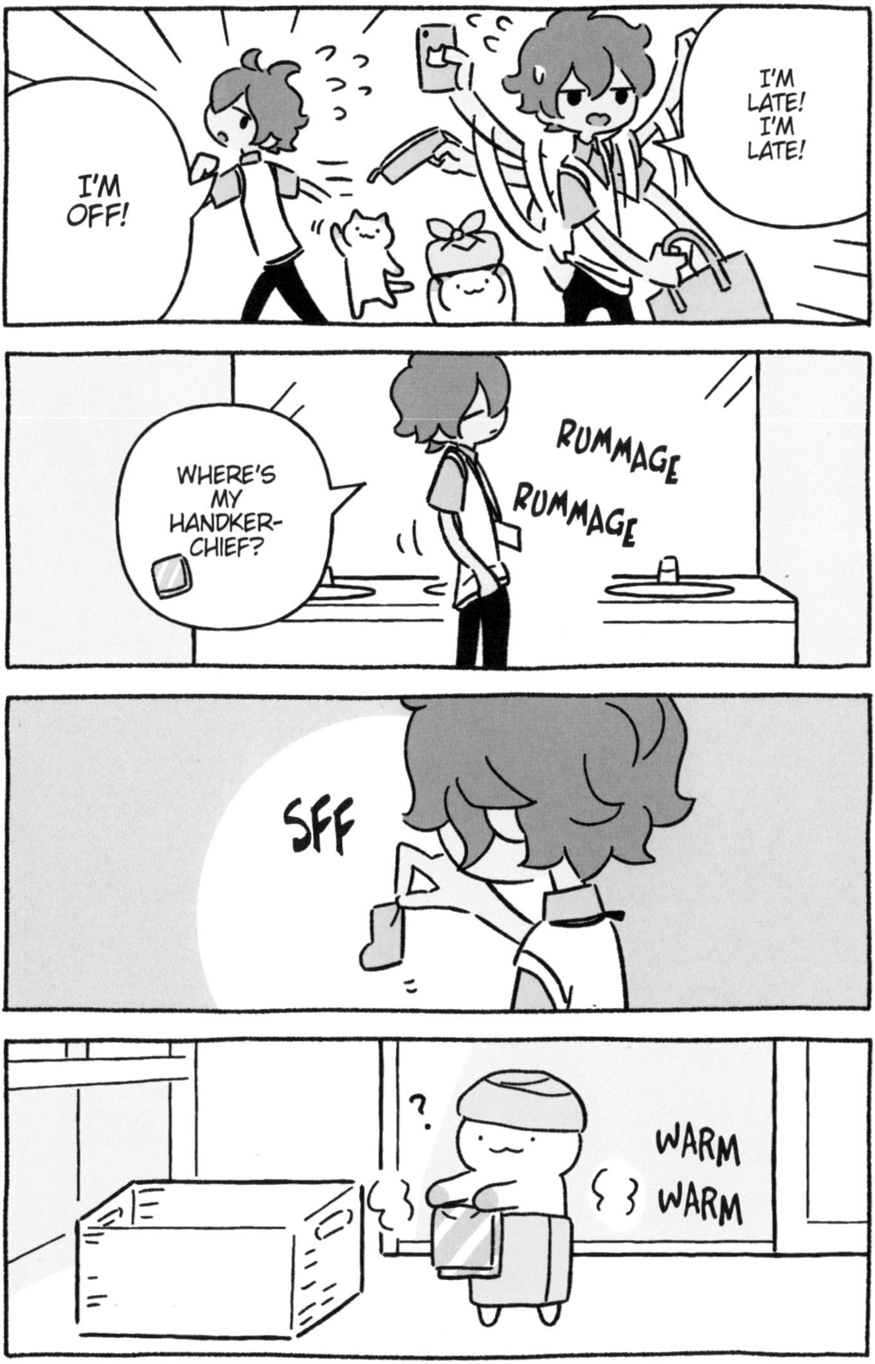
I'M LATE! I'M LATE!
I'M OFF!
RUMMAGE
RUMMAGE
WHERE'S MY HANDKERCHIEF?
SFF
WARM WARM
?

# FLOWERS AND MUSIC

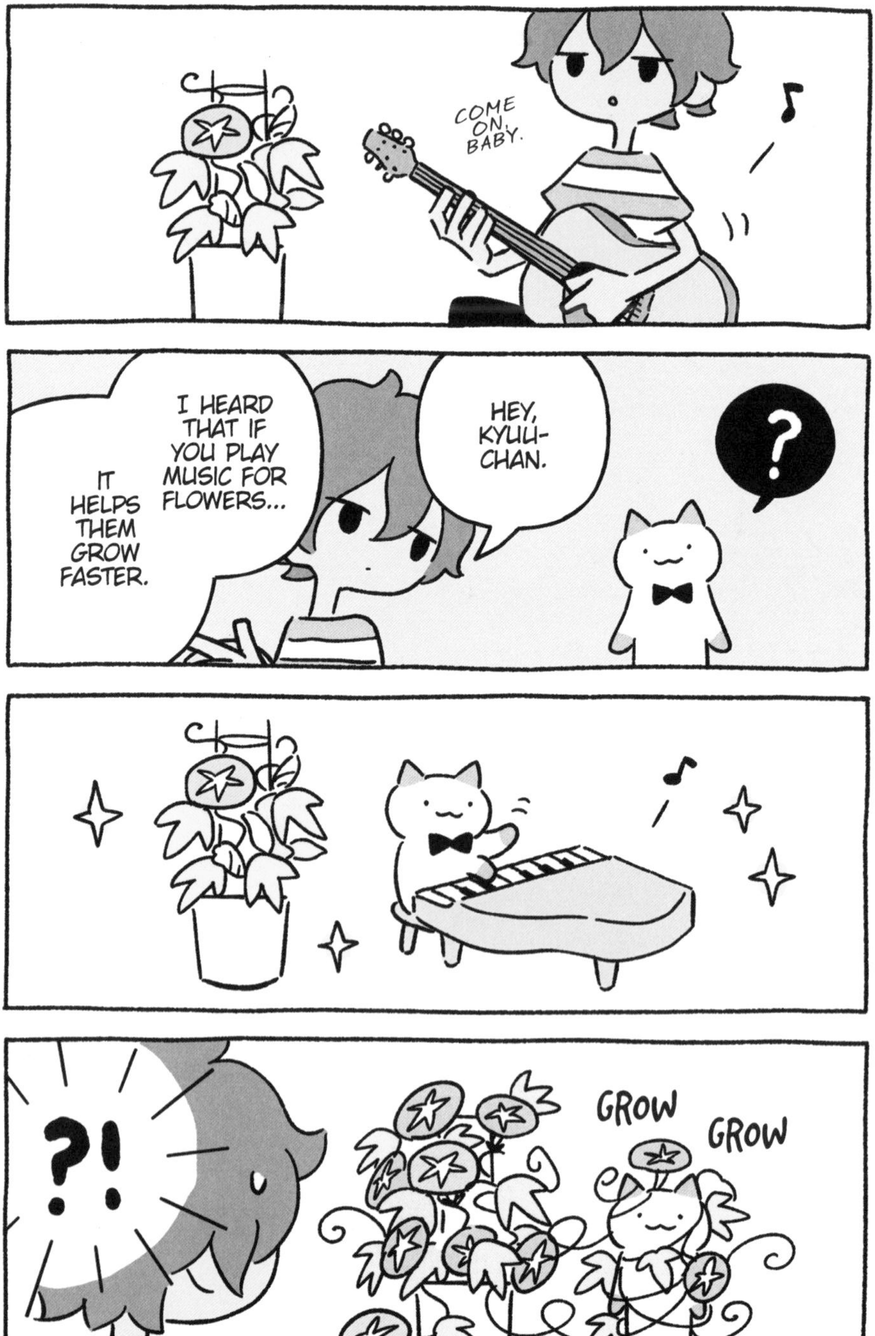
COME ON, BABY.
HEY, KYUU-CHAN.
?
I HEARD THAT IF YOU PLAY MUSIC FOR FLOWERS...
IT HELPS THEM GROW FASTER.
GROW
GROW
?!

# CHINESE LANTERN

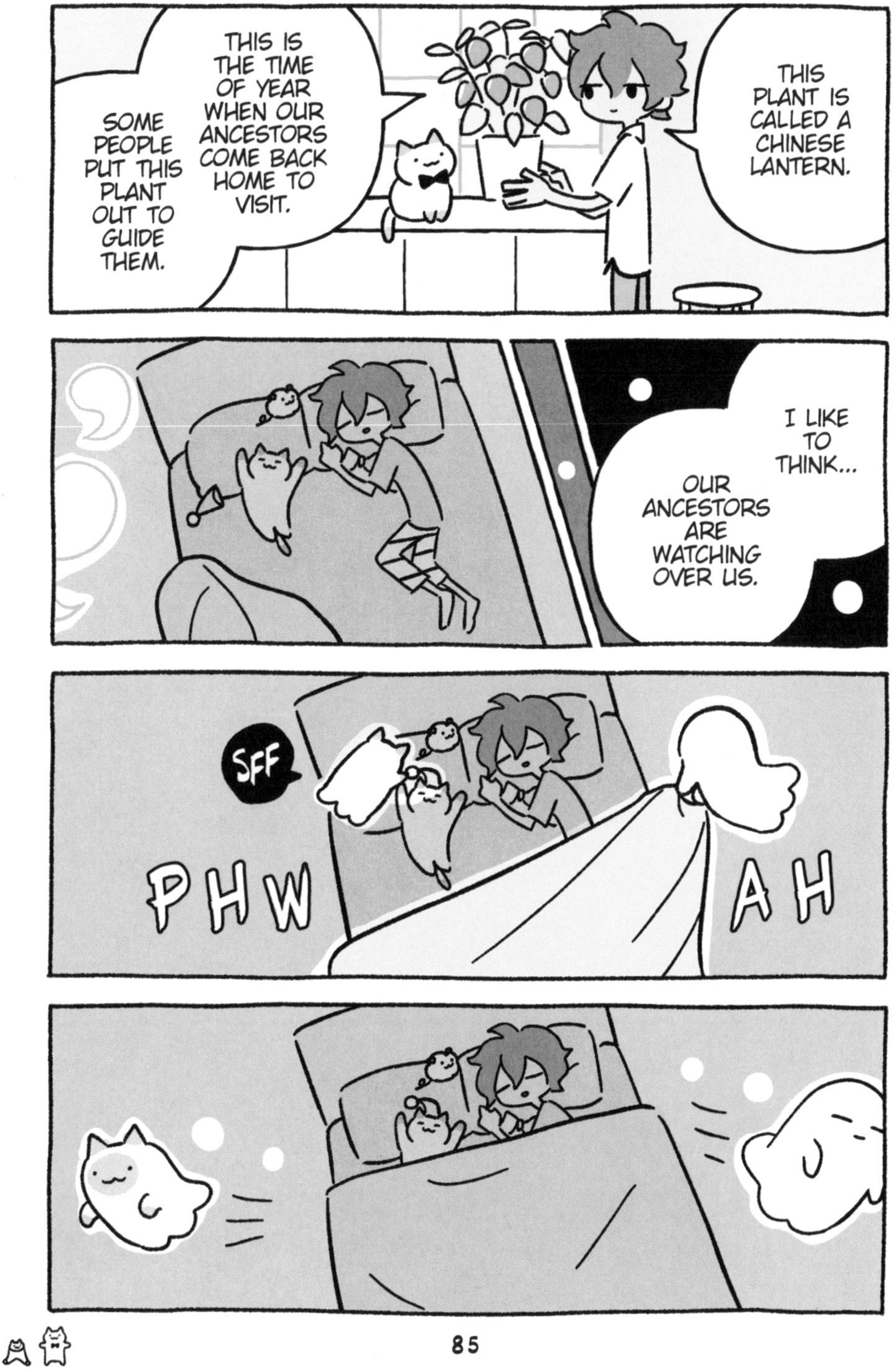
THIS PLANT IS CALLED A CHINESE LANTERN.
THIS IS THE TIME OF YEAR WHEN OUR ANCESTORS COME BACK HOME TO VISIT.
SOME PEOPLE PUT THIS PLANT OUT TO GUIDE THEM.
I LIKE TO THINK...
OUR ANCESTORS ARE WATCHING OVER US.
SFF
PHWAH

# AFTER THE SINGLE SOCK INCIDENT

I FEEL BAD FOR TAKING KYUU-CHAN'S SOCK.

I'LL GIVE IT BACK AT LUNCH-TIME.

SHOCK

# MULTIPLYING BUNS

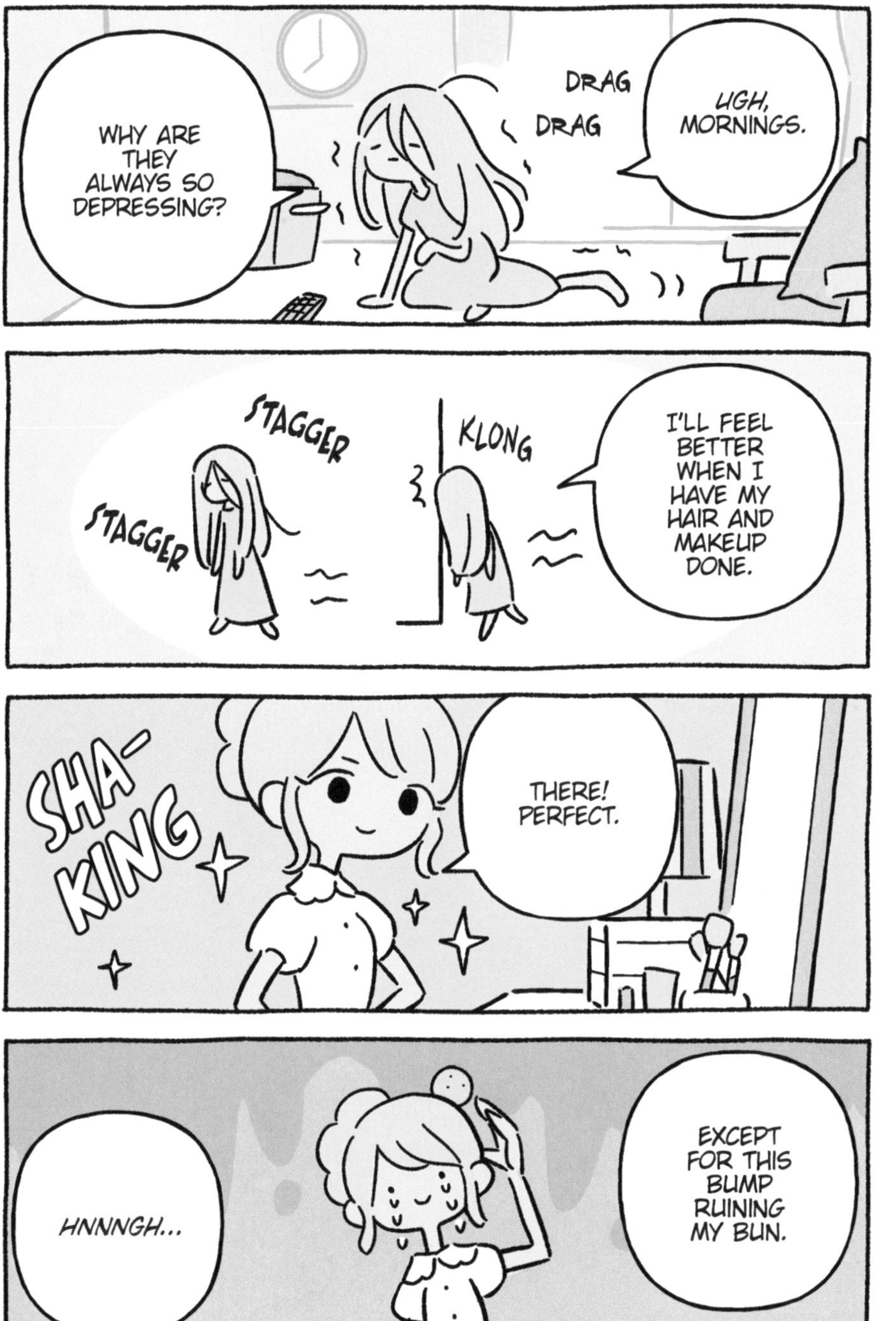
UGH, MORNINGS.
DRAG
DRAG
WHY ARE THEY ALWAYS SO DEPRESSING?
I'LL FEEL BETTER WHEN I HAVE MY HAIR AND MAKEUP DONE.
KLONG
STAGGER
STAGGER
THERE! PERFECT.
SHA-KING
EXCEPT FOR THIS BUMP RUINING MY BUN.
HNNNGH...

# BUMP

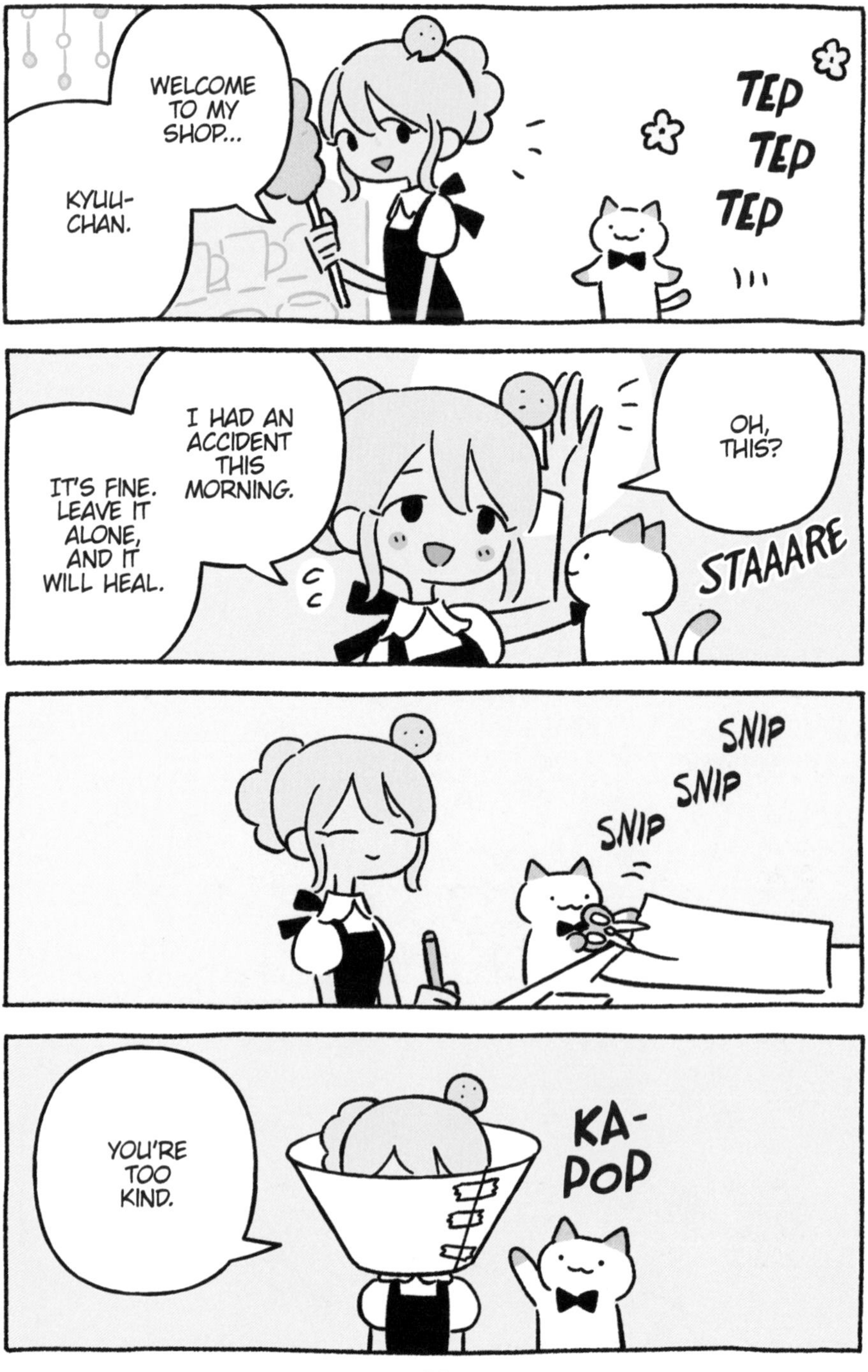
TEP TEP TEP
WELCOME TO MY SHOP... KYUU-CHAN.
OH, THIS?
STAAARE
I HAD AN ACCIDENT THIS MORNING. IT'S FINE. LEAVE IT ALONE, AND IT WILL HEAL.
SNIP SNIP SNIP
KA-POP
YOU'RE TOO KIND.

# CELEBRATION

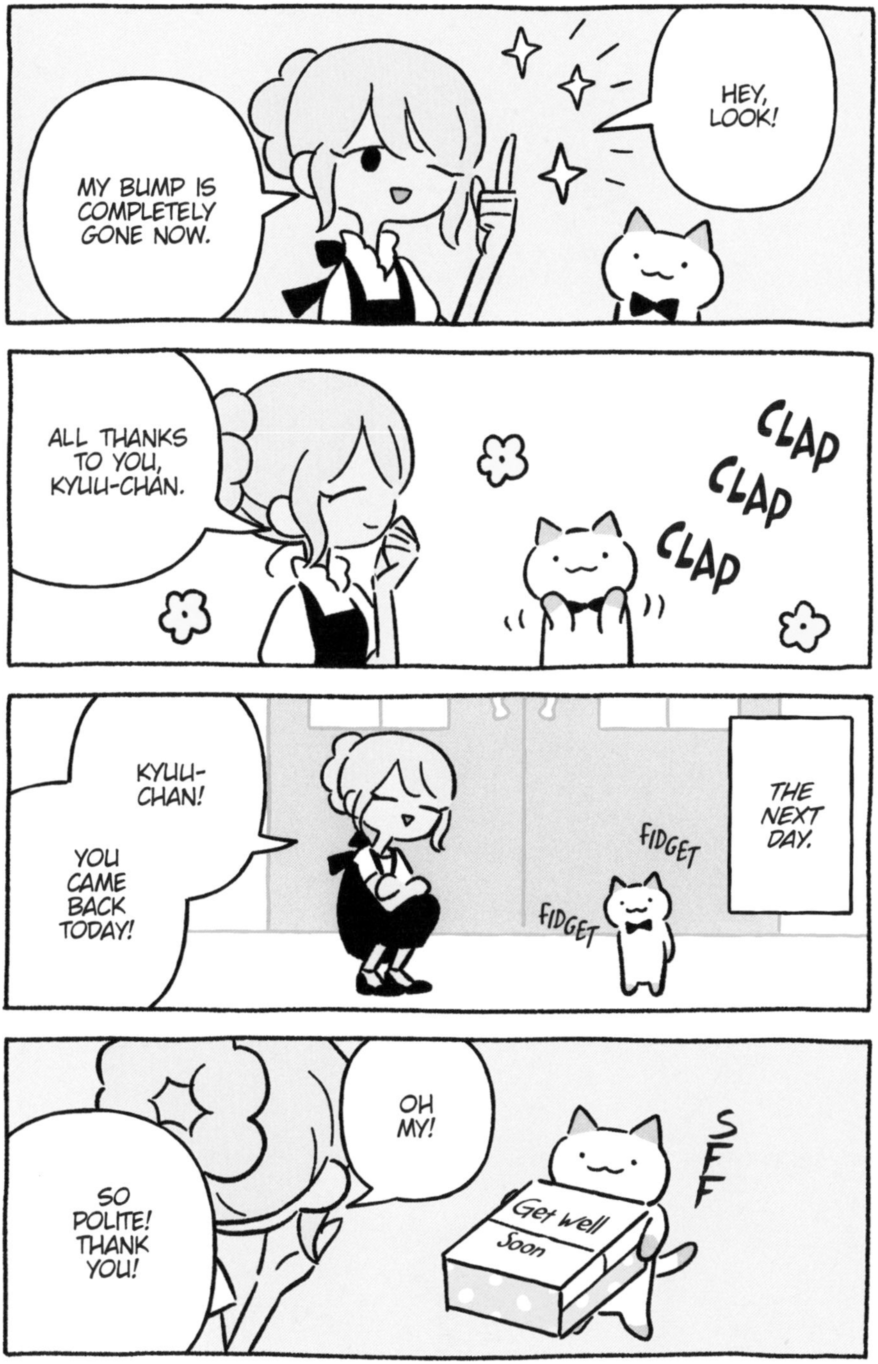
HEY, LOOK!
MY BUMP IS COMPLETELY GONE NOW.
CLAP CLAP CLAP
ALL THANKS TO YOU, KYUU-CHAN.
THE NEXT DAY.
FIDGET
FIDGET
KYUU-CHAN!
YOU CAME BACK TODAY!
SFF
OH MY!
Get well Soon
SO POLITE! THANK YOU!

# BASHFUL

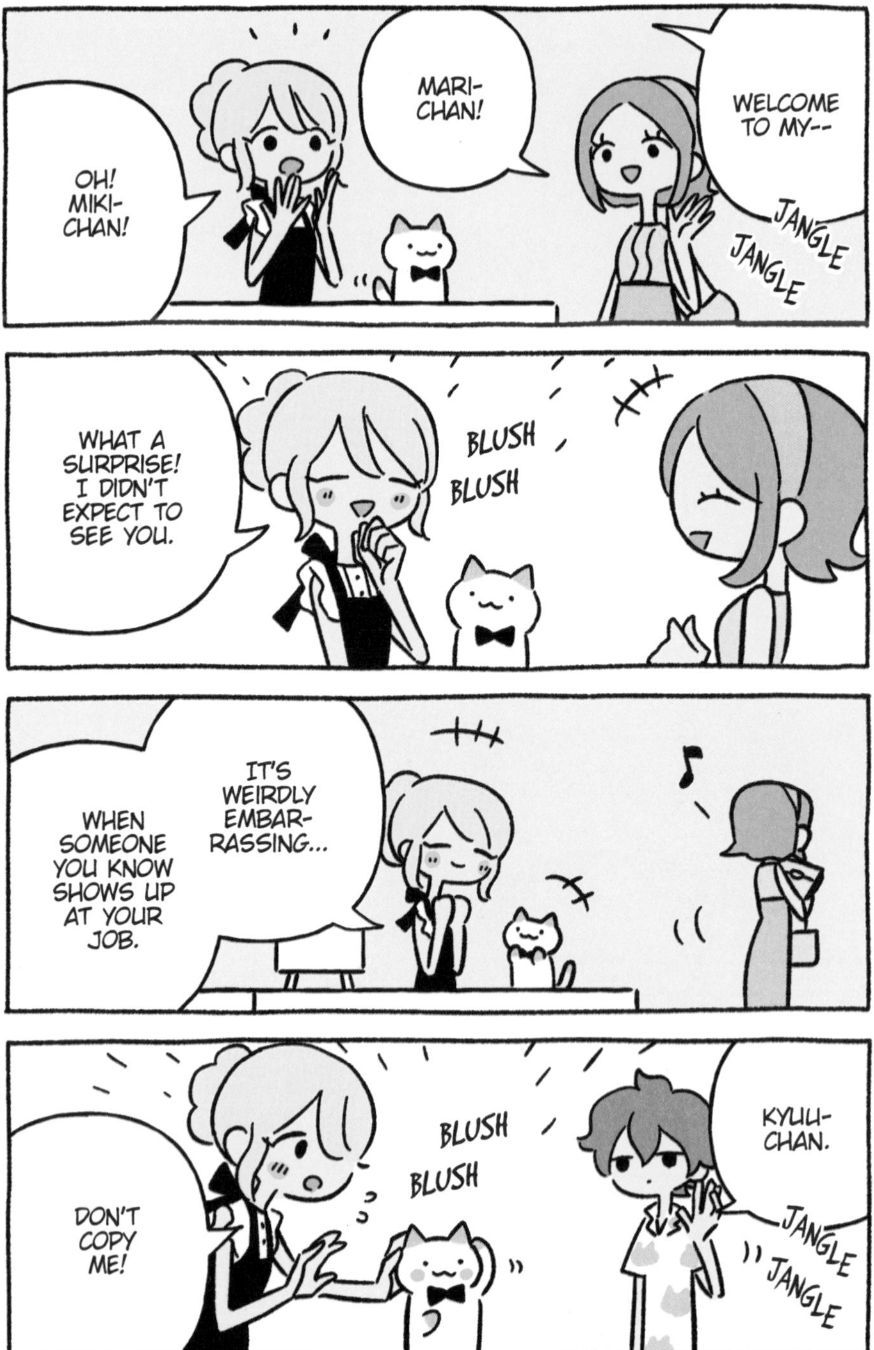
WELCOME TO MY--
JANGLE JANGLE
MARI-CHAN!
OH! MIKI-CHAN!
BLUSH BLUSH
WHAT A SURPRISE! I DIDN'T EXPECT TO SEE YOU.
IT'S WEIRDLY EMBARRASSING...
WHEN SOMEONE YOU KNOW SHOWS UP AT YOUR JOB.
KYUU-CHAN.
JANGLE JANGLE
BLUSH BLUSH
DON'T COPY ME!

# BOW TYING

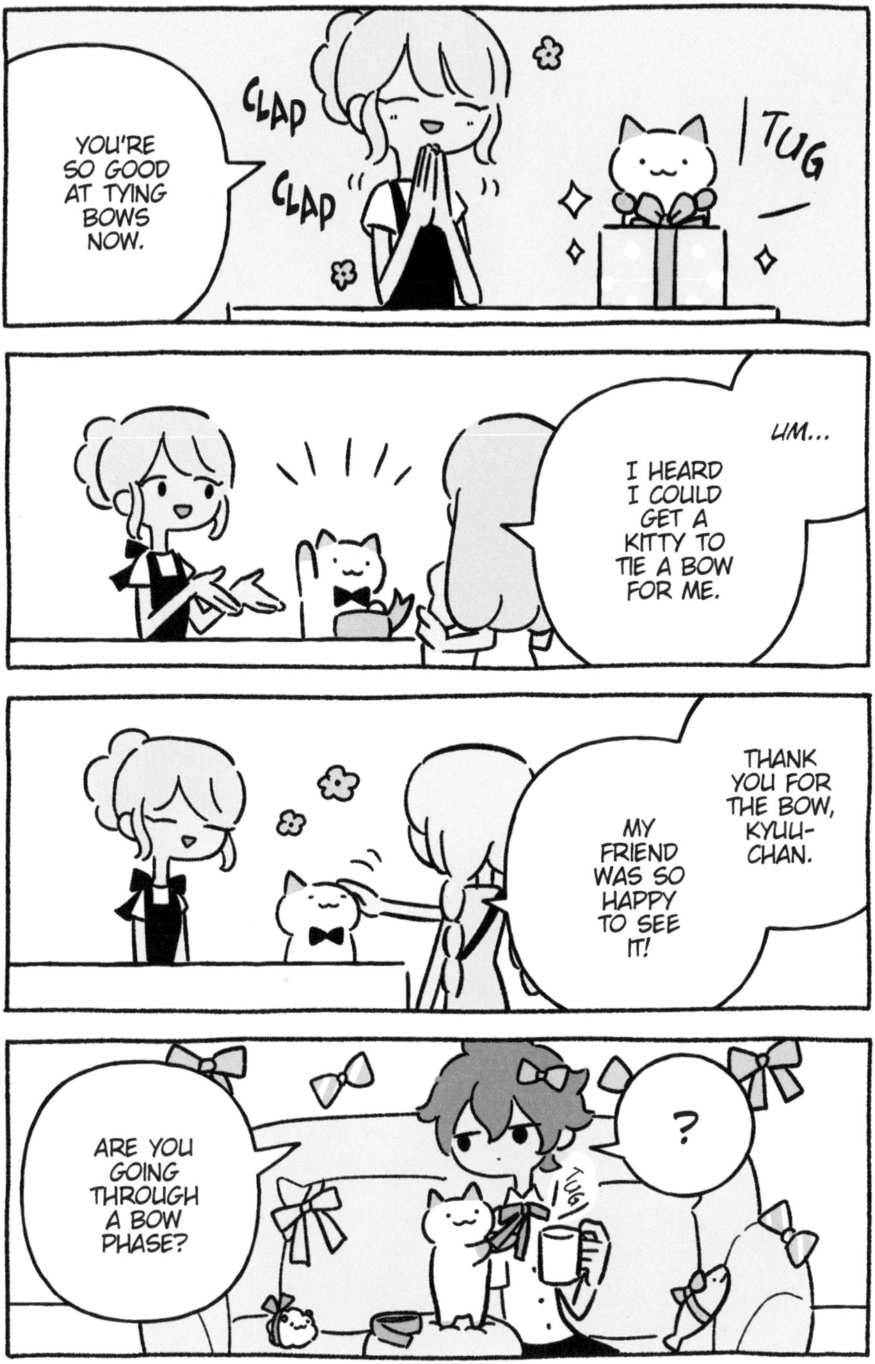
TUG
CLAP
CLAP
YOU'RE SO GOOD AT TYING BOWS NOW.
UM...
I HEARD I COULD GET A KITTY TO TIE A BOW FOR ME.
THANK YOU FOR THE BOW, KYUU-CHAN.
MY FRIEND WAS SO HAPPY TO SEE IT!
?
TUG
ARE YOU GOING THROUGH A BOW PHASE?

# COLD, COLD SHAVED ICE

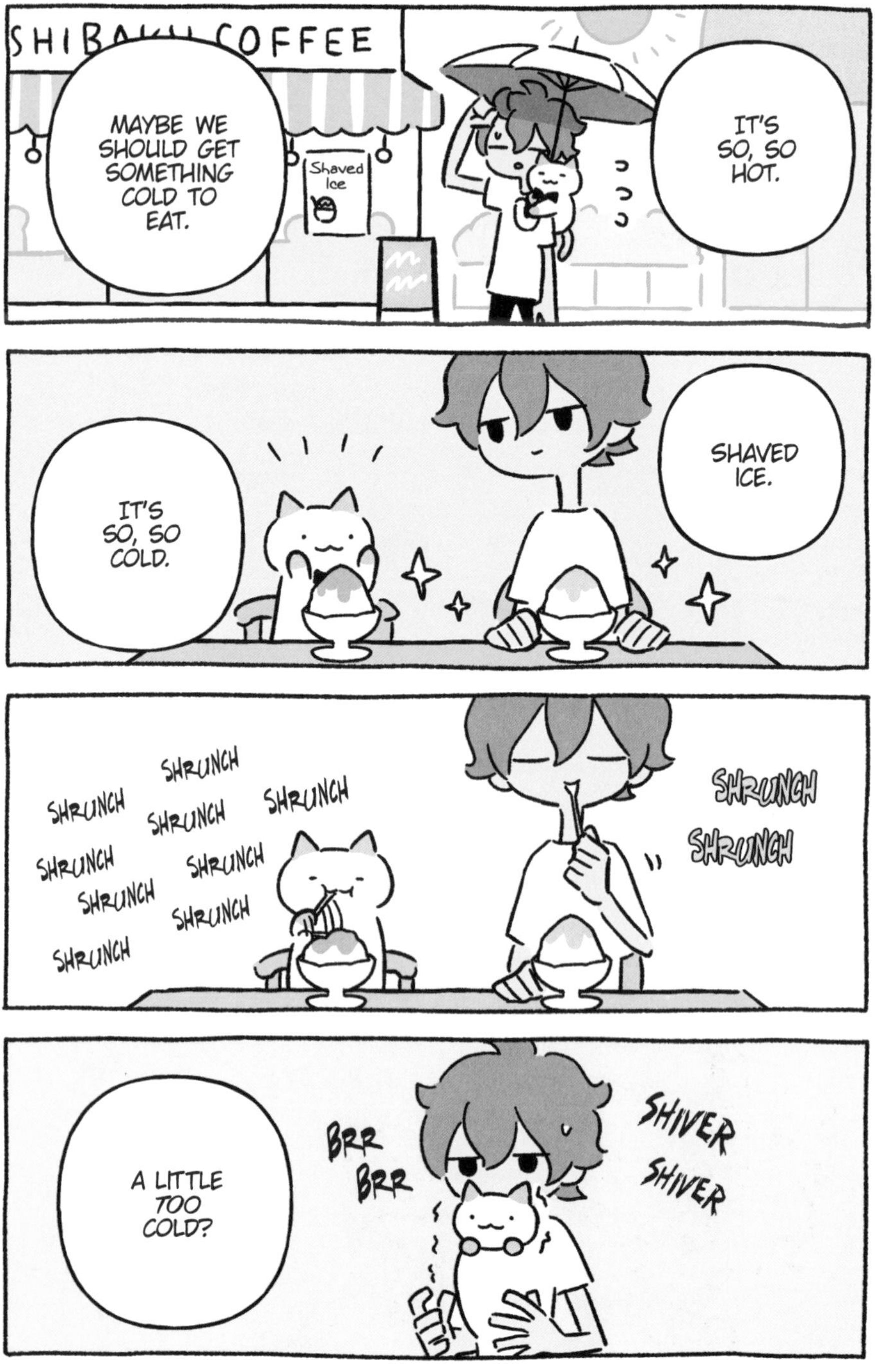
IT'S SO, SO HOT.
Shaved Ice
COFFEE
MAYBE WE SHOULD GET SOMETHING COLD TO EAT.
SHAVED ICE.
IT'S SO, SO COLD.
SHRUNCH
SHRUNCH
SHRUNCH
SHRUNCH
SHRUNCH
SHRUNCH
SHRUNCH
SHRUNCH
SHRUNCH
SHRUNCH
SHRUNCH
SHIVER
SHIVER
BRR
BRR
A LITTLE TOO COLD?

# MONA-CHAN TO THE RESCUE

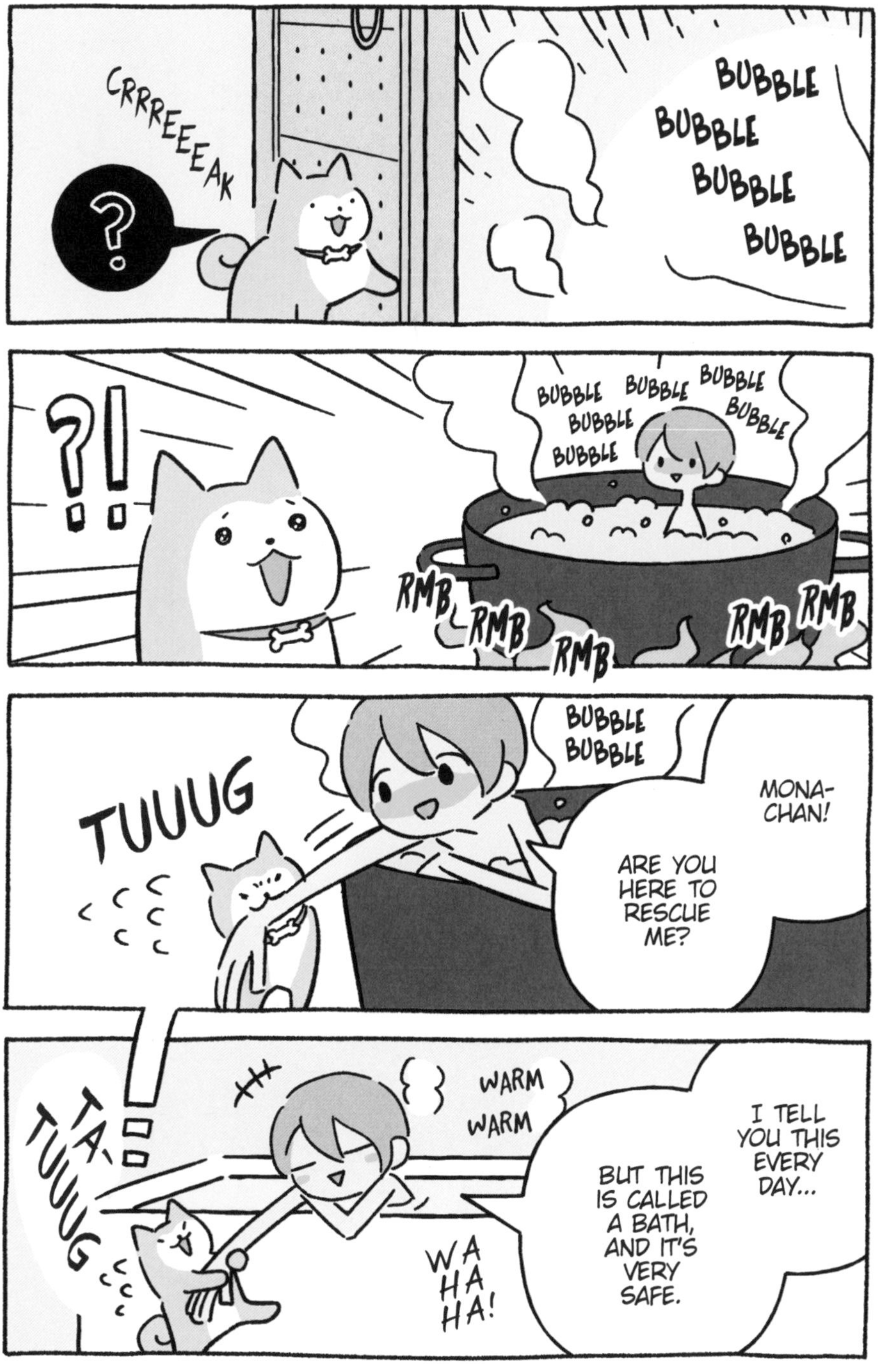
BUBBLE
BUBBLE
BUBBLE
BUBBLE
CRRREEEEAK
?
BUBBLE BUBBLE BUBBLE BUBBLE BUBBLE BUBBLE
?!
RMB RMB RMB RMB RMB
BUBBLE BUBBLE
MONA-CHAN!
ARE YOU HERE TO RESCUE ME?
TUUUG
I TELL YOU THIS EVERY DAY...
BUT THIS IS CALLED A BATH, AND IT'S VERY SAFE.
WARM WARM
WA HA HA!
TA-TUUUG

# SUPER COOL LIGHTS

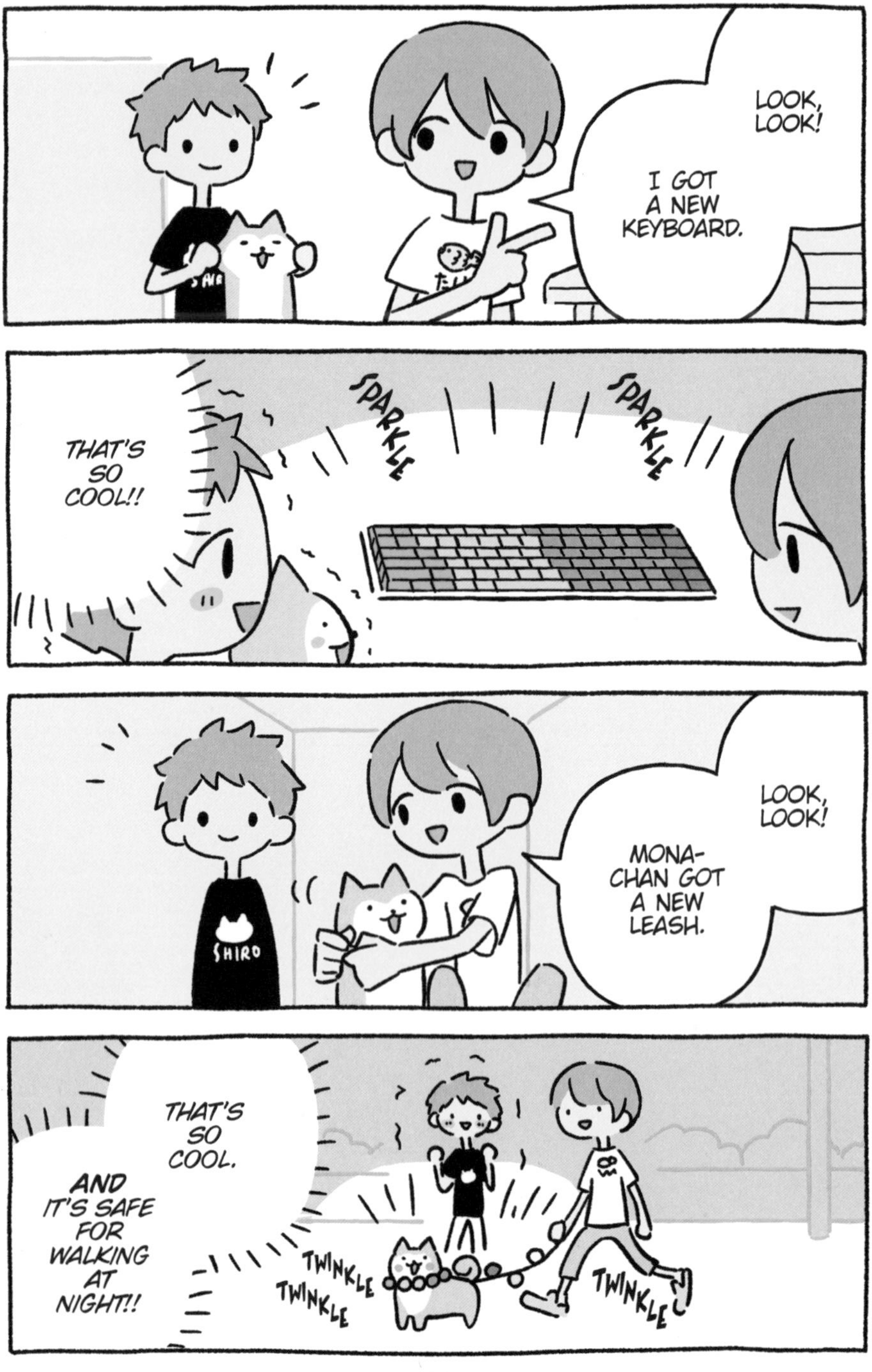
LOOK, LOOK!
I GOT A NEW KEYBOARD.
SPARKLE
SPARKLE
THAT'S SO COOL!!
LOOK, LOOK!
MONA-CHAN GOT A NEW LEASH.
THAT'S SO COOL.
AND IT'S SAFE FOR WALKING AT NIGHT!!
TWINKLE
TWINKLE
TWINKLE

# THE DAY BEFORE

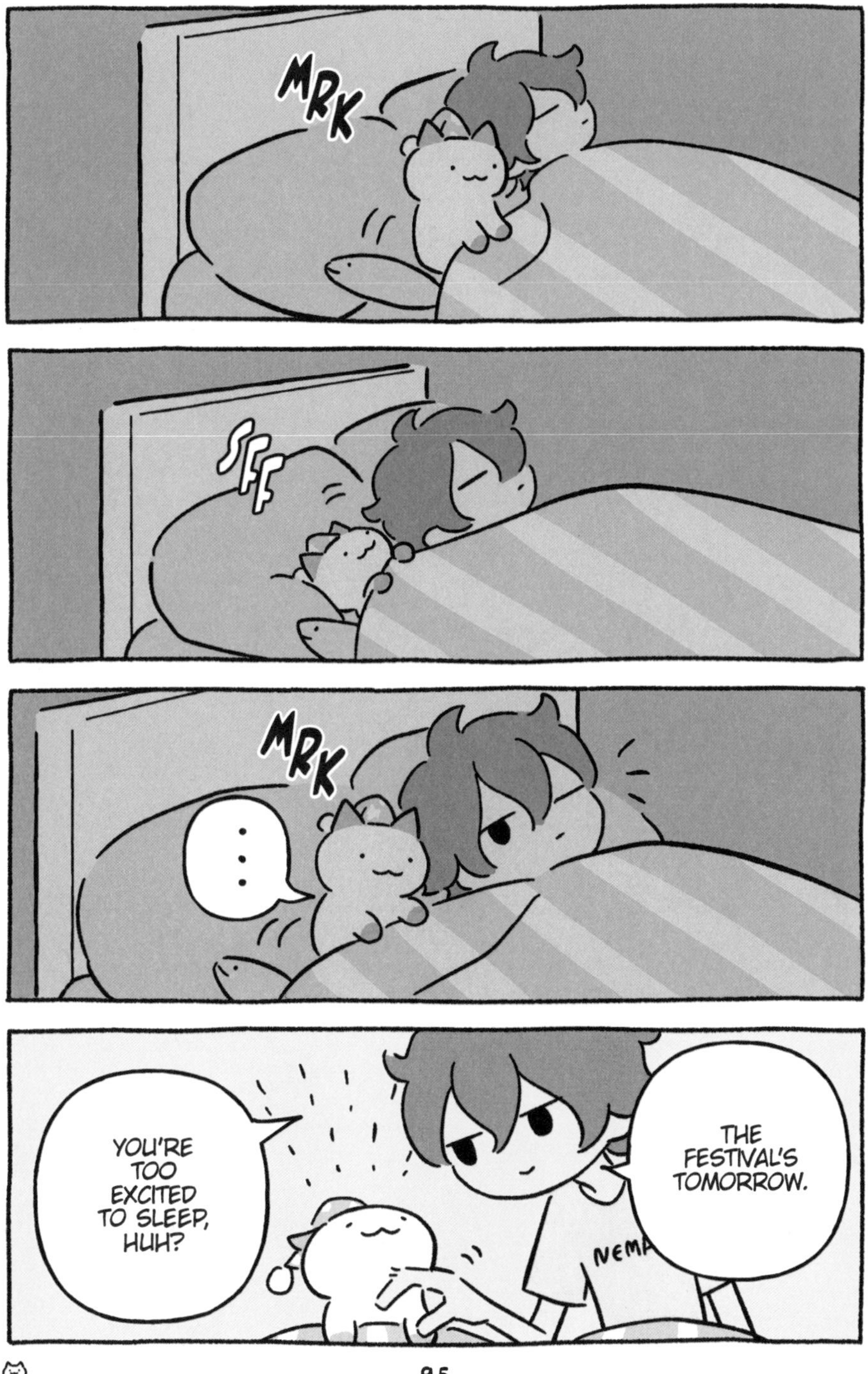
MRK
SFF
MRK
...
THE FESTIVAL'S TOMORROW.
YOU'RE TOO EXCITED TO SLEEP, HUH?
NEMA

# DISCOVERY

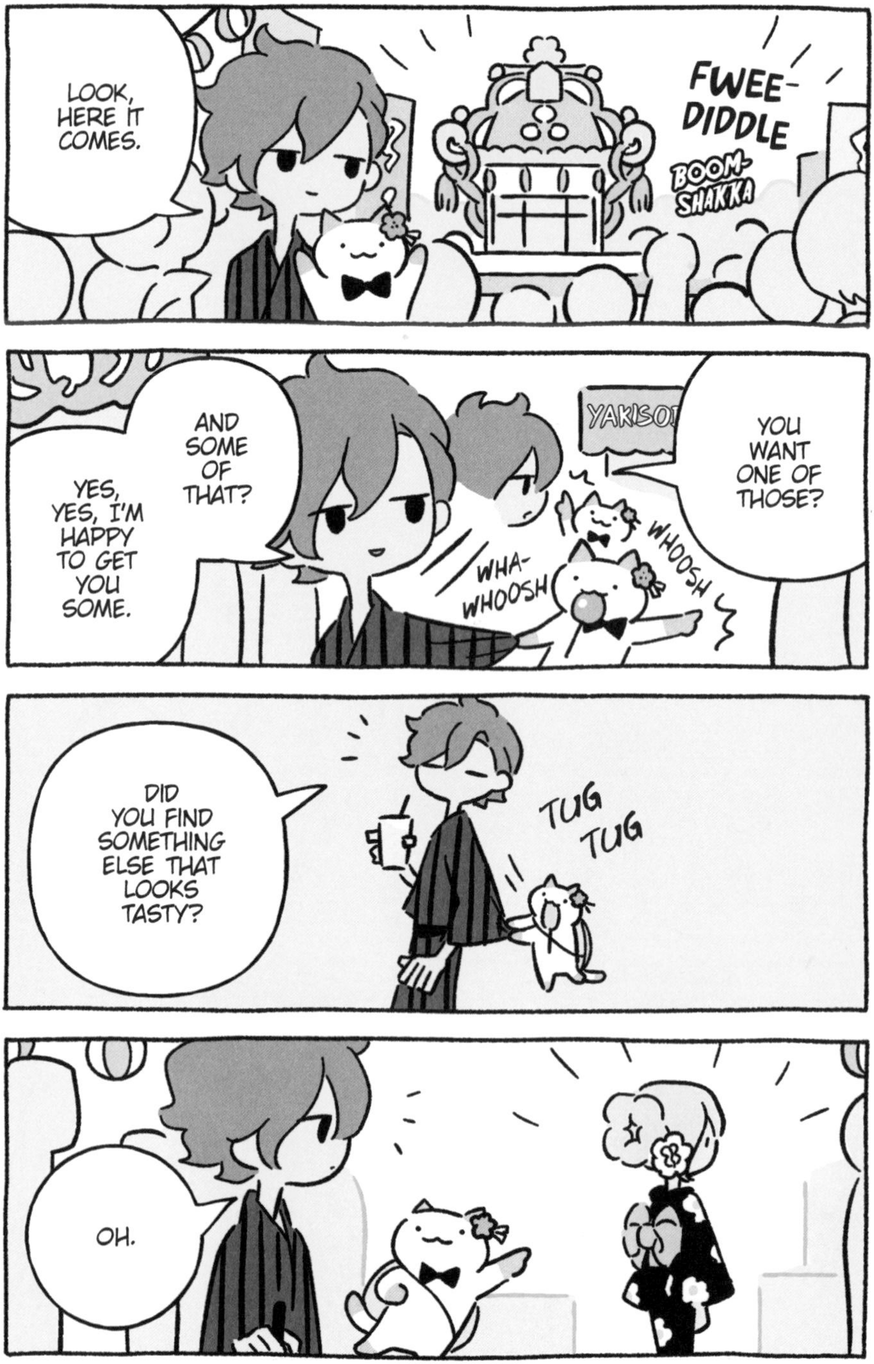
FWEE-DIDDLE
BOOM-SHAKKA
LOOK, HERE IT COMES.
YAKISO
YOU WANT ONE OF THOSE?
WHOOSH
WHA-WHOOSH
AND SOME OF THAT?
YES, YES, I'M HAPPY TO GET YOU SOME.
TUG TUG
DID YOU FIND SOMETHING ELSE THAT LOOKS TASTY?
OH.

# STRANGER DANGER

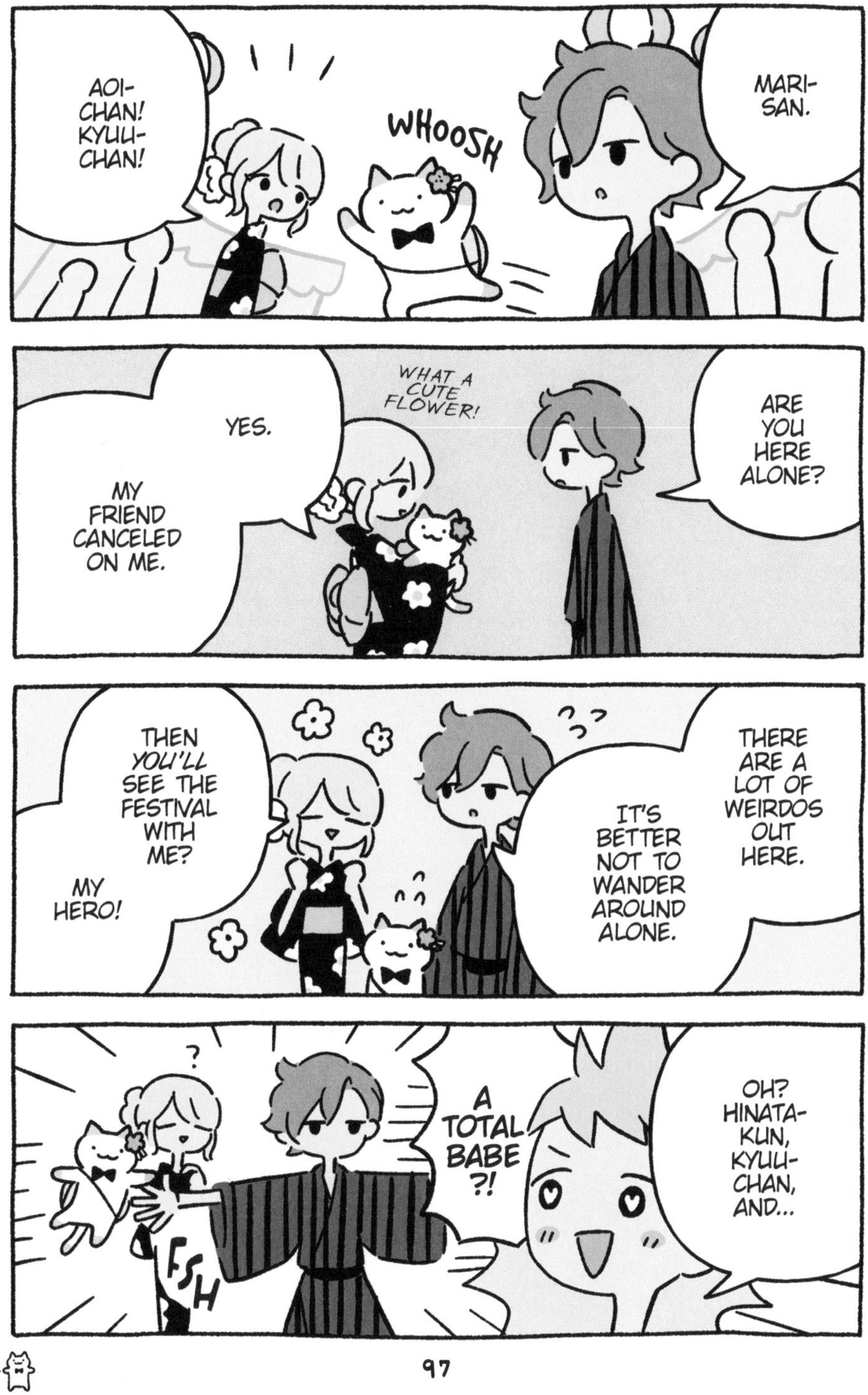

MARI-SAN.
WHOOSH
AOI-CHAN! KYUU-CHAN!
ARE YOU HERE ALONE?
WHAT A CUTE FLOWER!
YES.
MY FRIEND CANCELED ON ME.
THERE ARE A LOT OF WEIRDOS OUT HERE.
IT'S BETTER NOT TO WANDER AROUND ALONE.
THEN *YOU'LL* SEE THE FESTIVAL WITH ME?
MY HERO!
OH? HINATA-KUN, KYUU-CHAN, AND...
A TOTAL BABE?!
?
FSH

# EXPANDING CIRCLE ①

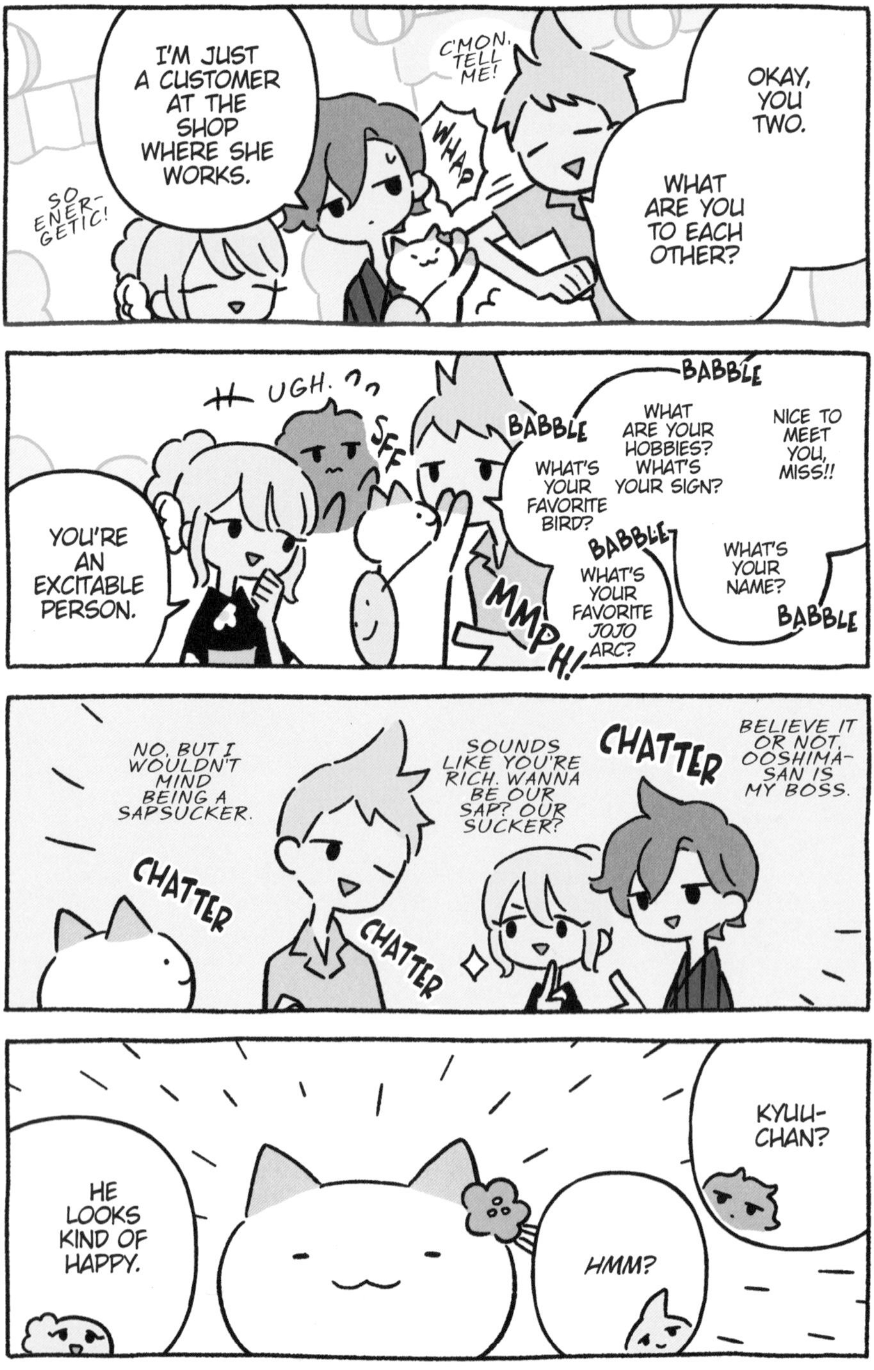
OKAY, YOU TWO.
WHAT ARE YOU TO EACH OTHER?
C'MON, TELL ME!
WHAP
I'M JUST A CUSTOMER AT THE SHOP WHERE SHE WORKS.
SO ENER-GETIC!
NICE TO MEET YOU, MISS!!
BABBLE
WHAT'S YOUR NAME?
BABBLE
WHAT ARE YOUR HOBBIES? WHAT'S YOUR SIGN?
BABBLE
WHAT'S YOUR FAVORITE BIRD?
BABBLE
WHAT'S YOUR FAVORITE JOJO ARC?
MMPH!
SFF
UGH.
YOU'RE AN EXCITABLE PERSON.
BELIEVE IT OR NOT, OOSHIMA-SAN IS MY BOSS.
CHATTER
SOUNDS LIKE YOU'RE RICH. WANNA BE OUR SAP? OUR SUCKER?
NO, BUT I WOULDN'T MIND BEING A SAPSUCKER.
CHATTER
CHATTER
KYUU-CHAN?
HMM?
HE LOOKS KIND OF HAPPY.

# EXPANDING CIRCLE ②

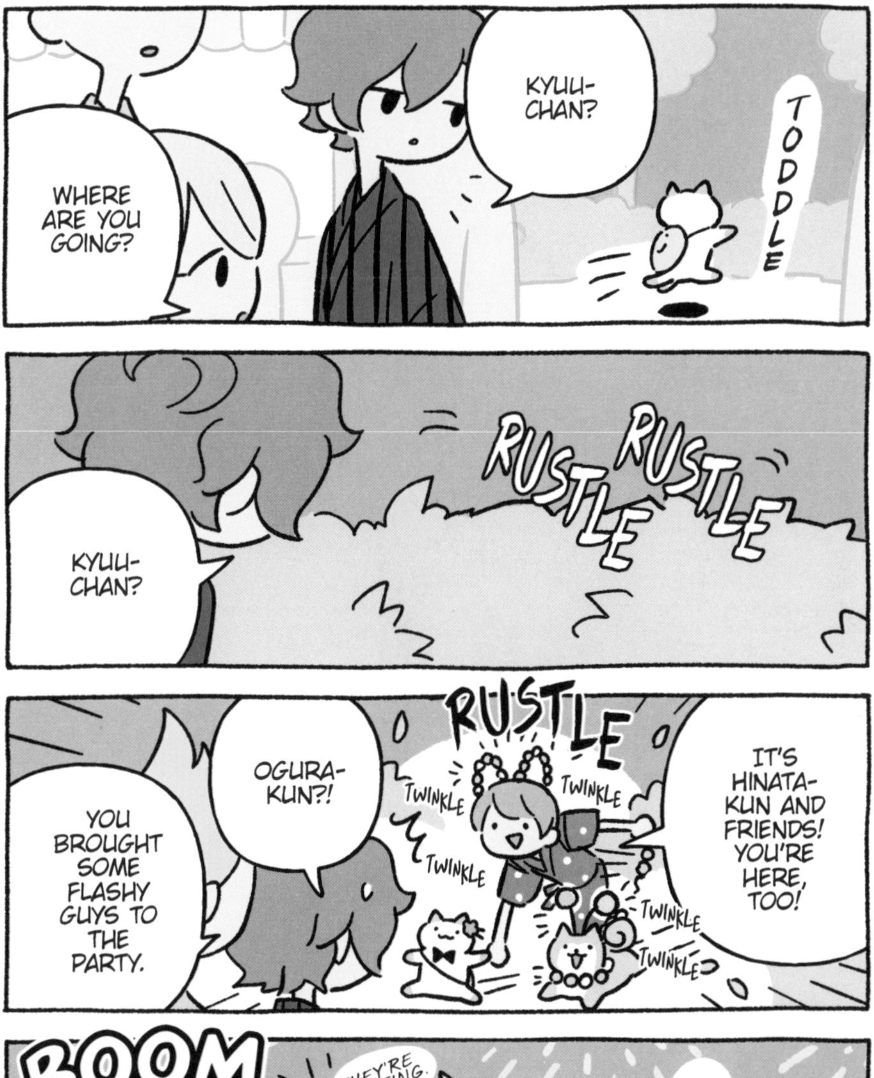

KYUU-CHAN?
TODDLE
WHERE ARE YOU GOING?
RUSTLE RUSTLE
KYUU-CHAN?
RUSTLE
IT'S HINATA-KUN AND FRIENDS! YOU'RE HERE, TOO!
TWINKLE
TWINKLE
TWINKLE
TWINKLE
TWINKLE
OGURA-KUN?!
YOU BROUGHT SOME FLASHY GUYS TO THE PARTY.
CHATTER
NICE TO MEET YOU!
CHATTER
MY PLEASURE!
THEY'RE STARTING.
BOOM
THE FIRE-WORKS SURE ARE FESTIVE THIS YEAR.

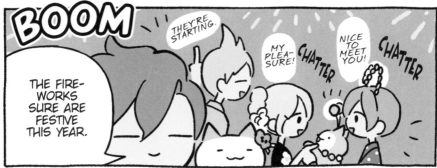

# SUMMER MEMORIES

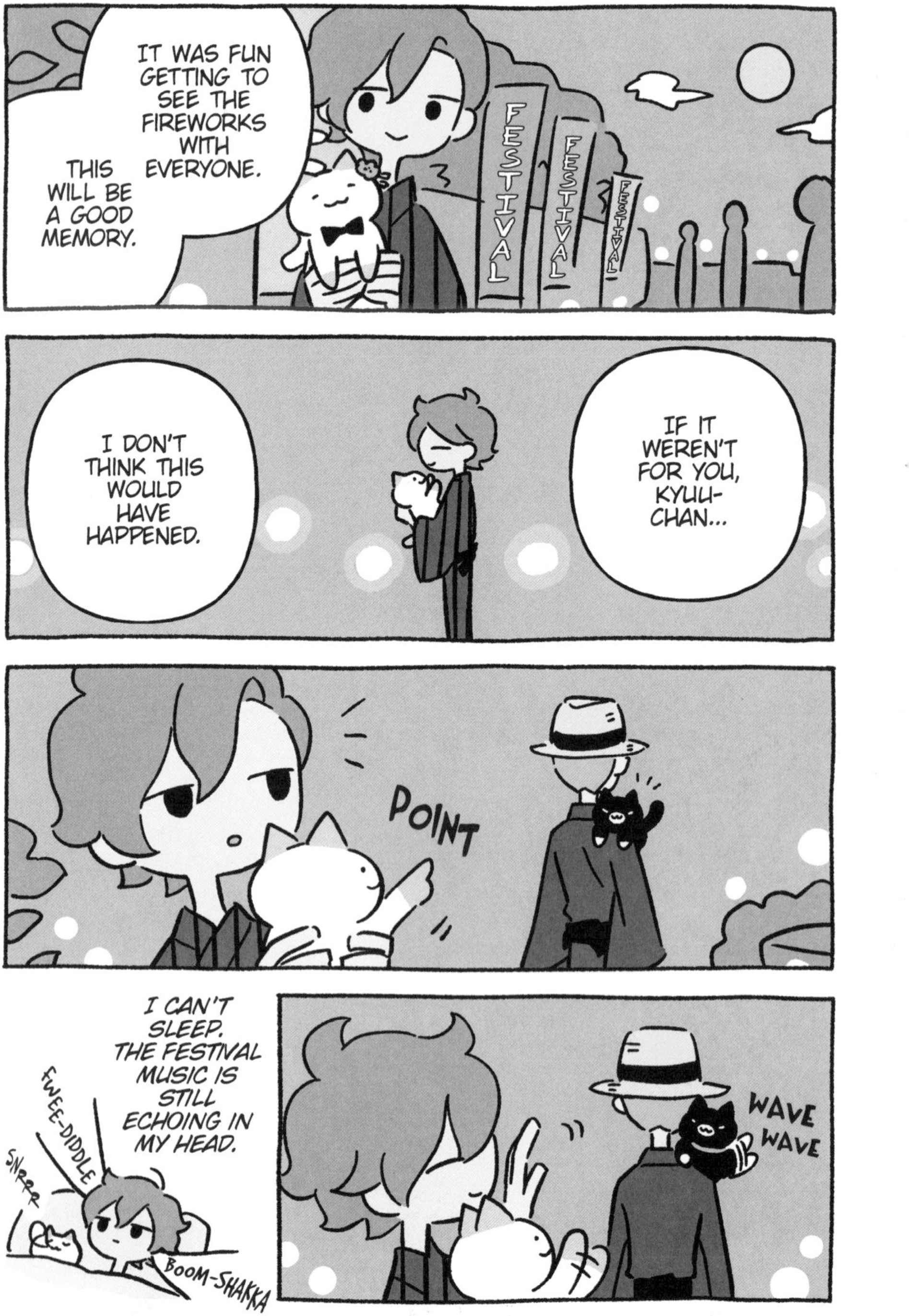
FESTIVAL
FESTIVAL
FESTIVAL
IT WAS FUN GETTING TO SEE THE FIREWORKS WITH EVERYONE.
THIS WILL BE A GOOD MEMORY.
IF IT WEREN'T FOR YOU, KYUU-CHAN...
I DON'T THINK THIS WOULD HAVE HAPPENED.
POINT
WAVE WAVE
I CAN'T SLEEP. THE FESTIVAL MUSIC IS STILL ECHOING IN MY HEAD.
FWEE-DIDDLE
SNRRR
BOOM-SHAKKA

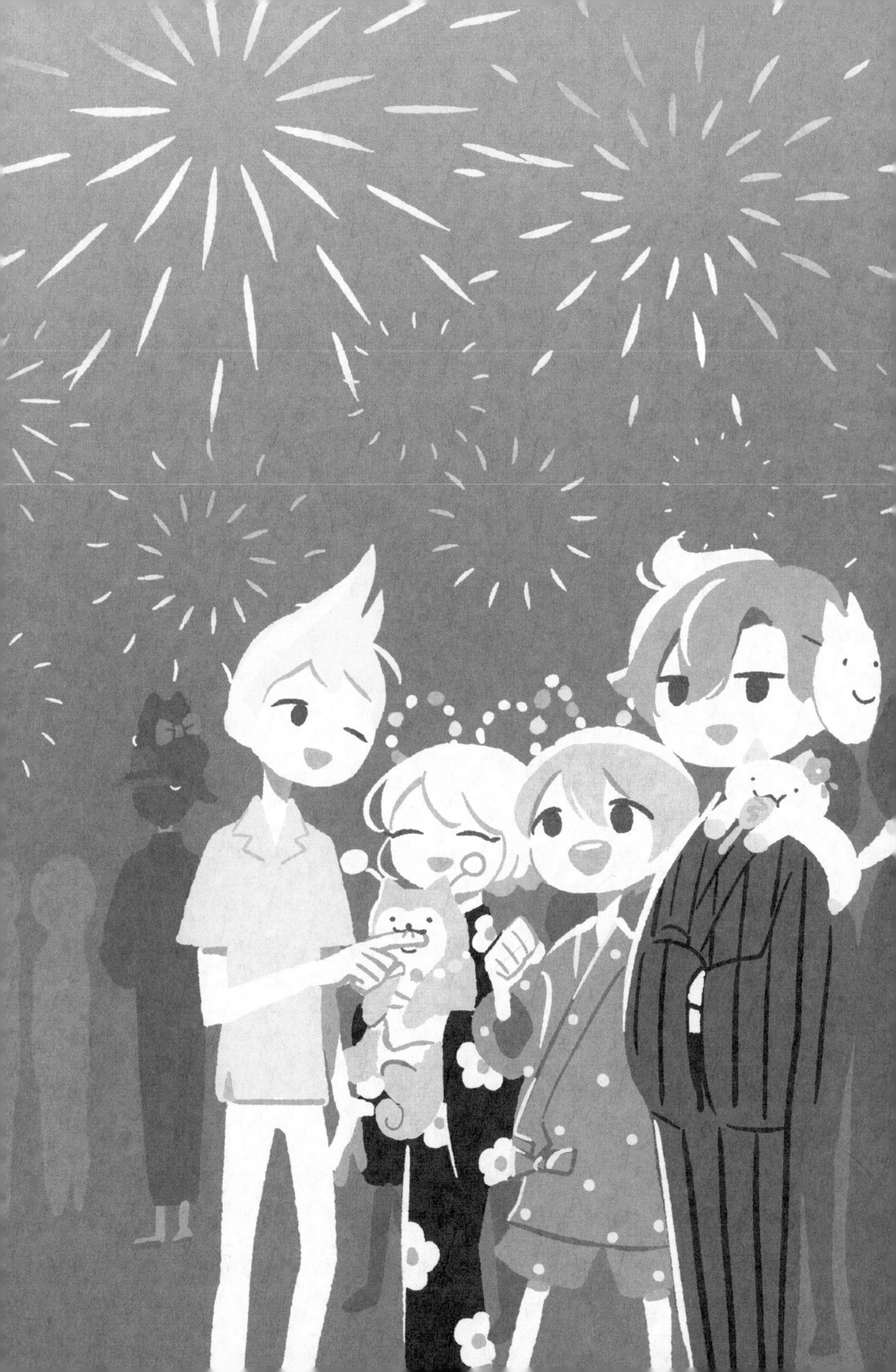

# BONDS OF FRIENDSHIP

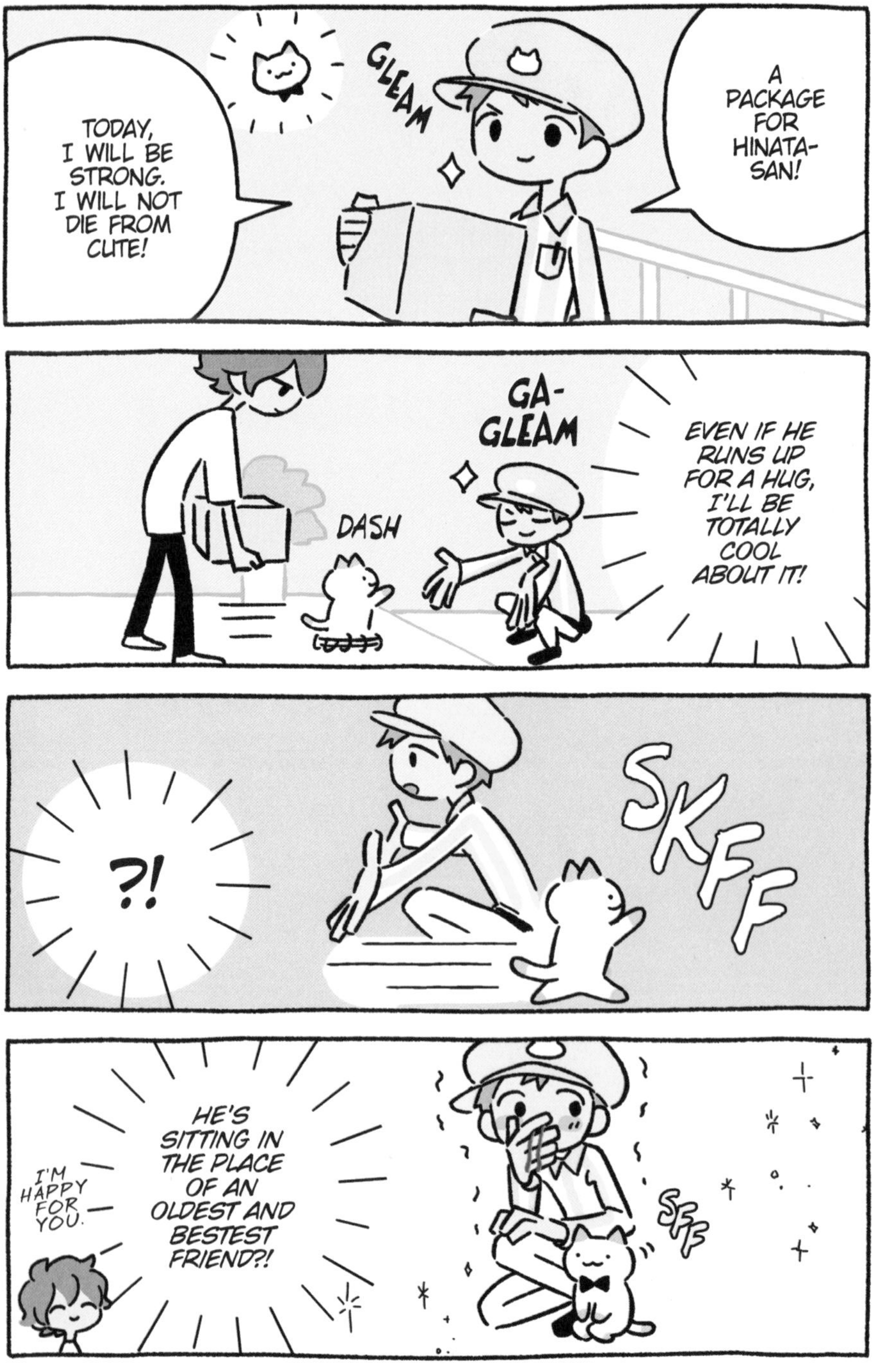
A PACKAGE FOR HINATA-SAN!
GLEAM
TODAY, I WILL BE STRONG. I WILL NOT DIE FROM CUTE!
EVEN IF HE RUNS UP FOR A HUG, I'LL BE TOTALLY COOL ABOUT IT!
GA-GLEAM
DASH
SKFF
?!
SFF
HE'S SITTING IN THE PLACE OF AN OLDEST AND BESTEST FRIEND?!
I'M HAPPY FOR YOU.

# REVENGE WINK

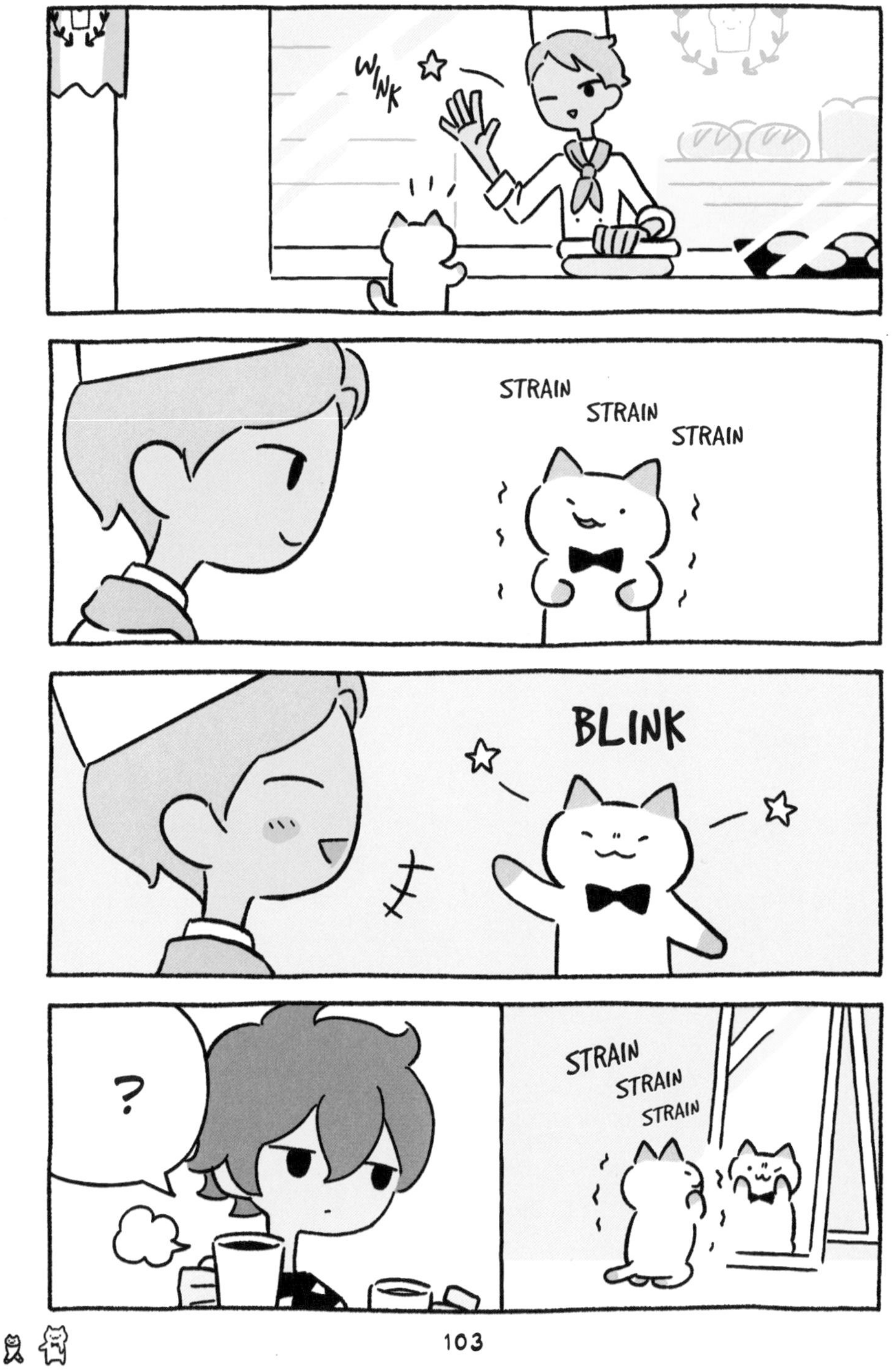
WINK
STRAIN
STRAIN
STRAIN
BLINK
STRAIN
STRAIN
STRAIN
?

# BLESSING

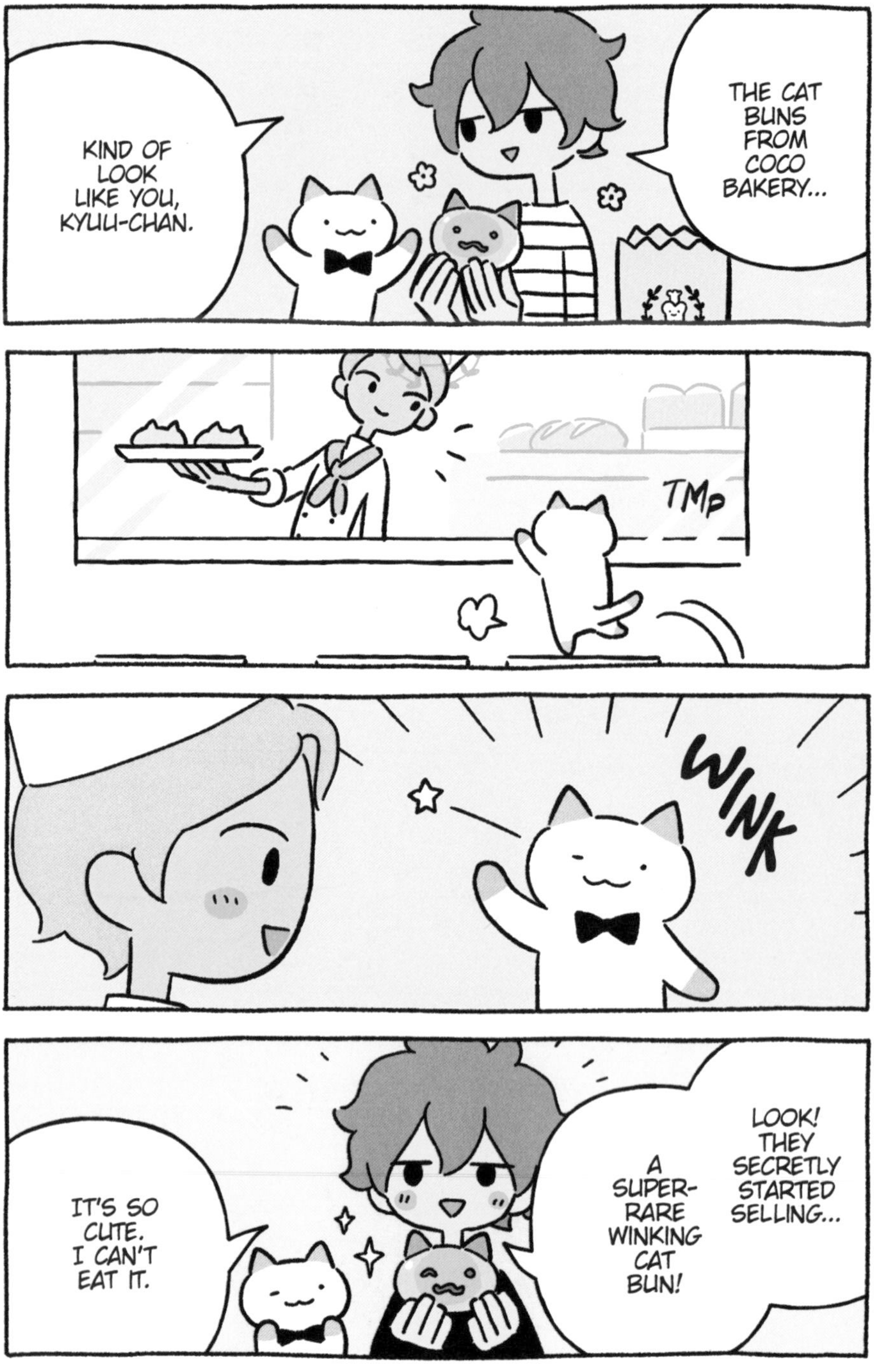
THE CAT BUNS FROM COCO BAKERY...
KIND OF LOOK LIKE YOU, KYUU-CHAN.
TMP
WINK
LOOK! THEY SECRETLY STARTED SELLING...
A SUPER-RARE WINKING CAT BUN!
IT'S SO CUTE. I CAN'T EAT IT.

# GROOMING

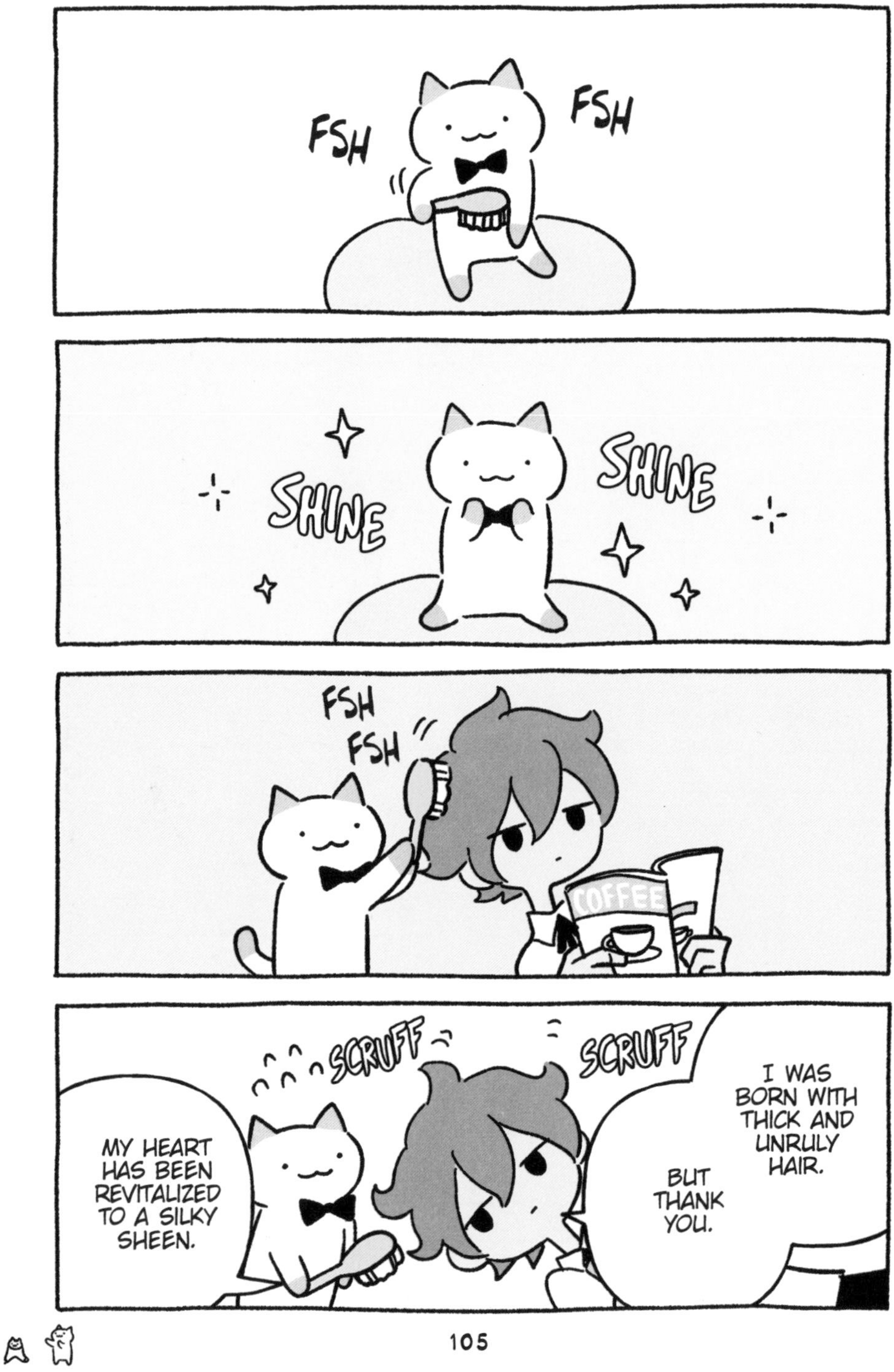
FSH
FSH
SHINE
SHINE
FSH
FSH
SCRUFF
SCRUFF
I WAS BORN WITH THICK AND UNRULY HAIR.
BUT THANK YOU.
MY HEART HAS BEEN REVITALIZED TO A SILKY SHEEN.

# USE OF TIME

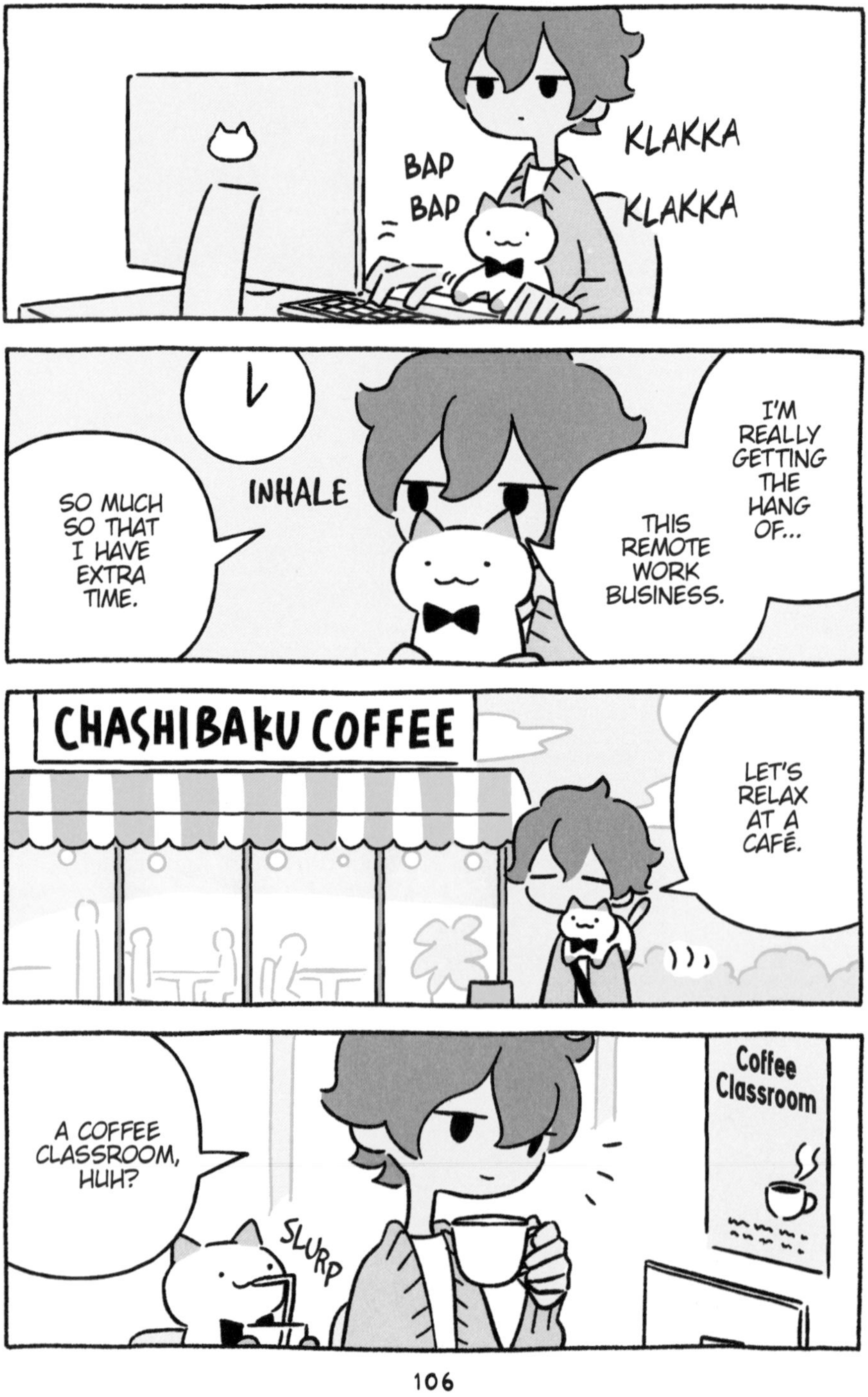
KLAKKA
KLAKKA
BAP
BAP
I'M REALLY GETTING THE HANG OF...
THIS REMOTE WORK BUSINESS.
INHALE
SO MUCH SO THAT I HAVE EXTRA TIME.
LET'S RELAX AT A CAFÉ.
CHASHIBAKU COFFEE
Coffee Classroom
A COFFEE CLASSROOM, HUH?
SLURP

# COFFEE CLASSROOM

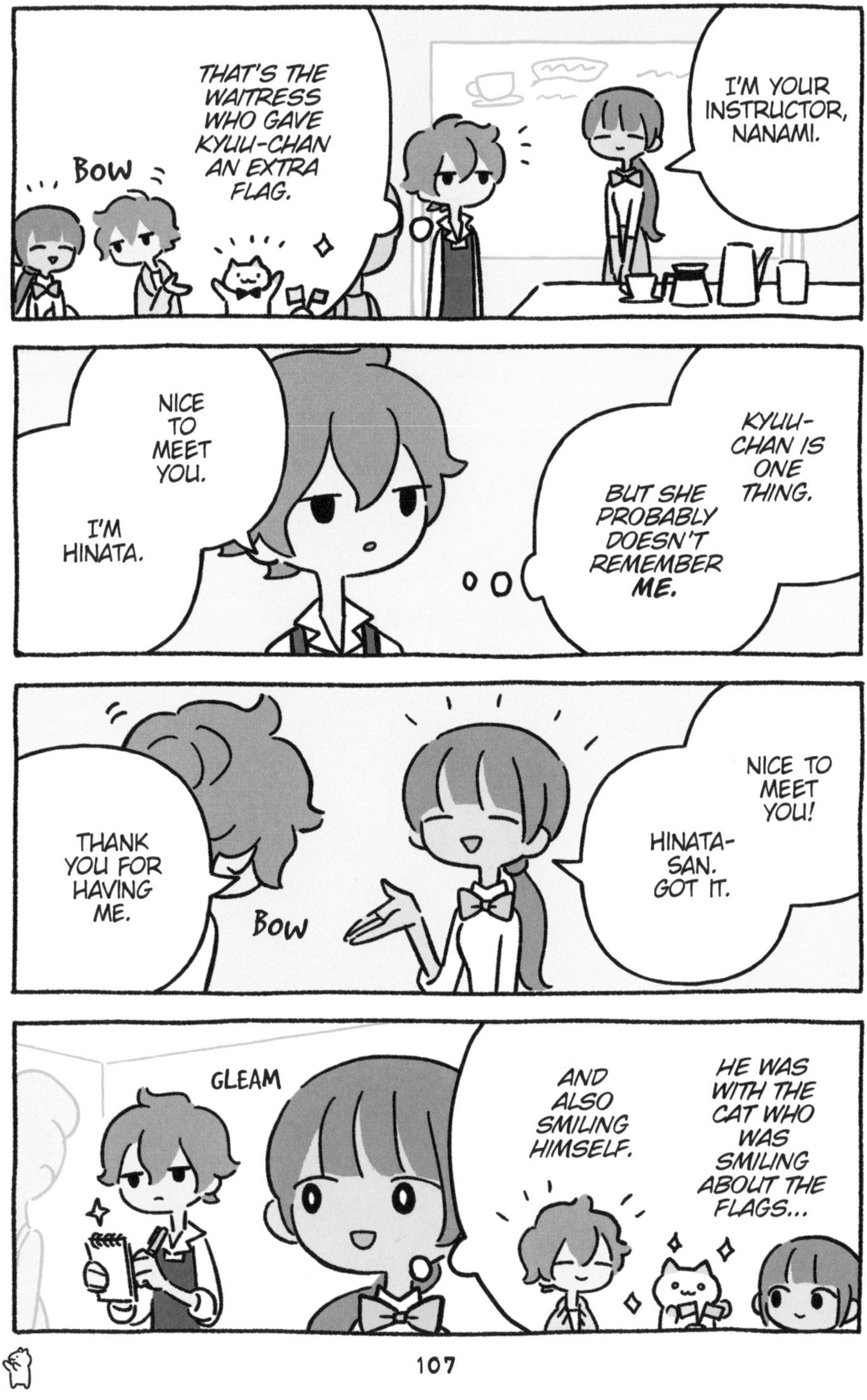
I'M YOUR INSTRUCTOR, NANAMI.
THAT'S THE WAITRESS WHO GAVE KYUU-CHAN AN EXTRA FLAG.
BOW
KYUU-CHAN IS ONE THING.
BUT SHE PROBABLY DOESN'T REMEMBER ME.
NICE TO MEET YOU.
I'M HINATA.
NICE TO MEET YOU!
HINATA-SAN. GOT IT.
BOW
THANK YOU FOR HAVING ME.
HE WAS WITH THE CAT WHO WAS SMILING ABOUT THE FLAGS...
AND ALSO SMILING HIMSELF.
GLEAM

# DELICIOUS COFFEE

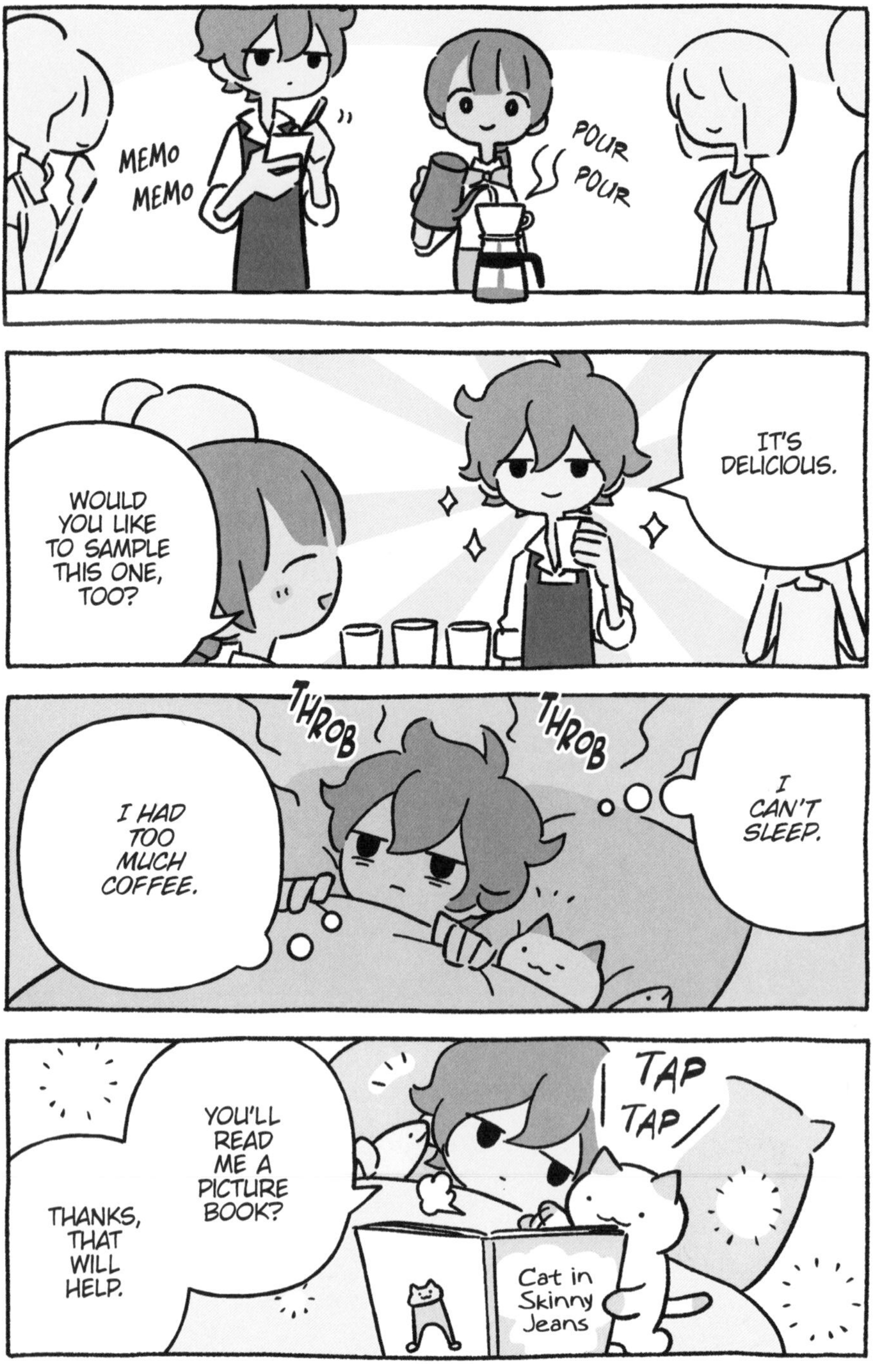
POUR POUR
MEMO MEMO
IT'S DELICIOUS.
WOULD YOU LIKE TO SAMPLE THIS ONE, TOO?
I CAN'T SLEEP.
THROB
THROB
I HAD TOO MUCH COFFEE.
TAP TAP
Cat in Skinny Jeans
YOU'LL READ ME A PICTURE BOOK?
THANKS, THAT WILL HELP.

# BAIT

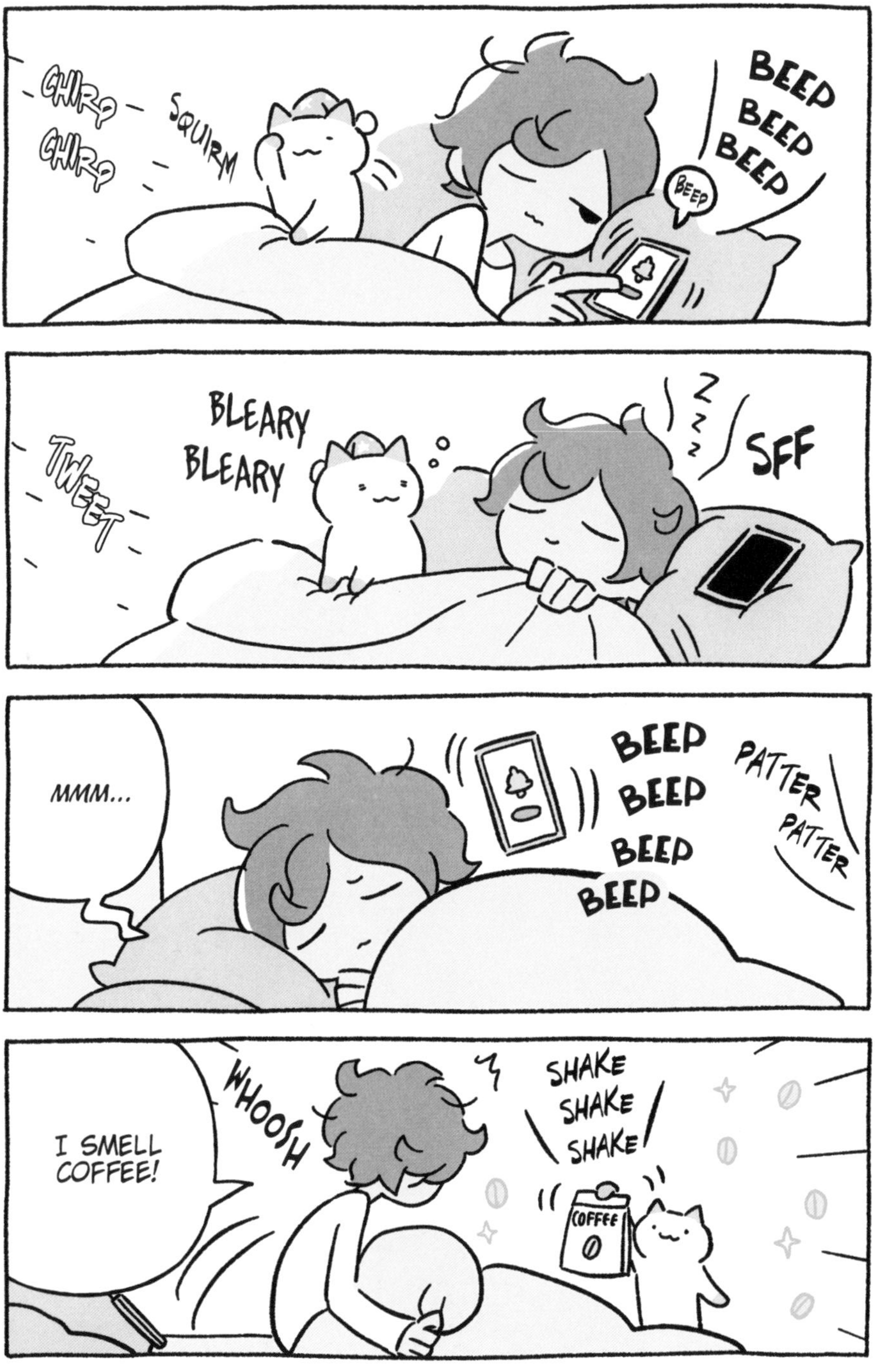
BEEP BEEP BEEP
BEEP
SQUIRM
CHIRP CHIRP
SFF
Z Z Z
BLEARY BLEARY
TWEET
PATTER PATTER
BEEP BEEP BEEP BEEP
MMM...
SHAKE SHAKE SHAKE
COFFEE
WHOOSH
I SMELL COFFEE!

# CHEER SQUAD

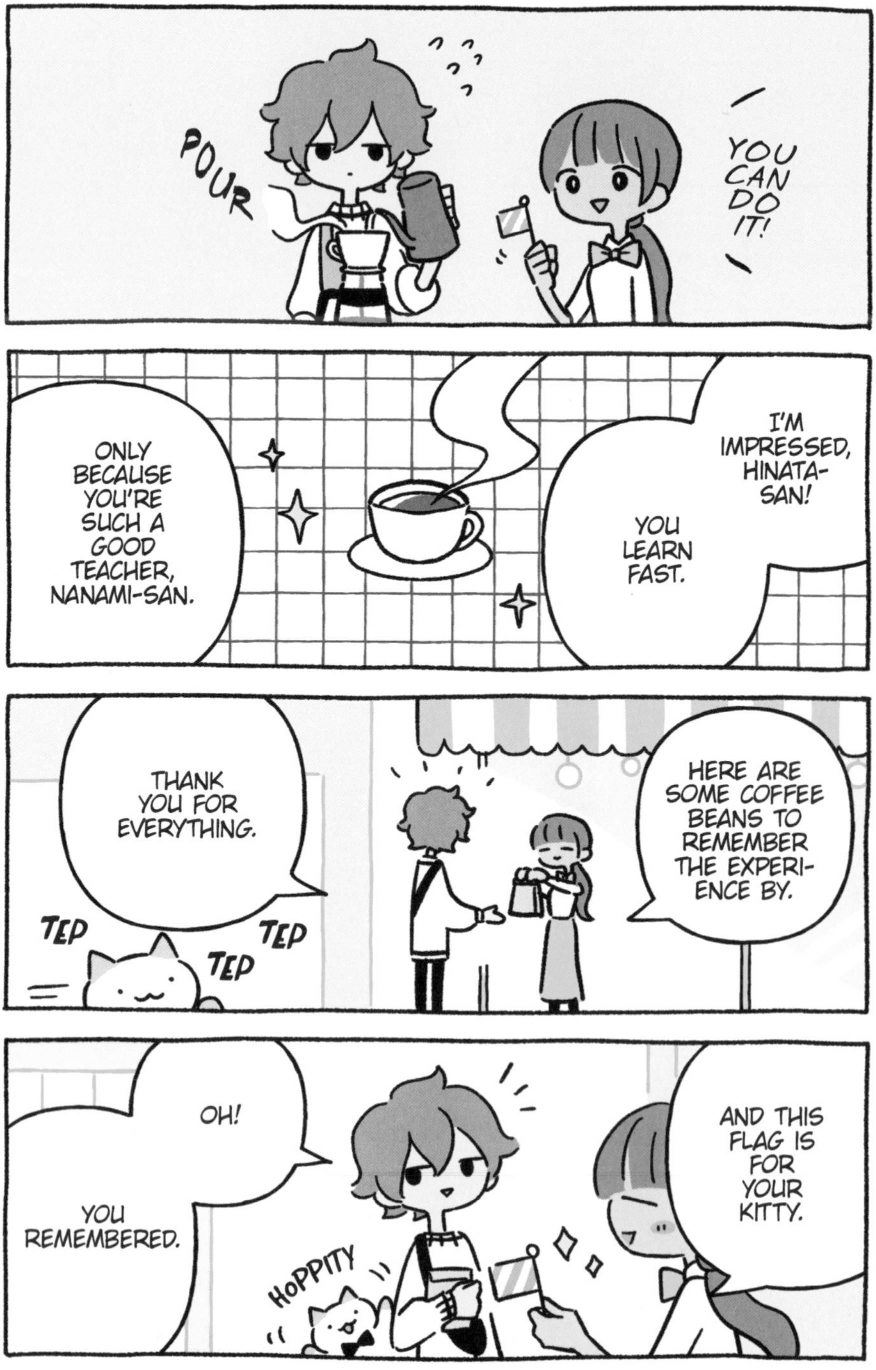
YOU CAN DO IT!
POUR
I'M IMPRESSED, HINATA-SAN!
YOU LEARN FAST.
ONLY BECAUSE YOU'RE SUCH A GOOD TEACHER, NANAMI-SAN.
HERE ARE SOME COFFEE BEANS TO REMEMBER THE EXPERIENCE BY.
THANK YOU FOR EVERYTHING.
TEP
TEP
TEP
AND THIS FLAG IS FOR YOUR KITTY.
OH!
YOU REMEMBERED.
HOPPITY

# INSECURE

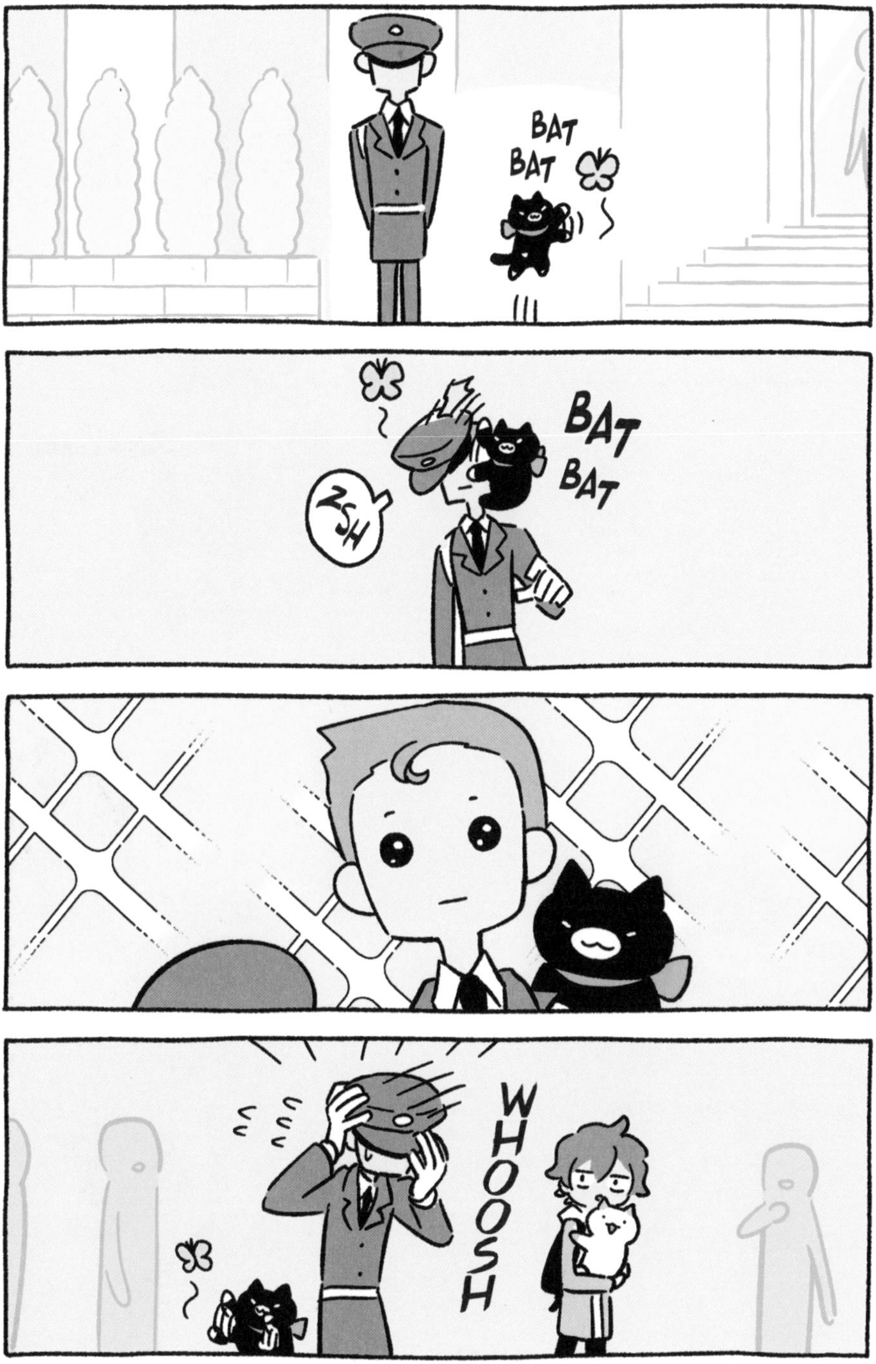

BAT
BAT
BAT
BAT
ZSH
WHOOOSH

# CANS

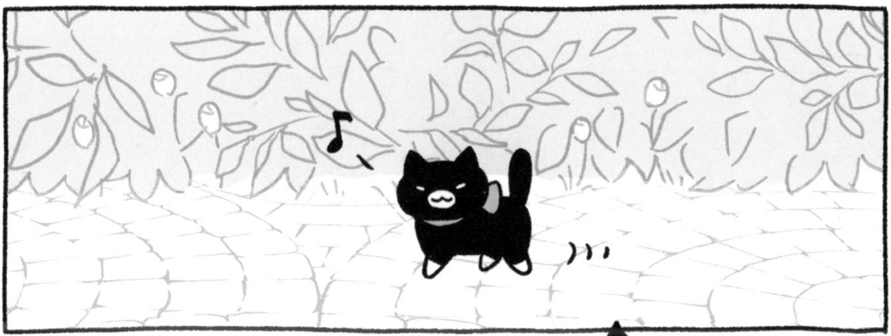

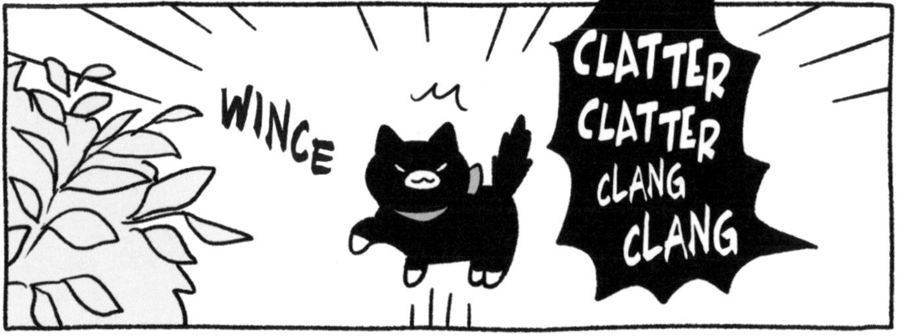
CLATTER CLATTER CLANG CLANG
WINCE

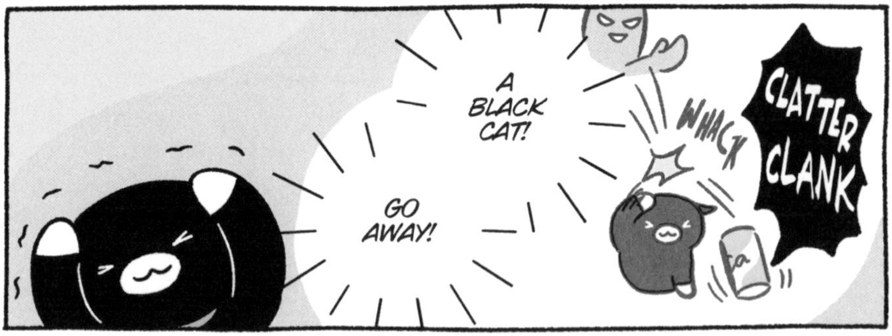
CLATTER CLANK
WHACK
A BLACK CAT!
GO AWAY!

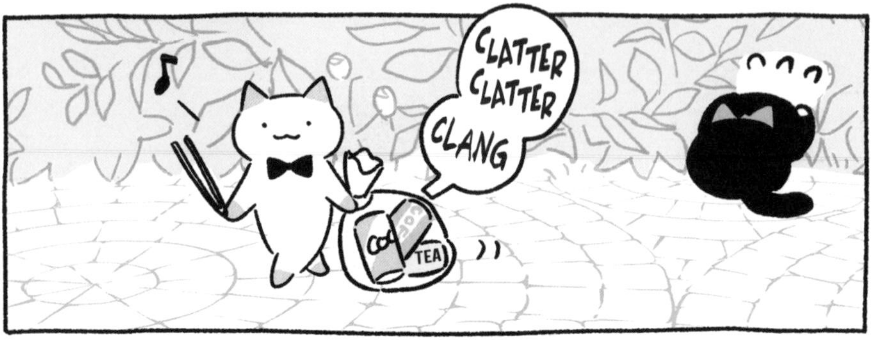
CLATTER CLATTER CLANG
TEA

# COME CLOSER

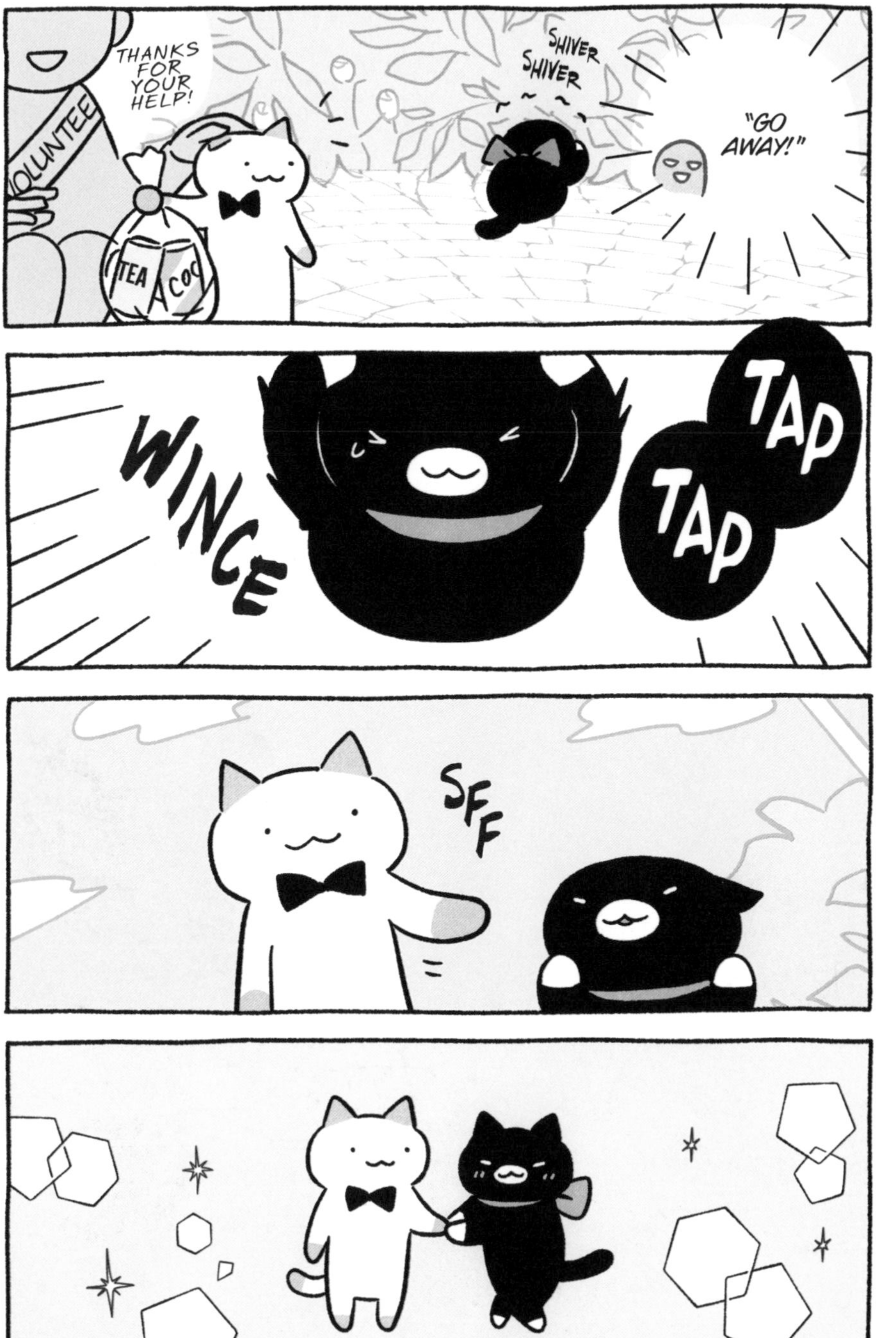
"GO AWAY!"
SHIVER
SHIVER
THANKS FOR YOUR HELP!
VOLUNTEE
TEA
COC
TAP
TAP
WINCE
SFF

# IT'S NOT ALL BAD

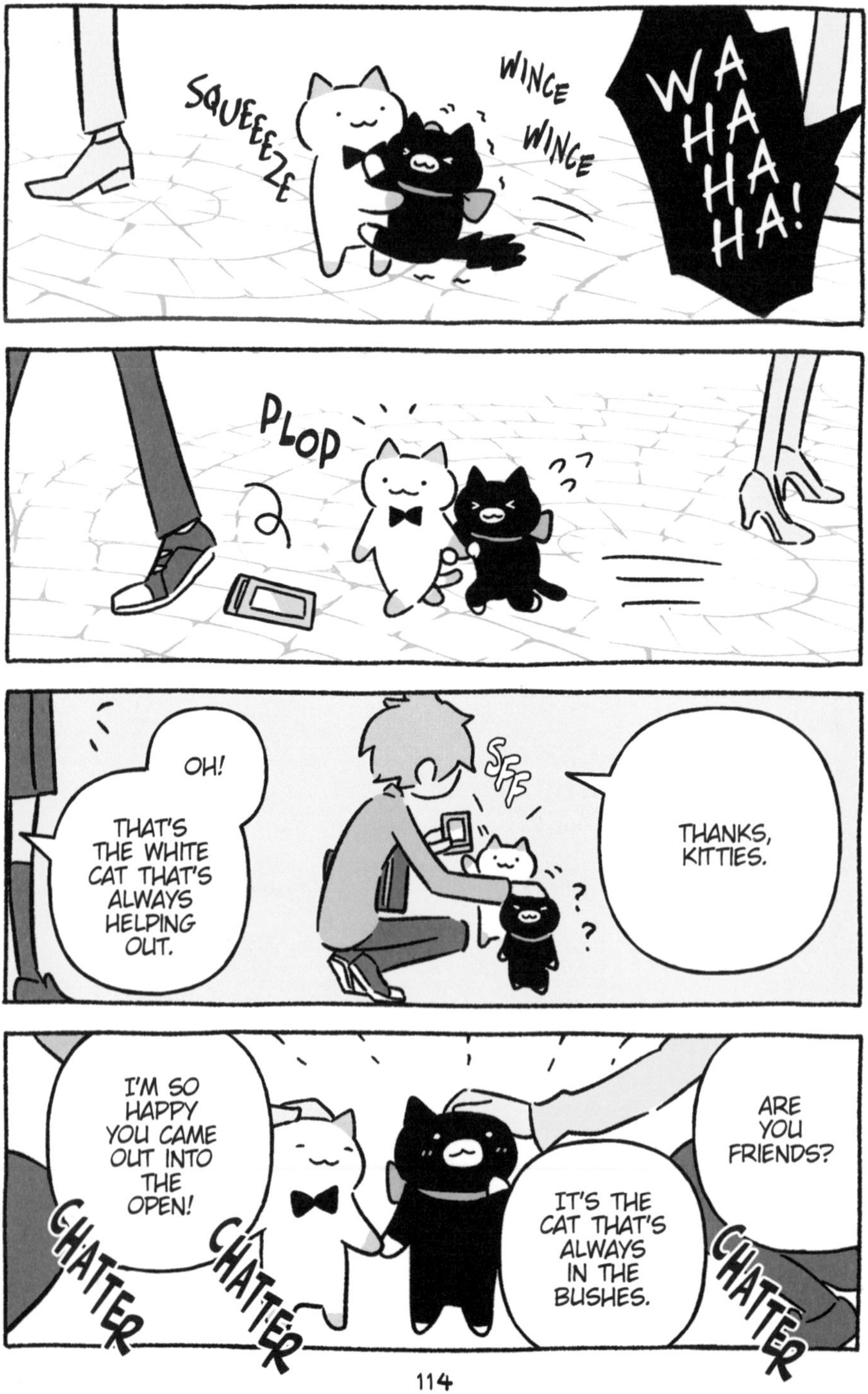

WA HA HA HA HA!
WINCE
WINCE
SQUEEEEZE
PLOP
THANKS, KITTIES.
SFF
OH!
THAT'S THE WHITE CAT THAT'S ALWAYS HELPING OUT.
ARE YOU FRIENDS?
CHATTER
IT'S THE CAT THAT'S ALWAYS IN THE BUSHES.
I'M SO HAPPY YOU CAME OUT INTO THE OPEN!
CHATTER
CHATTER

# WATCHING

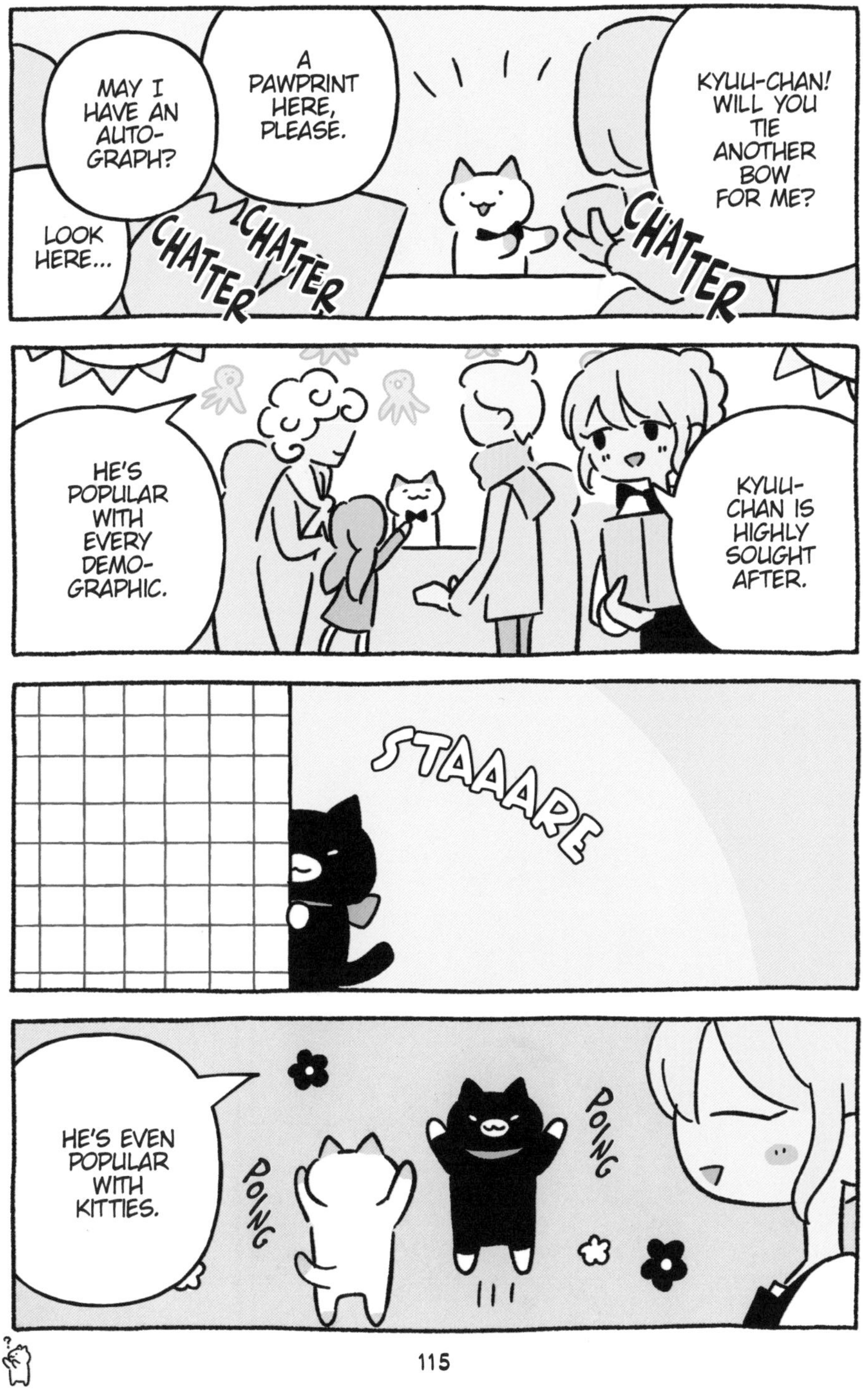

KYUU-CHAN! WILL YOU TIE ANOTHER BOW FOR ME?
CHATTER
A PAWPRINT HERE, PLEASE.
CHATTER
CHATTER
MAY I HAVE AN AUTO-GRAPH?
LOOK HERE...
KYUU-CHAN IS HIGHLY SOUGHT AFTER.
HE'S POPULAR WITH EVERY DEMO-GRAPHIC.
STAAAARE
POING
POING
HE'S EVEN POPULAR WITH KITTIES.

# NEW PERSON ON THE JOB

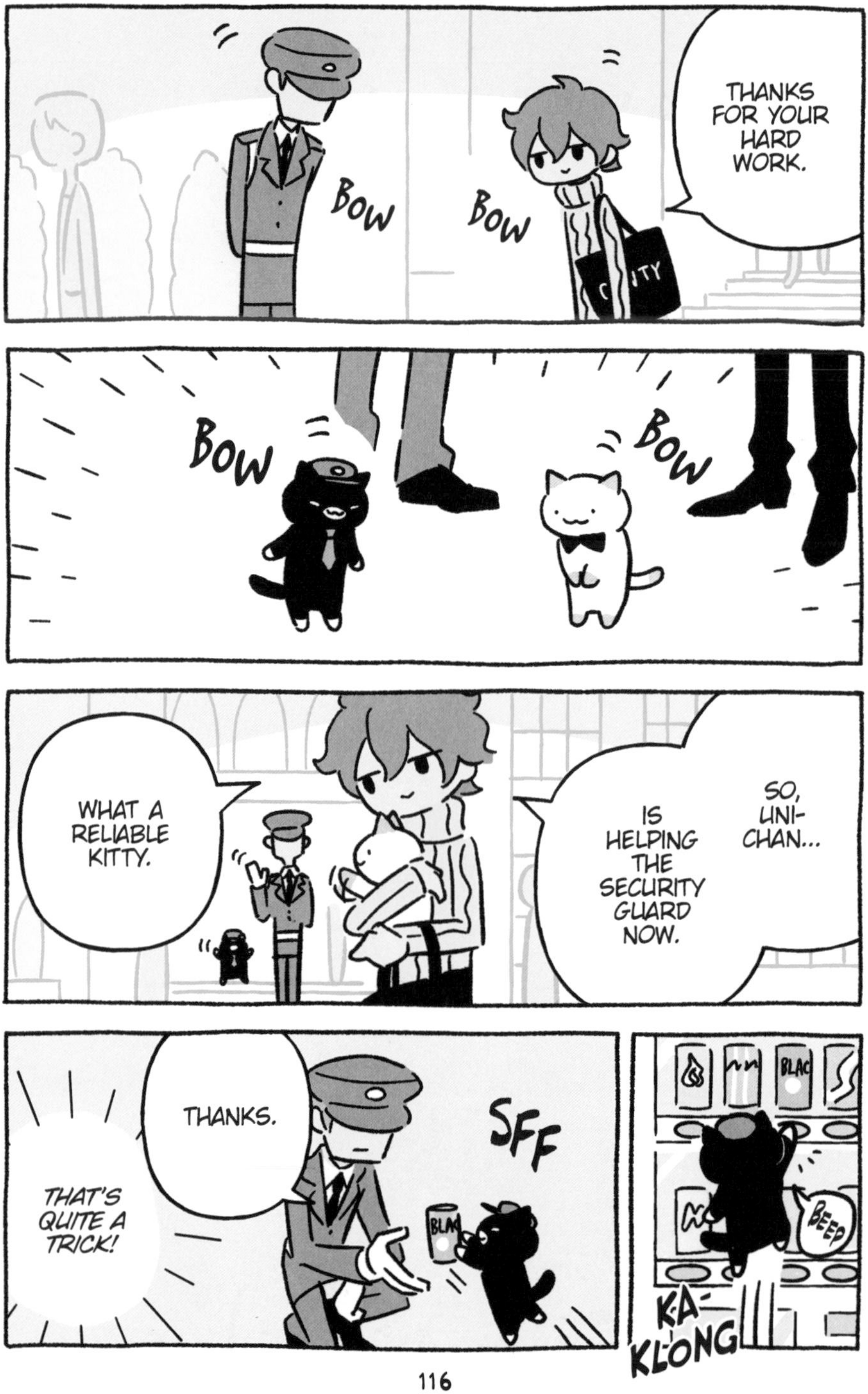
THANKS FOR YOUR HARD WORK.
BOW
BOW
BOW
BOW
SO, UNI-CHAN...
IS HELPING THE SECURITY GUARD NOW.
WHAT A RELIABLE KITTY.
BLAC
BEEP
KA-KLONG
SFF
THANKS.
BLAC
THAT'S QUITE A TRICK!

# FLUFFY STREET

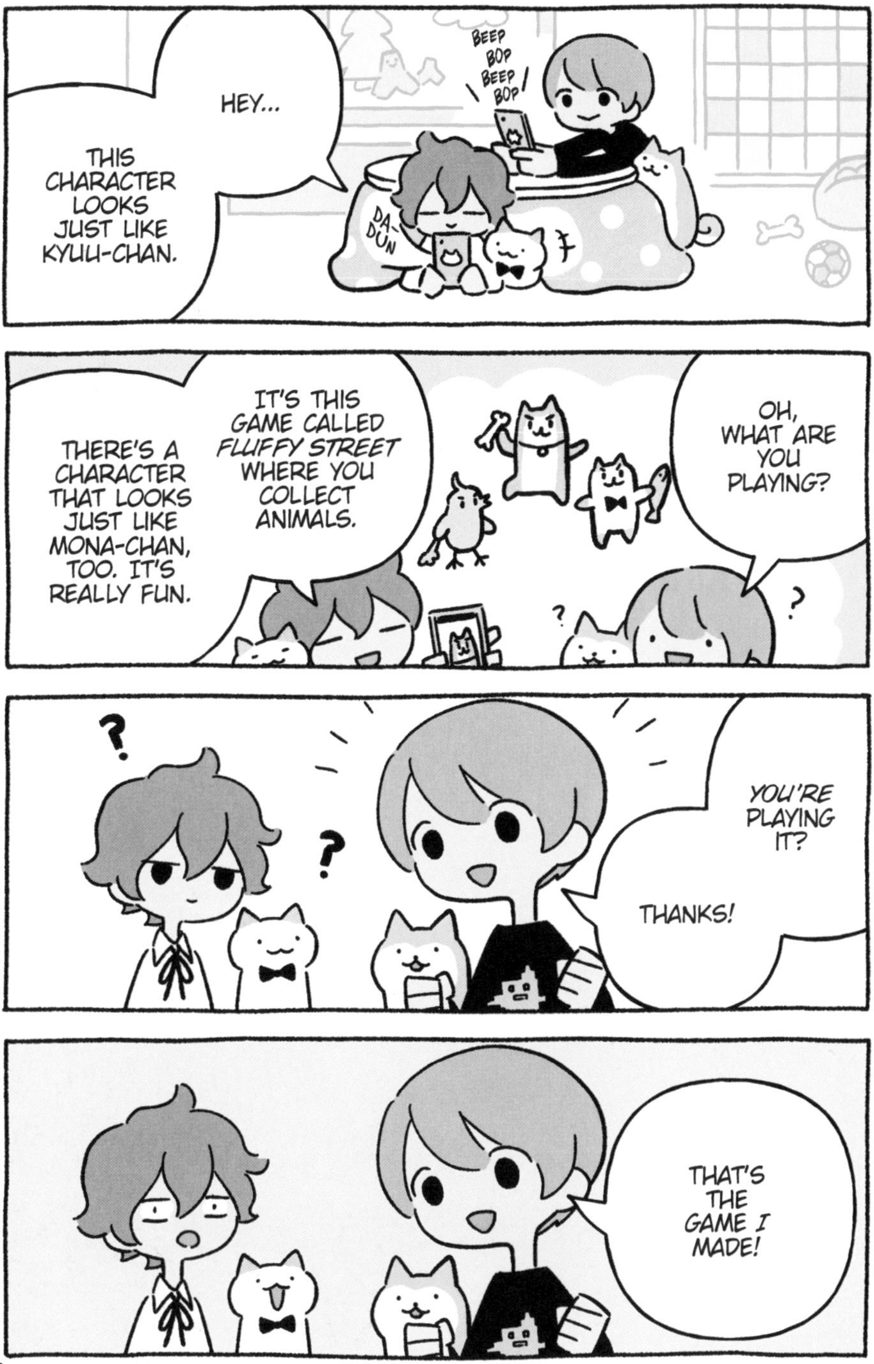
BEEP BOP BEEP BOP
HEY... THIS CHARACTER LOOKS JUST LIKE KYUU-CHAN.
DA-DUN
OH, WHAT ARE YOU PLAYING?
IT'S THIS GAME CALLED *FLUFFY STREET* WHERE YOU COLLECT ANIMALS.
THERE'S A CHARACTER THAT LOOKS JUST LIKE MONA-CHAN, TOO. IT'S REALLY FUN.
*YOU'RE* PLAYING IT?
THANKS!
THAT'S THE GAME *I* MADE!

# MOTIVATION

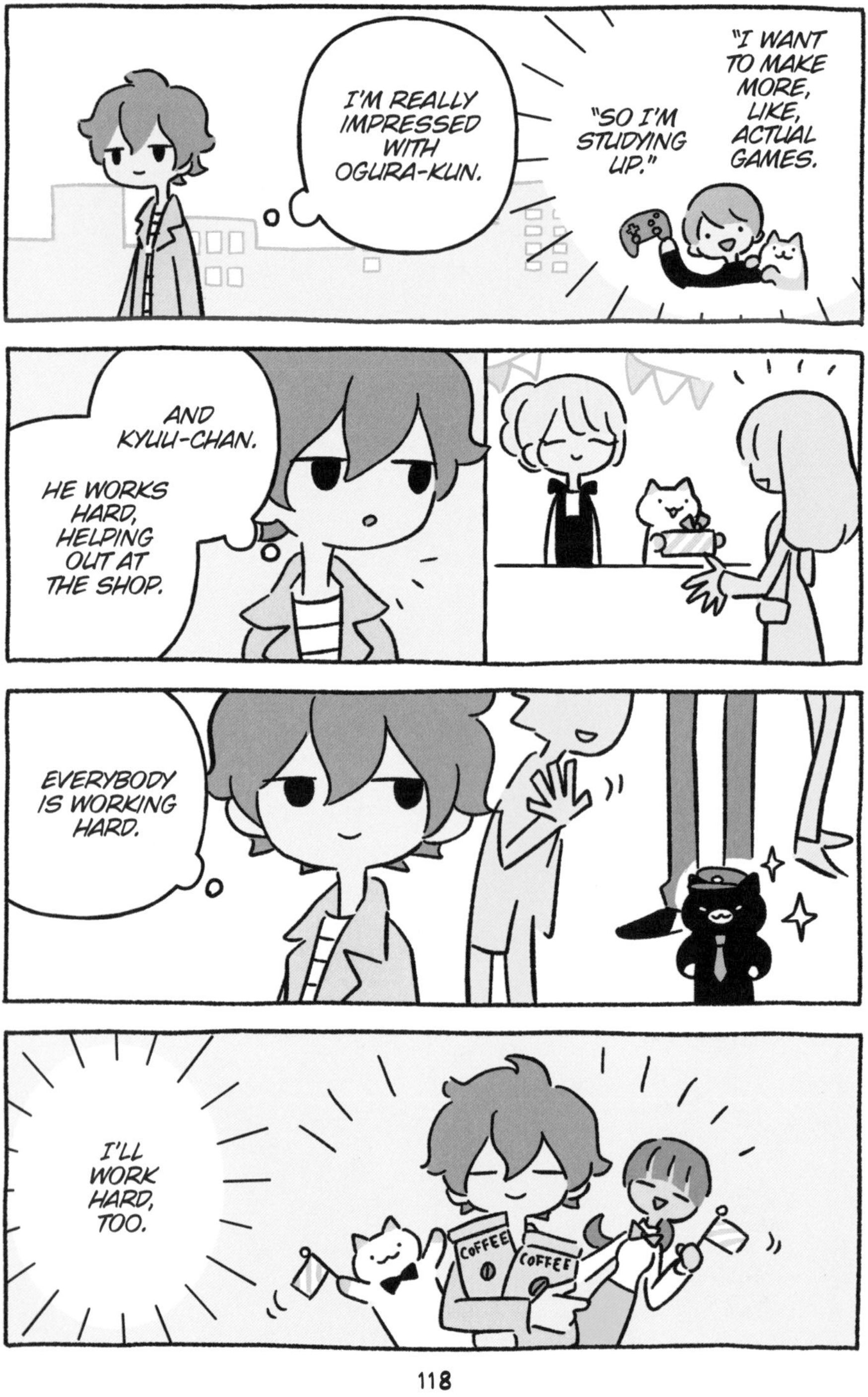
"I WANT TO MAKE MORE, LIKE, ACTUAL GAMES.
"SO I'M STUDYING UP."
I'M REALLY IMPRESSED WITH OGURA-KUN.
AND KYUU-CHAN.
HE WORKS HARD, HELPING OUT AT THE SHOP.
EVERYBODY IS WORKING HARD.
I'LL WORK HARD, TOO.
COFFEE
COFFEE

# LET'S PLAY FLUFFY STREET

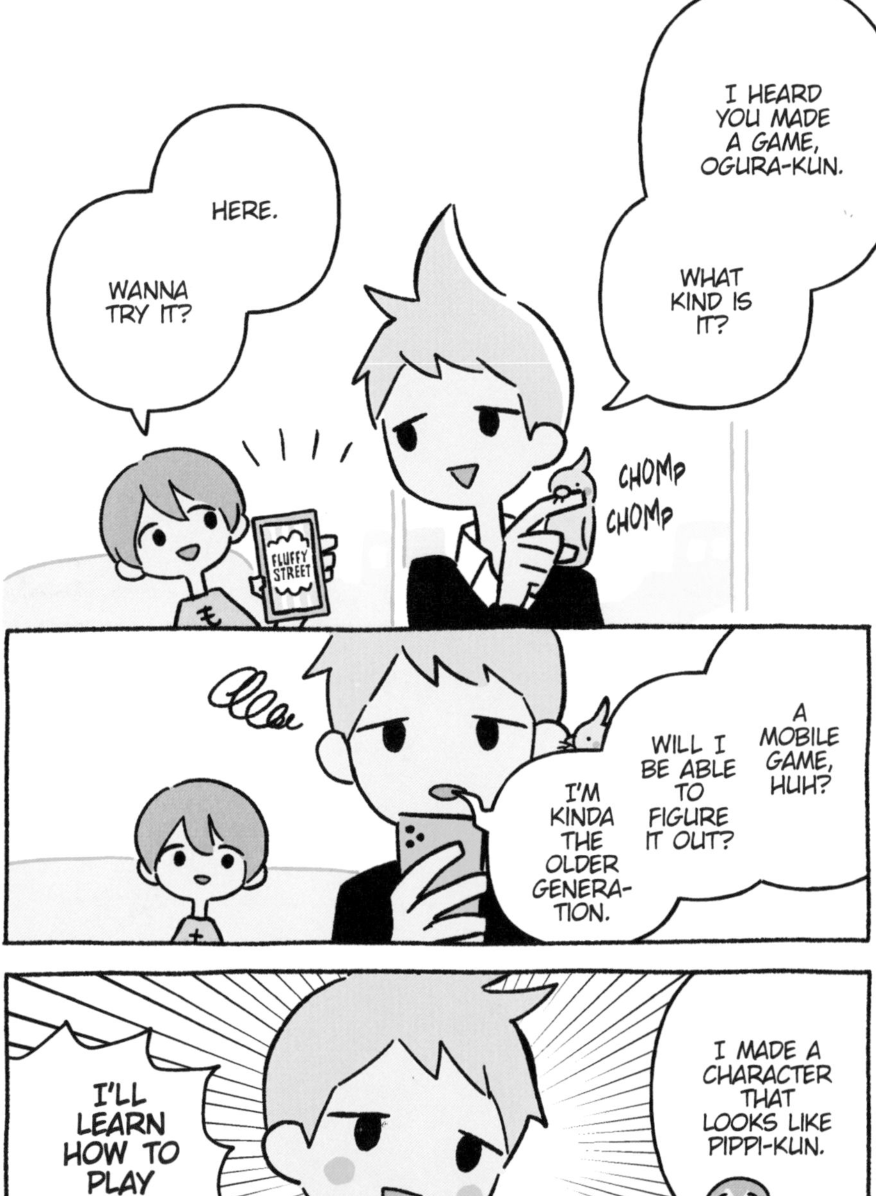
I HEARD YOU MADE A GAME, OGURA-KUN.
WHAT KIND IS IT?
HERE.
WANNA TRY IT?
CHOMP CHOMP
FLUFFY STREET
A MOBILE GAME, HUH?
WILL I BE ABLE TO FIGURE IT OUT?
I'M KINDA THE OLDER GENERATION.
I MADE A CHARACTER THAT LOOKS LIKE PIPPI-KUN.
I'LL LEARN HOW TO PLAY RIGHT NOW!!!

# FLUFF SEARCH

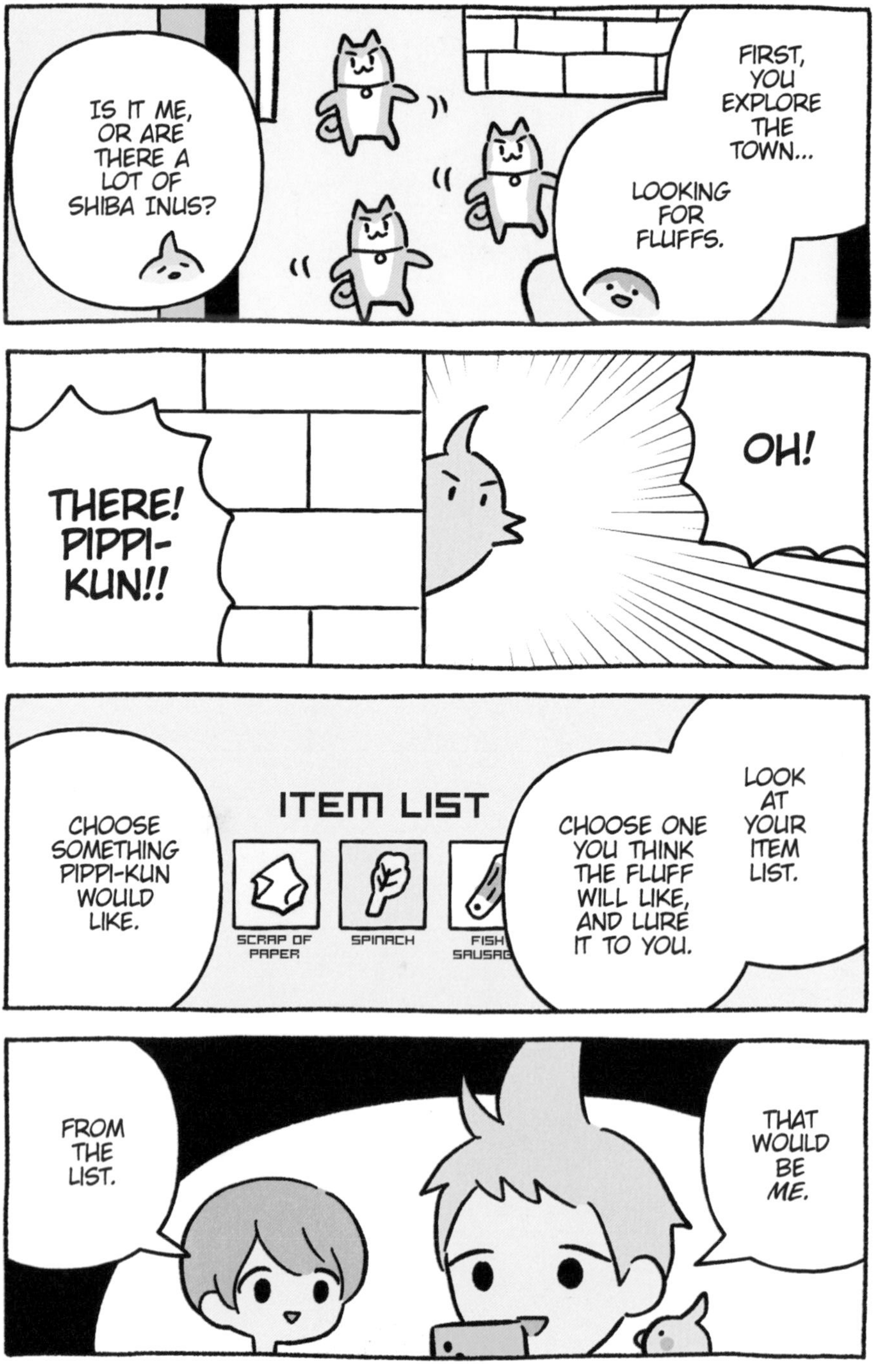
FIRST, YOU EXPLORE THE TOWN...
LOOKING FOR FLUFFS.
IS IT ME, OR ARE THERE A LOT OF SHIBA INUS?
OH!
THERE! PIPPI-KUN!!
LOOK AT YOUR ITEM LIST.
CHOOSE ONE YOU THINK THE FLUFF WILL LIKE, AND LURE IT TO YOU.
ITEM LIST
SCRAP OF PAPER
SPINACH
FISH
CHOOSE SOMETHING PIPPI-KUN WOULD LIKE.
THAT WOULD BE ME.
FROM THE LIST.

# BEAK ATTACK

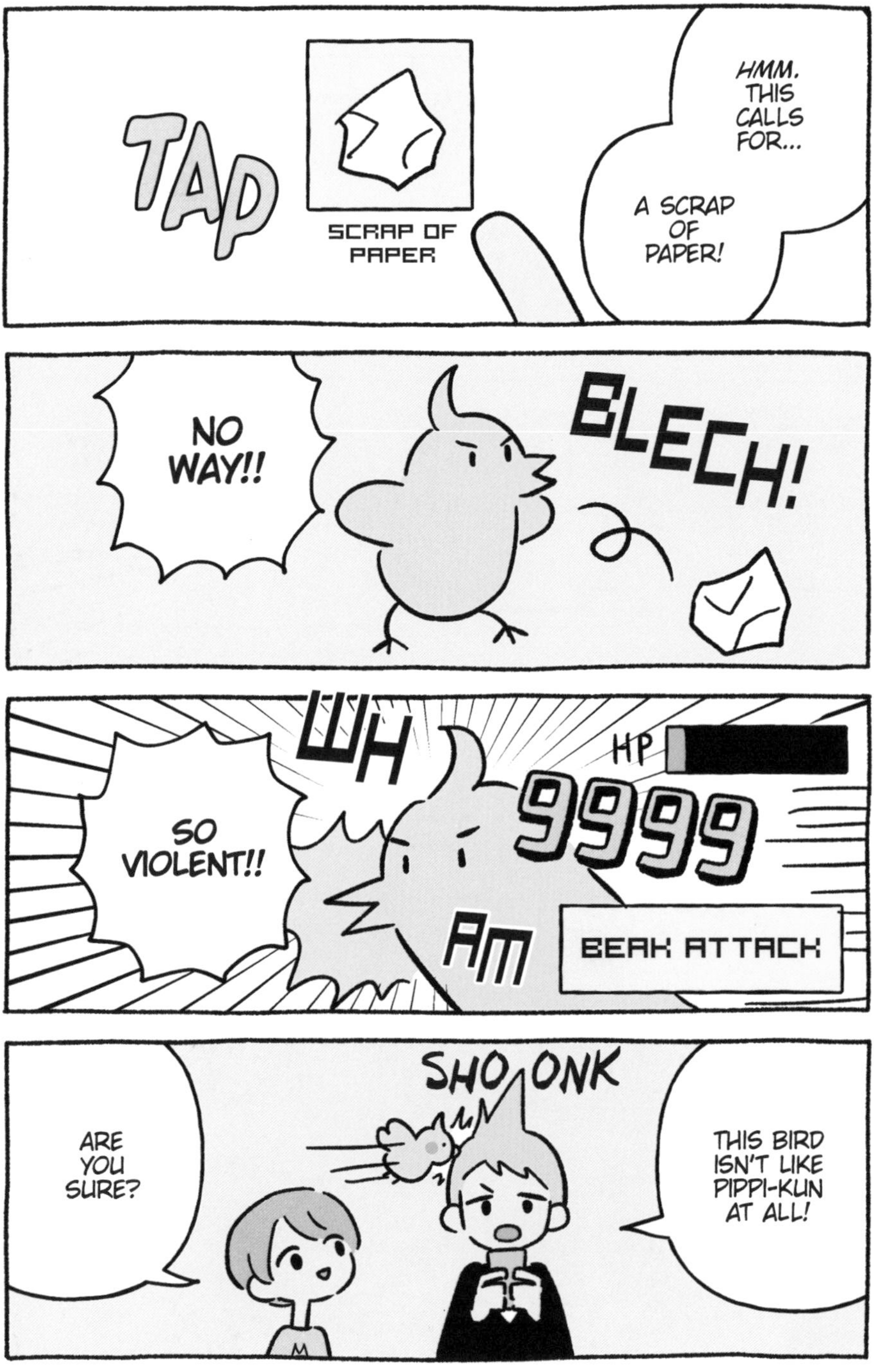
HMM. THIS CALLS FOR...
A SCRAP OF PAPER!
SCRAP OF PAPER
TAP
BLECH!
NO WAY!!
HP
9999
WH
BEAK ATTACK
AM
SO VIOLENT!!
THIS BIRD ISN'T LIKE PIPPI-KUN AT ALL!
SHO ONK
ARE YOU SURE?

# JEALOUSY

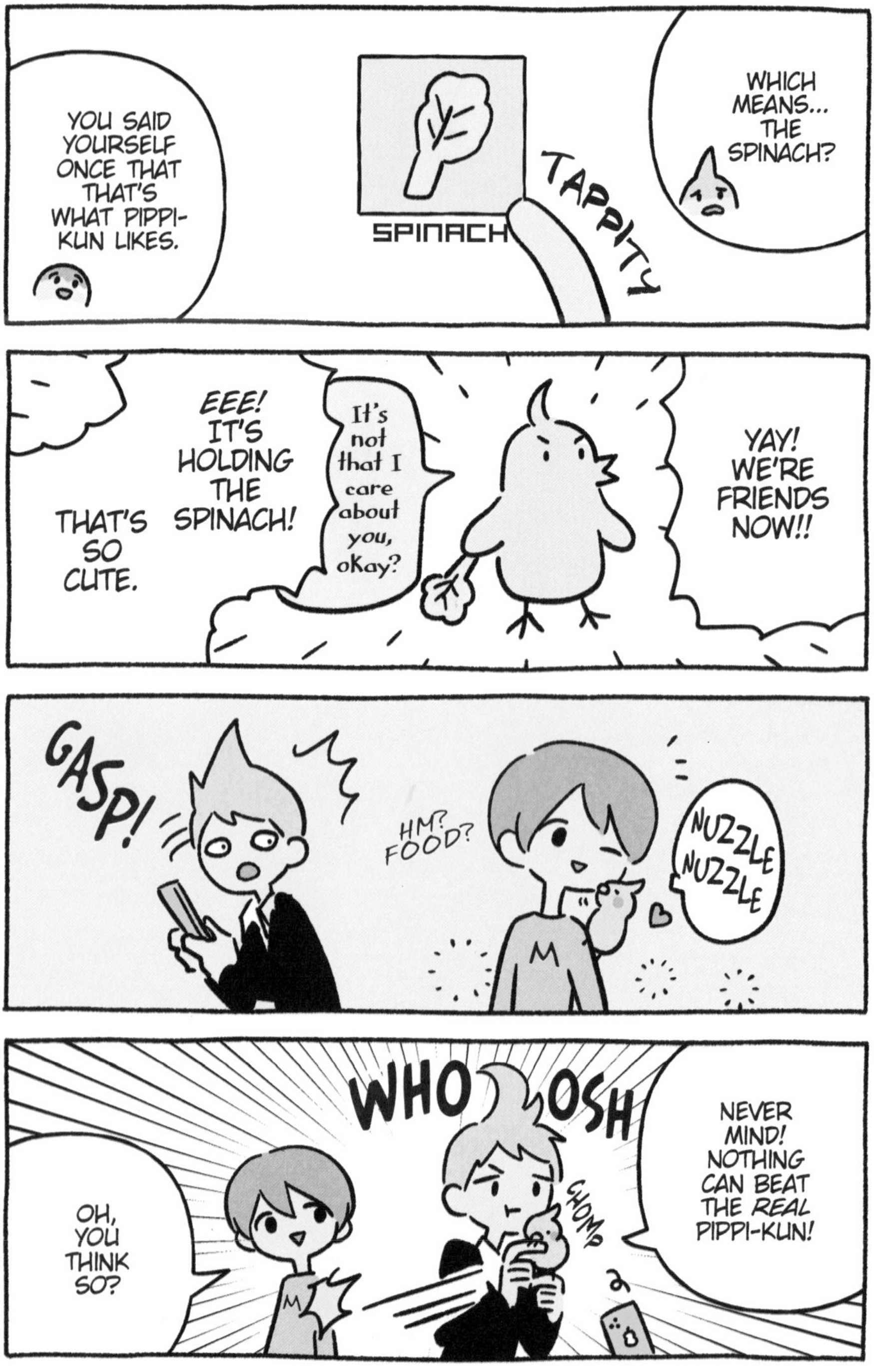
WHICH MEANS... THE SPINACH?
TAPPITY
SPINACH
YOU SAID YOURSELF ONCE THAT THAT'S WHAT PIPPI-KUN LIKES.
YAY! WE'RE FRIENDS NOW!!
It's not that I care about you, okay?
EEE! IT'S HOLDING THE SPINACH!
THAT'S SO CUTE.
NUZZLE NUZZLE
HM? FOOD?
GASP!
NEVER MIND! NOTHING CAN BEAT THE *REAL* PIPPI-KUN!
WHOOSH
CHOMP
OH, YOU THINK SO?

# SECURITY GUARDS

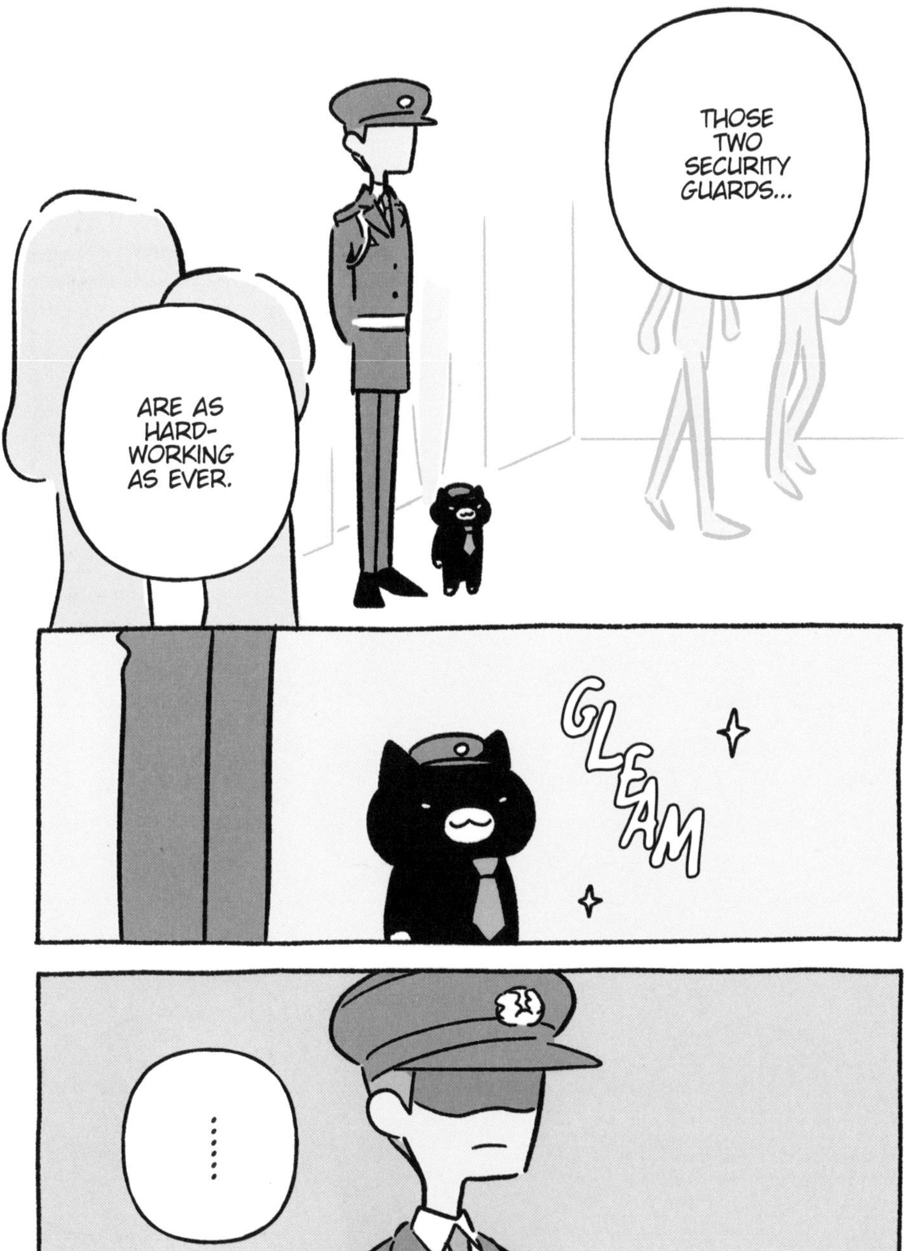
THOSE TWO SECURITY GUARDS...
ARE AS HARD-WORKING AS EVER.
GLEAM
......

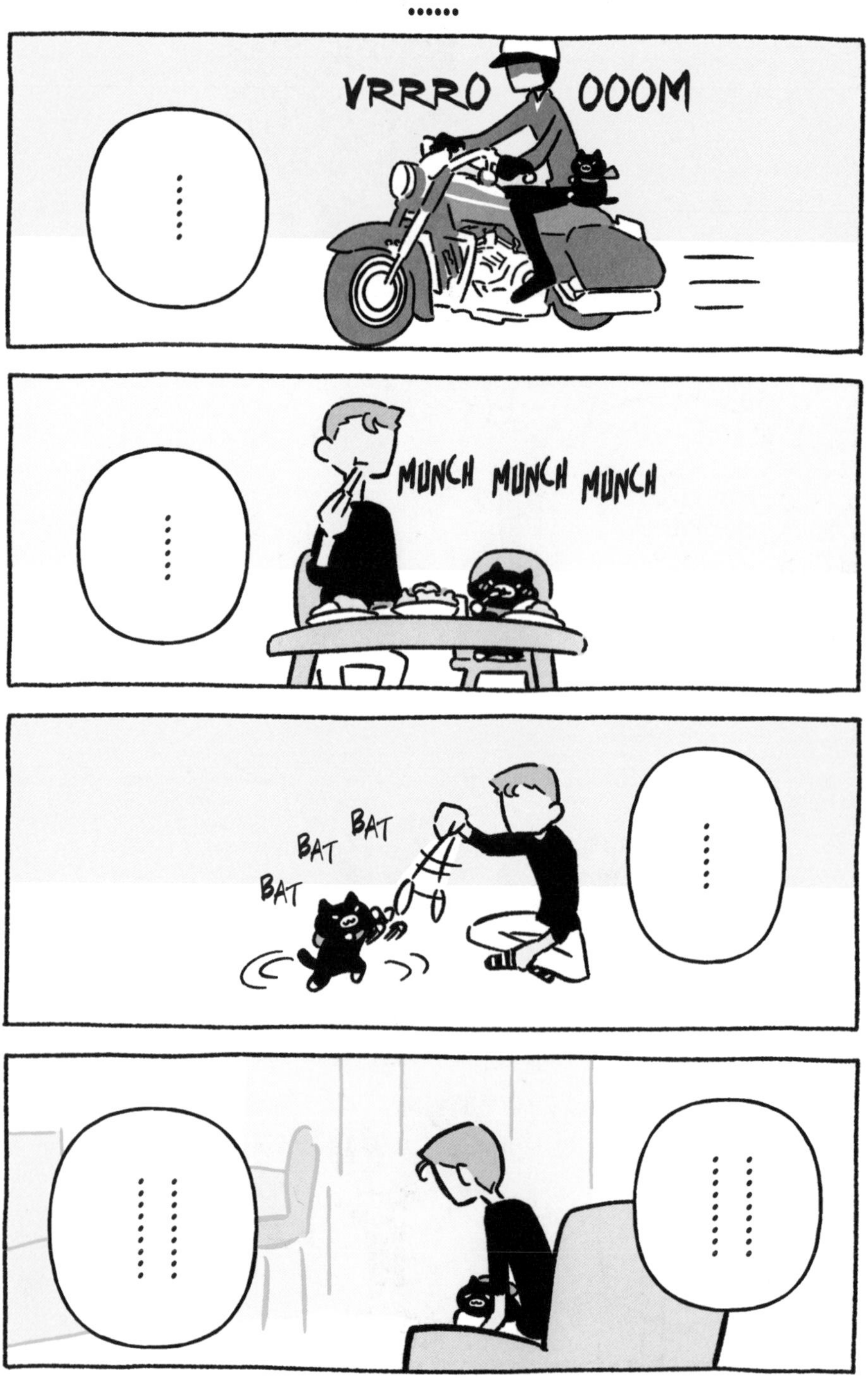
......
VRRRO OOOM
......
MUNCH MUNCH MUNCH
......
......
BAT
BAT
BAT
...... ......
...... ......

# BUT INWARDLY...

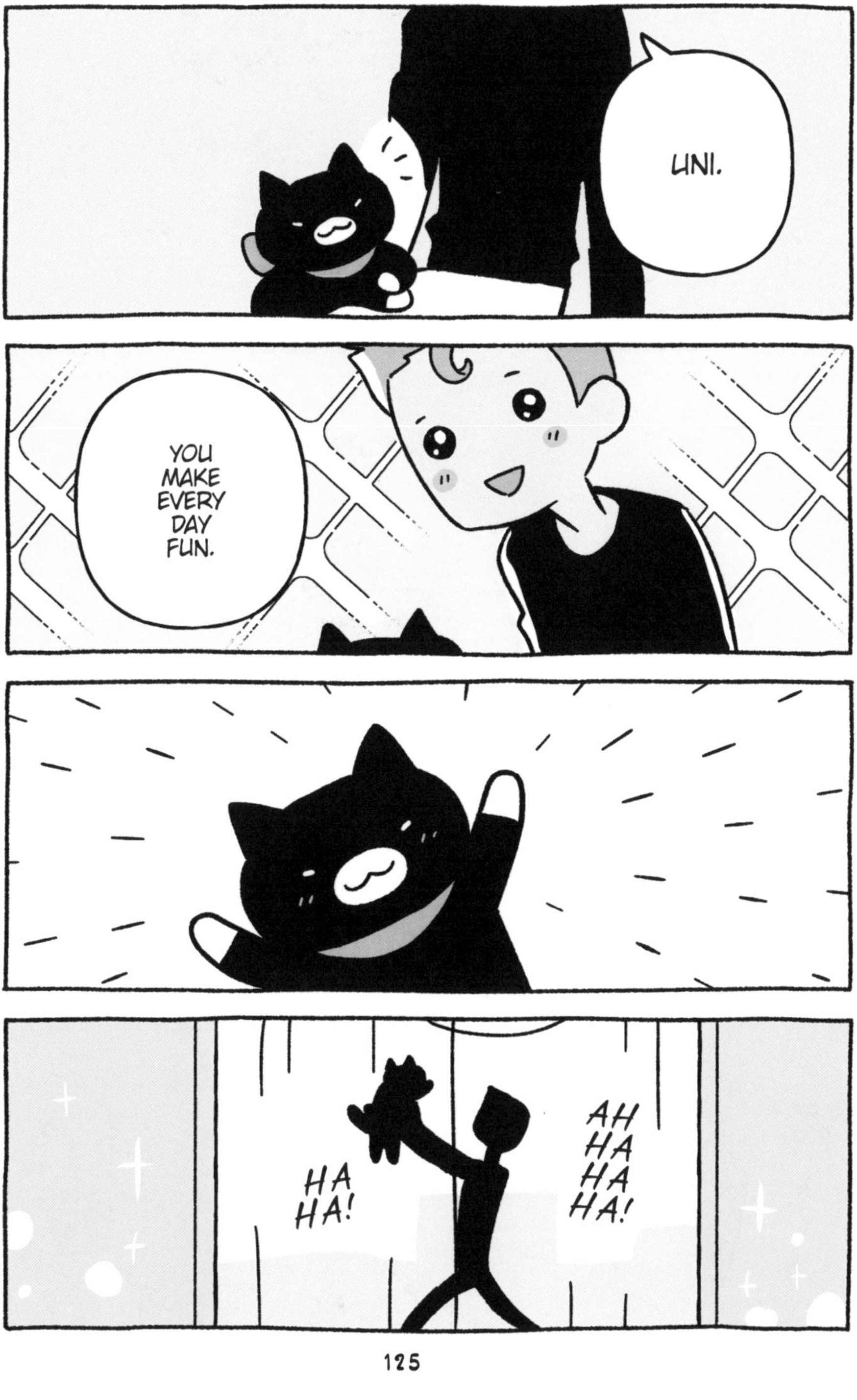
UNI.
YOU MAKE EVERY DAY FUN.
AH HA HA HA HA!
HA HA HA!

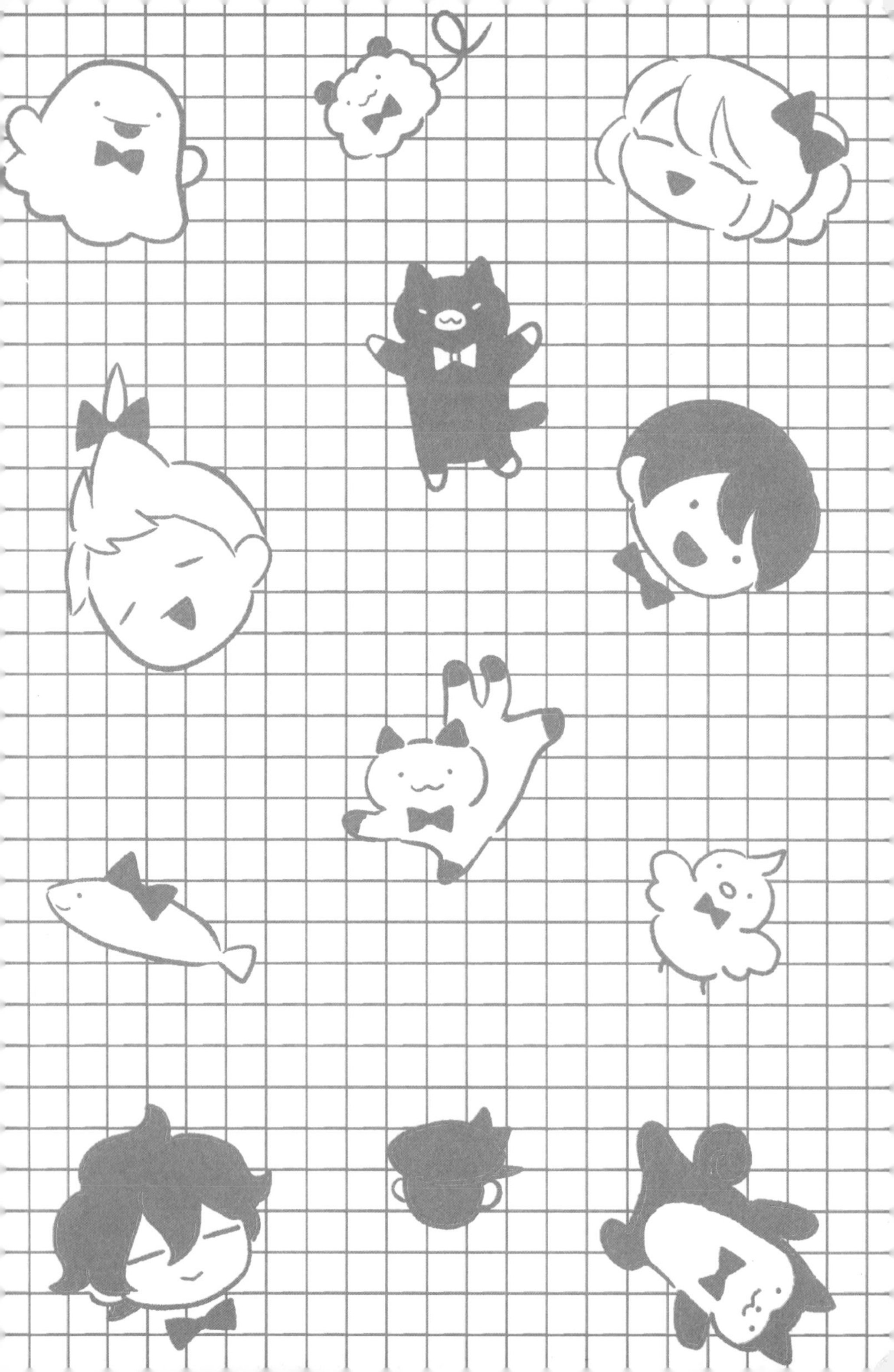

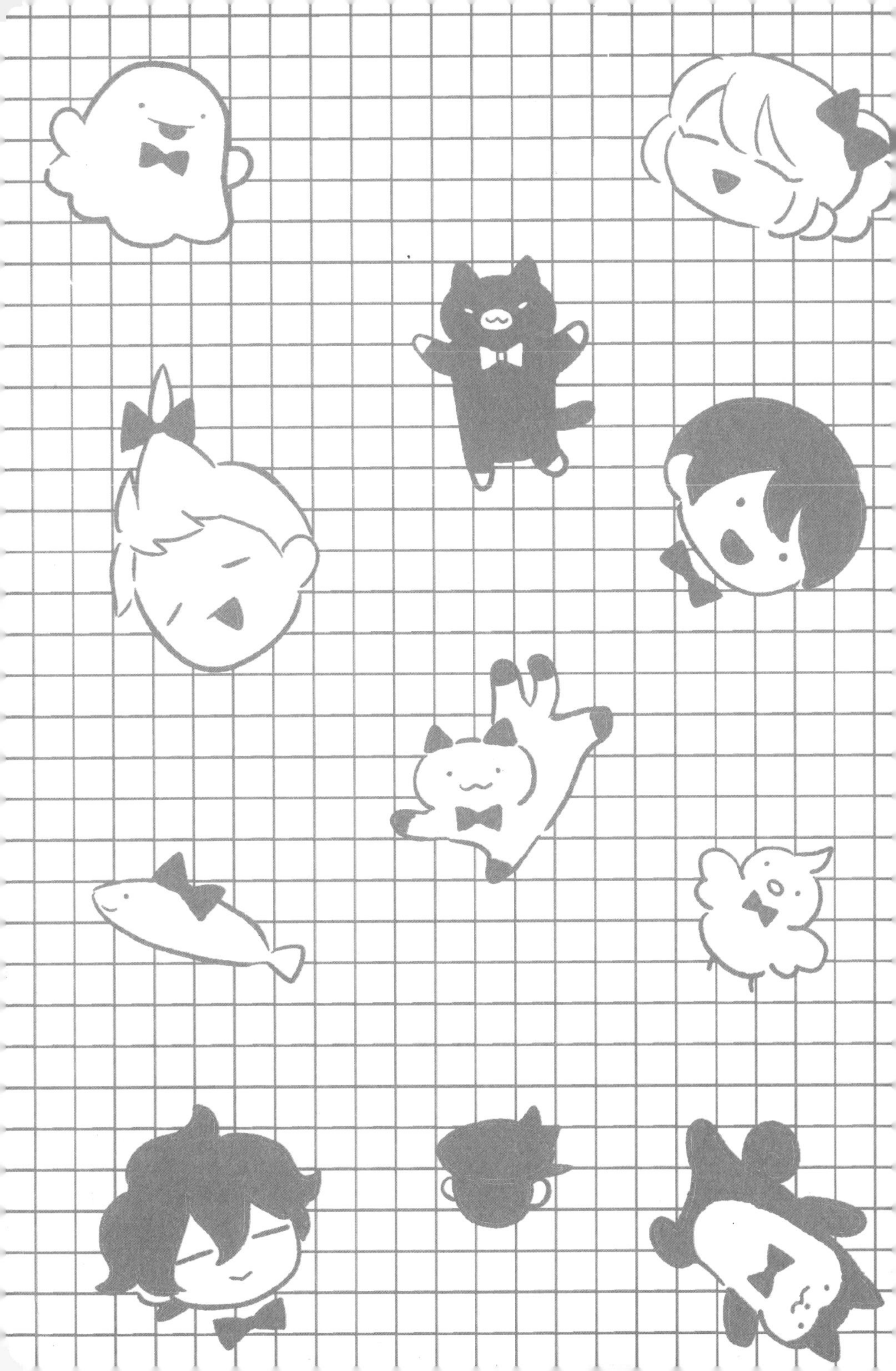

# SEVEN SEAS ENTERTAINMENT PRESENTS

## Wonder Cat KYUU-chan

### story and art by SASAMI NITORI          VOLUME 7

TRANSLATION
**Alethea & Athena Nibley**

LETTERING
**Roland Amago**
**Bambi Eloriaga-Amago**

COVER DESIGN
**H. Qi**

PROOFREADER
**Kurestin Armada**

SENIOR EDITOR
**Peter Adrian Behravesh**

PREPRESS TECHNICIAN
**Melanie Ujimori**
**Jules Valera**

PRODUCTION MANAGER
**Lissa Pattillo**

EDITOR-IN-CHIEF
**Julie Davis**

ASSOCIATE PUBLISHER
**Adam Arnold**

PUBLISHER
**Jason DeAngelis**

FUSHIGINEKO NO KYUU-CHAN VOL. 7
© SASAMI NITORI 2020 Printed in Japan
All rights reserved.
Original Japanese edition published by Star Seas Company.
English publishing rights arranged with Star Seas Company
through Kodansha Ltd., Tokyo.

Seven Seas press and purchase enquiries can be sent to Marketing Manager Lianne
Sentar at press@gomanga.com. Information regarding the distribution and purchase of
digital editions is available from Digital Manager CK Russell at digital@gomanga.com.

Seven Seas and the Seven Seas logo are trademarks of
Seven Seas Entertainment. All rights reserved.

ISBN: 978-1-63858-806-1
Printed in Canada
First Printing: December 2022
10 9 8 7 6 5 4 3 2 1

## ////// READING DIRECTIONS //////

This book reads from *right to left*,
Japanese style. If this is your first time
reading manga, you start reading from
the top right panel on each page and
take it from there. If you get lost, just
follow the numbered diagram here.
It may seem backwards at first,
but you'll get the hang of it! Have fun!!

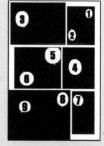